where
the
blue sky
begins

Books by Katie Powner

The Sowing Season

A Flicker of Light

Where the Blue Sky Begins

where the blue sky begins

a novel

Katie Powner

BETHANYHOUSE
a division of Baker Publishing Group
Minneapolis, Minnesota

© 2022 by Katie Powner

Published by Bethany House Publishers
11400 Hampshire Avenue South
Minneapolis, Minnesota 55438
www.bethanyhouse.com

Bethany House Publishers is a division of
Baker Publishing Group, Grand Rapids, Michigan

Printed in the United States of America

Library of Congress Cataloging-in-Publication Data
Names: Powner, Katie, author.
Title: Where the blue sky begins / Katie Powner.
Description: Minneapolis, Minnesota : Bethany House Publishers, a division of Baker Publishing Group, [2022]
Identifiers: LCCN 2022007642 | ISBN 9780764240393 (trade paperback) | ISBN 9780764240874 (casebound) | ISBN 9781493439126 (ebook)
Classification: LCC PS3616.O96 W54 2022 | DDC 813/.6—dc23
LC record available at https://lccn.loc.gov/2022007642

This is a work of fiction. Names, characters, incidents, and dialogues are products of the author's imagination and are not to be construed as real. Any resemblance to actual events or persons, living or dead, is entirely coincidental.

Cover design by Andrea Gjeldum

Author is represented by WordServe Literary Group.

Baker Publishing Group publications use paper produced from sustainable forestry practices and post-consumer waste whenever possible.

22 23 24 25 26 27 28   7 6 5 4 3 2 1

To my mom,
the strongest woman I know

one

Eric Larson had never seen such a sorry excuse for a town. He rubbed his eyes, weary from the ten-hour drive from Seattle, and blinked. This was it? This was the place Uncle Jack couldn't wait for him to see?

A sun-bleached *Welcome to Tukston* sign and five steel wheels the size of small houses greeted him and his brand-new Jeep. As he entered the dusty Montana hamlet, the street names on his navigation screen disappeared, and the car avatar stopped and turned sideways as if to say, "Your guess is as good as mine."

Eric laughed to himself. *"This navigation system is top of the line,"* the salesman had said. *"It will get you anywhere you need to go."*

Yeah. Anywhere except his home for the summer.

Tukston stretched languidly in front of him as he slowed down, and he couldn't help but frown. Was it really necessary for Uncle Jack to send him hundreds of miles away? Couldn't he have found him an office to run somewhere else? The outdated buildings, the absence of traffic lights, and the spectacular number of pickup trucks and cowboy hats reminded Eric of the Old West. His hydro-blue Jeep stood out like a polished sapphire in a gravel pit.

He pulled into a parking space in front of a diner to try his luck using Google Maps on his phone. His thumbs flew across the screen, searching for answers. How did he get to the rental his uncle had secured for him? He'd never thought to ask if the place had running water and electricity, but now that he was here, he couldn't help but wonder.

The June sun quickly heated the interior of the Jeep. When Eric lowered the window for a breath of fresh air, something caught his eye. *Hello.* What did we have here? A long-legged blonde in short denim cutoffs walked by on the sidewalk and glanced his way. She seemed a little perky for his taste, and her hair was kind of frizzy, but he lifted his sunglasses to give her a wink, making sure to flex the muscles in his bent arm. She brushed her hair over her shoulder and shot him a smile as she passed.

Tukston might be the redneckest town he'd ever seen, but at least the scenery wasn't half bad.

Eric watched the girl walk away before turning back to his phone. Typing in the address of his rental house produced a red arrow on Google maps, but the address was only partially the same as the one he'd typed in. Was that the place? The address his uncle had texted him said *West*. The one on Google said *East*. When he typed it in again, the arrow moved across town.

Great.

The phone rang as he stared at it. Uncle Jack. Perfect timing.

When he answered, his uncle didn't waste any time. "Hey, you get settled in yet?"

Eric kneaded his forehead. "It's like Tombstone over here. And the navigation system doesn't work."

Uncle Jack laughed. "You do realize people figured out how to find their way around long before cellular phones were invented, right?"

Eric had to smile. "You do realize people call them *cell*phones, right?"

"What people?"

"Everyone. Every single person in the country except you."

"That's hooey."

"You sound like you belong here, not me."

"No, no." Uncle Jack huffed the words as if he were out of breath. "You're the right man for the job."

"Are you climbing the stairs again? There's a perfectly good elevator in your building."

"And there's a perfectly good brain in your head that I expect you to use while you're in Tukston. I see big things on your horizon, my boy."

Eric's nose wrinkled. Big things? This town was too small for big things. But if he could make an impression at the office here, there would be no limit to his horizon once he got back to the big city.

"Where are you now?" Uncle Jack asked.

Eric sighed and read the sign above the diner. "The Good Food Diner."

"That's my favorite place to eat. You should try their Cowboy Deluxe burger, if you think you can handle it."

Eric bristled. He could handle a lot more than his uncle gave him credit for. "Right. Sure. Now, where's the house from here?"

"Don't know. Guess you'll have to ask for directions."

Eric rolled his eyes. His uncle had spent two years in Tukston setting up a local branch of Larson Financial back in the day. He knew exactly where the house was. "You're really not going to tell me?"

"Where would be the fun in that?" Uncle Jack chuckled. "Get off your phone and go talk to a real live person. They'll point you in the right direction. And try to be nice, please. My company's reputation is on the line."

It wasn't like any of this had been Eric's idea. When Uncle Jack had told him that he thought Eric was ready for the next step in his career, Eric had assumed he was being promoted. Not being sent to Hicktown, USA. But he hadn't been able to tell his uncle no. Despite never having kids of his own, the man had been more of a father to him than his own dad for years now. Eric would do whatever it took to prove himself to his uncle.

Except use an outhouse or wear cowboy boots.

"Fine." He opened the car door and stepped into the sunshine. "Talk to you later."

He was going to conquer this summer. He would find his rental house. He would charm the socks off all the clients at Larson Financial. He would make his uncle proud and rub it in his father's face. And then he'd get that tenth-floor office he'd been promised.

A bell above the door jangled as Eric entered Good Food. As his eyes adjusted to the dim light, he took in the dingy interior of the restaurant. Only three customers were here at four in the afternoon on a Saturday, and all three turned in their seats to gape at him. Two were older men who looked like they'd just returned from a week in the woods—make that two weeks. The third was a kid no more than ten who was nursing a strawberry milk shake.

Under the scrutiny of the locals, Eric wavered and ran a hand through his dark brown hair. None of these people seemed like the type to be impressed by his forty-dollar T-shirt.

The middle-aged waitress approached him with a wide smile and heavily hair-sprayed bangs. "Howdy there. You can sit wherever you'd like."

They even said *howdy* here. It figured. Eric returned her smile, calculating the probability as high that this woman would know where his rental was. "Thanks, but I'm just looking for some help. Can you tell me how to get to Prairie Dog Road?"

She tilted her head and raised an eyebrow. "You know someone over there?"

"Uh, no."

She looked him up and down, her eyes flicking toward his

Jeep parked outside after studying his Italian loafers. "I'm Dee. What'd you say your name was?"

And this was why he would rather rely on his phone for information. Phones did not ask questions. "I'm Eric." He held out his hand. "Eric Larson. The new senior advisor for Larson Financial."

Her eyes widened, and her broad smile returned. "You're Jack's nephew? I heard you were coming, but I didn't expect you to be so—" her eyes scanned his shoulders and biceps again, then studied his bare left hand—"young. And neat."

Eric shifted on his feet. He couldn't be the only man in Tukston who took good care of his appearance. He glanced at the other men in the diner. Well, maybe he could.

He gave Dee his best lopsided grin. "Perhaps you could draw me a map?"

"Sure, sure." She hurried to pull a small notebook and pen from her apron pocket. "I suppose you're renting the Gustafson place. We'll have you on your way in no time."

His calculations had been correct. As usual.

She quickly sketched a map on the paper with one X marking where the diner was and another X for the house. She explained the route to him and tore the page from her book. "There's a big propane tank painted like a pink pig in the yard near the end of Prairie Dog Road." She held out the page. "If you see that, you know you've gone too far."

"Thank you." He took hold of the paper. "I appreciate your help."

She didn't let go of the map until he looked up and met her eyes. Her expression was earnest. "You'll have to meet my niece sometime. She's about your age, and real pretty, too."

Eric swallowed before nodding. "Thank you, again."

She finally let go, and he quickly tucked the paper in his pocket before she could get any ideas about writing her niece's phone number on it. He liked to look, sure, but he wasn't looking for a relationship. He was only in town for the summer. Besides, he had Tiffani.

Sort of.

He hurried out the door and back to his vehicle. According to the hand-drawn map, Prairie Dog Road was southeast of the diner. His phone rang again as he glanced behind him to back onto the street. He perked up. It was Chase.

"Hey, bro." Eric would never talk on his phone while driving in Seattle without the hands-free feature on, but there weren't any other cars on the road here. "How was Burger King today?"

"Terrible. I messed up three orders and got yelled at twice."

Eric tried to keep the smile out of his voice. If handing someone the wrong size box of fries was his little brother's biggest problem, he was doing pretty well. "It's only your first week. Cut yourself some slack."

He had hoped Chase would aim a bit higher when he'd encouraged him to get a summer job before leaving for college, but at least he was working *somewhere*. With how shy Chase was, Eric was just glad he got a job after graduation at all.

"Did you make it to Tukston yet? What's it like?"

Eric took a right turn, guided by the waitress's map, and shook his head. "It's small. Quiet."

Dirty. Podunk.

Terrifying.

"It's weird to have you so far away. I don't like it."

"I moved out twelve years ago, Chase."

"Only to the other side of Seattle. Now you're a thousand miles away."

He'd only had six years at home with his younger half brother, since Chase wasn't born until two years after his parents' divorce. After his mom remarried. He still remembered how annoyed he'd been as a fourteen-year-old about having a baby brother, about his only-child status being disrupted, but

that hadn't lasted long. Chase's chubby cheeks and the inno-
cent way he'd gripped Eric's finger had won him over. Then as
soon as Chase could walk, he'd started following Eric around
everywhere he went, and they'd been close ever since.

Eric tapped the steering wheel. "It's only seven hundred and
thirteen miles. And I'll be back in time to help you move into
the dorms at U-Dub."

Chase had earned a scholarship to the University of Wash-
ington, and Eric couldn't be prouder, although it had taken
some convincing on Eric's part to get his brother to agree to
go. Chase was nervous about leaving home and being around
a bunch of new people, yet Eric knew his brother would find
his place on campus if he only gave it a chance.

"You promise?" Chase asked.

"Of course." Eric noticed a woman in a purple trench coat
driving a clunky Honda scooter ahead of him on the road and
slowed down. "I wouldn't miss it."

"My dad says you won't last two weeks in Montana. He says
you're too soft for rural living."

Eric wrinkled his nose. His stepdad, Steve, was a decent guy.
He'd stepped in and done his best after Eric's dad split. But
they'd never really connected.

"I think I can handle Montana for one summer."

"That's what I told him. You can handle anything."

The pride in Chase's voice gave Eric pause. He wasn't sure
he deserved Chase's admiration.

The phone beeped in his ear, and he glanced at the screen.
Another text from Tiffani. The fifth since he'd left Seattle this
morning.

"I gotta go, okay?" He switched the phone to his other hand.
"We'll talk again soon."

What was that woman on the scooter doing? She wobbled
back and forth on the road. As Eric closed the distance between them, he noticed that despite being closer to fifty, she

13

was wearing a glittery silver helmet with purple stars that matched her coat as if she were twelve.

"Okay," Chase said. "But don't forget you promised."

"I won't forget."

If there was one person in the world to whom he was sure to keep a promise, it was Chase. He said goodbye and tossed his phone on the passenger seat, knocking the waitress's map onto the floor.

"Oh, come on." He reached over to pick it up, pulling his eyes off the road for a second. The map was just beyond his fingertips.

He stretched his hand a little farther. He felt the paper and swiped at it. "Yes." When he straightened up, he was drifting into the other lane and a giant truck was barreling down on him. The driver laid on his horn, and Eric jerked on his steering wheel to correct course, almost clipping the crazy lady on the scooter as he passed her.

His pulse pounded. "Shoot."

That was close. He looked in his rearview mirror. The woman's scooter wobbled some more, then veered into the ditch and tipped over. Eric winced. What was she thinking driving that thing on this road? It was rough and uneven, and there was no shoulder. Maybe he'd gotten a little close to her, but it was hardly his fault she put herself in such a precarious position.

Should he stop to make sure she was okay? He looked in the rearview again and saw her stand up, dust herself off, and push the scooter back onto the road.

She was fine. He, on the other hand, was hungry and exhausted from driving all day and just wanted to find his new place and unload all the Trader Joe's food from his Jeep. He took another right and checked the map. House number 600. Just up ahead.

A small horse trailer was parked along the road in front of the house next door to his rental, and he cast a wary eye at the

Beware of Dog sign staked in the middle of the yard among an assortment of gaudy lawn ornaments. Great. He hated dogs. And where did his neighbor keep a horse?

He swung around the trailer and pulled into his driveway. The place wasn't much to look at. The siding hadn't been updated since the nineties from what he could tell, and if the front yard had any grass in it, it was well hidden by all the weeds. But he hopped out of the Jeep with a fistful of determination. It was only temporary. And he'd have lots of good stories to tell his buddies when he returned to Seattle.

Wait a minute.

What was that thing on his porch?

two

"You-*niece*. You-*niece*." Eunice Parker limped down the road muttering to herself. How was it possible the weekend nurse at the clinic still pronounced her name wrong after all this time? It rhymed with geese. Fleece. Henri Matisse. It wasn't that hard.

Maybe if she hadn't been so preoccupied with geese on her way home from her appointment, she wouldn't have ended up in the ditch. No, that wasn't correct. It was entirely, one hundred percent that blue Jeep's fault. Who was that guy, anyway? After living in Tukston all forty-six years of her life, she knew a stranger when she saw one.

She ought to report the car to the police. Her knee hurt, her coat had a tear, and the front wheel of her beat-up old Honda Spree scooter was now flat. It was a miracle her urostomy bag hadn't ripped off when she hit the ground, the stupid thing. As she pushed the Honda along, she looked at the scooter more closely. The right-side mirror was busted, too. Super.

She hadn't made note of the license plate number on the Jeep, but it had to be the only vehicle in town painted such an ostentatious color. Where did that guy think he was, anyway? Miami? The cops shouldn't have any trouble tracking him down. She turned down her street and spotted her house. So close yet so far away. Her whole body ached.

Dr. Mullins kept telling her she needed to quit riding her

scooter around town—that it was too dangerous in her condition—but she'd already sold her car. She didn't feel comfortable
behind the wheel anymore with how light-headed she could get.
She didn't want to hurt anyone. She'd settled for the scooter to
get around the past two months. But now?

The flat tire *fwop*, *fwop*, *fwop*ped against the pavement.
Now she was in trouble.

By the time she reached the dinged-up single-horse trailer in
front of her house, her arms were Jell-O. She leaned the scooter
against the trailer with a murmur of relief, then kicked the tire
weakly when a surge of anger sparked through her. How dare
that nurse mispronounce her name? How dare that Jeep run
her off the road?

How dare her body betray her?

Sweat dripped from her forehead and stung her eyes. She
trudged around the trailer and froze. The blue Jeep. It was right
there next door, parked in the Gustafsons' driveway. Blue Jeep
Guy was the new renter?

Suuuper.

Eunice sat on a stool and cradled her head in her hands,
elbows on her kitchen counter. She'd emptied her urostomy
bag—not so nicely referring to it as No-No in her frustration
instead of JoJo, her usual name for it—and taken some Tylenol
with water. And now she waited. The headache should start
to ease in another fifteen minutes or so. Then she would call
the police.

She opened one eye a tiny bit to study the piece of paper
in front of her. Maybe she should add Nurse Ratched's name
from Dr. Mullins's office to her list. Ha. Two could play the
name game. But no. This list was too important to be used for
something as frivolous as that. She moved her finger along the

page, counting names, though she knew exactly how many there were.

One, two, three, four, five, six, seven.

A groan escaped. Did she really want to spend what little time she had left on these seven people? It seemed such a daunting task. Impossible even. Especially if she couldn't get the Honda Spree fixed. And even if she could, the scooter couldn't take her any farther than the city limits. She studied the list again. Some of these people lived miles outside of Tukston. The last name she had written wasn't even . . .

She sat up a little straighter as the pain in her head began to lessen. "Oh, Lo-ord," she called out in a singsong voice, giving *Lord* two syllables. "You're not making this easy."

There was no response. Maybe she was crazy to think this whole thing was His idea in the first place. If it was, He wouldn't allow some guy to ride into town on his blue horse and ruin her plans, would He?

Well. He had allowed worse things.

She let her head sink to the counter, where the coolness of the cracked linoleum felt good against her temple. The headaches were becoming more frequent. The body aches more debilitating. How much longer before Tylenol no longer worked? Her urostomy bag rested on her lap as a constant reminder, something that still bothered her despite Dr. Mullins's assurance that she would get used to it in time.

Ah, time.

Her eyes lined up with the fish tank sitting across from her on a wooden stand. She'd had such big plans for it when she rescued it from the dump last summer. Had imagined it filled with multicolored rocks, plastic treasure chests, and decorative artificial plants. Had longed to see it bursting with colorful fish, teeming with life. But life—and its limits—had gotten in the way, and the tank was destined to remain empty. Just like the plastic dog dishes on the floor in her laundry room and the purple cat carrier on the top shelf of her closet.

Everything was empty.

Eunice lifted her head with renewed purpose. She couldn't allow the new guy in town to take her list away from her, as well. It was all she had left. He needed to pay for what he'd done. She pulled her phone from her back pocket and tapped it awake. After calling the police to make her report, her next call would be to a lawyer.

Unless . . .

Her finger froze in midair. No, no. She couldn't do that. It was a ridiculous idea. Then again, he was new to town and wouldn't know anything about her past. He probably wouldn't bother her with small talk or prying questions. And he had a perfectly functional vehicle and presumably a valid driver's license, which was more than she could say for herself.

Her list taunted her from the counter. *I will not let you rest.* Her sore knee taunted her from beneath the fabric of her pants. *I will not let you walk around town.*

Yes, it was a ridiculous idea, but what did she have to lose? She would talk to him. She would make her ultimatum. She would complete one final task before it was all over.

Her head sank back onto the counter.

But not until tomorrow.

three

$\mathcal{E}$ ric panted through his fourth and final set of twenty-five push-ups, twenty-five burpees, and twenty-five crunches. He'd found himself breathing hard during his two-mile jog earlier, as he wasn't used to the thinner air that came with a higher elevation.

He scrutinized his flexed and shirtless profile in the mirror before hopping in the shower. He was determined to return to Seattle in better shape than he left, to show his friends that country living hadn't changed him. If he went back after three months with flabby arms—or, heaven forbid, a can or two missing from his six-pack—they might think his ambitions had gone soft, as well.

His shower was quick and hot, and he dressed with more optimism than he'd had yesterday when he arrived. Just because he was stuck in Nowhereville for the summer didn't mean he couldn't make the most of it. He would exceed everyone's expectations. In fact, he would increase the Tukston branch's profits by ten percent, two percentage points more than the advisor Uncle Jack had sent to a different branch. How was that for a "big thing"? His uncle would wonder why he hadn't promoted Eric sooner.

Today held promise. The sun was shining, and there were all kinds of hills and mountains around for his new favorite toy to explore. Even though the GPS in his Jeep was unreliable, Eric was still happy with his purchase. Just think of the photos he'd be able to post on social media from up in the mountains.

He sat at the table with an acai bowl from Trader Joe's and sent a text to his brother.

Good luck at work today. You got this!

Chase was quick to respond.

I hate hamburgers.

Eric chuckled as he sent back two thumbs-up, then finished off a protein smoothie. He checked for other messages, but after she'd peppered him with texts the day before, there was nothing but silence from Tiffani today. It figured. She'd been impossible for him to figure out ever since they'd met. Ever since that benefit dinner where she'd saved him from making a fool of himself in front of Mr. Lindor. Yes, *the* Mr. Lindor, whom she later convinced to transfer his investments to Eric's care.

Tiffani might be impossible, but where would he be without her?

He quickly washed, rinsed, and dried his dishes and set them back in the cupboard to avoid any clutter on his countertops. Clutter made him nervous. Then he filled his water bottle and grabbed a couple of Clif Bars from the pantry. Time to get a move on. Daylight was a-wasting, as Uncle Jack would say.

He found his tennis shoes tucked neatly against the wall where he'd left them by the front door and bent to pull them on. A timid knock sounded, and he stilled, fingers on the laces. Who would be showing up at his house on a Sunday morning?

Eunice tugged on the front of her shirt to make sure JoJo was good and covered, then knocked again, harder this time. It

21

wasn't that early. He couldn't still be sleeping. And the Jeep was in the driveway in all its blue glory so she knew he was home.

Cinderella was on the front porch, pecking at ants. She was the strangest chicken Eunice had ever seen—a black Polish hen with a riot of black-and-white feathers on her head—and for some reason she thought she lived at the Gustafson house. Eunice kind of hoped Cinderella would leave a splatter of poop for Blue Jeep Man to step in next time he left the house. Wouldn't it just serve him right.

The knob turned, and Eunice jumped. A man she guessed to be in his mid-twenties opened the door, and she involuntarily took a step back. Muscular biceps poked out from the sleeves of his T-shirt, and bright blue eyes that rivaled the car in the driveway looked at her curiously. Oh, how fantastic. Good-looking men always thought they knew everything.

He leaned against the doorframe as he took in her ratty sweat-pants and purple Crocs. "Hello."

She raised her chin. "You ran me over with your Jeep."

"Excuse me?"

Eunice waved an arm toward the offending vehicle. "You knocked me into a ditch and broke my scooter."

Realization dawned on his chiseled cheekbones and perfectly proportioned nose. "Hey, I'm sorry about that. There was a truck coming at me, and—"

She held up a hand. "No excuses."

"Uh. Okay." He stood up straight. "How did you find me?"

"I live next door."

A look she could only interpret as disappointment twisted his face. Or maybe it was fear. "I really am sorry, but I never actually hit you."

Eunice's hands clenched. The *nerve*. "It was reckless endangerment. I'm going to report the incident to the police and then ask my lawyer to draw up papers for a lawsuit."

He blanched. Ha. Just the response she was hoping for.

"Unless."

His eyebrows raised. "Unless?"

She took a deep breath. Did she really want to do this? It had seemed like a good idea last night, but this man was a stranger. Could be a serial killer for all she knew. Or a tree hugger. But no, the Gustafsons were picky about who they rented to, and she had no other options. Eunice Parker did not exactly have a long queue of friends lined up at her door to help her in her time of trial.

"I need a driver."

The ridiculously handsome man tilted his head. "You need a ride somewhere?"

"I need a ride to seven somewheres, and you're going to take me. Now that I can no longer rely on my scooter."

He rubbed the back of his neck. She sensed his hesitation.

"My *vintage* Honda Spree scooter," she added. "Which *you* destroyed. Or else I'll sue."

The scooter had already been in bad shape before it took a nosedive into the ditch, but he didn't need to know that. And she'd never sued anyone before and had no idea how it worked or if she'd have a case, but he didn't need to know that either.

He crossed his arms over his chest. "Where are these seven places? And when are you supposed to go to them? I have to work tomorrow."

"Not today. Just . . . soon. One place at a time. I have a list of people I need to visit."

"Like a bucket list?"

She gulped. More like a *None of Your Business* list. "Will you help me or not?"

He gave her a crooked grin. Oh, didn't that just take the cake. He had the most adorable dimples she'd ever seen.

"I don't even know your name."

"My name is Eunice Eugenia Rasmussen Parker . . ."

His eyes widened.

"... and I almost deserve it."

"What does *that* mean?"

She grimaced. She should've known better than to try a literary joke on this guy. "I suppose you've never read C. S. Lewis."

The man shrugged.

"*The Voyage of the Dawn Treader?*"

"Is he a blogger?"

"Never mind. What's *your* name?"

"Eric. Eric Larson."

Larson? Eunice tugged at the front of her shirt again. It wasn't the name of a serial killer. She'd known a Larson once. "Well, now that you know my name, will you help me?"

The crack in her voice must have given her away because he looked up and studied her face. She didn't want to come across as desperate. Needy. But she was.

"All right."

She swallowed. Shifted on her feet. "All right?"

"I'll help you." He grinned. "In exchange for your silence about the scooter."

Those dimples, those eyes . . . they probably helped Eric get special treatment from other women. Women who still had time left to dream about handsome men. But they weren't going to work on her.

She forced her face into a serious expression, gave a curt nod, and held out her hand.

He shook it with a wink. "Deal."

"Deal."

What had she done?

four

ric's Jeep failed to direct him to Larson Financial on Monday morning, but he was willing to forgive it for that after the awesome time he'd had driving around yesterday. The weather and the scenery and the driving part had been awesome anyway. The stewing over the deal he'd made with Eunice? Not so much. He was *not* looking forward to following through on his end of the bargain.

What choice did he have, though? A reckless endangerment charge, lawsuit, or both would not exactly help with proving himself to Uncle Jack. If his uncle found out about it, he'd leave him to rot in Tukston forever, instead of moving him up the ladder in Seattle. That was not an option. *"Be nice,"* his uncle had said, and Eric was pretty sure he'd meant to everyone. Even crazy ladies on scooters.

Eric drove up and down Tukston's two main streets until he saw the *Larson Financial* sign. This was the smallest and farthest away of the company's four branches, but it had the same familiar custom-built sign with the bold blue letters. As he parked in front of the white one-story building, his phone rang.

He answered, "Don't you ever text?"

"Have you met the team yet?" Uncle Jack asked.

Eric checked the time. He was five minutes early, which was about ten minutes too late in Uncle Jack's mind.

"I just pulled up." Eric unbuckled and opened his door. The air was brisk this morning. "I'm heading in."

"Call me on your way home tonight, let me know how it goes. Tell everyone hello for me. And remember our motto: 'Your financial security tomorrow—'"

"'—is our leading goal today.' I remember."

His uncle was acting like a nervous parent on his child's first day of school. Why send him here if he didn't think Eric could handle it? Eric knew the loss of the senior financial advisor at the Tukston branch had been an unexpected blow, and he knew it would take time to find a suitable replacement out here in Isolation Nation. He just didn't know why *he* had to be the one to fill in.

Eric stepped onto the sidewalk. "Will do, Uncle Jack."

He dropped the phone in his unzipped briefcase and smoothed a hand down the front of his dark-blue tie. Time to meet his new team.

The air inside the office smelled of coffee and carpet cleaner. An elderly woman with short white curls sat behind the reception desk. Her glasses had silver chains attached to each arm, and she wore a red crewneck sweatshirt that said *World's Greatest Grandma*.

She greeted him with a bright smile and a loud voice. "Good morning. You must be Eric. We're glad you're here."

"And you must be Winnie." Eric returned her smile and raised his volume level to match hers. "Uncle Jack told me all about you."

It was partly true. He'd told Eric the receptionist was an older woman with great phone skills and an eye for detail who had retired three years ago with a "big to-do" and then kept showing up to work. He hadn't mentioned that Winnie was at least eighty and practically deaf.

Winnie pointed across the room. "Coffee's on, if you want."

Ah, coffee. He'd brewed some earlier with his French press—

two pumps of sugar-free hazelnut syrup and one tablespoon of almond milk—but he wouldn't turn down another cup. After all, as a born-and-bred Seattleite, coffee was his middle name, area of expertise, and birthright.

He glanced at the side table where Winnie pointed and swallowed hard. The pot looked about twenty years old, and if the name on the can sitting next to it was any indication, the stuff inside—which he would not deign to call coffee—was a long trip to the bathroom waiting to happen. Valu Brew. Such a bargain brand, they couldn't even afford the *e*.

He shook his head. "No, thanks."

"Okay, then let me show you where your desk is. You've got thirty minutes to get settled before your first appointment."

Eric frowned as he followed the tiny woman's squeaky white tennis shoes through a glass-paneled door to the back room. He hadn't anticipated receiving any clients on his first day. He'd planned to spend most of this week getting to know the other two advisors and familiarizing himself with his predecessor's caseload. But the sooner he started taking clients, the sooner he could begin racking up that ten-percent growth in profit he needed to impress Uncle Jack.

The beige room had a water cooler along the back wall. A plain wooden desk on each side of the room faced the other. There was a large black chair behind each desk and two smaller black chairs in front. Just enough room existed between the setup on the left and the setup on the right to walk through to get a cup of water.

Winnie gestured toward the desk on the right. "That one's for you." She waved to the left. "That's Max's over there."

"What about Benson? I thought there were three of us."

Winnie leaned her right ear closer. "What's that?"

Eric raised his voice. "I thought there would be three of us working here."

"Oh." She nodded. "You mean Benson. He's the part-time assistant. That's his table over there."

27

She pointed to the far left corner of the room. Eric hadn't even noticed the tiny table. Was that duct tape on the legs? How did anyone have any privacy around here?

"He doesn't meet with clients?"

That explained a lot. Though Uncle Jack had insisted there was a "measurable need for our services" in Tukston, Eric had wondered how this office could support two advisors, let alone three. The front door opened and shut, and he spun around.

Winnie followed suit. "There's Max now."

Max strolled through the glass door and approached them on bowed legs, gangly except for a paunch hanging over his leather belt. He removed his cowboy hat, and the fluorescent lighting shone off his balding head. Eric struggled to keep the surprise off his face. Not because Max was going bald, but because he was wearing jeans. Jeans—as in pants made from denim. Uncle Jack would never allow an employee wearing jeans into the building of Larson Financial in Seattle. Not even on their day off.

Max extended a hand, and when Eric shook it, Max pumped enthusiastically. "Well, well, well. Look what the cat drug in. You remind me of your uncle, all dressed up like that."

Eric looked down at his clothes. Standard office attire. Max wasn't even wearing a tie, although it would look pretty strange with his triangle-and-stripe western shirt if he was.

"It's mighty nice to see you, Eric," Max continued. "Mighty nice. I wasn't sure how much longer I could hold this place together by myself."

Winnie huffed, and Max winked at her. "I wasn't completely on my own, of course."

"Well, unlike you gentlemen, I don't have time to stand around and chat all day." Winnie patted Eric's arm. "Let me know if you need anything, hon. You know where to find me."

She walked back through the glass-paneled door and resumed her position at the reception desk with a spry little hop to get up on her ergonomic office chair. Eric shook his head. What kind of team was he working with here?

"If you're anything like your uncle, I imagine you're ready to get right down to business." Max clapped him on the shoulder. "I'll leave you to it, but holler if you have any questions."

Eric nodded and forced a smile. Yes, with the setup in here, all he would have to do was "holler" across the room to ask Max a question. His first business expense was going to be ordering a cubicle wall. He glanced around. And maybe a new table for poor Benson.

He checked the time: 8:24. He scrambled to his desk and searched for information about the client who would arrive any minute. What was their name? Had they been to the office before?

Nothing helpful.

He grumbled to himself. He preferred a meticulous approach to preparing for client meetings. Though he was thirty-two, people often mistook him for younger and assumed he was still wet behind the ears, which made them hesitant to put him in charge of their hard-earned money. It was a challenge he eagerly accepted, to earn each client's trust. He hated going into an appointment blind.

The phone on his desk rang, and he snatched it up. He could hear Winnie's voice coming from the lobby and through the phone at the same time.

"Your eight-thirty is here."

What would Uncle Jack do in this situation?

Eric put on a confident smile, cleared his throat, and straightened his tie. "Send them in."

Eric sat on an outdoor chaise lounge on his back deck and pulled on a sweatshirt. The evening sun was warm on his face, but the air was colder than he'd expected for June. Must be the elevation again. He relaxed into the chair, thankful the rental house came furnished.

It had been an interesting day. With the small number of clients who had been scheduled from eight-thirty to five-thirty, he'd assumed he would have plenty of time for administrative tasks and maybe even some research or prospecting. But almost everyone who came in to see him had settled in as if preparing to share their life story. He'd barely had twenty minutes to run to the grocery store down the street for a deli sandwich for lunch.

He would not be making that mistake again.

He'd placed an order for a sound-absorbing office partition as soon as he got home. After dinner, he'd placed another for an office-sized Keurig. It was time to give clients other options besides Valu Brew.

His phone alerted him to a notification, and he swiped to see the photo Tiffani had posted. A selfie of her in a sundress, posed along the rail of someone's shiny, pristine boat. He grunted. She worked hard not to let people see any other side of her besides the one she presented on social media. But he'd seen it. The other side that was clever and generous and sometimes insecure.

He looked closer at the photo. Was that Greg's boat? What was she doing with *him*?

Eric shut off the screen and leaned his head back. It didn't matter. She was free to do whatever she wanted with whomever she wanted. It's not like they were dating.

At the moment.

He turned his thoughts back to his clients. Most of the people he'd met had been friendly and understated. None of them was looking for a big payday or even a comfortable retirement. They had been concerned about one thing, and one thing only: their families. *Will my wife be able to keep our house if I die? How do I make sure my son with special needs will be taken care of? Is it possible to get out of the hole on my land so I won't burden my children with debt when I'm gone?*

He hadn't debriefed with Max at the end of the day, but he guessed his day had been much of the same. In Seattle, most of his clients already had a lot of money, and their main concern was how to make more. How to squeeze the most out of the system. How to capitalize on their capital. But here? It had only been one day, but it kind of seemed like most people were just trying to survive.

That might make it hard to squeeze additional profit out of the branch. Hard, but not impossible. Eric would find a way. He remembered the look on Uncle Jack's face when Brady the Brownnoser reported on the eight-percent growth he'd accomplished at a branch in Redmond. Eric wanted to earn that same look of affirmation.

A look he'd never received from his own father. Uncle Jack's self-absorbed, unreliable, and adulterous younger brother.

A gravelly sound caught his attention, and he spied that weird-looking chicken scratching at the ground by the chain-link fence. One glance at that fancy plumage on its head and he couldn't help but wonder if its mother had gotten frisky with a cockatiel. Would that make it a chickatiel? How did it get into his yard? Why was it always here? He needed to find out who it belonged to.

Through the fence, Eric noticed Eunice's backyard. It was the same size as his, but it was crowded with plants and raised garden beds and . . . were those bowling balls? It must take forever to mow around all those things. And he didn't know much about gardening, but if all those raised beds had vegetables planted in them, Eunice was going to end up with an awful lot of produce for one person.

Assuming she lived alone. Which he did.

His phone announced the arrival of a text, and he checked the screen. Tiffani again, asking him to call her. She blew him

31

off all day yesterday and now she wanted to talk? His neck muscles tightened. This was so Tiffani typical. Maybe he would call her later.

Speaking of phone calls, though, Uncle Jack would be eager to hear how the day went. Seattle was an hour behind Tukston, so Eric had waited to give his uncle time to wrap up his own day, yet he knew if he didn't call soon, Uncle Jack would beat him to it.

He punched the appropriate buttons on his phone.

"Eric." Uncle Jack picked up on the first ring. "How'd it go? Tell me everything."

five

By Friday morning, Eric's lungs had adjusted to the altitude, and he barely broke a sweat during his two-mile loop. By the time he was ready to leave for work at exactly seven-thirty, he felt as if he were king of the world. His body was doing everything he demanded of it, and the new Keurig and variety pack of K-Cup pods to go with it had been waiting on his front porch when he got home from work last night. He couldn't wait to see the look on Winnie's face when he brought the coffeemaker into the office.

He slung his briefcase strap over his shoulder and balanced the two boxes in his arms as he left the house. Which explained why he didn't see the poop on his porch until it was too late. His smile dimmed. His shoes were Salvatore Ferragamo, a gift from Tiffani. Did that chickatiel do this? How could such a little thing leave such a big mess?

He scraped his shoe along the edge of the grass on his way to the Jeep, muttering to himself about what kind of tacky shoes the town of Tukston might have to offer if his loafers were ruined. He swung the box toward his vehicle.

"Ouch."

He jumped, losing his grip on the bottom box. It plummeted to the ground, slamming into the concrete. He looked up with wide eyes. Eunice stood beside the Jeep like she owned it. What was she doing here?

His smile went from dim to nonexistent.

Eunice was not smiling either. "First you run me over on the road, and now in your driveway?"

"Sorry, I didn't see you there." Eric set the K-pods on the hood of the Jeep and gingerly picked up the Keurig box. "I also wasn't expecting anyone in my driveway this early in the morning."

"I wanted to catch you before you left. Where do you work anyway?"

He shook the box warily, and his heart sank when it rattled. He'd removed all the packaging and padding last night and only set the appliance back in the empty box for transportation purposes. A mistake, apparently.

"It's broken."

Eunice wrapped her arms around her stomach and looked down at her feet, which were clad in the same purple Crocs as yesterday. "I'd like to schedule our first outing for tomorrow."

Eric pressed his lips together. She said it as though she was booking an oil change.

"Tomorrow, I . . ." He scrambled for an excuse, yet he had no plans. Wasn't even sure what a plausible excuse would be around here. But he didn't want to "schedule an outing."

"I work at Larson Financial."

She fidgeted. "They're closed on Saturdays."

"You asked where I work."

"Oh." She narrowed her eyes. "That explains the tailored slacks. Just like Jack."

"You know my uncle?"

"I . . . knew him. Is he aware of your reckless behavior?"

Uh-oh. Seemed like everyone in town remembered Uncle Jack. Would Eunice call him up to tattle if he didn't do what she asked? He checked his watch. He needed to get to work. Maybe it wouldn't be so bad driving Eunice around tomorrow. The sooner he took her to visit all the people she wanted to visit, the sooner his obligation to her would end.

"What time do you want to leave?"

She took a step back as if he'd startled her. "Nine?"

Eric carried both boxes back to the porch and set them down. He'd have to deal with them later. "Okay."

A strange expression passed over her face. "Okay."

She tromped off toward her house without looking back. Eric shook his head. What a piece of work. Never even said she was sorry about the broken Keurig. Never even acknowledged it.

Eric hopped in the Jeep and started the engine. Desk work. That was what he wanted. Numbers and forms, statistics and percentages.

That was the easy stuff.

Eunice sat at the kitchen counter, trembling. Her list rested at her fingertips. Yes, it had been her idea to drag Eric into this, but what had she been thinking?

Her head ached, and her stoma's stony silence taunted her. The other types of ostomies—colostomies and ileostomies—made all kinds of noise, she'd learned. Gurgling, grumbling, growling . . . even whistling. But it figured JoJo was the silent type. Urostomies made nary a peep.

Even when someone moved in and literally took up residence on her body, Eunice still couldn't pull off a conversation.

Oh well. She'd always preferred talking with animals over people anyway. Had dreamed of becoming a vet and helping the creatures most people took for granted. But none of that mattered now.

Her shoulders sagged, and she fought the urge to lay her head down on the counter. Only eight-thirty in the morning and her strength was already used up.

She'd woken up early and spent almost an hour talking herself into going over to Eric's house. She'd felt like a fool, standing out there. Needing him. Then when he'd agreed to take her out tomorrow, she'd panicked. Now she *had* to do it. For the past month, it had all been a grand idea in her mind.

Now it was real.

The doorbell rang, and Eunice groaned. Was Bertie here already? At least it wasn't a Wanda week. Wanda was the worst.

Eunice tucked her list into the pocket of her bathrobe—had she really gone over to Eric's in her bathrobe?—and slowly slid off her stool and padded toward the door. Bertie let herself in before Eunice was halfway across the living room.

"Good morning." The home nurse greeted her with a wide smile. "It's a beautiful day."

Eunice grunted. Bertie always said that.

"Hi."

"Have you eaten breakfast yet?"

"Yes."

Bertie put her hands on her hips. "Did not."

Eunice ran her fingers through her thinning hair. "Okay, fine. Not yet."

"Let's get to it then."

Eunice wearily returned to her stool and watched as Bertie prepared 7-grain oatmeal on the stovetop and rinsed blueberries. The oatmeal was from Eunice's cupboard, the fruit from Bertie's bag. Bertie kept up a steady stream of chatter, going on about the weather forecast and her plans for the weekend and her son's upcoming thirteenth birthday.

"A teenager, can you believe it?"

What Eunice really couldn't believe was that she and Bertie were nearly the same age. Bertie was a couple of years younger, but they were both in their mid-forties. Bertie had a husband, two kids, and a full-time job as a home health nurse. Her biggest health complaint was perimenopause. Aside from occasional online work for Dusty's store, Eunice had no one, nothing, and less than six months to live.

She chuckled.

"What's so funny?" Bertie asked.

"Nothing." Eunice leaned her elbows on the counter. "I'm just dying over here and you're talking about a birthday party."

If she couldn't laugh about it, she'd have to cry. And she didn't want to do that.

Bertie harrumphed, put on a stern face, and pointed a finger at her. "Excuse me for not pretending to be as depressed as you."

This was why Eunice preferred Bertie to the other nurse, Wanda. When Bertie said stuff like that, Eunice knew it was because she cared and didn't want Eunice to give up on life before it gave up on her. When Wanda said stuff like that, she meant it.

Bertie's face softened. "Did you see Dr. Mullins this week?"

It made Eunice tired just thinking about it. With the scooter out of commission, she'd been forced to walk the half mile to the clinic, and her stamina had been sorely tested. She had clearly taken the Honda for granted.

"Yes."

Bertie slid Eunice's breakfast in front of her on the counter and waited. Eunice drew squares on the linoleum.

The nurse sprinkled more brown sugar on top and pushed the bowl closer. "And?"

Eunice sighed. Picked up the spoon. "And nothing. Everything's the same. My levels haven't changed."

Sometimes it felt like years since Dr. Mullins had opened her up to remove her diseased bladder and create a stoma only to find her cancer had spread far beyond what the scans had shown. But it had only been a few months.

"That's great news." Bertie scooped a bowl of oatmeal for herself and poured milk over it. "You want some of this?"

Eunice moved her spoon out of the way. "Just a little."

It should be good news. The fact that her numbers hadn't

gotten worse since last week. But she couldn't bring herself to get excited about it. The inevitability of her impending death scoffed at any attempt to wring false hope from a positive doctor's report. The only real positive thing she could wring out was that Dr. Mullins said she didn't have to keep coming in every week as long as she remained stable. "Once a month is fine," he'd said. "As long as the home nurses keep an eye on you."

Eunice wasn't sure how much eye-keeping the weekly Friday check-ins accomplished, yet she didn't mind seeing Bertie twice a month. Wanda, she minded.

"How's JoJo feeling today?" Bertie asked.

Eunice scooped a few blueberries with her spoon and dropped them in her oatmeal. "Out of sorts."

"Want me to take a look at her?"

"No."

"Are you keeping her clean?"

Eunice grunted. Of course she was. Usually. When she felt up to it. She lifted her eyes to the heavens. *Lord, do I smell? Is that why she's asking?*

"You know, my neighbor's cat just had kittens." Bertie kept on talking as she finished her oatmeal. "She's giving them away to good homes. They are the most adorable things you ever saw. Brown and white. You should think about it."

Eunice *had* thought about it, many times. She'd never been allowed a pet growing up because her mother thought they were too messy. Once Eunice was on her own, the first thing she did was rescue a dog from the shelter: Charlie, a spunky terrier mix with one missing ear and a big heart. And that had ended in a tragedy from which she had yet to recover.

She shuddered. She'd always meant to try again. Always yearned to provide sanctuary for all the animals no one else wanted. But . . .

"A kitten would cheer you up," Bertie prodded.

"I don't want to leave behind any orphans."

"Oh, for goodness' sake." Bertie shook her head. "It's a cat, not a child."

"JoJo would be covered in cat hair."

Bertie stood and set her bowl in the sink. "You're impossible."

For a fleeting, wistful moment, Eunice imagined rubbing her hand over a kitten's soft back. Filling a dish with food and having it come running over with a *purr*. Lifting it onto her lap for a snuggle while they watched her favorite show together. What would it be like to have a companion again? To be needed?

But it was no use. She knew what it felt like to be abandoned. She wasn't going to intentionally put anyone through that.

Not even a cat.

Eunice lay awake on her bed, eyes wide open, and checked the time again. Past midnight. Tick, tick, tick. Sleep never came when she wanted it to.

Her window was cracked open so she could hear the nighttime sounds and smell the fresh air. The world was quiet and still.

"Hey, God." She turned on her side. "You still up? Of course you are. Could you help me out? I need to get my beauty sleep so I can face Mr. Perfect tomorrow." She chuckled to herself. "Okay, maybe not *beauty* sleep. I'd settle for not-a-total-zombie sleep."

She'd been nice-looking once. No Miss America or anything, but she'd turned a few heads. That was long before years of loneliness and heartache had taken their toll. Before her body's gradual rebellion. Before illnesses and surgeries and diagnoses. Definitely before JoJo unceremoniously entered her life.

"I'm sorry, God." She turned to the other side. "I shouldn't be so vain. It doesn't matter what I look like."

Her eyes remained open as she mulled over the plans she'd made. Less than nine hours until she was supposed to meet Eric in his driveway. What if he noticed her ostomy pouch? What if he asked her questions? She'd assumed he wouldn't care to know anything about her, but what if she was wrong?

Then there was the first name on her list to worry about. Jane Brandel. Of all the people she felt compelled to reach out to, to reconcile with, Jane should be the easiest. She'd always been a gracious person. That was why Eunice had put her first on the list. But what if she laughed in her face? Or worse, felt sorry for her.

She turned onto her back and folded her hands over her stomach. Maybe if she actually closed her eyes it would help. She squeezed them shut. *Sleep, sleep, sleep.*

The hours ticked by.

six

*E*ric stepped out of his house at nine o'clock sharp. The chickatiel was by the door as if it had been waiting for him. When he walked down the steps and over to the driveway, it followed.

"Shoo." He waved his hands at it. "Go home."

It made a peculiar warbling sound and cocked its head to stare at him with one beady eye. Eric put his hands in his pockets and leaned his back against the Jeep to wait. How did lonely and desperate creatures always seem to find him? Speaking of which . . .

He fixed an eye on Eunice's house, watching for any signs of life. Maybe she'd forgotten and he was off the hook. He would give her five minutes. The grass in her front yard was nicer than his, but there were garish lawn ornaments everywhere. A giant ladybug on a metal stake with its eyes hanging from the sockets on springs. A sunflower wind chime clanging and clonging. And the bowling balls. Purple ones, silver ones, striped ones, speckled ones. They were everywhere.

The chickatiel pecked at his foot, and Eric kicked at it. Not enough to make his PETA friends upset or anything. Just enough to back it up a little.

"I see you've met Cinderella."

Eric looked up. Eunice was crossing her yard, wearing those

41

purple Crocs and holding a frumpy jacket closed across her chest as if it were December.

He pushed off the Jeep and took a step toward his neighbor. "This thing has a name?"

Eunice nodded, adjusting the purple messenger bag that hung from her shoulder. "She's a Polish hen."

"Where does it—*she* live?"

"On your porch, I guess."

Eric rubbed his temple. "But where does she belong?"

Eunice shrugged. "Some people down the road had a whole flock of chickens a couple years ago. Renters. One morning, they skipped town and left everything behind, including their hens. Cinderella's the only one left."

He stared at his neighbor for a moment. She appeared to be serious. His shoulders drooped. What was the statistical probability the dumb thing would end up at the house *he* was renting? "I guess that means no one's waiting for her to come home."

A ghost of a smile softened Eunice's worn face. "I guess not."

Eric fought off a groan. Fine. He could ignore a chicken for one summer. Was it really Polish? Chase would get a kick out of that.

He tried to put on a friendly face and opened the passenger door. "Well, are you ready to go?"

The ghost of a smile turned into a corporeal scowl. "Would I be over here if I wasn't?"

Yikes. Touchy. He gestured toward the Jeep, and she climbed in gingerly as if she'd never been inside a vehicle before. He walked around the front to get in the driver's side, muttering to himself that she could've just said *yes* like a normal person.

Hopefully her shoes were clean.

He buckled up and started the engine. Time to get this over with. "All right, where to?"

Eunice shifted in her seat. "The first name on my list is Jane Brandel."

A crinkling sound caught his ear, and he noticed a piece of yellow notebook paper in her hand. "Oh. You have an actual list."

And the personality of an ill-mannered mule. And the makings of a mustache.

She quickly stuffed the paper in her pocket. "She lives just outside of town. I'll give directions as we go."

He backed out of the driveway. "You're the boss."

She waved a hand to the left, so he went left. He pushed buttons on the dash as he drove, adjusting the temperature, the airflow, the music. Uncle Jack might have scoffed at his decision to upgrade to a jacked-up Jeep with all the bells and whistles for his move to Montana, but Chase and Tiffani had been impressed.

Eunice motioned left again, with a grunt this time. Eric complied but not without a secret smirk. How had he ended up with this woman again? The Jeep hit a rough patch in the road, and he cringed. Right. He'd almost run her over.

"How long is this going to take?" He glanced at her. "You want me to drop you off for your visit and come back in an hour, or what?"

She graced him with a withering glare.

"Two hours?" He grinned, secretly pleased to be pushing her buttons. "Didn't take you for a chatterbox, but how about I give you my number and you just text me when you're ready?"

"That won't be necessary." She turned away to look out the window. "I'll only be a few minutes. You can wait in the car. Turn right at the stop sign."

He scoffed. "I'm driving you all the way out to Jane Brandel's house for 'a few minutes'? What's the point of that?"

"I need to talk to her about something important."

"You couldn't call?"

Eunice leaned away from him. Seemed to shrink before his eyes. Or shrivel. "It's something I need to do in person."

"You got a beef with this lady or something?" He tried on his teasing voice. "Should I be worried, Eunice?"

The teasing didn't work. She didn't move. Didn't respond.

His scalp started to itch. It did that when he was irritated, but he never scratched at it because it might cause premature hair loss. "You're really not going to tell me what these visits are about?"

Eunice mumbled something.

He sat up straighter. "What was that?"

"I have a bit of reconciliation to take care of, okay? People from my past."

Eric's eyebrows rose. "Reconciliation. You mean I'm giving up my free time to help you bury hatchets?"

She spun around and fixed him with a look he could not interpret. Stared long enough he began to squirm. Then her body relaxed, and one side of her mouth twitched up. "Better than burying bodies."

Eunice hid her smile when Eric laughed out loud about the bodies. Didn't want to encourage him. He was like a six-month-old golden retriever: old enough to be house-trained and follow basic commands but still unfairly adorable and annoyingly energetic. As he made the final turn and they approached Jane's house, however, any hint of humor vanished. Was it *really* so important to confess all her sins before the Almighty said, "Time's up"? What if Jane wasn't even home?

"It's that green house on the left," she said.

Eric nodded. "Roger that."

She swallowed hard. Why did she feel so nervous about facing her old friend? She was dying, you know. She had nothing to lose. But as Eric parked the Jeep and turned to her expectantly, her heart raced with trepidation.

"Okay then." She opened the passenger door and hesitated. "I guess I'll, uh, be right back."

She shut the door and took one tentative step toward the house. Her body resisted even as a sense of urgency propelled her forward. Another step. Dr. Mullins had been telling her for years to avoid stressful situations to prevent flare-ups of her autoimmune disease. This would certainly qualify. She could turn back now and Jane would never have to know.

But Eric was sitting in the Jeep, watching and waiting. Super.

Eunice sighed. "You got me into this, God." She reached the front step. "You'll have to get me through it, too."

Standing in front of the door, she checked to make sure JoJo was covered. Why had she left her bag in the Jeep? The glorified purse she called her *survostobag*—it held the emergency ostomy supplies she took with her everywhere she went—gave her hands something to fiddle with. Something to hold.

She cleared her throat. "Here we go."

A short, solid knock, then a step back. She clasped her hands behind her, then stuck them in her pockets.

The door opened. Jane stared at her with wide eyes. "Oh. Hello, Eunice."

Eunice recoiled. Tukston was a small town so she'd seen Jane around over the years. It was unavoidable. But when was the last time she'd been this close to her? The lines on Jane's face and the gray in her hair reflected Eunice's own painful hurtle toward old age. A dagger of grief stabbed her heart. So many wasted years.

"Jane." She recognized the desperation that had been creeping into her voice more and more lately. "How are you?"

"Better than you, I expect." Jane paused and gave a small, wary smile. "You're wasting away."

Eunice pulled her hands from her pockets and looked down at herself. The clothes she was wearing had fit when she bought them, but now they hung on her like so many listless regrets.

"I guess I haven't been eating much lately."

Jane peered around Eunice's shoulder at the Jeep. "Who's that?"

"My neighbor."

An awkward moment passed. Jane tucked her hair behind her ears and shifted on her feet. Eunice tugged at her shirt. What was she doing? Her list burned a hole in her jacket. She could almost smell the smoke.

"I'm sorry."

Jane's eyebrows shot up. "You're sorry?"

"I was jealous when I called you a—" she shuddered, remembering every single awful word—"an uppity snob in garbage-bag clothes. You were so polished and refined when you came back from New York. All educated. I couldn't even manage to graduate from the tech school in Butte. I couldn't understand why you'd even come back here."

Jane pressed a hand to her chest. "I thought you hated me."

"I didn't mean a word I said. Your leather pants were fabulous." Eunice hung her head. "I'm so sorry."

Silence pressed in long enough that Eunice was forced to raise her head. Jane was looking wistfully into the distance. "I threw those pants away, you know. Never wore them again."

Tears stung Eunice's eyes. What an asinine jerk she had been. All because one of her closest friends had gone away to college and actually grown up while she wallowed around Tukston working part-time as a receptionist at the auto parts store.

"I could never hate you. But after everything I said, I figured *you* hated *me*."

"And that's why you've avoided me for twenty years?"

Eunice flinched. That and other things. By the time she'd finally begun to realize her attitude toward Jane had been a mistake, her health problems had started cropping up and her parents had pulled their disappearing act and . . .

"Well. Yes. Can you ever forgive me?"

Jane laughed. "Oh, Neecy." She reached out and pulled Eunice into a hug. "Of course I forgive you. I should've never let all this time go by without trying to reconnect. I just didn't want to force myself on you if you had decided to move on from our friendship. I'm sorry too."

It hurt, having Jane's arms around her. Her bones rattled at the pressure, and her lungs struggled to draw enough air to remain conscious. But Eunice hadn't felt so good in a long time.

She deserved scorn, not forgiveness. She'd expected to speak her piece and run, not hear her old nickname on her old friend's lips.

Jane released her and took a step back. "Why don't you come in? We have so much catching up to do."

Eunice looked back at the Jeep. Maybe she should have taken Eric up on his offer to drop her off. But her energy was already fading. "I can't today. My neighbor is waiting."

"Some other time?"

The hopeful expression on Jane's face ripped holes in Eunice's heart, as if it were an old and brittle pair of pantyhose. She swallowed. She could not tell Jane the truth.

"Sure," she lied. "Some other time."

Eunice shuffled back to the Jeep in a daze. She felt one seventh lighter than when she'd woken up this morning. She'd also never been more painfully aware of her mortality. Not when Dr. Mullins had solemnly given his fatal pronouncement after the bladder-removal surgery. Not when she'd printed off a DNR order and stuck it to the fridge. Not even when she'd flipped through the calendar to mark an X on the so-called limit of her life. Jane's face . . .

But the hatchet-burying part had been easier than she'd expected. She never should've put this off for so long.

When she opened the passenger door, Eric grinned. "Well? How'd it go?"

Eunice carefully positioned herself in the seat and arranged her seat belt so it wouldn't give JoJo any trouble. "Good."

"Good? You checked an item off your bucket list and that's all you have to say?"

Her lips twitched. It wasn't a bucket list. Still, she snagged a pen from her survostobag and made a show of pulling the paper from her pocket and crossing off the first name. "Really good."

"All right." Eric chuckled and put the Jeep in reverse. "Well, I'm glad."

It really had gone much better than she could've hoped. She quickly glanced at the next name on the list before sticking the piece of paper back in her jacket. Practically the whole day still lay ahead of them. Maybe they should make another stop. Keep the progress going.

"Do you need to be back at a certain time?" she asked.

Eric backed out of the driveway and pointed the Jeep toward Tukston. "Uh . . ."

"The next person on the list lives over past the post office. It's not that far. I thought—"

"You never said anything about making multiple stops."

"You don't want to chauffeur me around all summer long. I'll buy you a cinnamon roll from the diner on our way through town."

She used to love those cinnamon rolls, back when she still had an appetite. Cream cheese frosting heaped on top.

Eric hesitated. "I don't know . . ."

"I'm sure your uncle would agree with me."

It felt wrong, bringing Jack back up. But he was already part of this and mentioning him had the desired effect. A resigned expression replaced the uncertainty on Eric's face.

"Okay, you win."

seven

Turned out Eunice had not been referring to the Good Food place when she said "diner." She directed Eric to a tiny combination deli and coffee shop called Hoagies and Grinders. As he climbed out of the Jeep, he grimaced. The vehicle was filthy, the hydro blue hidden beneath layers of dust and dirt.

He joined Eunice on the sidewalk. "I don't suppose there's a car wash around here."

She looked back at the Jeep. "A self-serve one, near the gas station, but I think it's out of order. Seems a little pointless anyway."

Pointless? The Jeep had cost him half a year's salary. He saw plenty of point in keeping it sparkling clean. He held the door of the coffee shop open for her and followed close behind. The place was busy, and almost everyone turned to stare. Nosy bunch.

He flashed a smile around the room while Eunice kept her head down and trudged straight to a table for two in the corner. A teenager in—wouldn't you know it—cowboy boots met them at the table before they'd even settled in.

"Good morning," he said. "What can I get you to drink?"

Eunice didn't meet his eyes. "Water, please. And two cinnamon rolls."

Eric gulped. He'd let her talk him into this, but he didn't

actually want a cinnamon roll. Did she have any idea how many carbs were in one of those things?

The kid nodded. "Okay. Anything for you, sir?"

Eric hesitated. Did he dare try the coffee here? "Do you have almond milk? And sugar-free syrup?"

The kid nodded again.

"Great. I'll take a double-shot latte with almond milk and two pumps of sugar-free orange, please. Sixteen ounces."

The kid's face fell. "We don't have orange."

"No problem." Eric gave him a reassuring smile. "How about hazelnut?"

The kid looked relieved. "Yes, okay. I'll get that right out."

As he walked away, Eunice stood. "I'll be right back."

She cut for the bathroom before Eric could even respond. He shook his head. She reminded him a little of Chase. His little brother sometimes came across as rude and unfriendly because of how shy and timid he was. Being in a public place was practically torture for him. But with Eunice, Eric didn't think he could excuse her behavior so easily. He was pretty sure she was just weird and grumpy and trying to wreck his day off.

As Eric glanced around the little café, taking in the people and faux Parisian décor, a neatly dressed woman approached.

"Excuse me." She patted her dyed bob of hair and leaned close. "Are you the new man over at Larson Financial?"

Eric stood and held out his hand. "Yes, ma'am. Eric Larson, at your service. And you are?"

"Oh!" Her heavily powdered cheeks blushed as she shook his hand. "My, my, such manners. I'm Brenda Wallace. I heard you arrived, and I've been thinking maybe it's time to make an appointment. Get some advice about my financial situation, you know."

"Of course, Ms. Wallace." Eric nodded solemnly. "I would be happy to help. Just call the office and we'll get you scheduled."

"Wonderful." She patted her hair again. "I'll do that. And it's just Brenda."

"Okay, well, it was nice to meet you, Brenda." He took a step toward his seat, hoping she'd take the hint. He didn't mind meeting potential clients, but he didn't exactly want this woman joining him at the table or anything. What was taking Eunice so long?

"You know, there's this lovely young lady who walks Pumpkin for me on Tuesdays, and she's just the sweetest thing—"

"Pumpkin?"

"My Pomeranian. Anyway, she's about your age, and I bet you two would have so much in common. I'd love to introduce you."

He wasn't a hundred percent sure if she was referring to the dog or the dog-walker, but he wasn't interested either way. "I'm going to be busy all summer, getting the office back on track and everything. But I appreciate the thought."

Brenda looked disappointed, so he pulled out his dimples— they'd never failed him yet—and she waved a hand. "Oh, yes, of course. I'm sure you work very hard."

Eunice appeared and slid into her seat, eyes fixed on Brenda. "Oh. Hi, Brenda."

Brenda raised her chin. "Eunice."

The server appeared with a tall glass of water in one hand and a latte in the other and jostled around Brenda to get to the table. "Here you go."

"Thank you," Eric said.

Eunice continued to stare at Brenda until Brenda fidgeted with her purse. She looked back and forth between Eric and Eunice with a clear question in her eyes. "Well, I better be going. See you soon, Eric."

As she hurried off, he eased himself into his chair and looked at Eunice. "You know her?"

"It's a small town."

51

"Is she on your list?"

Eunice looked down at her hands folded on the table. It was fascinating to him, her list. All these people she wanted to reconcile with. After spending half a day with her, it was no stretch for him to believe she had her fair share of enemies. What he couldn't understand was her desire to put herself through this whole process of tracking them down to supposedly set things right. Why start caring about these people now?

Eunice took a sip of water. "No. She's not."

The overeager kid returned and set two cinnamon rolls, two forks, and two napkins on the table. Each roll was the size of a small country. "Enjoy."

Eric swallowed. "Thanks."

The kid hurried away, the café still bustling with customers. Eric eyed the carbohydrate monstrosity before him with suspicion. Tiffani would turn her nose up and say, "Straight from the lips to the hips." Chase would down it in three bites with no effect on his scrawny build. His father . . . well, his father would scoff at Eric's hesitation and say something to belittle him.

He'd abandoned Eric and his mom twenty years ago. Why did Eric still hear his father's voice in his head?

Eunice took another drink of water and narrowed her eyes at him. "Something wrong?"

He picked up his fork and banished all thoughts of his father. "No."

She kept her jacket pulled tight and scanned the small, crowded space rather than take a bite of the roll that had been her idea. "The girl at the counter is ogling you."

"Ogling?" Sounded like a word Uncle Jack would use.

Eunice swirled the ice in her glass. "She's cute."

A large bite of cinnamony goodness kept him from responding, but he couldn't resist a glance over there. The girl was in her early twenties, he guessed, probably fresh out of college.

She caught him looking and smiled. He had no choice but to smile back.

Eunice snickered. "Now you're both drooling. You should ask if she has plans for dinner."

"Uh, no." He sipped his latte. "I don't date girls with short hair."

Not to mention when she pushed her bangs out of her eyes, her fingernails were covered in chipped black nail polish.

Eunice stared at her plate. "I suppose you can afford to be picky and only pay attention to supermodels."

She made it sound like he was shallow. But knowing what he wanted in a woman didn't make him shallow, did it? "I'm not picky. She's just too young for me."

"She can't be more than five years younger than you."

"Try ten years."

Eunice looked at him. Looked over at the girl. "How old are you?"

He sighed. No one ever believed him. "Thirty-two."

She turned to study him. "Ten years isn't that big of a difference. Do you already have a girlfriend?"

When he didn't respond, she pressed. "Maybe you left her behind when you moved here?"

"She's not exactly my girlfriend."

He didn't know what Tiffani was anymore. He'd thought maybe the time apart would make it clear.

"Whatever she is, I bet she's tall and skinny and beautiful."

Eric's forehead wrinkled. He wasn't sure he liked where this was going.

"And I bet she has a name like Ashley or Maci with an *i*, doesn't she?"

His face heated. Where did this woman come off being so nosy all of a sudden? He would refuse to answer her prying questions if their relationship wasn't already tenuous. And if he wasn't stuck in her service for the foreseeable future. "Tiffani."

Eunice raised one eyebrow. "With an *i*?"

He pressed his lips together, but then chuckled. "Yes." It really was funny. "Tall, long-haired, Tiffani with an *i*."

Eunice gave him a half smile. "I knew it."

He laughed out loud this time. Why did she care? But she'd nailed it. How had she known? Maybe he was as predictable as Tiffani always said.

Eric took another bite of his cinnamon roll and blinked. Apparently, he had finished it with hardly a thought. It had been delicious. The latte hadn't been half bad either. He glanced at Eunice's plate. She'd barely eaten a third of her roll, but her water was gone.

"You must've been thirsty."

Eunice straightened and appeared as surprised at her empty glass as he'd been at his empty plate. "Huh."

He checked the time on his phone. Three texts from Tiffani. Speak of the devil. "Are you planning to finish?"

Suddenly somber, Eunice shook her head.

"Okay, ready to go then?"

"Yeah."

"You want me to box that up?"

She hesitated. "Okay."

He requested a box from the young woman at the counter, who smiled at him again and touched his fingers with hers when she handed it over. Eunice had been right. She was cute. But those *fingernails*. He winked and walked away, knowing her eyes were on his back.

While he slid her roll into the box, Eunice went for the cash register. Eric frowned. He didn't really want her to pay. Sure, it had been her idea to stop for food and everything, but he didn't feel right about her spending money on him. Didn't want to take advantage.

He hurried over and pulled out his wallet. "Let me."

She didn't look at him. "I said I would do it."

"At least let me pay for my latte."

"I got it."

"Coffee wasn't part of the deal."

She pushed away the five-dollar bill he held out. "I said I got it."

How would he ever win with this woman? Not wanting to cause a scene, he acquiesced. Why did it seem like Eunice was two different people? Sometimes she was funny and almost normal. Other times . . .

They headed for the door. He had high hopes this mission would be completed before lunch and he'd still have half a day to himself. Brenda Wallace waved from her table as they passed, and the three other ladies sitting with her turned to gawk, whispering among themselves. Eric gave them a nod, and they tittered to one another.

Eunice wrapped her arms around her stomach and muttered, "You've only been here one week and you're already more popular than me."

At Eunice's direction, Eric pulled up to a white house with a chain-link fence around the yard. Two large German shepherds ran around inside the fence.

"Same drill as before?" he asked.

Eunice nodded, looking considerably paler than ten minutes ago. "I'll be right back."

She slid out of the Jeep as if her muscles were stiff and sore. He waited until she closed the door, then picked up his phone. A fourth text from Tiffani had come in since they left Hoagies and Grinders, this one with specific instructions. He watched Eunice slowly make her way through the gate and tapped his screen to start a video call as Tiffani had requested.

It took only one ring before her tan face appeared. "Hello, lover."

He cringed behind his sunglasses. He hated it when she called him that. "Hey."

"I was beginning to think there were no cell towers out there in Montana."

"There aren't, up in the mountains."

She pulled her own sunglasses down to scrutinize him. "Is your house in the mountains?"

"No, but I've been busy."

She made the little sound she always made when she was annoyed, then ran her French-manicured fingers through her hair. "So, what's it like? Are there cowboys everywhere?"

He glanced up to see Eunice almost get knocked over by the long wagging tail of one of the overfriendly dogs. He waited until she safely reached the front door before returning his attention to Tiffani. "Some. Everything is . . ."

"What?"

"Different." He didn't know how else to explain it.

"Different good or different bad?"

That felt like a loaded question. He shrugged. "I'm not sure yet. What about you? What have I missed?"

Her eyebrows arched. "Well, Le Magnifique is closing down, can you believe it? Some sort of scandal with their bookkeeper or whatever. I heard it from Piper. I swear she goes in there like every other day."

Eric scratched at his cheek. "Is that a restaurant?"

"Don't be ridiculous. It's the nail salon on Seventh Street. The one with all the black-and-white artwork on the walls?"

"Oh. Right."

Her full, shiny lips turned down in a pout. "I can't believe you don't remember. It's my favorite salon."

"Sorry, I—"

"Anyway, now I have to break in a new nail tech somewhere else. But it's not as bad as what happened to Greg."

She let Greg's name hang there for a second—just long enough to make Eric wonder—but jumped back in before Eric could reply. "His personal trainer quit out of the blue. He's joining a team that's going to work for the Olympics or something. Some people are so flaky. Did you see the picture of my new dress?"

"Yes." He knew what she was fishing for. "You looked amazing, as usual."

It was true. She had all the right curves in all the right places. She was the perfect height. Her hair was the perfect length. Even her social connections were perfect.

She pulled her phone closer to her face and gave him a sultry smile. "Do you miss me yet?"

Did he? They'd had an on-again-off-again relationship for over four years now. They'd technically been off-again when he left Seattle, neither of them interested in the long-distance thing, but it was probably only a matter of time before they—

The passenger door of the Jeep flew open, and Eric jumped.

Eunice climbed in. "Let's go."

Tiffani scowled. "Who's *that*?"

"Look, I gotta run." Eric held the phone close to his face and lowered his voice. "I'll call you back later."

She huffed. "Don't bother. I've got plans."

The call clicked off, and Eric stifled a growl.

"Sorry to interrupt," Eunice mumbled.

"It's fine." He would smooth things over with Tiffani later. He started the Jeep. "How did it go?"

When she'd returned from the first house, she seemed pretty happy. But now she looked sullen. Well, she often looked sullen, but this time more than usual.

She turned her face toward the window. "Fine."

Her voice was tight.

"Doesn't sound like it went fine."

"Were you talking to Tiffani with an *i*?"

He pulled away from the house and did a U-turn to head back toward Prairie Dog Road. "Yes."

"How is she?"

He lifted one side of his mouth. "Fine."

Eunice wrapped her arms around her stomach. Why was she always doing that?

"Did you work everything out with this person?" He didn't even know if it was a man or woman she wanted to talk to at this house. She was sure stingy with details.

"I guess."

"You *guess*?" Eric rolled his eyes to himself. Guessing wasn't good enough. He wanted to make sure *she* was sure so he wouldn't have to bring her back here again. "Well, did they forgive you? Or you forgive them? Or whatever you were looking for?"

He would go back right this second if he needed to, just to get it over with. What was one more U-turn?

Eunice muttered something he couldn't make out.

"What was that?"

"No, okay?" He could see her face pinch from the corner of his eye. "Nothing really happened. She didn't remember."

He scoffed. "You were upset enough about something that happened with this person that you wrote her name on your list, and she didn't even remember?"

No answer.

Unbelievable.

He wanted to laugh at the absurdity of it all, but something held him back. The set of Eunice's jaw maybe. Or the unreadable lines of her face. She stared at the world outside as if it were a disturbing mystery, and he shook his head. She was an odd one. Even smelled weird.

He let out a long breath as he turned toward their street.

Two names down. Five more to go.

eight

Beneath her shirt, Eunice could feel the bulge of her urostomy bag. JoJo didn't like to be this full. Didn't like the way she drooped as the urine collected and she became heavier and heavier.

Eunice held every muscle taut, afraid to jostle the bag more than necessary. How could she have been so stupid as to drink that entire glass of water at the coffee shop? She should've paid more attention. *This* was why she never left the house unless absolutely necessary.

Well, it wasn't her only stupid move today. The blank look on Marlene's face as she tried to apologize for that outrageous shellfish incident several years ago troubled Eunice's mind like a haunting. She'd been mortified when it happened. The way she'd caused such a scene in the grocery store and poor Marlene had been caught in the middle of it. But it seemed the whole thing had failed to leave as much of an impression on Marlene as it had on her.

Eric drove the Jeep over a bump, and Eunice lurched in her seat, sweat beginning to form on her upper lip. She held her breath. *Hang on, JoJo. We're almost home.*

As they turned onto Prairie Dog Road, Eunice released the air trapped in her chest. Next time she would be more careful. If there was a next time. She wasn't sure she wanted to keep putting herself through this. Maybe this whole idea was as foolish as she'd feared from the beginning.

Eric parked the Jeep in his driveway, then turned and fixed her with a concerned look. "Are you feeling okay?"

She opened her door and slid out carefully. "Thanks for the ride."

If he gave any kind of response, it was cut off by the slamming of the door. Eunice kept her arms around her stomach, giving JoJo as much support as she could while she hurried across her yard into her house. Her hands shook as she let herself in and shut the door behind her. She leaned her back against it with a grumble. How close had she come to spilling pee all over Eric's Jeep?

Emotions gathered in her throat, choking her. Anger, disgust, shame. Sorrow. It was bad enough she was living her last days on earth. Why'd she have to live them like this? And how could she have alienated so many people that Eric, practically a stranger, was the only one around to witness them?

A knock on the door made her gasp. What the—? She didn't have time for visitors. She needed to get to the bathroom. Another knock came, and she scowled. Whoever it was could wait. Better yet, she could pretend she wasn't home.

She carefully pushed off the door and crept toward the bathroom.

Another knock. "I know you're home, Eunice."

She froze. Eric. Super.

"Everything okay in there?"

A frustrated growl escaped her lips. What did he want? Had she not been humiliated enough for one day?

Bang, bang, bang. "Eunice?"

This was not happening. JoJo was not interested in what Eric had to say. But what if he wouldn't leave? Eunice's shirt was long enough to cover her waist. Maybe she'd better just deal with him quickly and be done with it.

She returned to the door and opened it with a glare. "What?"

Eric took a step back. "Oh. Hey. When you didn't answer, I thought . . ."

"Did you need something?" The sharpness in her voice was more than she'd intended, but this conversation needed to end as soon as possible.

He held up a white Styrofoam box. "You forgot your cinnamon roll."

Her stomach churned. "Keep it."

She'd started to close the door when he braced it with his arm. "Are you sure you're okay?"

"Yes, I'm fine."

The sharpness had turned to pure venom. What kind of monster was she?

The kind who was going to have a mess on her hands if she didn't get to the toilet, and fast. Her body tensed as she felt a sudden growing warmth around the waistband of her pants and underwear. JoJo had begun to leak.

Panic set in. "Can you leave me alone now?"

Eric's face scrunched with an indecipherable expression. "As soon as I'm sure you're okay, I'll get out of your hair."

She tried to shut the door again, but he was far too strong. That old, familiar desperation overtook her, coursing through her veins and strangling her lungs. She barely held back a sob. "Please. Leave. Me. Alone."

Each word was like a pant, the effort to maintain control of herself sapping what little strength she had left.

His arm dropped. His shoulders fell. "Okay. All right. Sorry."

He turned away. Finally. But why did he seem dejected? People like him didn't care about people like her. She paused for a second, remorse over her harsh words begging a small part of her to call after him and apologize, but no. She had no time to lose.

Shutting the door with a thud, she turned toward the bathroom, her whole body trembling now. But it was too late. With
a sickening slide, the adhesive pulled loose from her skin. Her
heart squeezed and fell and flipped inside out as urine soaked
her shirt and pants, filling the air with the odor of the wretched.
And she crumpled to the floor in a puddle of pungent liquid
waste and bitter tears.

nine

ric breathed in Monday morning like the aroma coming off freshly ground beans from Lighthouse Roasters. Ahh. Back to work.

Aside from his outing with Eunice Saturday morning—which had been, uh, *interesting*—and his conversation with Tiffani—which had resulted in a silent treatment she had yet to end—his weekend had consisted of hand-washing his Jeep with a hose, going for three extra runs, reassuring Uncle Jack that he had everything under control, and sitting on the back deck with Cinderella while she pecked at Eunice's leftover cinnamon roll.

If he put in forty hours a week at Larson Financial and slept seven hours a night, that left . . . ugh, seventy-nine hours a week to kill.

He couldn't get to the office soon enough.

He checked his hair in the bathroom mirror one last time and adjusted his tie. Max had ribbed him about his "power ties" last week, but he wasn't about to relax his high standard of attire just because he was in Podunk City. Dress for the job you want, not the job you have, they always said. And he wanted that tenth-floor office in Seattle.

As he walked to the Jeep, he looked over at Eunice's house. He'd seen her working in her backyard yesterday, but only when he was inside. He'd like to think she was avoiding him out of embarrassment over the way she'd acted on Saturday, though it was also possible she was avoiding him purely out of distaste for his company.

Fine with him.

At Larson Financial, Eric grabbed his briefcase and strode into the office, already feeling more confident. Even though the world of finance could be a roller coaster, it was far more predictable than the world outside.

Winnie greeted him with a smile. "Good morning, hon."

No matter how early he was, Winnie was always there before him. Despite the warm temperatures predicted, she wore a crewneck sweatshirt like always. This one was white with a picture of cats.

He nodded. "Good morning."

After a week of polite declines, she no longer brought up the coffeepot. The reordered Keurig should arrive by the end of the day Wednesday according to the online tracking. The tracking for the cubicle wall, however, made no such promises.

"Did you have a good weekend?" Winnie asked.

Eric paused by her desk. That was not a subject he wanted to get into. "Yes."

Winnie narrowed her eyes and leaned closer. "Did I tell you I have a granddaughter about your age?"

She had. Twice. "I believe so. But I'm keeping pretty busy, so—"

"She's actually my best friend's granddaughter." Her voice rose several decibels. "But we're very close."

That he did not know. But it was just as irrelevant. "I'm sure she's a wonderful person."

Winnie settled back in her chair, pleased. "As sweet as a summer day. Lovely personality."

Yikes. He knew what that meant. "Well, I'll just be at my desk. Let me know when my first appointment arrives."

She peered at him over her glasses for a moment, then waved

him away. He passed through the glass-paneled door and settled himself at his desk. One week had not been enough time for him to get used to sitting directly opposite his partner, trying to pretend he couldn't hear Max's long-winded conversations that had nothing to do with finance. Nor enough time to get used to Max's jeans. He'd noticed his clients didn't dress up either. One man had shown up to his appointment in oil-stained coveralls without the slightest hint of embarrassment.

The door opened and Benson slipped through, head down. That's the only way Eric had ever seen him.

"Good morning, Benson."

The lanky kid's head shot up as if he'd been startled. "Uh, good morning, Mr. Larson."

Eric had asked the kid to call him by his first name, but the request had gone unheeded. "Is the Borderman file ready?"

Benson scurried to the corner and picked up a folder from the rickety table. Eric hadn't yet ordered a new one. He made a mental note to ask Winnie on his lunch break about finding a local store that carried tables.

The kid handed Eric the folder without looking at him and turned away.

Eric nodded. "Thanks."

Though he appeared barely old enough to drive, Eric had learned Benson was twenty, was taking community college classes, and had been hired by the last senior advisor simply because he'd been the only applicant for the job. But Eric had also learned Benson had a great head for numbers and stats. He was skittish around people, though, and seemed content serving as an assistant, despite all Uncle Jack's talk about Benson's "potential."

Eric wondered again where his uncle had found the people keeping Larson Financial afloat. None of them had the drive he'd expected. The ambition for "big things." And none of them seemed to be what Uncle Jack had made them out to be.

Max came trundling through the door two minutes after eight and waved at Eric as he settled into his big black chair with an *oof*. He was medium-statured and built like he'd been an athlete once upon a time, but he moved like he'd recently been struck by a car. Or, more likely around here, a tractor.

"Gonna be a beautiful day," Max said. "Too bad we have to spend it cooped up inside."

Eric chuckled. He couldn't think of a better place to be than in an office. "And where would you rather spend it?"

Max grinned. "On the back of a horse."

A horse? Eric tried to hide his surprise. Why would anyone want to do *that*?

His desk phone rang, and he answered it.

"Your eight-fifteen is here," Winnie shouted, her voice resounding from two places at once.

Eric cracked his knuckles and nodded to himself. "Send them in."

Eric fought to keep his mouth from falling open as he listened to his client's wild tale at the end of the day. He'd been scheduled to head home twenty minutes ago—Max and Winnie were long gone and only Benson remained in the office—but Bob Crowley's story just kept going, turning more incredible with every detail.

Bob chuckled and threw up his gnarled hands. "And that's when I snapped the raccoon's neck, I tell you what."

Eric sat back in his chair. "Wow. That was quite a story. I had no idea mules could climb trees."

Bob raised his wiry gray eyebrows. "Not just any mule."

"No, no, of course not." Eric stifled a smile. "Now, what was it you wanted to see me about today, Mr. Crowley?"

"Better call me Bob."

"All right, Bob. What can I do for you?"

"Well." Bob gripped his knees and looked down at the floor. "It's my will, you see."

Eric scooted closer to the desk. Many people asked him for advice about estate planning, especially when they reached a certain mature age. "I'd be happy to look it over. Did you bring a copy with you today?"

Bob's already-wrinkled forehead creased further. "No, I didn't."

Eric shuffled through the papers on his desk, hoping it was already on file. "I'm sorry, I don't see it here. If you'll give me a moment, I can ask Benson to look it up."

"Not sure what good that'll do. He ain't gonna find it."

Eric paused midway through raising a hand to get Benson's attention and looked back at his client.

Bob fiddled with the buttons of his ragged leather vest. "I don't got one, you see."

Ah. So that was the problem. Eric tapped his pen against the desk. "It's a good thing you survived that whole raccoon incident, then."

"Ha." Bob's grin revealed crooked yellow teeth. "I reckon you're right about that. So, you'll help me?"

"I wish I could, but a will is a legal document, and I'm not a lawyer. You'll need an attorney, preferably one who specializes in estate planning. I can refer you to one here in town." Eric clicked on his laptop to search the business directory for the information he needed.

"Now hold on, hold on." Bob raised one hand. "No need for that. I got no interest in lawyers. Knew one once and he bled me dry in my divorce, even though I told the judge there was a conflict of interest."

"I'm sure he was just doing his job."

"He was sleeping with my wife."

Eric's eyes widened. "Oh. I'm sorry, I—"

"Not to mention he was my brother. Yeah, I got no use for lawyers. Anyway, I only come here because I knew Jack back in the day, and he was a real straight shooter. I figured you would be, too. Can you help me or not?"

Eric drew a deep breath. He had no basis for offering legal advice. He really shouldn't get involved in this. But he had a feeling if he didn't, Bob would continue with no will at all. The motto Uncle Jack had chosen for Larson Financial came to mind. *Your financial security tomorrow is our leading goal today*. That was the guiding principle of the company, but would helping Bob with his will get Eric any closer to his own goal of growing a ten-percent profit?

"Look, Bob . . ." Eric leaned closer. "I can't draw up a will for you, but I can give you a list of websites that provide templates and instructions to help you make one on your own. If you do that, you can bring it in, and I can look it over and help you determine whether it lines up with your financial goals."

"You're not making any sense, son." Bob scratched his head. "Aren't you a financial advisor?"

"Yes, but—"

"And ain't my will supposed to be all about what happens to my finances?"

Eric sighed. "Yes, but a will is a legal document." He tore a sheet of paper off the top of his notepad and began writing down the websites. "I'm sorry I can't be of more help."

Bob slowly pushed himself out of his chair and took the paper from Eric's outstretched hand. He squinted at it, then shoved it in his vest pocket.

"Thanks for coming in," Eric said. "Let me walk you out."

He fought back pangs of guilt as the old man trudged to the front door just ahead of him. He'd help him if he could. Really.

Once he had seen Bob out of the office, he returned to his desk for his briefcase. Benson was there.

"You didn't have to wait. You could've left at five-thirty with everyone else."

Benson stuck his hands in his pockets. "He doesn't have a computer."

Eric gathered his things and loosened his tie. "I'm sure he has a family member who can help him."

"Not that I know of."

Eric ushered Benson out of the office ahead of him and locked up, his stomach sinking. What was he supposed to do? He could get sued for involving himself in the creation of Bob's will. Talk about a conflict of interest. And Bob's request was confidential. Benson shouldn't know anything about it.

Eric really needed to check on the status of that portable privacy wall he'd ordered.

ten

ric stood at the back door of his house, holding a sesame quinoa salad and watching Eunice work in her garden. Once he'd gotten used to the rambling design of it and the bowling balls, he'd realized it was well taken care of and kind of beautiful. Especially now that some flowers were beginning to bloom. Funny how someone so mean could create something so nice.

She moved around the backyard slowly. Did she not have a job? Why did she never leave her house?

And another thing. Where was her dog?

His phone jangled from the kitchen table. When he jogged over to see who the call was from, he set his bowl down and snatched it up. "Hey, bro. How's it going?"

"Good, I guess."

"You don't sound like it."

"Mom's driving me crazy."

Eric laughed. "She does that sometimes. Go easy on her, she means well. How's Burger King these days?"

"It's okay. But I don't think my car is ever going to stop smelling like fries."

"Don't worry about it. No one else rides in that rattrap anyway."

Chase paused. "Well, someone *could* ride in it."

Eric's ears picked up something different in Chase's voice. "Did you have a certain someone in mind?"

"No." His answer came too quickly and with too much force. Eric pounced. "Is it someone you work with?"

Burger King wouldn't be his first choice as a place to meet girls, but Chase had rarely shown any interest in dating, so Eric was willing to go with it.

"No." There was a smile in his brother's voice. "But she comes in a lot when I'm there. It's like maybe she knows when my shifts are."

"Dude." Eric pumped a fist in the air. "That's awesome. You've got to ask her out."

"I don't know . . ."

"Is she cute?"

"Yes."

"Then what's to know?"

"I don't know what she likes to do. Maybe she's still in high school. Maybe she's leaving for college in a couple months, and we'll never see each other again."

Eric shook his head. "You're overthinking it, man. Just start with her phone number."

He spent another few minutes pulling details out of his brother—she had pink hair, always ordered the number two combo, and used an obscene amount of ketchup on her fries—then tried to convince his brother to make a move before Chase had to go. When Eric hung up, there were still no messages from Tiffani, but someone had left a voicemail. He didn't have to check the call log to know it was from Uncle Jack. No one else in America left voicemails anymore.

Eric grunted. He didn't feel like talking to his uncle right now. He punched the buttons to listen to the message, hoping there would be no reason to call Uncle Jack back, but no such luck. *"Call me back as soon as you get this"* was kind of hard to ignore.

71

Uncle Jack answered right away. "Eric. My boy. I see from the charge account you haven't wasted any time making improvements at the office."

"Nothing major." Eric snapped his fingers to himself. That reminded him, he still hadn't looked for a table for Benson. "Just a Keurig and a cubicle wall. Oh, and new client chairs."

He'd ordered those when he got home today. The longer poor old Bob had sat across from him in his chair, the more Eric noticed how shabby it was. How thin the padding. How narrow the seat. He hadn't been able to help Bob with his will situation, but he could at least ensure he'd be more comfortable if he ever came in again. Clients hoping to increase their wealth expected luxury.

Did someone like Bob have any wealth to increase, though?

"Just take it slow." Uncle Jack's voice took on a serious tone. "You might find people resistant to a bunch of changes all at once."

He wasn't really *changing* anything. More like updating things that were already there. Except the wall, but that was a necessity. Clients also expected privacy.

No need to mention his request to Winnie that she start scheduling appointments closer together for better efficiency.

"It's fine, Uncle Jack. Don't worry."

"Everything's fine, huh? Well, that's good to hear." His uncle's voice held a hint of doubt. "Any other impending purchases I should be aware of?"

Eric hesitated. "I do need to find a new table for Benson. The duct-taped leg is not a good look. I saw a furniture store downtown." It felt ludicrous calling it *downtown* when a single mall in Seattle had more going on. "Sofas and More, I think?"

"Ah. A fine place. But I'd consider it a favor if you'd try another place first. The Kitchen Sink."

"Huh?"

"It's a store called Everything But the Kitchen Sink. The owner and I go way back."

Eric smiled to himself. How had his uncle managed to make so many friends and connections in only two years? "Okay, will do."

"Now, about business. Any interesting clients today?"

Should he tell his uncle about Bob? If he was already skeptical about how *fine* things were, Eric didn't want to give him any reason to wonder if Eric was doing his best. He believed he'd done the only thing he could for Bob today. The right thing. Brady the Brownnoser hadn't pulled off an eight-percent increase by wasting his time on unprofitable tasks. Yet Eric was hesitant to bring that up. Somewhere deep in his heart he feared his uncle might see it differently.

"No, just standard stuff."

"All right. Well, don't forget to get out there and pound some pavement." Uncle Jack chuckled. "Don't expect people to come to you. They won't know how much they need you until you tell them."

Eric wasn't sure of the best strategy to drum up more clients in a place like Tukston, but he nodded. "Will do."

After they said goodbye, Eric traded his phone for his salad and returned to the back door. Eunice had gone inside, so he let himself out onto the deck to claim his chaise lounge. Cinderella soon found him as if she had a radar for his presence, and he flicked some of the quinoa from his fork onto the ground for her.

Quite the social life he had all of a sudden.

He finished his dinner to the sound of gentle scratching. The quiet stretched around him, tugging at his chest. He couldn't remember the last time he'd spent so much time with himself. In Seattle, there was always something to do. Somewhere to go. Someone to meet up with. But here?

He'd almost be tempted to space out on social media, but

he didn't feel like looking at all his friends' posts showing off the life he was currently missing. And he'd almost mistake the ache in his heart for loneliness, but he was far too secure and independent for that.

Right?

Maybe he'd go for a run after he finished his dinner. Or a drive. Or . . . something.

What would his friends say if they could see him now?

It was eleven o'clock and finally good and dark. Summer days up here in Montana seemed to last forever. Eunice's body screamed for rest, for her bed, but she stood in the backyard and surveyed her work. She was proud of her garden. The neatness and extent of it. The one normal thing left about her life, even if it was pointless to grow vegetables she might never have the chance to harvest. Maybe she could talk to Bertie about making sure all the produce was donated to the food bank.

She shivered in her sweatpants and sweatshirt. Though it was a cool evening, the chill she was feeling went deeper than that. It seeped under her skin and settled into her bones. She'd spent many years alone but had never experienced the weight of loneliness she carried now. Not even when her parents died overseas without a chance to say goodbye. Not even after she'd pushed away the only man she'd ever loved for the second and final time, knowing he would never come back for a third.

The stars were out in force, and she wrapped her arms around herself and stared at them. It all made more sense now. Why she'd lost everyone in her life. Maybe even why Charlie had been taken from her in such a violent way. It was so she herself could be lost to the world with no strings attached, right? Nothing left behind, except maybe some beans, zucchini, and tomatoes.

She could almost accept it, on a night like tonight. Almost

dive into the vastness of the inexplicable sky and convince herself dying wasn't going to be so bad. There were eternal worlds of stars and light to explore outside of her fading husk of a body. A Creator to meet and lifetimes of new things she could not begin to imagine from her backyard.

Yes, she could almost look up there and say, "I'm ready."

Almost.

eleven

Thursday morning, Eric left his house just before seven, determined to beat Winnie to the office. The second Keurig had arrived yesterday as scheduled, and he hadn't even opened the box this time. He'd left it safely ensconced in its packaging and now set it carefully on the passenger seat of the Jeep with the box of K-pods on the floor. After a moment's hesitation, he buckled it in. Coffee was not something to be careless with.

The air coming in the open window as he drove was already warm and smelled like cut grass. He parked in front of Larson Financial with a huff. The light was on inside. Why would Winnie be here a full hour before they opened? So much for setting up the Keurig as a surprise.

Entering the office took a little work with his briefcase and the two big boxes, but he got himself inside and smiled at Winnie triumphantly. "Good morning."

"You're awfully early today." She pointed at the Keurig box. "What do you got there?"

"A new coffeemaker."

She watched him set the boxes on the floor next to the side table. "We *have* a coffeemaker."

"But this one is better."

"How do you know? You don't even drink coffee."

Eric gestured toward the ancient coffeepot. "I don't drink *that* coffee."

Winnie slid from her chair and scurried over. "What's wrong with *that* coffee?"

Uh-oh. She did not sound pleased. He brought out his dimples. "Just wait until you try this kind. You're going to love it."

"It's huge. And what are all those little cup thingies?"

"Those are the pods." Eric opened the Keurig box and pulled out the appliance. "You choose which kind you want and stick it in the brew chamber, then you press the button. A fresh cup every time."

Winnie's eyes narrowed, incredulous. "You mean to tell me, if someone was sitting out here waiting for their appointment and they wanted a cup of coffee, they'd have to brew it themselves?"

"Uh . . ."

"How long does it take?"

He removed the packaging from the machine and shoved it back into the box. "Only a minute."

She harrumphed. "The table's not big enough for that thing."

"We might need to get a bigger table." He winked at her and pushed the old coffee machine aside to make room. "Speaking of which, I'd like to buy a new table for Benson, too. Do you know where a store called Everything But the Kitchen Sink is?"

Winnie kept her eyes fixed on the Keurig as if it might spontaneously combust, but she nodded. "I'll write down the address."

"Thanks, Winnie." Eric smiled at her. She'd get used to it in no time. "You're the best."

Eric stood on the sidewalk in front of the furniture store and chewed the inside of his cheek. Under the large lit-up sign that read *Everything But the Kitchen Sink* was a smaller, hand-painted one that said *Actually, we have those too*. He shook his head and checked the time on his phone. He had a one-thirty appointment. Better make this quick.

A tinny *ding-dong* rang in the rear of the store as he entered. Eric was the only customer. The showroom, if you could call it that, was crammed with items. Furniture, sure. Couches and dressers, tables and chairs, bed frames and nightstands. There were also piles of knickknacks, stacks of books, and—aha. Bowling balls. Eunice must shop here.

"Good afternoon." A tall, lean man with a gray ponytail ambled through the obstacle course and spoke to Eric through his unruly handlebar mustache. "Name's Dusty. What can I help you with today?"

Eric shook Dusty's outstretched hand. People sure did a lot of hand-shaking around here. "Eric. I'm in the market for a couple of tables. Is everything here, uh . . ."

"Used? Yes indeed. We get all the best donations."

Eric shoved his hands in his pockets. Uncle Jack had sent him to a thrift store? "I see. Well, I'm looking for a small desk table and a console table."

Dusty scratched his head. "One of them ones that sit up against the wall?"

Eric nodded.

"Don't get many of those, but I have something that might work." Dusty motioned for Eric to follow him to the right side of the store. "Are you setting up a house? Did you recently move to town?"

Eric chuckled to himself. He probably did stand out as a stranger. There were only, what, two thousand people in Tukston? "I'm only here for the summer. The tables are for my office, Larson Financial."

Dusty's face brightened. "You must know Jack. I bet they're glad to have you. Max said Stan left big shoes to fill."

"You know Max?"

Dusty nodded, and Eric mentally face-palmed himself. Of course Dusty knew Max. Only two thousand people, remember?

"Here's a nice little desk table." Dusty pointed, then pointed again. "And here's what I was thinking for the other."

The desk should suffice. It was the right size and appeared sturdy. But the "other" . . .

"That's a bench."

"Well, sure." Dusty shrugged. "But with a little creativity and a few adjustments, you'd have yourself a console table."

Uncle Jack must have been crazy when he recommended this place. But Eric didn't have time to stop at Sofas and More now. He pulled a credit card from his wallet and handed it over. "I'll just take the desk for now."

"Oh." Dusty nodded. "All right."

Eric eyed the desk again and pictured the back of his Jeep. It would be a tight squeeze. Really tight. "Do you have delivery service by any chance?"

"Sure do." Dusty moved toward the rear of the store. "My son, Nate, will help you with that part while I ring you up."

He reached the back wall and flipped a light switch off and on three times before making his way to the cash register. Eric stood by the desk, unsure what to do. No Nate appeared. He didn't want to be late for his appointment.

As he tapped his foot and waited, his phone beeped. Probably Chase. Or maybe Tiffani, who had finally given up her silent treatment yesterday. He pulled it from his pocket to check and stiffened. Nope. He'd been way off.

His dad.

Really? He hadn't heard from him since his last obligatory "Happy birthday" text.

Heard you're in Tukston.

79

That was it? The guy hadn't contacted him in months and that was all he had to say? Eric's jaw clenched. He had no interest in communicating with his father. He'd disappeared from Eric's life just when Eric had needed him most—as a boy on the verge of manhood.

He read the message again, then shoved the phone back in his pocket. Leave it to his dad to come out of nowhere and ruin a perfectly good day.

A man the spitting image of Dusty but about Eric's age and fifty pounds bulkier came out of the back room. Must be Nate. Finally.

"Would you be able to drop this off at Larson Financial?" Eric tapped the desk with his knuckle and glanced at the time. "I'm happy to pay a delivery fee, but I've got to get going."

Nate's sleeves were rolled up, and his thick arms were greasy like he'd been working on an engine. He strode over with a smile and picked up the desk as if it were made of cardboard.

He turned to walk away with it, so Eric scrambled after him. "Hey. Do you want to follow me back to the office? I'm headed there now."

Nate didn't respond, only carried the desk through the back door and disappeared. Eric threw up his hands and turned to Dusty in exasperation.

"He can't hear nothin'." Dusty handed him a receipt and his card back. "Been deaf since he was little. Not that he was ever *little*."

Eric pocketed the items. "Oh. Sorry."

"Nothin' for anyone to be sorry about, except his mama. She's the one that done it. But it's just been Nate and me ever since."

Seemed like a strange thing to tell a stranger. Was everyone around here so . . . open?

Eric shifted on his feet. "Well, thanks for your help."

"Sure, sure." Dusty waved a long arm toward the door. "You go on and get back to work. Nate knows where the office is."

Eric hurried to his Jeep, feeling like an idiot. How was he supposed to know Nate was deaf? He hopped in the car and fired it up, thankful it would take all of three minutes to drive across town to the office. His phone felt like a grenade in his pocket as he pulled onto the road. Why had his dad texted him out of the blue? What did he *really* want?

Why had Eric and his mom not been enough for him?

When he reached the office, it smelled like burnt oil. He found his Keurig tucked under the coffee table and the old coffeemaker noisily brewing a fresh pot of Valu Brew.

twelve

ometimes I wonder if you're killing me off just to force me into these horrible situations." Eunice nervously ran a comb through her hair after her afternoon shower, careful not to pull on any snags. She didn't need to lose any more hair than she already had. "We both know I wouldn't be doing this otherwise."

Her talks with God had increased lately, ever since JoJo had spewed all over the entryway. As she faced another outing with Eric, this time to see a man she never thought she'd speak to again—ever—Eunice wondered if it was really true. Was having certain and imminent death hanging over her head the only reason she was trying to complete the task she felt God had given her to do? Would she have ignored the nudge He so clearly gave her to make peace with those she'd hurt if she hadn't been facing the end?

"You could've at least brought me a chauffeur with something interesting to say." She pulled a light sweater over her T-shirt and looked down at her feet. Yes, she was trying a little harder to look presentable in penance for her horrible behavior the last time she was with Eric, but was she willing to give up her purple Crocs?

Nope.

In the kitchen, Eunice turned up her nose at the precut bowl of honeydew melon in the fridge. She wished she could forget yesterday had been a Wanda day, but the repulsive green fruit was a constant reminder. Eunice was certain she'd told Wanda how much she hated honeydew. It was just like her to conveniently forget.

If only Dr. Mullins hadn't insisted a home health nurse come *every* week. Why wasn't twice a month with Bertie enough? Why did she need help at all? She could die just fine by herself, thank you very much. But she supposed she should be thankful. The fact the online work she did for the Kitchen Sink somehow provided health insurance was reason enough to be grateful.

She settled for a small glass of apple juice—couldn't afford a repeat of last time—and a piece of plain toast, the same thing she'd had for breakfast. And lunch. She just didn't want anything else. Her body didn't want food at all really, but her teeth still enjoyed crunching. *Crunch, crunch, crunch.* She tapped her chin. What if . . .

She took another bite of toast, but this time chewed with her mouth wide open. *Crunch, crunch, crunch.* Ah. Very satisfying. Her mother would turn over in her grave. When Eunice joined her there in a few short months, she hoped she would have toast in her teeth.

She finished eating and checked the time. Ten minutes until she and Eric had agreed to meet. She wanted to be early this time. Outside, the mid-June sun was shining bright and heating up the world, though her body could rarely stay warm anymore. She tugged her shirt down and slogged over to his driveway. If only Dick Samson's house were far enough away that she could've convinced herself to leave him off her list.

The Jeep was sparkling clean when she reached Eric's driveway, the blue paint glinting in the sun like gemstones. Super. Eric was not going to be happy when he saw the road they'd be traveling today.

"Hello."

She spun around. He was wearing black gym shorts and a T-shirt, and his hair had an intentionally mussed look. He looked so young and bold, like he had his whole life ahead of him. Like he'd never once wondered about what happened after.

"Hi."

"Ready to go?" He flinched. "I mean, of course you are. Otherwise you wouldn't be over here, right?"

Her shoulders drooped. "I'm sorry about last time. I wasn't good company."

His eyebrows rose. "You noticed?"

She felt her cheeks flush. Of course she'd noticed. She wasn't *actually* a heartless witch. She only played one on TV. Or, you know, in real life when she was in over her head and worried about spilling urine all over Fancy Man's leather interior.

She hung her head. "I was having a bad day. I was . . ."

Scared.

He tilted his head, waiting for her to finish. He really was like a puppy. "You were what?"

He would never understand.

"Nothing."

"Okay." He shrugged. "Shall we?" She nodded, and he opened the passenger side door for her. "Your chariot awaits."

Oh, brother.

As they drove out of town, Eunice gave directions and racked her brain for something to say, partly to keep her mind off what she was about to do and partly to make up for the way she'd acted last time. She'd avoided Eric all week, up until last night when she saw him on his back deck and forced herself to go out in her yard and bring up their agreement over the fence. It was that whole death-hanging-over-her-head thing that gave her the courage. Or the madness.

He already had plans for the morning, he'd said, but he'd agreed in a very pathetic, resigned manner to drive her at four o'clock. Like he was doing her a favor instead of working off a debt.

"What were you doing earlier?" she asked.

The muscles in Eric's arms twitched as he gripped the wheel. How was he so tan when he worked indoors all day?

His voice was noncommittal. "Just had to take care of a few things."

Fine. She couldn't really blame him for being vague. Why should he tell her anything? "Have you talked to Tiffani lately?"

It was the only other thing she could think of to say, the only other thing she knew about his life besides Larson Financial.

The corners of his mouth turned down ever so slightly. "No."

She couldn't see his eyes behind those expensive-looking sunglasses. Was he upset? About Tiffani or about her prying? Or both? Eunice fiddled with her seat belt. This was too exhausting. Better stick to the basics.

She pointed. "Turn right on that gravel road."

She could've sworn she heard him groan. The Jeep slowed to a crawl as they took the turn and continued, though the reduced speed did nothing to keep the dust from swirling around the car. It would be gray by the time they reached Dick's house.

Eric still didn't speak. Maybe it had nothing to do with her or the last day they'd spent together. He seemed preoccupied. JoJo shifted on her lap, and Eunice winced. What would Eric say if he knew she'd brought a bag of urine into his brand-new car? It was part of who she was now, but she had her doubts about whether he could accept that.

After a minute, she tried again, if only to keep Eric's attention off the bulge under her shirt. "It's a nice day."

He looked around as if he hadn't noticed. "Yeah," he admitted. "The sky's so blue. I mean, it's blue in Seattle, too, but there's so much of it here."

The sky in Montana on a summer day was the kind of thing that made Eunice wonder if she would ever really be ready to leave this earth.

"You see that cabin on the left?"

Eric nodded.

"That's where he lives."

"He?"

Her cheeks burned. Her chest and stomach, too. "Yes."

Eric's eyebrows popped up above his sunglasses, but he kept his thoughts to himself. Good thing or she'd probably say something she would regret. He turned onto Dick's long driveway and slowly approached the house. The truck parked in front was unfamiliar. Eunice's insides roiled.

Eric parked the Jeep, and every bite of toast Eunice had eaten that day threatened to make a reappearance. She would rather give an impromptu speech on the North American gopher in front of ten thousand people than face Dick Samson again. She didn't want to do this.

But.

Her hand rested on the door handle. She'd wronged the man. Truly and unquestionably.

"I'll just wait here, then," Eric said, urging her along.

Her voice was a pathetic squeak. "Okay."

She slid from the Jeep and took a deep breath. Was it going to be like this every time? She still had four names to go after this. Her nerves were never going to survive her list. A yellow Lab appeared out of nowhere and ran up to her barking, curious and excited.

"Good dog." She scratched his ears for a long minute, happy for the distraction. Though he'd only had one, Charlie had always loved a thorough ear scratch. "Good boy."

She took a look around as she walked toward the front door. It was definitely the residence of a single man. No feminine touches in sight.

That was her fault.

She paused and glanced at the sky. "Why'd you let me do so many dumb things?"

The only reply was the scream of a hawk circling the field behind Dick's house, but in her heart she knew God wasn't to blame for the lies she'd told. Well, just one lie really. One really big, life-altering lie.

Her head swam as she knocked on the front door, bracing herself on the doorframe with her free hand. Wouldn't it just figure for her to faint on Dick's doorstep.

The Jeep idled in the driveway, and the dog sniffed Eunice's Crocs, but no other signs of life were forthcoming. She knocked again, as hard as she could with arms as limp as sleeping cats.

Nothing.

She rubbed her temples as she turned away from the house. A headache was forming.

"You'd think I'd feel relieved," she muttered. "But if I don't do this now . . ."

The thought of working up the guts to face Dick a second time made her body shudder. What if she couldn't do it? And they'd come all this way.

She opened the Jeep door and climbed in. "I guess no one's home."

Eric glanced at the time. "So that's it? You want me to take you somewhere else?"

Eunice carefully buckled, silently reminding JoJo to be on her best behavior. "I know where to find him."

If Dick Samson wasn't putzing around his cabin on a Saturday afternoon, she could bet there was only one other place he would be.

Eric sighed. "Is it far?"

"No." She folded her arms over her stomach. "Just a couple miles from here."

As Eric shifted the Jeep in reverse, she steeled herself. If Dick really was blowing off steam in Logan's field like she suspected, he probably wasn't alone. But her destruction of his life eight years ago had been a public affair. It was only fair her apology should be, as well.

thirteen

*E*ric drummed his fingers on the steering wheel. Eunice must have directed him to the wrong place. There was nothing here but empty fields and scraggly bushes. Not even what he'd call a road.

She pointed. "Over there."

He craned his neck and saw three trucks parked next to a bit of barbwire fence. What were they doing? How did she know they'd be here? As the Jeep crept closer to the trucks, four men sitting in camping chairs turned to look at them. They were all wearing ball caps and jeans despite the heat and holding beer cans.

And guns.

"Um . . ." He glanced at Eunice. "I don't know about this."

She blew out a breath. "They're here to shoot gophers. Not people."

"Do they know that?"

"It's a summer sport around here."

Basketball was a sport. Football was a sport. He'd even go so far as to say canoeing was a sport. But shooting gophers?

One of the men stood as Eric brought the Jeep to a stop at a safe distance, and Eric let out a breath of relief when the man set his gun down in his chair before taking a couple of steps closer.

Eunice's voice was small, like a child's. "That's him. Dick Samson."

Eric left the Jeep running. The man looked to be about fifty and had a scowl on his face as he peered into the Jeep. Eric glanced at his neighbor. She was resolutely unbuckling her seat belt, but fear creased her face. He wouldn't want to be in her shoes.

She opened the door, glancing back at him once, and her eyes looked like they were pleading. But she'd gotten herself into this mess, whatever it was. It had nothing to do with him, right? After the way she'd treated him last time, she was on her own.

The door shut behind her with a pathetic thud.

He huffed. Checked his phone. No service.

Oh, fine.

He lowered the windows and killed the engine. Dick the gopher guy *might* kill him, but Uncle Jack would kill him for sure if he ever found out he'd let a woman face a situation like this alone. He wasn't completely heartless. Besides, this could be interesting.

Eunice walked—or maybe *trudged* would be a better word—over to where Dick stood. Eric hurried after her but stayed a little behind. As he drew closer, his eyes widened. One of the other men was barely more than a boy. Wait . . . was that Benson? He wasn't old enough to be drinking. What was going on?

Dick crossed his arms over his chest as his scowl deepened. "What're you doing here, *You*-niss?"

Ha. Eunice wasn't the only one who could dish out harsh words. Looked like she'd met her match.

She tugged on her shirt but held his gaze. "It's Eu-*niece*, and you know it."

Dick gave Eric a quick once-over, then turned back to Eunice. "I got nothin' to say to you."

Her fingers rolled the edge of her sweater. "Then you can just listen."

"Oh, that's rich." Dick called over his shoulder to his buddies, "You hear that, guys? First she talks my wife into listening to her, and now she wants *me* to listen."

One of the other men looked uncomfortable, and one of them chuckled. Benson was silent, frozen, his eyes fixed on Eric with a question. Eric had plenty of questions of his own, but he kept quiet.

Eunice held her head high with what appeared to be great effort. "I came here to, uh, apologize. For—"

"I know what for," Dick interrupted. "You think I could ever forget what you did? The lies you spread about me, *Youniss?*"

Eric shifted on his feet. It was no stretch to believe Eunice had offended Dick, yet Dick's reaction seemed to go way beyond offense. And watching this guy berate Eunice wasn't as entertaining as he'd thought it was going to be. Eric was glad once again that Dick had left his gun in his chair. He was scary enough without a rifle in his hands.

Eunice took a step back. "I'm sorry. I shouldn't have done what I did. I was wrong. But you can't blame me for anything that happened after that."

"I sure can." Dick balled his fists and raised his voice. "You think you can ruin people's lives and then just show up and say sorry?"

"Come on, Dick," one of the men said. "Chill out."

Dick waved the words away. "Listen here, *You*-niss. I don't plan to ever forgive you, and my kids won't either. You can take that to your grave."

Yikes. Eunice's face paled, and her body stiffened. Eric thought for a second she might pass out, but instead she hung her head. "Okay." She looked back up. "I'm sorry, Dick."

She turned and walked back to the Jeep. Eric easily beat her there and started it up, not wanting to stick around and take the chance Dick's gun would find its way back into his hands.

He hoped Benson would be okay. Why was he hanging out with those guys?

The moment Eunice closed her door, he pulled out, not waiting for her to buckle. Gravel flew and dust rose around them like a shield as they sped away. So much for the thorough cleaning he'd given the Jeep last night. Eunice struggled to fasten her seat belt as they jerked and jolted over rough terrain, that sick look back on her face.

When they were out of gunshot range, he slowed. Just wait until he told Chase about this. It really was like the Wild West out here.

He took his hands off the wheel one at a time and shook them out. Whew. That was intense. "What was *that* all about?"

Eunice wrapped her arms around her stomach and looked out the window. "I've made a lot of mistakes."

The way she said it made him think of his dad. *A lot of mistakes.* He shook that off. "I guess that wasn't the response you were hoping for."

No answer. She seemed tired and lost in thought. He was dying to know what the deal was with Dick, but it didn't look like he'd be getting any more information out of her.

He drove back to the gravel road Dick's house was on, imagining all kinds of outlandish scenarios about what Eunice might have done to the man, and was almost back to the pavement before she spoke again.

"I guess not."

They drove the rest of the way in silence. As he pulled into his driveway, his stomach reminded him of his five-mile run this morning and how the protein shake he had for lunch was a long time ago. He didn't remember there being much waiting for him in his fridge, but he was eager to scope it out anyway.

He turned off the Jeep, pocketed the keys, and opened the door. Eunice didn't move. Her face was pinched.

He dropped one foot to the concrete. "So . . ."

She shook her head and turned to him as if just realizing he was there. "I'll let you know when I'm ready to go out again."

He gaped. She wanted to do this *again*? He would've bet a hundred bucks she'd want to give up on this whole list thing after her encounter with Dick. He sure would. And had he not put in enough time to pay off his debt to her by now?

"Are you sure?"

"I'm sure."

"But why? That guy wasn't worth the time it took to drive out there."

"Doesn't matter. I need to do this." As if to prove it to both of them, she pulled the crumpled yellow paper from her pocket and gave him a small, wry smile. "Got a pen?"

He hesitated, then pulled one from the side door pocket and held it out to her. "What's the point of putting yourself through this? Why do you *need* to?"

She drew a line across the page. "I just do."

He studied her face. He'd dated a lot of women in his thirty-two years. He'd learned to read their eyes, the set of their jaws. The tilt of their heads. They never told the whole story with their lips, yet their bodies usually told him everything he needed to know.

Eunice was hiding something.

He tried the humorous approach. "Did you lose a bet or something? Truth or dare gone wrong?"

"No."

"You have to complete a series of tasks before you can inherit your grandmother's money?"

He'd seen that in a movie once.

She looked him in the face and held his gaze. "No."

He pulled off his sunglasses and shined his baby blues at her. "Oh, come on. I'm part of this now, too. Something must be driving you. Besides me, of course."

Her eyes dropped. Her shoulders sagged. She was going to give in. He could feel it.

"I won't tell anyone. I promise."

"Okay." Her voice was soft. Almost reverent. He leaned closer to hear. "I'm dying. Soon."

It took a minute for her words to sink in. Did she say *dying*? That couldn't be. She wasn't old enough to be dying. But she just sat there, waiting for him to respond.

He shifted in his seat. "You're sick?"

She nodded, her hands clenched in her lap.

"Cancer?"

"Yes."

Okay. He sat back. Pulled his foot back in the car. Stared out the windshield.

Holy crap.

This was real.

"How . . . uh, how long . . . ?"

"The doctor gave me a few months. Said there's nothing he can do."

An unfamiliar emotion wobbled inside Eric's chest. He didn't even know what it was, but he didn't like it. "I'm sorry, Eunice. Really sorry. I don't know what to say."

She gave a short, humorless laugh. "There's not much else to say, is there? I won't make it to my forty-seventh birthday." She turned to look him in the eye. "This is my last summer on earth, can you believe that?"

No. He couldn't. She was in her forties, and he was in his thirties. Only one decade ahead of him and she was dying?

"I know the whole thing probably seems stupid to you, but this list is important to me." Her voice was tight now. Strained. "When God gives you a mission, you don't ignore it. I need to right a few wrongs. I need to cross every name off my list before . . ."

Eric rubbed his chin. The God stuff made him squirm—his

94

family never talked about that kind of thing—but her revelation explained a lot. If she believed this was her last mission in life, no wonder she was taking it so seriously. "It's not stupid."

She turned wide, troubled eyes on him. "I don't think I can do it without your help. I thought I'd have more time."

He swallowed. There were so many questions he wanted to ask. Where was her family? Why was she living alone? How did she *know* God wanted her to do this? But he didn't have the heart to badger her right now.

"Of course." He took a deep breath and let it out. "Of course I'll help you."

fourteen

It took four days for Eunice to even consider going outside to check her plants. Getting out of bed was so exhausting. Emptying her ostomy bag was so exhausting. Researching the items her boss had asked her to value online was so exhausting.

Saturday had taken its toll. But by Wednesday, she could even smell herself in her sleep.

The shower felt good, although standing and lifting her arms was . . . you know, so exhausting. She cut it short, found some clean clothes, and looked out the back window. Everything needed water, including the grass. June had been warmer than usual, and it hadn't rained since May. The hose was attached to the outdoor spigot. The watering can sat beside one of the raised beds. It shouldn't be that hard.

Then why did the thought of going out there make her want to cry?

She slumped onto a stool in the kitchen and laid her head on the counter in what had become a familiar pose. Something about the cool linoleum soothed her.

Why had she told Eric the truth? No one but her doctor, Bertie, and Wanda knew how numbered her days were. She hadn't even taken a medical leave from her work, such as it was. Eric had no business knowing such intimate information. He was a stranger. A naïve, cocky yuppie who was more concerned about his Jeep than her.

Maybe she was being unfair to him. He hadn't recoiled in disgust, and he'd said he would help. But what if he told everyone at work? She groaned. No one at Larson Financial could know about this. How could she be sure he kept his promise?

She could see the sun shining through the window. Her poor garden was probably dying of thirst. Ha. Dying. She forced her body to slide off the stool and plod to the back door. It wouldn't be right to let her garden fend for itself after she'd brought it to life. Wasn't it the responsibility of the creator of a life to care for it?

"Yeah, God, isn't it?" The words sounded hollow, bouncing off the sliding glass door and back at her. "I'm not going to let my plants just waste away."

The door made a swooshing sound as she slid it open, and warm air hit her face. It felt good. Through the chain-link fence, she saw Cinderella scratching at the ground in Eric's yard. She found it inordinately satisfying that his grass looked worse than hers.

She carefully made her way to the spigot and turned on the water. Lifting the hose was like lifting the branch of a tree. Her arms shook as she pulled it over to the watering can, and she hesitated. If she filled the can, she'd have to pick it up. A bunch of times. Better to just use the spray from the hose.

She leaned against the first bed and held the hose in front of her, using her thumb to create a spray that hit several of the beds at once. Her plants were definitely looking peaked. Poor things.

The mist from the spray struck her face like tiny sharp rocks, stinging and causing her to flinch. She used to enjoy cool mist on her skin on a hot day. How long would she be able to stand here?

Cinderella made a loud squawking sound, and Eunice started. She secretly wished Cinderella had chosen to live at

her house. Chosen *her* company. Eric didn't give the chicken
the appreciation she deserved. Speaking of her neighbor, she
saw him approaching the fence out of the corner of her eye.
Why was he off work already? And how did he get his hair to
look so effortlessly tousled? She shuddered to think what her
own hair looked like.

He leaned his forearms on the fence and gave her a half
smile. "Hi."

Her voice was rusty from disuse. "Hi."

"Haven't seen you out here lately."

Her mortality stood between them like the proverbial el-
ephant. "I've been busy."

Her face heated. What a stupid thing to say. She looked down
to avoid his eyes. Well, super. She wasn't wearing any shoes.

"You need help?"

Water seeped through her socks. Her toes were suddenly very
cold. She began to shiver. "No, thanks. I'm good."

When he didn't answer right away, she chanced a glance over.
He looked skeptical.

"Really." Her voice shook as her teeth chattered. "I'm f-fine."

"Um." He pushed off the fence. "Sure. By the way, what kind
of dog do you have?"

She stilled, her heart free-falling off a cliff as she pictured
Charlie's sweet, mischievous face. How did Eric know about
that? "What do you mean?"

"Your sign." He pointed toward the front yard. "It says 'Beware of Dog.'"

Oh. That. She'd put it up after losing Charlie and her parents
only six months apart. To keep people away. She didn't know
if she could survive losing anyone else.

"I . . . don't."

"You don't have a sign?"

"I don't have a dog."

His expression was bewildered. "Do you have a cat?"

She shook her head. Why would he ask her that? He reached to scratch his scalp but stopped short, his eyes darting to the bottom of her shirt. She quickly tugged her sweater down. Oh no. Had JoJo been hanging out in the open for all the world to see?

Eunice cringed.

Eric looked uncomfortable. "Maybe I should give you my phone number."

Her eyebrows shot up. "What?"

"In case you need anything." He pulled out his phone. "Or if you want another ride. That way you don't have to walk over."

She looked over at his house. It wasn't that far. She could walk a few measly yards, couldn't she? Well, maybe not today. Or any day so far this week. But she'd bounce back and be walking around in no time. Right? She still had five more months left. Dr. Mullins promised.

"Just give me your number and I'll text you," Eric said. "Then my number will be in your phone."

She swallowed. Dr. Mullins had promised nothing.

She tried to stand up straight. "All right." Her voice came out in a croak. Ha, croak. She was on a roll with the death puns today. She recited her number, and Eric punched it into his phone.

He jabbed at his screen a few more times, then put his phone back in his pocket. "There. Text sent."

She wasn't sure what to say. "Thanks?"

"Well, I'm going to go find some dinner." He took a couple of steps toward his house and stopped. "Are you sure you don't . . . ?" His words faded away, presumably at the look on her face. "Right. Okay. See you later."

She watched him for a moment, her mind racing. Had her sickly urine just been on display in front of Mr. Debonair? Every time she thought she couldn't sink any lower . . .

Her feet were soaked. Her thumb was numb where it pressed

against the mouth of the hose. But the two farthest raised beds still needed a drink. She moved forward, pulling the hose along, willing it to come. A couple steps—*squish, squish*—and she switched thumbs. The water just barely reached the beds if she tilted the hose high enough.

Had Eric said dinner? Was it dinnertime already? She looked around and realized the small neighborhood was alive with activity. Kids riding bikes up and down the street. Cars pulling into driveways. People firing up their grills.

The smell of meat cooking made her stomach clench. Another whole day was gone. And she'd done nothing but water some plants. It was an overwhelming feeling.

Tick, tick, tick.

When Dr. Mullins had told her the shocking news, she had taken it pretty well. Had been almost philosophical about it. Later, when she talked about it with Bertie and Wanda, she was matter-of-fact, though maybe a little morbid. But something about seeing the reality of her terminal illness reflected back at her from Eric's face hit her in a whole new way.

She dropped the hose and slogged back to the spigot, every step an effort. Pain stabbed her wrist as she twisted, twisted until the water stopped.

"God?" She reached the sliding door and turned back to look out over her neighborhood one more time. Somewhere a child laughed. A screen door slammed. "I'm scared."

fifteen

During his lunch break Thursday afternoon, Eric sat at a picnic table in a small park across the street from the office. It was unimaginatively named Tukston Park. He'd been packing his own food lately, having found most of the options for grabbing a quick bite not up to his standards. All the restaurants and stores were fine enough but didn't offer much in the way of low-carb, high-protein organic food.

And his Trader Joe's stash was getting perilously low.

It was hot, even though the table was in the shade. Eric rolled up the sleeves of his button-down, then used his phone to check the status of the cubicle wall he'd ordered. The "Track Package" feature still didn't seem to be working. It said the package had shipped over a week ago, but there had been no updates since then. He was going to have to call someone about it. Or cancel the order.

He checked his messages while he was at it. A couple of new texts from Chase said he'd found out who his roommate at UW was going to be.

I looked him up online. Seems pretty cool.

Eric smiled. Yes, Chase had needed a little push, but Eric was confident he was going to hit his stride in college.

Farther down the screen, Eric saw Tiffani's name. And his

101

dad's. No new messages from them, but his shoulder muscles tightened as he stared at their names. Eunice's words from the other day in the Jeep sparked in his mind. *"I need to right a few wrongs. I thought I'd have more time."*

What would *he* do if he found out he had only a few months to live? What would he want to say to Tiffani? To Chase?

To his dad?

He shook his head. Eunice was the one dying, not him.

A movement caught his eye, and he looked up to see a young woman in shorts and a tank top walking a long-haired collie. She smiled at him as she followed the dog into the park, and he smiled back. She was cute. Late twenties. Nice legs. But those shoes. They were almost as bad as Eunice's.

She slowed down. "Hi."

He flashed his dimples. "Hi."

"Rusty likes this park."

"I don't blame him." Eric put his phone away. "I like it, too."

She let the dog off his leash and watched him run around, sniffing bushes. Eric admired the curvy profile of her body. Maybe he should ask her name. He couldn't see himself taking her to dinner or anything, but meeting for coffee might be a possibility. Her curly black hair was kind of wild, but it was getting old having no one to hang out with except Eunice, who was apparently not the crazy cat lady he'd thought she was.

He remembered how rough she'd looked last night out in her yard. And had that been a . . . a . . . he didn't know the right term for it, but it had looked like a pee bag under her shirt. Yikes. How did that even work?

He should stop at the hardware store on his way home and buy her one of those big oscillating sprinklers so she wouldn't have to stand out there with the hose like that.

The collie ran up to him and sniffed his pants. Ugh. This was why he hated dogs. He didn't need dog snot on his Ted Baker slacks. They were dry-clean only.

Another gift from Tiffani.

"Rusty, stop." The girl rushed over and tugged on Rusty's collar. "Sorry, he doesn't know about personal boundaries."

"It's okay. Not many dogs do."

She giggled and tucked her hair behind her ear. Her laugh was high-pitched and tinny. Not adorable. But she was nice to look at and the right age.

She moved a little closer. "So, what are you doing out here?"

"I—" Before he could decide how much information to divulge, another person walking briskly past caught his attention. Benson. He'd been trying to talk with him all week.

"Hey. Benson." Eric jumped up from the table and gave the girl an apologetic look. "I've got to run. See you later." He turned away as she opened her mouth in protest. "Benson, wait up."

Benson slowed his pace but kept his head down.

Eric caught up and fell in beside him. "Where are you headed?"

Benson shrugged. "Just killing time."

"Did you eat lunch already?"

Another shrug.

"I've been wanting to ask you about Saturday." Benson's jaw muscle twitched, but Eric pressed on. "What were you doing out there with those guys?"

Benson stuck his hands in his pockets. "Shooting gophers."

"I know, but were you drinking?"

Benson stopped walking. "My dad likes it when I hang out with him. And he thinks if I hang out with him and his friends, I should act like them. What were *you* doing out there?"

"Eunice is my neighbor. She needed a ride. You were with your dad? Was he the one . . . ?"

Benson started walking again. "Yeah. That was him."

Eric fought to keep his face from giving anything away. Benson's dad was Dick Samson? Guess Eric wasn't the only one whose dad set a less-than-stellar example for his son. "What was he so mad about? What happened between him and Eunice?"

"It's a long story."

"Give me the short version."

Benson stopped again, and this time he turned to face Eric. "Eunice saw my dad snuggled up with some lady at a bar in Butte and told my mom. Dad said he and the lady were just talking and that Eunice made it sound worse than it was to get back at him for dumping her in high school. My parents ended up getting divorced."

Eric's eyebrows shot up. "Because of what Eunice said?"

"Not really. My mom found out about all kinds of other stuff after that and lost it. But my dad blamed it all on Eunice and tried to turn everyone against her. Said we'd all still be together if it wasn't for her."

Whoa. Seemed like Dick should be the one apologizing to Eunice, not the other way around.

Benson scratched the back of his head. "Look, I shouldn't have told you. It was a long time ago. I'd rather just forget it ever happened."

"Didn't seem like your dad wanted to forget."

"It hasn't been easy for him, okay?"

His own father's face appeared in his mind. Eric had never been able to defend him like Benson was doing for his dad. He'd been too angry to try and justify what he'd done.

"Okay." He checked the time. "We better head back. But go easy on the alcohol, all right? I don't want you to get in trouble. I need you at the office."

"I only pretend to drink it."

Eric narrowed his eyes as they turned around to go back. "Pretend?"

"Yeah." Benson gave him a sidelong glance. "I've seen what drinking can do to a person's life, and I'm not interested."

Eric nodded. He'd seen it, too, and he'd worked too hard for what he had to throw it away on alcohol.

"Besides." Benson smiled. "That stuff's disgusting."

Eric packed up his briefcase at the end of the day with a frown. Winnie was still only scheduling the bare minimum number of clients per day, despite his repeated requests to add more. "Max doesn't drive people through here like livestock," she'd muttered the last time he brought it up.

On top of that, his last client had been a single mother with three kids. A sweet, quiet woman he couldn't stop thinking about. Her aging parents had given her ten thousand dollars from the sale of some property they'd been holding on to, and she'd come to him hoping to find a way to turn the ten thousand into three college tuitions.

She'd been excited about the options he'd confidently presented, but now, as he adjusted his tie and smoothed his hair, the weight of her children's future weighed on him. He knew all the right moves to make her investment pay off big for both her and Larson Financial.

But there were no guarantees.

When some bigwig client in Seattle lost ten thousand dollars, it didn't keep Eric up at night. It was part of the game. And the client usually had another ten thousand to replace what was lost. How was a single mother working in Tukston going to come by another ten thousand dollars?

Max appeared at his desk. "You okay?"

Eric nodded. "Just thinking."

"I couldn't help but overhear what you were saying to Ladonna at the end there." Max rubbed his chin. "You've got to be careful getting their hopes up, you know? It takes a lot of courage for some of these folks to even come in here."

Eric thought about Bob and Ladonna and other clients he'd met. Maybe it took a lot of courage just living in a place like this. "Duly noted."

Max tapped Eric's desk with his knuckles. "What're you doing tonight?"

Eric slung the briefcase strap over his shoulder. "I've got to stop at the hardware store on my way home, but that's about it. You need something?"

"No, no." Max hooked his thumbs in his belt. "Just wondered if you'd want to hit up Good Food with me. The missus is at some church meeting tonight and said I was on my own for supper."

Eric pictured the shabby diner and hesitated. A greasy burger wasn't going to do his abs any favors.

"Come on, it's my treat." Max slapped him on the shoulder as he came around his desk. "Jack told me to make sure you're getting out into the community. Meeting people."

"You talked to my uncle?"

"He and I check in once in a while. What do you say?"

Eric could hardly refuse if his uncle was behind this. He was determined not to give Uncle Jack any reason to believe he wasn't doing his part around here. Brady the Brownnoser wouldn't turn down a chance to schmooze the man reporting back to Uncle Jack about him.

He tried to sound pleased instead of resigned as he and Max made their way out of the office. "Okay."

In the lobby, Eric was relieved to see Winnie had already left. Things had been a little tense between them since he'd brought in the Keurig. "Where does she run off to so fast every day?"

She was always first to arrive and first to leave.

Max threw up his hands. "Well, let's see. Mondays she's got bridge club. Tuesdays she's got that water aerobics in Butte. I don't know what she's got going Thursdays."

"She's a busy woman."

"More like a force of nature. I hope I'm running around like that when I'm eighty." Max pointed at the side table. "It's looking a little crowded over here these days."

Eric chuckled. The other morning, he had arranged and re-arranged until he was able to fit both coffee machines on the table, Winnie's old pot and his new Keurig. She'd scowled at him the whole time.

"I'm on the lookout for a bigger table," he said.

"You got Benson's desk from the Kitchen Sink, didn't you? They didn't have any tables?"

"Nothing to go up against the wall like this. He tried to talk me into this wooden bench he had, but it wasn't tall enough."

"You could always make a few adjustments."

Eric dipped his head. "That's what he said. But I wasn't too impressed with the selection over there. Not sure why Uncle Jack recommended them."

Max gave him an inscrutable look. "Only used furniture store in town."

"I'm more interested in new furniture."

Max acted like he had more to say, but he kept his mouth shut. Eric wasn't sure he wanted to hear whatever it was. Max was a good guy and everything, but he'd lived his whole life here in Backwater, USA. What did he know?

When they walked into Good Food together a few minutes later, the place was bustling. Apparently, this was the place to be on a Thursday night. A chalkboard sign read SEAT YOUR-SELF.

"The Cowboy Deluxe is on special every Thursday," Max explained.

Eric remembered Uncle Jack saying something about the Cowboy Deluxe. *"If you think you can handle it."* Eric had no doubt he could.

He and Max took one of the last open booths. The sounds of chatter, laughter, and food frying, the hominess of it, almost made Eric a little homesick. When was the last time he'd been to family dinner at his mom's?

The waitress Eric had met on his first day in Tukston stopped at the table and gave Eric a smile. "You just missed my niece. Such a nice girl."

Not that again. Eric tried to look polite but uninterested. "I'm sure she is."

"She likes to take a slice of pie to go every now and then. We've got peach, apple, and banana cream today."

Max rubbed his stomach. "You're killing me, Dee."

"You survived all those years on the back of a bull." Dee scrutinized Max over her glasses. "I don't think a piece of pie's going to do you in."

Max grinned. "In that case, I'll take one of each."

Dee raised her eyebrows but wrote it down on her notepad. "Anything else to go with that, Max?"

"Just a grilled cheese, please. With extra pickles on the side."

"You got it." Dee turned her attention to Eric. "And for you?"

He hadn't even looked at the one-page menu stuck between the ketchup bottle and napkin dispenser at the end of the table. "I'll have the special, please."

Now Max raised his eyebrows. "You sure about that?"

This from a man who was about to eat three pieces of pie. Eric sat up straight. "Of course. Uncle Jack recommended it."

"Alrighty then." Dee tucked the notepad in the pocket of her apron. "I'll have that right out."

She walked away, and Eric felt Max's eyes on him. He didn't want to talk about work. Or furniture. Or burgers.

"What was all that about how you survived on the back of a bull?"

Max leaned his elbows on the table. "Oh, I rode the circuit for a while."

"The circuit?"

"Rodeo. Started in high school, got recruited for college.

108

Went pro for a few years, but my wife convinced me to give it up. She said if my skull got bashed in, she'd leave me."

Eric gave a low whistle.

Max waved a hand. "She didn't mean it. She just didn't want me to get hurt. Rodeo's dangerous, and nobody wore a helmet back then. 'Course, a helmet won't keep your side from being gored."

Eric had a hard time picturing Max on the back of a raging bull. He was so affable and easygoing. But that probably explained why some mornings Max moved like a ninety-year-old man. "So you retired from rodeo and became a financial advisor?"

Max laughed. "Something like that. I mean, if Jack hadn't—"

"Here you go, boys." Dee set two plates down on the table.

"Oh." Eric eyed the burger in front of him, a stab of doubt suddenly poking his stomach. "That was fast."

"We crank 'em out on Thursdays." Dee smiled. "Enjoy."

She hurried off, and Eric stared at his plate. Nestled among a pile of steak fries was the biggest burger he'd ever seen. It started with a sauce-coated bottom bun, then a patty covered in yellow cheese, a layer of fried onions, a pile of jalapeño slices, another patty with white cheese, four strips of bacon, and then the top bun.

"That's local, grass fed beef right there." Max took a bite of his grilled cheese sandwich. "You're in for a treat."

Sweat formed on Eric's upper lip as he picked up the sandwich. Melted cheese dripped from the side. A whole day's worth of calories, right here in one meal.

Max pointed a pickle spear at him. "Your uncle used to love those."

There was no turning back.

He took a bite.

sixteen

Eunice wearily dragged the big black trash bag down the hall toward the living room. Almost there. Who knew a few old clothes could be so heavy? JoJo made a muted slapping noise in protest as she swung against Eunice's waist in between her grunts of exertion.

"I don't feel so good either, JoJo." Eunice stopped to catch her breath, still gripping the bag's plastic drawstring. "But we must push on."

In JoJo's silence, Eunice heard a question. Something along the lines of *And why exactly must we push on again?* Eunice took a deep breath, steeled herself, and resumed her slow trek down the hall. Because she had no time to waste, that's why.

She reached the back of the couch and leaned against it. When the doorbell rang, her lean morphed into a slump. Oh, thank goodness. Bertie was here.

"Come in," she shouted. She tried to shout anyway. It came out with far less force than she'd intended.

Bertie burst through the door on a surge of energy and enthusiasm. "Good morning, good morning." Her bright smile froze on her face. "And what do we have here?"

Eunice looked around at the random stuff she'd piled up. "Just putting together some boxes to donate."

"Okaaay." Bertie dropped her tote onto the couch and surveyed the room. "Then where are the boxes?"

"I haven't gotten that far yet." Eunice had spent all day yesterday gathering odds and ends, bits and pieces from all over her house, and sorting them into piles on the floor. But she'd discovered in the process that she didn't have any actual boxes.

"I see." Bertie flicked a strand of hair from her forehead and eyed the black bag at Eunice's feet. "And what's in there?"

"My clothes."

Bertie raised one eyebrow. "You planning to join a nudist colony?"

Eunice scoffed. "I kept a couple things."

"I should hope so. Now, where exactly were you planning to donate all this . . . stuff?"

"I don't know. I was hoping . . ."

Bertie moved closer and patted Eunice's hand. "That I'd help you?"

Eunice nodded. After Wednesday evening, she hadn't been able to shake a sense of urgency about being productive with her days. Thursday morning she'd woken up with a fire in her belly that counteracted her soul-deep fatigue just enough to help her see her house—more specifically all the *stuff* in her house—in a new light.

"I don't need any of this." She made a weak gesture with her arm. "And I don't want anyone else to have to deal with the mess. You know. *Later*."

Compassion softened Bertie's face. "Have you eaten breakfast yet?"

Eunice shook her head.

"Okay." Bertie clapped her hands twice. "First, breakfast. Then we'll get to work."

Bertie was long gone. She'd accomplished more in a couple of hours than Eunice had in an entire day, and she'd promised to bring boxes next time. Eunice sat on her favorite stool and laid her head on the counter. She was utterly spent, but it felt good to have accomplished something.

Her eyes lined up with the fish tank she had insisted on keeping. She'd been ruthless about everything else. Wall hangings? In the pile. Books? It hurt, but they had to go. Miscellaneous kitchen gear? She never used it anyway. But she'd drawn the line at her assortment of pet supplies. Maybe because they represented a different life—the one where she had a thriving veterinary practice and animals scampering all over her house. Or maybe because tossing them in a discard pile would feel too much like tossing aside any last remaining hope.

But hope for what? That Dr. Mullins was wrong? That God would send a miracle? Or just that she still had enough time for something that mattered?

"Oh, Lo-ord." Her voice carried across the counter and dropped off the edge. "What do you want from me?"

She shifted on the stool, and the crinkling of paper in her pocket raised the hair on the back of her neck. Her list.

"Okay, okay." She looked up. "I can take a hint."

She pulled out the list and tried to smooth the creases with no success. Touching the last name, she wondered if she really had the guts. Then she slid from the stool and walked over to the fridge.

An Eiffel Tower magnet her parents had mailed her from Paris before their accident was stuck to the old appliance. She used it to secure her list to the fridge door. Front and center.

"There."

She couldn't chicken out now.

Eunice slowly pulled a box of frozen corn dogs from the freezer. In addition to making great strides with Eunice's donation quest, Bertie had also gone to the grocery store to pick up some food Eunice could easily prepare to make a few quick meals. She'd been aghast at Eunice's food situation.

112

The corn dogs had been Eunice's one special request. Bertie had not been thrilled—she said only teenage boys ate frozen corn dogs—but she'd eventually given in.

Eunice set two of the corn dogs on the tray of her toaster oven and turned it on. The little oven droned like a distant semi on the highway as she returned to her stool. She was hungry, which didn't happen often anymore. That was good, right?

She laid her head back on the counter to wait.

Eric slipped off his loafers and loosened his tie with one hand as he walked through the door. In the other hand he held his phone, expecting a call from Uncle Jack any—

Ring, ring.

His uncle was nothing if not punctual.

"Hello."

Uncle Jack's voice was animated. "It's been three weeks already, can you believe it?"

Yes. Yes, he could. He'd been painstakingly counting down every passing day. "I miss the water."

"Montana has water. There are rivers everywhere."

"I miss the noise."

"Montana has plenty to say. You just can't hear it yet."

"What does that mean?"

"Keep listening. You'll figure it out. Have you met any nice girls?"

Eric rolled his eyes. Uncle Jack would never understand his desire to enjoy the local scenery from a safe distance. His uncle was always pushing Eric to think about "settling down," even though he was a confirmed bachelor himself.

"The women in Tukston aren't really my type."

"Oh? And what is your type?"

Eric fiddled with the top button of his shirt. He remembered a time when he was twelve, just before his dad left. They'd been at the store, and he'd pointed out a girl he knew from his class who he thought was nice. *"You can do better,"* his dad had said.

Anger flared in Eric's chest, but he tamped it down. He didn't want to think about his dad. "I'm only here for a little while, Uncle Jack. No point in getting attached to anyone."

Uncle Jack's response was a long moment in coming. "Okay. Well, how's it going at the office?"

"Great." Eric was grateful for the change of subject. "I've been recommending more high-yield investments and looking through the files of clients who've been around awhile to see if we can give their portfolios a boost. I know Max likes to play it safe, but it feels like the office is stuck in a rut. I think we can do more."

"More?" Uncle Jack's voice took on a thoughtful tone. "Did these clients ask for a boost?"

Eric hesitated. "No, but you said they won't know how much they need me until I tell them."

"I see."

"I'm taking the initiative."

Uncle Jack cleared his throat. "Just remember, what's best for Larson Financial is whatever's best for the client, not the other way around."

Eric shook his head. Did Uncle Jack speak to Brady the Brownnoser in riddles, too? "Right. So, have you had any luck finding my replacement?"

Uncle Jack chuckled. "Patience, my boy. Patience. It takes time to find the right person."

"But you're still planning to transfer me by the end of the summer, right?"

"We'll see."

We'll see? That was a hundred percent not what Eric wanted to hear. He plopped down on the couch. "I thought—"

"Have you been to the Kitchen Sink yet?"

Eric sighed. "Yes. I found a desk for Benson, but they didn't have the kind of table I was looking for. You didn't tell me it was a *used* furniture store."

"Everything there's in good shape."

"Yeah, but secondhand style isn't the look we're going for at Larson Financial, is it?"

"Did you meet Dusty and Nate?"

Eric stifled a frustrated groan. His uncle was always doing this. Changing the subject. Avoiding the issue. "Yes."

"Good folks. Amazing how Dusty's been able to support himself and his son by shaping up other people's castoffs. I left every piece of furniture I had there with them when I left town. Knew they'd put it to good use."

"That's great, but I might have to go to Sofas and More for the table."

Uncle Jack paused. "Do whatever you think is best."

They chatted for another minute before Uncle Jack had to go. Eric changed into gym shorts and a T-shirt and fixed himself a protein shake. His stomach was still recovering from dinner out with Max last night. Not only had he failed to finish his burger, even after Max said Uncle Jack *always* finished, but he'd also spent the rest of his evening on the toilet.

He looked out back and saw Cinderella poking around the yard. Her funny feathers still made him chuckle. Chase had sent a dozen ROFL emojis after Eric texted him a picture of the weird animal. Eric's eyes swept past the chicken to Eunice's yard. He swallowed the rest of his shake and set the empty glass in the sink. He should go deliver that sprinkler.

When he reached Eunice's front yard, he hesitated. The last time he'd knocked on her door, she totally freaked out. He looked around. Maybe he should leave the package there on the porch, next to that potted plant. But what if she didn't leave her house for a few days?

He took a step closer to the house and hesitated again. The

sound of a shrieking alarm came from inside. What was going on? He hurried to the door and sniffed.

Smoke.

"Eunice." He pounded on the door. "Eunice, open up."

No answer. He tried the knob, and it was locked. Jamming his fingers into his hair, he paced. Should he call 911?

He pulled his phone out, ready to make the call, but on a hunch he ran around to the back of the house first. Aha. The sliding door was open. He burst into the house, waving an arm in front of his face. Smoke was everywhere. His eyes burned.

"Eunice?"

The shrill warning of the alarm ignited the adrenaline in Eric's body. Heart pounding, he followed the sound to the kitchen where he found his neighbor with a wet towel in her hand, feebly slapping at a blazing toaster oven.

"Charlie," she whimpered. "Charlie."

He grabbed the towel from her hand, pushed her aside, and put the fire out with a few well-aimed blows. *Smack, smack, smack.*

He unplugged the unit and stepped back, panting. The door of the toaster oven hung open, and a charred lump of something sat inside, sizzling.

Eunice coughed. Her voice was hoarse. "I fell asleep."

Eric dropped the towel in the sink and slumped against the counter. "You could've burned your whole house down."

She took a shuddering breath and wiped her eyes.

"Who's Charlie?" he asked.

Without looking at him, she turned on the faucet and held her left hand under the cold water. "I burned my hand."

Eric huffed. Fine, she didn't want to talk about Charlie. But did she have any idea how reckless she'd been? "Fire will do that."

"Fire will do a lot of things."

"Yeah." He gestured around the kitchen. "Exactly."

She stared at the water as it ran over her hand. "No, I mean, it makes everything clear."

He looked around. Smoke still lingered, making the air anything but clear. He wondered how much of it she'd inhaled.

"Do you need me to take you to the doctor?"

Her shoulders drooped. She turned off the water and examined the angry red mark across her fingers. "No."

"That doesn't look good."

"I'll be fine."

Eric wasn't so sure, but how did you make a grown woman go to the doctor if she didn't want to go, short of throwing her over your shoulder and stuffing her in your car?

He worked his way around her house opening windows. The smoke began to dissipate, revealing half a dozen piles of stuff on the living room floor. He didn't even want to know.

"I brought you something." He retrieved the sprinkler from the front porch and set it on the counter. "To help you with your garden."

Her injured hand was clutched to her chest, leaving wet streaks on her shirt. "Thank you."

She stared at the sprinkler, then at him. Then at the door. But he couldn't just leave her like this. "Do you have a first-aid kit or something? Can I wrap that for you?"

She looked like she wanted to refuse, but then she sank onto one of the stools and pointed down the hall. "In the bathroom."

He marched down the hall, on edge. It was lucky he'd shown up when he did. Eunice shouldn't be living alone in her condition.

He didn't like snooping around someone else's house, and he *really* didn't like fire. But he found the bathroom and began a search for ointment and bandages.

What was this? He held up a box. *Skin Barrier Prep*, it said. It must have something to do with her pee bag. Did she have to change the bag every day? How did she empty it? Would she be able to do whatever she needed to do—whatever that was—with an injured hand? And what the heck did *this* thing do?

He moved a skin-colored cummerbund thing aside and shook his head. This was way more than he wanted to know about his neighbor.

He found a zippered pouch and was almost afraid to look inside, unsure what strange things he might find, but it turned out to be the items he'd been looking for. He brought the pouch to the kitchen and made quick work of covering Eunice's burn in antibiotic ointment and a gauze wrap.

She let her hand rest on the counter. "That feels better."

He'd done the same treatment for Chase one time when a bonfire at the beach got out of hand. He'd never been so scared in his life as when he saw the giant ball of paper someone threw in the flames jump out and start rolling toward his little brother. Chase had begged to go to Mukilteo Beach with Eric and his friends.

"Don't you have any family who can stay with you?" he asked.

She stared at her hand. "No."

"No brothers or sisters?"

When she didn't respond, he continued, hoping to get her to talk. "I've got a younger brother. Chase. I'm helping him move to college at the end of the summer."

Her voice was small and distant. "I've got no one."

He swallowed. Thanks to his dad, he knew what it felt like to be abandoned. Thanks to Uncle Jack banishing him to Tukston, he knew what it felt like to be lonely. But he'd never been all alone.

He hesitated, wanting to say he was sorry but not sure how she'd take it.

She held up her bandaged hand. "Thanks for your help."

"You're welcome."

Two thank-yous from Eunice in one day. That had to be

some sort of record. Maybe she was becoming less irritated with his very existence.

She waved her uninjured hand toward the door. "You can go now."

Maybe not.

He put the supplies he'd used back in the pouch and zipped it closed, chuckling to himself as he realized it didn't actually offend him anymore when she talked like that.

"Call me if you have any more problems." He took one last look at the smoldering mass in the toaster oven. "You've got my number."

She didn't respond, but as he walked away, he heard her mutter to herself, "All this over a corn dog."

seventeen

Eunice stood in her small garage and shivered. Though the temperature outside was over eighty degrees, the concrete floor in here gave the air a chilled feeling. She studied her Honda Spree with a critical eye. She hadn't driven it since the day Eric forced her into the ditch, but she still had a small shred of confidence in the old girl. It wouldn't be pretty, but if she could pump up the flat tire with her portable air compressor, she was sure it would take her to Diane Butler's house.

The next name on her list. Only five blocks away.

Her hand throbbed where it had been burned, and her mind seared with the image of a scruffy, trusting face. Why had she brought Charlie up there when the hill caught fire? Why had he run away from her? She shook her head. Reliving it wouldn't bring him back. She had a job to do now.

She'd taken a couple of Tylenol for the pain—okay, four or five—over the last half hour, and relief should arrive soon. Maybe it wasn't the best idea to go out by herself in the shape she was in, but Eric had helped her enough lately, hadn't he? She could do this one on her own.

When the tire was filled with air, she opened the garage door and squinted at the brightness. The FedEx driver was pulling away, and a plain brown box sat by her front door.

Must be her monthly shipment of urostomy supplies. Bertie was always telling her how lucky she was that Eunice's boss took care of all that through his store. That everything she needed, even the more expensive extended-wear wafers she liked, showed up on her doorstep like clockwork every month. No hassles. But the brown box didn't make her feel lucky.

It was a sweltering Sunday afternoon. She pushed her sparkly helmet on her head and clumsily snapped the buckle into place with her one good hand. How much hair was this thing going to take with it when she took it off? Better leave it on at Diane's house so she only had to remove it once.

The Honda sputtered to life with a snarling protest on the third attempt, and Eunice warily set out. What was that awful noise coming from the scooter? She sniffed. And what was that smell? Thank goodness she was going only a few blocks.

Her stomach knotted as she drew close to her destination, though the pain in her hand, which was now shooting up her arm, outdid it for discomfort. The scooter's vibrations were killing her.

Ha. She'd never noticed before how many common expressions had to do with death.

Diane's pretty red Camry was parked in front of the house. The yard was immaculate, the grass thick and green and uniform from one side to the other. An ornate floral wreath hung on the door. It was the home of a woman who knew exactly what she wanted. A woman in complete control of her life.

A woman Eunice had hurt.

She rang the doorbell. If she talked with Diane today, her list would be more than halfway completed. A small part of her wanted to believe her list would be all the way completed if it hadn't been for Eric wrecking her scooter. A larger, more insistent part knew she wouldn't even be this far if not for him.

A man opened the door and furrowed his brow at her. "Can I help you?"

Diane's husband, Wes. He didn't recognize her. She must look ridiculous.

She tried to smile, or at least not grimace. "Is Diane home?"

"Sure." Wes looked suspicious, but he left the door open and turned. "I'll go get her."

When Diane appeared, she was drying her hands on a dish towel with a smile plastered on her face. Her hair was styled in a short bob Eunice figured even a hurricane-force wind couldn't muss.

"Why, Eunice." Diane's eyes flicked from Eunice's Crocs to her bandaged hand to her helmet. Her voice was strained as if forced through a politeness grinder. "What a surprise."

Eunice shifted on her feet. "Hope I'm not interrupting anything."

"Oh, no. Just doing the dishes. I like to make a nice dinner on Sundays. Wes is partial to pork roast."

Eunice didn't come here to talk about pork roast, and she supposed Diane knew it. Better cut to the chase.

"I wanted to say I'm sorry. For everything that happened at church. I shouldn't have . . ."

Her voice trailed off. There were a dozen ways she could finish that sentence. Shouldn't have listened to those other ladies. Shouldn't have signed that petition. Shouldn't have believed for one second that Diane's daughter was somehow less of a person because of her mistakes.

Diane fidgeted with the towel. "It's not like you led the charge or anything."

"I did nothing to stop it either."

She'd been a fool. Had gotten swept up in the drama when she started attending Grace and Truth Church, where a certain group of ladies had taken an interest in her. They did all kinds of things together and for a time made Eunice feel like maybe

122

she belonged. A feeling she'd sorely needed after her parents died, leaving her utterly alone in the world.

"No one did." Diane's voice was no longer strained. Just quiet and hollow.

"They should have." Eunice tugged on her shirt. "I should have. Paige didn't deserve to be treated like that."

She hadn't been the first seventeen-year-old girl to wind up pregnant, and she surely wouldn't be the last. But the ladies who had befriended Eunice were so piously enraged by Paige's indiscretion that they started a petition to ban Paige from attending youth group. *"She'll be a bad influence on our children,"* they'd insisted.

Eunice had gone along with it, but the whole thing had left a foul and confusing taste in her mouth. She'd stopped attending church not long after. But Diane hadn't.

Neither had Paige.

"You and Paige were so brave."

"Those other ladies didn't stick around either. They moved on to some other church not long after you left. The congregation has been nothing but supportive of Paige and her daughter since then."

"But everyone just watched while they— we—hurt you."

Even Diane's own sister had remained silent.

Diane looked at the floor. "I can't expect others to be perfect when I'm not. But you're right. It hurt."

Eunice hung her head as well. "I'm sorry."

"You should come back to church. There are a lot of great people at Grace and Truth, even if we don't get everything right all the time."

Eunice could not imagine sitting through a Sunday morning service, trying to keep JoJo hidden and suffering through the agony of the wooden pew against her bony rear end. It might be nice to find that feeling again, the feeling that she belonged, but even if her body could physically endure it, everyone would stare at her. Wonder about her. Ask questions.

"Maybe." She raised her head and forced herself to look Diane in the eyes. "But, please, Diane, will you forgive me?"

Diane looked over her shoulder and back. "I want to, Eunice. I appreciate you coming here. But it's been so long. I need a little time."

Time? Eunice didn't have time.

She swallowed, her mouth dry and her body aching. "Okay."

"I better get back to my roast." Diane put one hand on the door. "Bye, Eunice."

The door shut, and Eunice slumped. It took a lot of energy to stand upright for a whole conversation. Shuffling sluggishly back to the scooter, she turned Diane's words over in her mind, this way and that. Why would Diane want Eunice to come back to church if she wasn't even sure she could forgive her? *Even if we don't get everything right all the time.* Ha. Eunice could relate to that.

She sat down on the scooter with a groan, not knowing how to feel. She could cross another name off her list. That was good. But she couldn't force people to forgive her. That was . . . hard. Diane's forgiveness suddenly meant a lot more to her than it had even this morning.

"I guess you'd probably say that part is for you to handle, huh, God?" The Honda turned over on the second try, and Eunice wobbled onto the road. "I do the apologizing. You do the heart stuff."

Yes, hearts were definitely God's territory, not hers. But still, she would come back another day and try again.

If she had the time.

As she rode home, struggling to grip the handlebar with her bandaged hand, a car approached from behind. She tensed. She was already as far over on the road as she could go, but that hadn't kept her out of the ditch last time. She chanced a glance over her shoulder.

A blue Jeep.

Wouldn't you know it.

Eric slowed the Jeep to a crawl and gave her as wide a berth as the road would allow.

eighteen

Eric held out a blueberry scone from Hoagies and Grinders. "Good morning."

Winnie huffed but snatched the scone from his hand. "It will be as soon as you take care of that mess in my lobby."

Eric's smile wavered. It wasn't his fault he hadn't been able to find a suitable table. And it wasn't *her* last name on the door. "Why don't you choose a coffee flavor you like, and I'll make it for you in the Keurig? To go with your scone."

"I've already had two cups. From *my* pot. And what are you hiding behind your back?"

He swallowed and set the small box on the table. "Oh, this? Uh, this is sugar substitute."

She heaved a heavy sigh and shook her head. This was probably not the right moment to bring up his idea about purchasing a small refrigerator in which to store milk and creamer. Or his plan to add recycling bins to the lobby.

"You either use sugar or you don't use sugar," Winnie grumbled. "There's no room for sugar substitute."

Yesterday, the usual Monday morning chaos had been amplified by an incident involving the crowded coffee table and a young child. Luckily no one had been hurt, but Winnie had blamed the whole thing on Eric's "newfangled contraption."

He wanted to say something about how more and more clients were trying out the Keurig as they waited and it seemed to be a hit, but he opted for a more diplomatic approach. "We could certainly use a bigger table. I'll keep looking."

That bench from the Kitchen Sink was looking more and more appealing.

He pushed through the glass door and set his briefcase on his desk. His workout this morning had been intense, so he did one more quick set of stretches before sitting down. One of the perks of being the first to arrive—well, first besides Winnie—was not having anyone around to see him get settled in. He wouldn't mind if the whole town of Tukston thought he was always prepared, always ready to work, always professional. But of course he did have to be seen at the grocery store once in a while.

His mind wandered for a second while his laptop fired up. The conversation he'd had with Tiffani last night had left him confused. She said she missed him and wanted to see him. She'd used her sexy voice, and he'd allowed himself to imagine being close to her again. Kissing those pouty lips and running his fingers through her perfectly coiffed hair. Yet he felt so far away from her—farther than 713 miles—and he wasn't sure why.

The laptop was ready for action with ten minutes left before office hours, so he decided to give his email a quick check. There was one message from the company he'd used to order the cubicle wall. He sat up straighter. Maybe it had finally shipped. He was tired of feeling exposed in his own office.

He opened the email and groaned. They regretted that they could not ship the item to the given address at this time and were issuing a full refund. What? Shoot. So much for acquiring a little privacy anytime soon.

Benson arrived, walking briskly to the back of the room with only a brief nod in Eric's direction.

Max followed a minute later and pulled right up to Eric's desk. "Howdy."

"Good morning."

"Winnie looks fit to be tied out there."

Eric kept up a professional demeanor but rolled his eyes on the inside. "Once we find a bigger table, everything will be fine."

"If you say so. Hey, do you have any plans for Monday?"

Eric shuffled some papers. His first client would be arriving any moment. "Monday?"

"Fourth of July?"

"Oh." Eric checked his watch rather obviously. "I forgot all about that. Does Tukston have a fireworks show or something?"

Max laughed. Loudly. "You better plan on coming to my house."

"I—"

His desk phone rang.

"I'll let you get that." Max pointed at Eric. "Four o'clock on Monday. Bring a friend. Don't forget."

Eric picked up the phone and heard Winnie's double voice. "Brenda Wallace is here to see you."

Before he could respond, the glass door flung open and Brenda entered the room, a well-brushed Pomeranian in her arms.

"Hello, hello." She parked herself in the chair across from him. "I thought Winnie retired? I went to her party and everything. What's she doing here?"

Eric blinked. "Uh—"

"She told me to wait, but Pumpkin is kind of impatient. I think he knows it's Tuesday."

"I see." Eric tried not to show he was flustered. Dogs were not allowed in the office as a rule. This one wore a red-and-black plaid bandanna around its neck. "Pumpkin likes Tuesdays?"

"Of course." She held the dog up and rubbed noses with it. "That's when he gets to go on a walk with his bestest friend in the world, isn't that right, Mr. Muffin?"

She said that last part in a baby voice. Was the creature's full name Pumpkin Muffin? Did it have a middle name? Eric didn't dare ask.

"The dog walker takes him on Tuesdays, remember?" Brenda ruffled the fur on Pumpkin's head. "I would still love to introduce the two of you. I just think—"

"Thank you, Ms. Wallace, but—"

"It's Brenda."

"Right. Brenda. Thank you, but I'm very busy, like I told you before. Now—"

"Not too busy to drive Eunice Parker around, though."

Her smile was bright, but there was an undercurrent to her words that made Eric want to fidget.

"It's nice of you to help her, of course," Brenda continued. "Very generous. I just can't understand why she feels the need to go around stirring up trouble after all these years."

Eric clenched his jaw. What did Brenda Wallace know about it? Part of him wanted to tell this woman that Eunice had a very good reason for "stirring up trouble," but he'd promised he wouldn't say anything.

"I don't—"

"She was at my sister's just the other day." Brenda lowered her voice and leaned closer with a conspiratorial expression. "Poor Diane is still shaken up about it."

So that was where Eunice took her scooter Sunday afternoon. He'd been surprised to see her driving it down the street. And concerned frankly. Why hadn't she called him? He would've taken her. His heart pinched a tiny bit. Probably because he'd never acted too thrilled about being around her, that's why.

"Now, we better get down to business." Brenda set the Pomeranian on her lap. "Before Pumpkin needs to piddle."

Sweat drenched Eric's face and neck as he ran, soaking the top of his shirt in a V shape. He'd waited until after nine to take an evening run, hoping it would've cooled off by then, but it was still warm. He pushed himself, letting the pavement take another bit of tension away from him with every footfall.

Though his wireless earbuds blasted music in his ears, his thoughts turned to Eunice. She hadn't given any details about her cancer, but it must be bad if it was draining her life away so quickly. What was she like before? Did she drive a car? Go for runs? Wear normal clothes?

He'd made so many assumptions about her when he first met her. Being able to read people was important in his line of work. If he'd been wrong about Eunice, what else had he been wrong about? *Who* else?

Tukston was not what he had expected. It was rougher and smaller and rednecker than he could've imagined, but it was the pace of life that got to him the most. People talked slower, drove slower. They took forever to finish their meals in the diner because they kept talking to other people and asking for refills on their coffee. He'd thought Seattleites drank a lot of coffee, but he'd watched an old man with weathered hands drain seven cups in one sitting the other day. Black.

He reached the last stretch of his five-mile loop and slowed to a light jog to cool down. If he kept this up, he'd need to extend his run to six miles. Maybe seven. Five miles found him back at his house far too quickly and gave him too much time to think about his life.

By the time he got to his driveway, he was walking, alternately swinging his arms in circles, and pulling one knee at a time to his chest to stretch out. His body was bending to his will. While he'd always been in good shape, his muscles were even more defined now that he had so much extra time on his hands. Because he was not even close to what he would consider busy, despite what he'd told Brenda Wallace.

In Seattle, he'd been busy. And he'd liked it that way.

Once his arms and legs were adequately stretched, he headed

for his front porch. His three-and-a-half-minute post-run shower awaited. Cinderella met him on the top step with the weird gurgling sound she always made that he took for a greeting, but today it sounded a little more urgent than usual. When he climbed the steps, he saw why.

An egg. Sitting on the rustic brown *Welcome Home* doormat was a small white egg.

He cocked his head at the chicken. "Did you do this?"

What would make her decide to lay an egg all of a sudden? He'd been here a month, and this was the first time he'd seen one.

"Is this because of all the scraps I've been giving you?" He squatted to get a closer look. "Aren't farm-fresh eggs supposed to be brown?"

Cinderella bobbed her head, the fancy feathers on top swooshing back and forth. What was he supposed to do with it? He couldn't leave it sitting here. Someone might step on it. Should he—gulp—eat it?

He touched it and grimaced. It was warm. Gross.

He nudged it to one side with his foot and then went inside. He would deal with that later. After setting his shoes in the correct place, he pulled his phone from the running belt around his torso and saw he'd missed a text from Chase. The text sounded a bit desperate.

He tapped his brother's name on the screen and smiled when Chase answered after one ring. "Hey, bro."

"You got my message?"

"Yeah." Eric filled a glass with water from the sink. "What's the big emergency?"

"I didn't say it was an emergency."

Eric grinned to himself. Chase was so easy to rile up. "Okay, well, if it's not important . . ."

"Cut it out." Chase laughed. "Okay, it's sort of an emergency. You remember that girl I told you about?"

Eric was all ears now. "The one with the pink hair?"

"We talked. A lot. And she gave me her number."

It sounded like great news to Eric, but Chase's voice was broody. "What's so bad about that? Isn't that what you wanted?"

"Yeah, but she kind of sort of hinted that she maybe didn't have any plans for Fourth of July. Now I'm freaking out. Did she want me to ask her out? What could I possibly do with her on Fourth of July that wouldn't be lame? I don't want her to think I'm a loser. But if I don't text her, she'll think . . ."

Eric raised his eyebrows. "She'll think what?"

"That I don't like her or something."

"Do you?"

Eric could practically see his brother's face work its way through a slew of expressions, most of which were probably heavy on insecurity and angst. Oh, to be eighteen again.

"Yes. What should I do?"

"When did all this happen?"

"Today. She came in as my shift was ending, and we sat at a table and talked for like an hour."

Eric didn't think Chase had ever in his life had a conversation that lasted an hour. This was serious. He knew what he would do in the same situation. In fact, he'd probably be out on the town with the girl right now. But this was Chase.

"What do you *want* to do?"

Chase hesitated. "Just hang out with her somewhere that doesn't smell like fries and watch some fireworks, I guess."

"Then that's what you should do."

"But what if she thinks that's lame?"

"Then she might not be the girl for you, bro."

Even as he said the words, Eric's chest tightened. It was easy to give relationship advice to someone else. When it wasn't his heart that would break if he got it all wrong. He thought of the only relationship advice his dad had ever given him—"*You can do better*"—and cringed.

"Should I wear my *God Bless America* T-shirt?" Chase asked.

Eric shook his head. Was his brother trying to be a dork or did it just come naturally? "Maybe save that for the second date."

"This is why I need you to come back. I need your help."

"You'll be fine."

"But I've got no one to talk to."

"We can talk on the phone anytime you want."

"It's not the same."

Eric missed Chase, too. Not that he would admit it. "Only two more months. Then I'll be back."

He ran the calculation in his head. Only 1,416 hours left in Tukston. Uncle Jack had said "We'll see" about Eric's assignment being over by summer's end, but Eric had no plans to stick around longer than that. He would return to Seattle by move-in weekend at UW whether Uncle Jack liked it or not.

"Promise?" Chase asked.

Sometimes it felt like Chase was still a little kid, and Eric was still trying to reassure him he wouldn't let go of the back of his bike until he was ready.

"Promise."

nineteen

Eric tried to sleep in Monday morning, but the sunshine and the heat woke him early. Why couldn't his rental have come with A/C? Twenty-three percent of home break-ins occurred at a first-floor window, but if this high-temperature streak continued, he might have to start sleeping with his window open anyway.

Today was the party at Max's house, and Eric had some seriously conflicted feelings about it. He knew Uncle Jack would be happy he was going. He knew it was good for business. He knew he had nothing else to do. But he also knew going to a party in Tukston would be nothing like going to a party in Seattle. In Seattle, he'd had years to learn exactly where he fit. What would impress people. What wouldn't.

But here?

He put himself through an extreme workout and showered, all the while thinking about the party. Uncle Jack had taught him to always have three questions ready for any situation so he would never find himself unable to carry a conversation. Eric racked his brain for suitable questions, but he had no idea what type of people he might encounter. Did everyone shoot gophers in open fields? Was that something to bring up?

No, nothing involving weapons or dead animals.

He dressed and opened the vanity cupboard in the bathroom for his hair paste. When he screwed off the lid, he grunted.

That's right. He'd forgotten he was going to pick up more from the store, and shampoo, too. He rubbed what was left of the paste into his hair and grabbed his keys. Plenty of time to hit up the grocery store before the party. There were some other things he needed, as well.

He slipped on sunglasses and flip-flops and hurried out the front door. His foot came down with a *crunch*. Oh no. Another egg. Now crushed. Cinderella was stalking ants in the driveway, but she looked up at the disturbance. Was it his imagination or did she appear . . . disgruntled?

He wiped his foot on the mat. "Sorry."

She stared at him with one beady eye, which was somehow more disturbing than two.

"This is not a good place to lay your eggs."

He shouldn't be talking to a chicken. His friends would tease him up and down for that. He carried the mat to the spigot on the front of the house and ran it under the water, then pulled off his yolk-covered sandal and did the same.

"What are you doing?"

He spun around. Eunice was standing in her front yard, a newspaper in her hand.

"That chicken laid an egg on my doorstep. What are *you* doing?"

She'd better not be heading out on her own again. What if something happened? What if she got stranded somewhere?

She held up the paper. "The letters to the editor are entertaining."

She was wearing her purple Crocs and a long bathrobe he remembered from the first time they met. Did she sit around the house in her pajamas all day? What a sad way to spend your last few months. She probably didn't want his pity, but it was hard not to feel sorry for her.

"You got any plans today?"

She blinked. "Uh . . ."

"It's the Fourth of July."

"I realize that."

"Why don't you come with me to this Fourth of July party I'm going to?"

Max had said to bring a friend. Eric wasn't sure if Eunice counted as a friend or not, but who else did he have? Cinderella?

Eunice looked past him at the Jeep. "I pumped up the tire on the Honda. It took me the five blocks I needed to go, but it's flat again."

Why was she telling him that? "Okay."

She pulled her bathrobe tighter around her body. "It was one more name crossed off my list."

Oh. That made four, right? Three more to go.

"Good." Was it good? Nothing about her situation seemed good exactly. "The party's at four."

She looked down at her robe. "I don't know . . ."

"Oh, come on." He shot her a smile. "It'll be good for you to get out of the house. I won't know anyone either."

She tucked the newspaper under one arm and gaped at him. He winked. "Meet me back out here at four-thirty."

"I thought the party was at four."

"We'll be fashionably late."

She puckered her lips in a sour expression but made a motion with her head he took as a nod. Then she turned and shuffled back into her house.

Was he going to regret this?

Eleven o'clock? What did it mean Joe had to step out, and the grocery store wouldn't reopen until eleven o'clock? Who was Joe?

Eric turned away from the handwritten note on the door

with a huff. He'd just have to kill some time. Maybe if he took a nice long walk around town, he'd find something interesting.

Hey, a guy could hope.

He'd noticed the red, white, and blue decorations going up on storefronts, lampposts, and signs all over town in the last week, but as he walked around in the already hot air, he got a closer look. Tukston was apparently a very patriotic place.

On a large digital reader board by the four-way stop, he read the announcement, *Fourth of July Schedule*. His eyes widened as the board flashed through a list of events. Parade at noon. Face-painting in the gazebo. A dunk tank to raise money for the fire department. Cornhole game tournament at three. A duck race? Really? Maybe he could use that as one of his three questions. *Have you ever competed in the duck race?*

The whole day would be capped off by a fireworks display at the high school football stadium at ten o'clock. Eric was impressed. Tukston did not take their celebrations lightly. As he made his way back toward the grocery store, he saw food vendors setting up trucks and a bunch of kids preparing tables for a lemonade stand. It was like a movie from the fifties. And someone somewhere must be planning to sell funnel cakes because he could smell them.

There was another conversation question. *What is your favorite fair food?*

Ugh. So lame.

He was waiting at the door when Joe returned at eleven. He tossed a few more items he needed into a shopping basket and made his way to the hair-care aisle. His expectations were low, but not low enough. This was it? These were the only options?

They didn't carry the brand he used for hair paste or anything remotely resembling it. He picked up a generic brand of shampoo that described itself as "invigorating." He grumbled to himself as he dropped it into the basket. Not only did he need the right kind of paste to keep his hair looking like the perfect combination of professional yet playful, he also needed to start thinking seriously about a haircut. He'd gone to the same stylist every six weeks for the past seven years. If Tukston had an airport, he'd be tempted to fly back to Seattle for a hair appointment.

Maybe that should be his third question. *Do you cut hair?*

He shuddered. How would he ever trust his wavy locks to anyone in Tukston?

A man appeared at his side and reached for the same shampoo Eric had chosen. "I like this one. Not that I have much hair left to wash."

Bob Crowley.

The grizzled old man grinned, causing his jowls to sway. "Smells like the mint gum my Betty used to chew after she would chew her chew, I tell you what."

Bob laughed at the look on Eric's face and slapped him on the shoulder. "She was a wild woman, that one."

Eric picked a hair gel at random and threw it in his basket. "Hi, Bob. Good to see you. Didn't you tell me you were divorced?"

"That was my first wife. Only lasted fifteen months. I was with Betty fifty-two years. All glorious, 'cept maybe the year we lost our boy. I miss them both."

"I'm very sorry to hear that," Eric said.

Bob nodded, clutching the shampoo bottle to his chest.

Eric shifted on his feet. Should he bring up the issue of Bob's will? Ask him how it was coming along? Benson had insinuated Bob had no computer and no family. But he seemed like a smart, resourceful guy. He'd solved that problem with the raccoon, albeit in an unconventional way.

"Been meaning to come by the office," Bob said.

Aha. So it was on Bob's mind, too.

"Great." Eric smiled. "Call anytime and we'll get you on the books."

Bob scratched at the stubble on his face with gnarled fingers. "I was hoping I could just stop in. I got rid of my phone. Too much of a nuisance."

No computer and no phone? How did this man survive?

"I see. Well, if you stop in, we'll see what we can do. If nothing else, you can make an appointment while you're there."

Bob reached out a hand. "Much obliged."

Eric shook it, and Bob ambled away. His worn jeans and long-sleeved shirt seemed incongruous to the sunny July day, but although Eric had only met Bob twice, he couldn't help but think the attire suited him. Bob looked like he would be most at home in a cabin in the woods. A cabin he'd built by hand, with a pump outside to draw water.

After purchasing his items, Eric headed for the Jeep to the *crack* and *pop* of roadside-stand fireworks being set off. Apparently the celebrating had begun.

Eunice fiddled with her oversized sunglasses as Eric parked the Jeep along the road at Max's place up in the hills. There were over a dozen other cars here. It had been a moment of weakness, agreeing to this. It wasn't at all like Eric had said: *"I won't know anyone either."* She would know *everyone*.

Hopefully her sunglasses were big enough to hide behind.

A headache began to form as she climbed out of the car with her survostobag. The sun was blinding. The air stifling. She wasn't going to last long out here, and she certainly wasn't going to be good company. She should have told Eric she would be nothing but dead weight if he brought her along.

She winced. Dead weight.

Eric pulled two cases of Coke from the back seat of the Jeep, and she followed as he carried them across the front yard toward the smell of burgers and the sound of laughter. Everyone appeared to be congregated in the back. Eric let himself through a side gate as if he owned the place. Had she ever had that much confidence?

Maybe. A long time ago.

A couple of people shouted Eric's name. He greeted them with a smile, but it was his surface smile. That was how she'd begun to think of it. He had an outgoing, charming demeanor, but the more time she spent around him, the more she suspected it was all for show. An act. The fitted T-shirts and flexed muscles might even be part of it. Maybe they were like her sunglasses. Something to hide behind.

Max took the Cokes from Eric's hands. "Glad you could make it. Thanks for the drinks. Hello, Eunice. Long time no see."

Max had been several years ahead of her in school, but they knew each other from around town. "Hi."

Her throat was dry. Her voice flat.

"Help yourselves to the food and make yourselves at home." Max gestured around the property. His backyard was about an acre in size, though the whole property was at least five. "There's all kinds of yard games going on. I don't even know what all Ceci's put out."

Max and Ceci had married right after their graduation. The way Eunice had heard it, the only way Ceci's dad would let her ride the circuit with Max was if they were hitched. Max hadn't hesitated.

"Thanks," Eric said.

Max walked off, playing the gracious host role with utter sincerity, and Eric glanced at her. "Can I get you something to drink?"

She'd emptied her ostomy pouch right before leaving the

house and didn't relish the thought of having to do it again while she was here. "No, thanks. I'm just going to find a shady spot to sit for now."

"You sure?"

The sun scorched her scalp through her thinning hair. Why had she washed and styled it instead of wearing a hat like Wanda was always nagging her about doing if she went out?

"I'm sure."

When Eric hesitated, she looked around until she saw an empty lawn chair under a tree and pointed. "I'll be right over there. I'll be fine."

"Okay, but flag me down if you need anything. Or text me, if you don't want to get up."

She muttered "I'm not an invalid" to herself as he walked away. But she kind of was.

Children ran shrieking around her legs, chasing a goat—was that Smellie Mellie?—and someone shouted "Boo-yah" after a good hit over the volleyball net. She was going to get knocked over if she didn't move. Her skin prickled as she made her way over to the chair, as if a pair of eyes were watching her. Or multiple pairs. Everyone here was probably watching and scrutinizing.

Her deteriorating health must be starting to affect her clarity of mind, as Dr. Mullins had warned. That was the only logical explanation for how she could've thought this party wouldn't be so bad.

The lawn chair was on uneven ground and shifted to one side when she sat down, almost dumping her out. Super. Whoever was watching her must have seen that. At least the shade felt good. Maybe she could take a nap behind her sunglasses until Eric was ready to leave and no one would notice. She gingerly laid her left hand in her lap. It had been over a week, but her burn still hadn't healed. Wanda had made quite a fuss about it.

"Is that you, Neecy?" A woman in a *God Bless America*

tank top and red shorts appeared at her elbow, with a camping chair slung over her shoulder. "How can you stand those long sleeves in this heat?"

Better than letting anyone see her scrawny, discolored arms, but she wasn't about to tell Marianne Taylor that. "I didn't want to get sunburned."

Marianne set up her chair next to Eunice and plopped into it. "Fat chance of that in the shade. I haven't seen you in ages— what have you been up to?"

They'd worked together once. Years ago. Marianne's dad owned the auto-parts store where Eunice worked after high school.

"Not much." After a moment's awkward pause, Eunice scratched at her arm and continued, "How about you?"

Marianne adjusted the red visor on her head that matched her shorts. "The kids are keeping me busy. Even in the summer, they've got sports. Sports, sports, sports. I swear, all I do is drive kids to practice. You know how it is."

No, she most certainly did not.

"Oh, there's Ginny." Marianne pointed with a squeal, then waved her arm. "Ginny, over here!"

The cold pit in Eunice's stomach grew colder. Ginny had been in her graduating class. As she walked over to join them, she grabbed another woman's arm and dragged her over, too. The other woman was younger than she and Ginny. Maybe late thirties.

"Hello, Marianne. Hello, Eunice," Ginny said. "You know Pickles, right?"

Marianne nodded that she did, in fact, know the other woman with the petite nose and long legs. Eunice almost choked on her own spit. Pickles?

"We just got here," Ginny continued. "Is this the hottest Fourth of July we've ever had or what?"

Pickles giggled behind her hand. "Almost as hot as Eric."

142

Eunice stiffened. Eric? *Her* Eric?

"You got that right." Ginny fanned herself as she and Pickles set themselves down on the grass. "How do we convince the men to play a shirtless game of volleyball?"

Marianne laughed. "If anyone could figure out a way to make it happen, it's you."

"I haven't seen a butt that tight since Max was still riding bulls." Ginny leaned closer to Pickles and smirked. "Imagine what his abs must look like."

Eunice scowled as the three women watched Eric work the crowd, making people smile but never talking with anyone too long. Sure, he was a fine specimen of a man, but she did *not* like the way the ladies were talking about him. He didn't exist for their enjoyment.

"I wonder what he's saying." Ginny sighed wistfully. "He has such a beautiful mouth."

Pickles eyed him like he was a three-tiered chocolate cake and she was about to break a thirty-day sugar fast. "Guys like that don't usually have much to say. But they sure look good not saying it."

"He has a good job, you know," Eunice sputtered, unable to keep quiet any longer. "He's a financial advisor, not just a—a pair of biceps. He helps people. He's . . . he's *nice*."

"Whoa." Ginny held up her hands. "Easy there, Eunice. We're just admiring him from afar, that's all. No need to get all defensive. You got a thing for him or something?"

Pickles snorted.

Eunice huffed, indignation warming her cheeks. "No. I just happen to know he has plenty to say. He's actually a really smart person." She lowered her voice and mumbled under her breath, "Smart enough to never let anyone call him Pickles."

Pickles raised one dainty eyebrow and glowered. "Says the woman named *Eunice*."

Ginny covered up a chuckle while Marianne waved an arm

in front of herself as if clearing the air. "Ladies, ladies. Can't we just enjoy the view in peace?"

"I can do better than that." Pickles unfolded her never-ending legs and stood. "It's about time I found a second husband."

As Eunice watched openmouthed, Pickles sashayed over to Eric's side with a smile. In less than a minute, she was touching his arm and laughing.

"She's never been able to keep her hands off a good-looking man," Marianne said.

Ginny gave Eunice a pointed look. "As long as she stays away from *my* man."

Eunice leaned back. Was Ginny still hung up on that? That was years ago, and he had never been Ginny's man, as much as Ginny had wished he was. It had always bothered Ginny that he chose Eunice.

And then she let him go.

"She's welcome to my man," Marianne chuckled. "But Steve hates pickles."

Eunice wanted to ask where this Pickles person had come from. What happened to her first husband? Why was she named after a sour cucumber? Instead, she watched with dread as Pickles worked her magic on poor, unsuspecting Eric. He really was easy on the eyes. But that didn't mean he was shallow enough for someone like Pickles, did it? Eunice remembered with unease the time she'd insinuated he was. She'd been so quick to judge.

Ginny's overly cheerful voice pulled Eunice's attention away from Eric. "So, Eunice, do you have a man?"

Really? Eunice tried to keep from grimacing. "No."

"Didn't you ever want to get married?"

It felt as if a sinkhole had opened up in the middle of Max's yard and swallowed Eunice. She wished it would. And she would fall and fall and fall . . .

Marianne *tsk*ed. "Don't be so nosy."

Ginny threw up her hands. "What? I was just wondering."

Eunice couldn't take it anymore. With great effort, she pushed herself up from her chair. "I need a drink."

Marianne pouted at Ginny. "Now look what you did."

"Can I have your chair?" Ginny asked.

Eunice walked away. Pickles was still doing everything she could to hold Eric's attention, although Eunice noted with some satisfaction that it didn't seem to be working. He was very charming with women, her included, but he never let it go too far. Was it because of Tiffani? Was he in love with her? Or was there another reason he kept clearly interested women at arm's length?

The kids and the goat ran past again as Eunice approached a giant Yeti cooler, and she caught a whiff of the creature. It really was Smellie Mellie. Max's uncle from up in Moose Creek had begged him to take the goat in when no fence he constructed proved capable of keeping Mellie from escaping night after night to raid the garbage can behind the bar and grill.

She opened the cooler lid and perused the offerings. Some of Eric's Cokes were there. Some Diet Sprites. A vast assortment of beer.

She shouldn't. She had vowed to herself she would not take a single sip of liquid while at this party. But she was so *thirsty*.

Glancing over her shoulder, she saw Ginny talking behind her hand to Marianne and pointing at Eunice with a sneer. Eunice's cheeks burned. She was nothing but a big joke to them, and she was nothing but a fool for letting Eric sweet-talk her into coming here. She reached in and grabbed a pretty pink bottle of Mike's Hard Raspberry Lemonade. It felt good in her injured hand.

She *really* shouldn't.

The sun burned the top of her head. The smell of overcooked

bratwurst turned her stomach. A high-pitched laugh coming from Pickles ricocheted around the yard like a well-manicured pinball.

Eunice twisted off the cap.

She was dying anyway, right?

twenty

Pickles had been hanging around him for almost an hour now, and Eric had to give her props for persistence. And for looks. She was undoubtedly attractive. But he was pretty sure she was a few years older than he was interested in, though she did everything she could to hide the fact. And that laugh. Yikes.

Words Eunice had said returned to his mind. *"I suppose you can afford to be picky and only pay attention to supermodels."* Was he picky for not wanting to get involved with an older woman? He didn't think so. And he didn't *only* pay attention to supermodels, but he did enjoy looking at them. What was so bad about that?

Pickles moved close enough to him that he could see the fine lines hiding underneath her makeup. Her voice was sultry, or trying to be anyway. "We should go check out the horseshoe pit. Horseshoes are my favorite."

She touched his hand and drew out the word *favorite*. The pit was on the far end of the property, away from everybody except three old ladies who appeared to be taking the game very seriously. Eric wasn't falling for that.

"I'm terrible at horseshoes. But don't let me stop you." He pulled out his dimples and gestured toward the pit. "I bet you're a ringer."

"Well, I . . . uh . . ."

"I wouldn't dream of keeping you from your *favorite* game. And they look like they need another player to make teams." He put his hands on her shoulders and spun her toward the pit. "You're going to save the day."

He gave a little nudge, and she took a reluctant step in that direction. Then he bolted as nonchalantly as he could before she changed her mind. A familiar gentleman with a handlebar mustache caught his eye as Eric moved to put a tree between himself and Pickles in case she turned back around. The man from Everything But the Kitchen Sink. What was his name again?

The man nodded toward Pickles and chuckled. "Well done."

Eric gave a sheepish grin. "I don't even know her. She just—"

"Latched on like a rainbow trout to a hopper?" The man's chuckle turned into a belly laugh. "Can't say as I blame her. Aren't many eligible bachelors around here. Other than me and Bob Crowley, of course, but I don't think we're her type."

It figured this guy would bring up Bob Crowley. Eric wouldn't even be able to wash his hair without thinking about Bob Crowley after today.

He stuck out his hand. "I believe we met at your store. I'm Eric Larson."

"I remember." The mustachioed man shook his hand. "Dusty Dillard, at your service. You ever find that console table you were looking for?"

Eric had stopped at Sofas and More after work not long ago. They didn't have any console tables in stock but had said they'd be happy to special-order one. All he had to do was say the word. So far, he hadn't said it.

He shook his head. "Not yet."

"We still got that bench I showed you. I know we could fix 'er up for you." Dusty looked him in the eye. "My boy Nate is real handy."

Winnie was still miffed about the Keurig and had taken to

adding little things to the table when he wasn't looking to make it even more crowded. Maybe Eric should take Dusty up on his offer. "I'll think about it."

Dusty nodded. An awkward silence followed. Eric noted the large knife hanging from the back of Dusty's belt and swallowed.

He cleared his throat. "Have you ever competed in the duck race?"

Dusty stared at him.

Eric panicked. "What's your favorite fair food?"

Dusty laughed, and his mustache pulled back on each side like curtains, revealing big teeth. "I like you, Eric, you know that? You ever try one of them fried cheesecakes on a stick?"

Eric almost melted with relief as Dusty went on to delineate the merits of every type of deep-fried food. He glanced around as Dusty talked and spotted Eunice leaning against a picnic table. What was she doing? Maybe he shouldn't have brought her. He thought it'd be good for her to get out of the house, but she looked miserable.

Dusty followed his gaze. "You know Eunice?"

Eric nodded. "We're neighbors."

"She and I go way back. She buys all my bowling balls."

He'd figured as much.

"She used to work with me at the store," Dusty continued, "Then her autoimmune problems made it too hard, and she started doing online sales for me from home. I hardly see her anymore, but I got a swirly purple ball waiting on her."

So she did have a job. He had a hard time picturing Eunice at a store helping customers, working alongside other people. And he doubted she would feel up to going in to get the ball anytime soon.

He wiped sweat from his face with his forearm. "Man, it's hot."

"I wouldn't mind a dip in the river right about now."

"You swim in the river?"

"Well, mostly I fish in it. But when the summer really starts cooking, sometimes you just gotta dive in. They got rivers where you come from?"

"Yes, but I spent all my time at the beach. Puget Sound. I don't think I've ever been to a river."

Dusty's bushy eyebrows rose. "Never been to a river? Did you fish in that Puget Sound at least?"

"No."

"That's a sad state of affairs, Eric." Dusty smoothed his mustache with one hand. "You ought to come fishing with me sometime. I know a good spot that's nice and remote."

Eric looked around. Max's nearest neighbor was a half mile away. Max probably saw more deer than humans up here most days. "More remote than this?"

Dusty laughed. "You come by the store and we'll set up a time. You won't regret it."

Fishing sounded kind of fun. How hard could it be? And Chase would love seeing pictures. "Okay."

Dusty nodded like it was a done deal. "I'm going to go rustle up some grub, but it was nice running into you."

As Dusty made a beeline for the food, Eric turned his attention back to Eunice. She was sitting cross-legged on the grass now, halfway under the table. What was she holding? Was that . . . ?

She seemed lost in her own world, but when his shadow fell across her lap, she looked up. "Oh. Hi."

He squatted beside her. "What are you doing down here? Are you okay?"

"My head is shpinning."

"How much have you had to drink?"

She held up a bottle. It was nearly empty, but one bottle wouldn't be enough to get her drunk, would it? On second thought, she weighed next to nothing. Even a small amount of alcohol, not to

150

mention the loads of sugar involved in a Mike's, could make her light-headed. And that wasn't even considering whatever illnesses she had. Eric hoped her cancer wasn't the liver variety.

"I think it's time for me to take you home." He took her by the hand and helped her to her feet, revealing another empty bottle of Mike's that had been tucked behind her. "You shouldn't be out in this heat."

Several people had started paying attention to them, and Eric's scalp itched furiously. He hadn't brought Eunice out here to make a spectacle of her.

"Don't you wanna eat first?" Eunice leaned against him to steady herself. "There's shamburgers. And Picklesss."

Eunice gave him a pointed look, and he had to bite back a laugh. "I'm not hungry right now. Are you?"

He didn't like that more people had begun watching them, though it might be a good idea to get some food into her.

She gripped his arm as her face fell and turned green. "No."

A woman in red shorts and a red visor appeared. "Goodness, Neecy, what's going on?"

Another woman, whom Eric had seen with Pickles earlier, elbowed her way through the gathering crowd. "Real nice, Eunice. You always have to go after the guy, don't you?"

"Nothing's going on." Eric put on the most charming smile he could muster. "I'm just giving Eunice a ride home."

The crowd parted to allow him to lead Eunice out front to the Jeep. He didn't turn around but felt plenty of eyes on his back.

She was quiet as he helped her into the passenger seat. Her face was flushed. He hurried around to the driver's side, started the engine, and cranked up the A/C. The digital temperature on the dash read ninety-four degrees. She leaned her head back against the seat and closed her eyes.

He flipped the Jeep around and headed back to Tukston. Two miles passed. Four. He thought she might've fallen asleep, but then she spoke.

"I'm shorry you had to leave the party."

"It's no big deal. I'll go back in a bit."

"I'm shorry I . . ."

Her voice faded, though whether from losing her train of thought or losing her courage, he couldn't tell. He'd never met anyone who felt she had so much to be sorry for. Then again, he'd never met anyone who knew they were about to die either.

His phone buzzed from the center console, and he glanced at it. Shoot, Chase was calling. Was he going out with pink-hair girl tonight? Eric knew Chase would want to talk about his plans, but now was not a good time. He'd have to catch up with him later.

He glanced at Eunice, and it struck him that he and his neighbor were fourteen years apart, just like him and Chase. He knew what the extra fourteen years he had on Chase had been like. The good and the bad. But what about the fourteen years Eunice had on him?

twenty-one

It had been nearly two weeks since the Fourth of July and Eunice still hadn't stopped kicking herself. How could she have been so stupid? She'd never been a drinker, and then suddenly when she was overstressed, overheated, and terminally ill, she thought she should give it a go? *Drink up, Eunice! What have you got to lose!*

Stupid woman. She never should've let those ladies get to her like that. Her only solace was that her mother had not been around to see it. She would've been disappointed.

She was always disappointed.

Three sharp raps on the door made Eunice groan. It was a Wanda day.

Super.

Unlike Bertie, Wanda always waited for Eunice to answer the door. Eunice took her time. With her hand on the doorknob, she took a deep breath. One other point of solace was that neither Wanda nor Bertie lived in Tukston so they would probably never hear about Eunice's Fourth of July adventure. Thank goodness the only home nurses available who were experienced in stoma care had been from out of town.

She opened the door.

Wanda gave a curt nod, her hands crossed over each other and holding the handle of a large tote bag. "Good morning, Eunice."

"Hi." Eunice stepped aside and gestured for the nurse to enter.

Eunice had made sure to have a piece of toast and half a banana earlier. Bertie's forced breakfasts were predictable, but there was no telling what Wanda might expect Eunice to eat. She probably had more honeydew in that bag.

Wanda shut the door behind her. "And how are we today?"

She always said "we." Maybe in her home nurse training class they taught people to do that so they would sound more sympathetic. Like they were in it together with their patients. But Eunice found it annoying.

She leaned against the kitchen counter. "Still dying."

Wanda set her tote on the table and gave Eunice a look. "You're extremely fortunate to still be living independently like you are. I wish you would make better use of your time."

Eunice scoffed inwardly. Just last Friday, Bertie had helped her finish boxing up every last item in her house she didn't have an immediate use for. Bertie had loaded the boxes into her truck with instructions to bring them to the battered women's shelter in Butte.

"You don't know how I spend my time."

Wanda's black hair was pulled back in a tight bun. She smoothed a hand over her head as if any of her hairs had a chance of escaping. "I'm not referring to how you *spend* your time."

Eunice scowled. Wanda's words reminded Eunice of her mother. She used to go on for hours about how Eunice spent her time. "At that filthy animal shelter." "On that rusty old scooter." "With that rascal of a man." Eunice's childhood had been pretty good as far as childhoods go—no tragedies, no divorce, no abuse—but for some reason it had been difficult for her mother to let her grow up. Maybe because Eunice was an only child. Maybe because her mother had no real life of her own and felt obligated to live Eunice's for her.

"I'm referring to your attitude," Wanda continued. "What you do with your heart and your mind, not what you do with your day."

Eunice's heart and mind were none of Wanda's business, thank you very much, and yet the words hit hard nonetheless. She was trying to make amends with people she'd wronged, wasn't she? She'd even made a new friend . . . sort of. What more did Wanda want from her?

"What difference does it make to you? You get paid regardless of my attitude."

Wanda blinked. "Have you eaten breakfast?"

"Yes."

"Have you changed your pouch since Bertie was here?"

That was a rhetorical question.

Wanda pulled a pair of medical gloves from her bag and headed down the hall with a jerk of her head. Eunice followed resignedly. She resented Wanda's presence in her home, but she couldn't deny Wanda was better at replacing her stoma equipment than she was. Even better than Bertie, and faster. It would feel good to get a fresh barrier. Her current one had started to itch.

Wanda pulled up Eunice's shirt and carefully tugged on the adhesive removal tab. "Have you showered since Bertie was here?"

"Not technically."

"Not technically?"

Eunice murmured in relief as Wanda washed her stoma and the skin around it. "I sprayed my feet with water from the hose. And I washed my face a couple times."

She'd also used a washcloth on her armpits and under her breasts. But it was a lot of work to take an actual shower these days. A lot of work to get in, and a lot of work to get out. And what if she slipped?

Wanda patted Eunice's stomach dry with a clean towel while

simultaneously inspecting the skin for any irritation. "I'm glad you washed your face, but you really should take better care of your privates."

Eunice scowled and gestured at her stomach. "They're not exactly private anymore."

It was maddening, having a pee hole in a place it felt like the whole world could see. Yes, urination was *supposed* to be a private matter. But it didn't feel like it was now. If she was facing years and years of living with JoJo, she'd make the effort to adjust. But she wasn't.

Wanda traced the stoma shape onto the new barrier. "See what I mean about your attitude?"

Another thing her mother always used to harp on. Her attitude. Until her mom inherited a large sum of money from Eunice's grandpa. Her parents had always lived frugally, but when that three hundred thousand dollars landed in their bank account, they started planning a "once-in-a-lifetime trip" to Europe. Her mom spent eighteen months organizing every detail. Sparing no expense. And, blessedly, giving Eunice some room to breathe.

That was why her mother never knew the real reason she broke it off with her blue-eyed man the second time. Never knew about her autoimmune diagnosis or the devastating news about her barrenness. Eunice had planned to wait and tell her parents when they returned so she wouldn't ruin their trip.

By the time her parents left for their dream vacation across the pond, Eunice's downward spiral had already begun, but she and her mom had a better relationship than they'd had in years.

Go figure.

Wanda cut out the new barrier and applied a thin layer of skin barrier powder. Eunice stood there holding her shirt up without a word. Why could she not stop thinking about her mom today?

As Wanda removed the backing from the new barrier and

applied it to Eunice's skin with an expert hand, Eunice felt tears begin to sting the back of her eyes. Because she missed her, that's why.

"Is your mom still around?" she asked.

She'd never asked Wanda any personal questions before, but Wanda's attention did not waver from her task. "No."

Eunice guessed Wanda was at least ten years older than she, but she wasn't sure. Her neat, trim appearance and beautiful olive skin made it hard to tell. "I'm sorry."

"I'm sorry for you, too." Wanda's voice softened. "I know you have no one left."

She knew? Then why was she so hard on her?

Wanda must have read the question on her face. "The last thing you need is my pity. You've already given yourself more than enough of that."

"What do you know about it?" A flicker of anger sparked in Eunice's chest. "You're not the one dying."

"Sure I am." Wanda finished the pouch-system change, peeled off her gloves, and threw them in the trash can. "We're all dying."

Eunice bit back a growl as she pulled her shirt back down. "You know what I mean."

"And you know what I mean. Everyone faces death every day. I could be called home before you. We just don't know."

"We" again. Eunice followed Wanda out of the bathroom and back to the kitchen. "You don't think you'd feel even a little bit sorry for yourself if you were in my shoes?"

Wanda reached into her tote and pulled out a honeydew. Eunice scrunched up her nose. She *knew* it.

"I'm sure I would."

Eunice sank onto her favorite stool. "Then how can you nag me about it?"

It came out like a whine. She sounded like a petulant child, but she was past caring about things like that.

"Because if I were in your shoes, as you put it, I would want someone to push me to make the most of my time. Not just to fill it with activity, but to put it to good use. Although at this point, I'd settle for a little activity. When was the last time you left the house? Talked to someone who wasn't your doctor or nurse?"

Eunice had been out in her garden every day. Eric's sprinkler had been a lifesaver. Ha. *Lifesaver.*

"I go outside."

Wanda slid a large knife from the knife block and began cutting the melon. "That's good. Fresh air."

"I talk to my plants."

Wanda's hand paused in midair as she glanced around the house. "What plants?"

"My garden. It's all in the back."

Wanda's face brightened as her hand came down and the knife sliced through the light green flesh. "I didn't realize you were a gardener. You never mentioned it."

Yeah, well, she'd never mentioned a lot of things. But her garden had been on her mind since last week when she'd asked Bertie about taking care of it if she . . . you know. Bertie had been happy to help her with the sorting and packing and donating of household items, but she'd held up her hands at talk of the garden. *"I've got the brownest thumb on earth, Eunice,"* she'd said. *"And not brown like dirt. Brown like dead plants."*

"I've got carrots, beans, tomatoes, zucchini, potatoes." She sat up a little straighter. "Cucumbers, too, but I've never been able to get one to reach maturity. I don't know why I keep trying."

"Where are they located?"

"The cucumbers? In one of the raised beds next to the potatoes."

"Well, there's your problem." Wanda slid the cut pieces of melon from the cutting board into a container. "Cucumbers and potatoes don't get along."

158

Eunice leaned her elbows on the counter. "You know about plants?"

Wanda set the knife in the sink. "We had quite a garden growing up. It was half an acre, not including the fruit trees. As a child, I hated it because it was so much work. But I grew to appreciate it eventually."

She'd never spoken of her childhood. The words felt like a peace offering.

"I don't have nearly that much." Eunice gestured toward the backyard. "Just a few raised beds. But . . ."

Her voice faded. It was still important to her, was what she wanted to say. But she didn't know if she was ready to talk like that around Wanda. Didn't know if she wanted to mention that in addition to the garden, she had a dozen perennials that would need to be cut back and tucked in for the winter. And if she didn't do it, who would?

"But you still want to take good care of it." Wanda nodded matter-of-factly. "I can help you, although your plants will need more attention than twice a month."

"I give them plenty of attention." Eunice's back straightened. "I have a new sprinkler. I check them every day. I'm not worried about that part. I'm worried about . . ."

Again the words wouldn't come. She thought back to what Wanda had said about putting her time to good use. Ensuring her modest harvest would not go to waste when the fall came seemed like a good use of time. But admitting that to Wanda? Saying it out loud?

Wanda gave her a knowing look. "Worried about what?"

"Nothing."

Emotions she couldn't name burned twisted paths along the underside of her rib cage.

She would figure it out. She would make her remaining days count.

twenty-two

noticed a refund on the account."

Eric could hear Uncle Jack chewing gum through the phone. He'd picked up the habit after Pete Carroll became coach of the Seahawks. Uncle Jack said it helped him concentrate.

"Yeah." Eric sat sweltering in the shade at Tukston Park on his lunch break. "For that cubicle wall I ordered."

"You changed your mind, huh?" Uncle Jack chewed and chewed. "Good."

Eric made a face. "No, I didn't. They said they couldn't deliver it for some reason. They issued a refund, but I'm going to update the address and order a new one."

"Oh."

Eric did not like the sound of that "oh."

"Are you sure that's necessary?" Uncle Jack asked.

Eric did not want to argue about this. It was too hot. "There is zero privacy in there. People are not going to share confidential information in a room where any random person might hear it."

"Our clients are not random people, my boy. Not to us, and not to one another."

Eric rolled his eyes. Surely his uncle knew what he meant. But everything was a lesson with Uncle Jack. Every moment a teachable moment.

"Yes, I know."

"And how about the table situation? Any resolution?" Eric winced, but before he could reply, Uncle Jack continued, "I heard you decided to go with Sofas and More."

Eric's neck tensed. "You heard—? How—?"

"I don't want to tell you how to run the office, but I think our Tukston clients would view a frugal furniture purchase as a sign we will be careful with their money and not frivolous. Don't you think?"

He didn't want to tell Eric how to run the office, huh? As if any of their clients would even notice if he got a new table. And he hadn't made a decision yet.

"The prices at Sofas and More are reasonable."

"So, it's true?"

"No, I—"

"Remember what I said. Take it slow."

Eric's voice rose. "It's a table."

"It's not about the table, my boy."

"Then what is this all about? You never scrutinized my charge account when I was in Seattle. Don't you trust me?"

Uncle Jack kept chewing in Eric's ear. Eric pulled the phone away in disgust. Ever since he moved here, Uncle Jack had been more involved in his life than usual. Why did his uncle care about the Tukston branch so much? Yes, this was technically Eric's first time acting as senior advisor, but Uncle Jack knew his work ethic. Knew about all the hours he'd put in over the past eight years. Had trained Eric himself and hinted that Eric would take over as owner someday so that Larson Financial would stay in the family.

It felt like too long before Uncle Jack responded, but maybe it was just the heat and the gum playing tricks on Eric's mind.

"I wouldn't have sent you there if I didn't trust you."

"Okay, but—"

"I heard something else."

Oh, brother. What now? Had Winnie called him about the Keurig?

"You never returned your father's message."

Eric's nostrils flared. He wasn't hot anymore. No, now his blood was ice cold. Was this the real reason Uncle Jack had called?

"You talked to him?"

"I understand you're still angry with him. I know he was wrong, but it's been twenty years."

Eric couldn't believe what he was hearing. "Yeah. Exactly. He's been missing from my life for *twenty years*."

"I don't think it's fair to say he's been missing. Not as involved as he should've been, yes. But he's tried."

"Calling on my birthday and sending my mom money once in a while does not count as trying."

"Twelve years old is a hard age to go through all that, I know." The compassion in Uncle Jack's voice did nothing to curb Eric's anger. "But you've both changed a lot since then. Maybe it's time to get to know each other again."

Betrayed. That was how he felt. Had Uncle Jack been reporting back to his dad about Eric all this time? Telling him how Eric was doing so his dad didn't have to put in the effort to find out for himself?

"I've got to get back to the office." Eric stood and brushed off his pants. "I've got a one-thirty appointment."

"Okay, but think about what I said."

Eric was not about to agree to that. "Talk to you later."

His loafers crunched the dry, brittle grass as he walked through the park back to Larson Financial. The city watered the lawn occasionally, but not enough for this heat. And the thunderstorms that often rumbled through in the late afternoons rarely brought rain with them, though he'd heard the lightning strikes brought risk of wildfires.

He woke up the screen on his phone and scrolled back to his

father's message: *Heard you're in Tukston.* His scalp itched, and he barely resisted the urge to scratch it. When the text message had first arrived, he'd been too surprised to wonder how his dad had heard about where he was. Now he knew.

Uncle Jack.

"Thanks for coming in, Jerry." Eric rose from his desk and shook the middle-aged man's hand to conclude their meeting. "Try to stay cool on your way home."

Eric's newest prospective client laughed. "It's hotter'n a 'lectric fence out there. They're forecasting more thunderstorms over the weekend, though. Maybe it'll rain."

From across the room, Max piped up. "That would be nice. Hasn't been this dry since '06. Remember that, Jerry?"

"Boy, do I ever."

Jerry ambled over to Max's desk so they could reminisce about the drought of '06, and Eric shuffled some papers into his briefcase. Jerry was his last appointment of the week, and his Friday night plans consisted of nothing but going for a run and sitting on his back deck with a chicken until dark. He wished Larson Financial had evening hours. And Saturday hours. He had a fishing trip planned with Dusty for next weekend, but this weekend was going to be brutal.

His desk phone rang, and he suppressed a sigh. Why couldn't Winnie just come talk to him?

He picked it up. "Yes?"

Winnie's double voice rang out loud and clear. "Bob Crowley wants to know if you'll see him before you leave."

Eric perked up. He'd been wondering when Bob might show up. It was the perfect excuse not to go home.

"Sure, send him in."

Eric was relieved when Max and Jerry walked out of the

office as Bob walked in. He didn't need anybody overhearing him navigate the sticky situation with Bob. Benson wasn't even around. He only worked half days most Fridays because of the community college classes he was taking.

Eric came around his desk and motioned for Bob to have a seat. "I'll be right with you."

He stuck his head through the glass doors and gave Winnie a meaningful look. "No need to wait around. I'll lock up."

Her crewneck sweatshirt was light gray today, with a sunflower on the front. She must not have any plans for the evening either since she usually lit out at exactly five-thirty.

She glared at him over her glasses. "People can't just show up whenever they want, you know. We have office hours. Appointments."

"Yes, I know." Eric gave her a small wave as she scooted to the edge of her chair and dropped off. "It's all right. Have a nice weekend."

He could hear her mutter "Appointments, people, *appointments*" as she pulled the strap of her large beige purse over her shoulder and headed for the door.

Eric returned to his desk. "How are you, Bob?"

"Fine, fine." He wore a stained white T-shirt under denim overalls. "Got no complaints. And you?"

Eric's smile froze for a second. Clients rarely asked how Eric was doing. They came to him to have their financial needs met, not inquire after his personal life. But Bob seemed sincere.

"I'm okay."

Bob dug a grimy finger in his ear. "You settling into country life?"

Eric realized he was jiggling his knee and forced his leg to be still. "It's . . . different."

Bob laughed. "That's what they all say at first. But you'll be all right. I been here my whole life, and I can always tell if someone's cut out fer it or not."

Eric thought back to what Chase had said about his step-dad, Steve. He thought Eric wouldn't last two weeks in Montana. Well, he'd already made it six weeks. But he had no plans to be "cut out fer it." A little over a month and he was out of here.

"Have you made any progress getting your will together, Bob?"

Bob reached into the front pocket of his overalls and pulled out a piece of lined notebook paper. "I wrote a few things down. Haven't signed it yet 'cause I figure I should wait till I got a notary, right? They got them at the bank, but I wanted you to see it first."

He unfolded the paper and held it out to Eric. Eric took it reluctantly. "This really should be typed."

"What difference does it make?"

"It'd be easier to read, for one." Eric squinted at the slanted writing. "And less likely to be smudged or tampered with. More likely to stand up in court."

Bob scratched the top of his head, causing Eric to think about the shampoo they'd both purchased from the grocery store. He'd had his doubts, but it really was invigorating.

"I don't got a computer."

The writing didn't even fill one page, despite Bob's statements and property descriptions being surprisingly detailed. It would only take Eric a couple of minutes to type it up. Yet he didn't want to run the risk of being sued or accused of coercion by some family member coming out of the woodwork should Bob pass away.

On the other hand, everything seemed straightforward. Bob's twenty acres of land would go to his neighbor. His 1982 Ford Bronco would go to some guy named Larry. His personal effects were to be liquidated, and the sum of his bank accounts—one checking and one savings—were to be split evenly between three nonprofit organizations.

Eric set the paper on his desk and pointed. "You don't have any family members listed here."

Bob shrugged. "My three older sisters passed on a while ago. I was the baby. Only my brother and me are left, and you know how I feel about him."

"Right, but—"

"I got a couple nieces and nephews spread out across the country, but we don't keep in touch."

Eric took a deep breath. Leaned back in his chair. "And you don't have any other accounts? Investments?"

Bob shook his head. Eric inwardly cringed. It should be a simple matter to type up Bob's words and send him off to the bank to have the will notarized. But this was anything but simple.

Bob set his hands on the grass-stained knees of his pants. "I just want to make sure my brother can't lay hold of it."

Eric knew he shouldn't even engage with Bob about this, but he was curious now.

"Is it family land or something? You think he might feel entitled to it?"

"No, not the land. He don't care about that."

"Oh." Eric rubbed his chin. "Do you have family heirlooms in your possession? Or antiques?"

Eric felt he could follow the trials of Bob's life in the lines on his face as Bob fixed him with a somber expression. "Nothing I own is valuable 'cept to me."

"What exactly are you worried about, then?"

"My accounts, son." The tone of Bob's voice changed. "What if he finds a way to get his grubby hands on 'em? He done it before."

Eric studied the handwritten will on his desk to avoid the desperate look in Bob's eyes. Bob's brother sounded like a real donkey's behind. It would be a shame for him to get ahold of Bob's money and keep it from reaching the charities, but was it really that big of a deal? By the time the money was split three ways . . .

So far, Eric hadn't met anyone in Tukston with a net worth that would make any of his Seattle clients even pause. But it seemed like a lot to them, he supposed. They'd worked for it. Scraped for it. Who was he to say how much value it had?

"I can see you're very concerned about this, but it seems unlikely your brother would go through all the trouble." Eric's finger landed on the line in the will that referred to Bob's accounts. "How much money are we talking about here?"

Bob shifted in his chair and looked nervously around the room. "I don't like discussing figures."

"You came to me, Bob. You asked for my help."

"I know, I know." His shoulders drooped. "Dusty said I could trust you."

"And you can."

"Well, here's the thing." Bob scooted to the edge of his chair and leaned closer to Eric's desk to examine the piece of paper. "It's a small town. Folks talk. My brother still knows people here, and I gave my word to a friend that I would—"

"How much, Bob?"

He looked up, and his eyes sparked with a flash of resolve. "Just over two million dollars."

twenty-three

*E*ric rummaged through his backpack the next Saturday morning, trying to focus on what he might need to go fishing with Dusty rather than on the bombshell Bob Crowley had dropped a week ago. It was still on his mind. Two million dollars? It could be the answer to Eric's ten-percent problem. But how did a guy like Bob Crowley end up with two million dollars?

He'd been too surprised to ask last Friday, and their conversation had ended rather abruptly when someone called Eric's desk phone because they'd seen Bob's Bronco parked out front and wondered if Bob would give them a jump. Even when everyone else had left the office, Eric still couldn't get any privacy. Bob had said "Duty calls" and promised to return a different day.

Eric checked the time. Dusty would be here to pick him up in ten minutes. He'd have to put his questions about Bob on the back burner for now.

Eric was eager to send Chase pictures of all the trout he was going to catch today. Maybe he'd send them to his stepdad, too. Prove he was most certainly *not* too soft for rural living.

A knock on the door interrupted his daydreaming. Was Dusty here already? He didn't see Dusty's truck in the driveway as he jogged to the front door with his backpack. Oh no, what if it wasn't Dusty? What if it was—

"Eunice." She jumped back, startled, when he swung open

the door. He leaned one hand against the doorframe. "What are you doing here? Is everything okay?"

She wrapped her arms around her stomach. "I think I'm ready to cross off another name."

No, no, no. Not today. "Sorry, I already have plans." Why couldn't she have brought this up earlier in the week? "How about we go out tomorrow afternoon?"

"I'd like to do it today. When will you be back?"

"I'm not sure. It could be a while."

Her face fell. He hated to disappoint her, but Dusty had said this was the only Saturday he would have free for a while. And Eric had only purchased a two-day fishing license.

"Look." He softened his voice. "If there's any daylight left when I get home, I'll take you. Okay?"

She blew out a breath. "It's just . . . I've been really struggling later in the day. The morning is when I have the most energy. I feel pretty good right *now*, but later . . ."

"How about tomorrow morning, then? First thing."

Eunice hung her head. "She'll be at church tomorrow morning."

Eric looked at the backpack he'd set on the floor. This could be his only chance to do some real Montana fishing with a real Montana fisherman. A once-in-a-lifetime opportunity.

"Eunice, I—"

A roaring truck engine cut him off. Dusty pulled his rusty black Ford into the driveway and parked next to the Jeep. When he hopped out, he had a purple bowling ball tucked under his arm and a grin on his face.

"Howdy," he called.

Eric waved. "Good morning."

"Lucky you're here, Eunice." Dusty climbed the front steps and held the ball out to her. "I brought you something."

Her face lit up. "Thank you. I've never seen one like that before. Look at the swirls!"

Eric had never seen her so excited. Dusty kept holding it out, but Eunice made no move to take it. She glanced at Eric nervously.

Eric reached for it himself. "I'll carry it over later. It's pretty heavy."

Eunice's smile wavered. "I don't have any money on me, but maybe I can—"

"No, no. It's a gift." Dusty waved her words away. "Soon as they brought it in, I knew it was for you."

She watched as Eric set it gently on the floor inside his door. "Thank you."

"My pleasure." Dusty turned his attention to Eric. "Well, champ, you almost ready?"

Eric cringed. His dad used to call him that.

He picked up his backpack. "I'm ready right now. Just need to lock up the house."

"Oh." Dusty gestured toward Eric's clothes. "You're going in that?"

Eric looked down. He was wearing a ratty lime-green T-shirt and lightweight black sweats over swim trunks and a tank top. Perfect for a day at the river, right? He'd take his outer layers off when he got to the water.

"Should I *not* wear this?"

Dusty chuckled. "You're going to scare the fish away in that shirt."

Did bright clothes scare fish away? Eric had no idea. "I can change."

"Nah, I'm just teasing." Dusty elbowed Eunice like they were in on a joke together. "You got a hat in that bag?"

Eric nodded and stepped out of the house, closing the door behind him.

"Sunscreen?"

Eric bristled. "Don't need it."

"Huh. Alright then." Dusty glanced over at Eunice as the

three of them made their way to the driveway. "You want to come fishing with us, Neecy?"

Eunice shifted on her feet. "No, I better not. I was just trying to get a ride to—"

"Your scooter out of commission? You need us to drop you off somewhere?"

"Then I won't have a ride home."

"Eric's riding with me." Dusty reached his truck and jerked a thumb at the Jeep. "Why don't you take the Jeep? I'm sure Eric won't mind, will you?"

He raised his eyebrows at Eric. Eric swallowed. Uh, yes. He did mind. If Eunice's scooter maneuvering was any indication, she was not what he would call a dependable driver.

"I don't know . . ."

"I'll be really careful." Eunice's face was suddenly eager. "I won't be going far."

She and Dusty stood there looking at him, and he tried not to scowl. This was not fair. He didn't want to seem like a jerk, but he'd paid a lot of money for that vehicle. What if she wrecked it? It wasn't unreasonable to worry she might end up in the ditch.

And was it normal for people to lend their cars to other people they barely knew around here?

It probably was. Darn overfriendly Montanans.

He wanted to say no with every fiber of his being, but the expectation on Dusty's face and the hopefulness on Eunice's were impossible to ignore.

"Fine." He pulled his key ring from the front pocket of his backpack. "As long as you're not going far, and you're very, very careful."

"Thank you." She took the keys when he held them out. "I will be."

"Good. Now that's settled"—Dusty smacked the hood of his truck—"let's get a move on, Eric. Those fish aren't going to catch themselves."

For the first half of the drive, Eric couldn't stop thinking about Eunice driving his Jeep into a ditch. And he'd just washed it two days ago. Exactly how far was "not far"?

For the second half of the drive, he forgot about his Jeep. As Dusty's truck ambled slowly along a winding road farther and farther from Tukston, Eric found himself mesmerized by the landscape. He'd seen hills and trees before. He'd seen rivers. But something about the way it all came together here, set against the immense blue sky, felt like he'd stepped out of a photograph and into real life.

Seattle was beautiful, too. Puget Sound and broken shells shining on the beach. A ferry glinting in the sun as it chugged back and forth between the islands. But this place had a beauty all its own.

Dusty pulled to a stop along a gravel road, rolled the windows down halfway, and turned off the truck. The murmur of the river was the only sound.

"Today's going to be a good day." Dusty hopped out and tossed his keys onto the front seat. "I can feel it."

The temperature was already high, yet the gentle breeze was enough to keep it from feeling unbearable. No other people or vehicles were in sight. Eric took a deep breath of fresh air. Dusty hadn't been kidding when he'd said this place was remote.

Eric met Dusty at the back of the truck to help unload the gear. "What is all this stuff?"

"You'll see." Dusty slipped on a dark gray vest overrun by pockets and handed Eric a small cooler. "You'll learn as we go."

When they started walking away with the keys still resting on the front seat, Eric hesitated. "You're going to leave your keys in there?"

He didn't like the idea of anyone stealing the truck and leav-

172

ing them stranded this far from civilization. Not that Tukston counted as civilization.

Dusty shrugged. "Don't need 'em in the water."

Eric looked back a couple of times as they navigated a barely-there path down an embankment. They were really going to leave the keys in the truck? It's not like Dusty didn't have enough pockets in his vest to keep them in.

Then again, Eric hadn't seen another single soul yet.

The next hour passed quickly. Dusty showed Eric the basics of reeling and casting and tying on flies as Eric tried not to think too much about how it should've been his dad teaching him how to fish. He peeled off his T-shirt and sweats and stuffed them in his bag as the temperature climbed, revealing Hawaiian-print swim trunks and a matching orange tank top that read *Sun's Out, Guns Out*.

They gradually worked their way up the river, and only once did another vehicle go by. It was an older model green truck that puttered past on the other side of the water, leaving a cloud of dust that lingered long after it was gone. Dusty caught two trout, which he called "browns," and Eric thought that was a suitable yet boring name for a brown fish. Eric snapped pictures of them with his phone before Dusty let them go.

"I'm only going to keep the best ones," Dusty said. "We've got all day."

As the second hour began, Eric felt the skin on his shoulders begin to burn, and he shook his head. The altitude again. He hadn't considered that he was almost a mile closer to the sun than he was used to.

The quiet expanded around him as Dusty's instructions dropped off—"Stop whipping the water!" and "Ten and two! Ten and two!"—and their conversation dwindled to nothing. The passing of time stalled. He fumbled a cast and pressed his lips together. Being in nature gave him too much time to think.

About Eunice and his Jeep and her terminal illness. About Bob and his will and two million dollars. About Tiffani and his dad. The rushing water whispered urgently to him but couldn't drown out the noise in his head.

Eric remembered that Bob had mentioned Dusty in his office. If the two men were friends, Dusty might know something about Bob's mystery fortune.

"How long have you known Bob Crowley?" he called.

Dusty's face didn't change. "Just about forever, I guess."

"What did he do before he retired?"

"You think he's retired?"

Eric hesitated. Did Dusty know how much money Bob had? Did anyone? "Okay, then what does he do now?"

Dusty gave him a lazy smile. "It's a secret."

Eric huffed. That only made him want to know more, but he tried to make a joke out of it. "He's got you keeping secrets for him, huh?"

Dusty was quiet for a minute. "Me and Bob, we share all kinds of secrets."

Eric's eyes narrowed. Secrets? What kinds of secrets was Dusty talking about? Maybe he *did* know what the deal was with Bob's money. But one look at the man's face told him he wasn't going to get any more information out of Dusty.

The quiet pressed in on Eric again. Big, black horseflies found him wherever he went, buzzing around his face and trying to bite his arms before he could swat them away. Sweat stung his eyes. He was glad he'd worn his swim trunks so he could wade into the water once in a while and cool off, even though the weeds along the bank scratched up his legs.

He was not as glad about his choice of footwear. The flimsy sandals he'd picked up at the IGA weren't cutting it. He'd been expecting a sandy beach, but it was rocks, rocks, and more rocks. They were slippery and dug into his feet. The few patches of sand he did come across smelled like the overflow from a septic tank mixed with wet dog. This was not the idyllic relaxing day he'd envisioned.

"You doing okay down there?" Dusty called from twenty yards upriver.

Eric had set his pole down and was windmilling both arms. "Just trying to scare off the flies."

"You must smell good." Dusty grinned. "Or they want a piece of those big buff arms."

When Eric had seen Dusty's long sleeves, he'd inwardly scoffed. But what he wouldn't give for a lightweight long-sleeved shirt right about now.

"How deep does it get?" he asked. "Maybe I'll cross over and see if the other side's any better."

"Oh, I don't know, up to your waist maybe." Dusty adjusted his ball cap. "Can't always tell. And the current can really get moving out there."

"Haven't you fished here before?"

"Well, sure, but the river changes all the time. She's alive, and she ain't tame."

Eric studied the river. She seemed pretty tame to him. Just nice, cool water flowing along and glittering in the sun. No tide. No waves. "I'm going to cross."

Dusty executed a perfect cast without looking at him, and the fly landed gently on the water with hardly a sound. "All right."

Eric considered his backpack for a second before deciding to leave it where it was near Dusty's cooler. But he pulled his phone from the front pouch and tucked it inside the chest pocket of his tank top. If he ever did catch anything, he'd need pictures as proof or no one would ever believe it.

He held his pole high and waded into the water.

"Watch out for moose," Dusty called.

The water rushing against Eric's legs grew louder the deeper he went. Did he say *moose*? "What?"

Dusty waved an arm. "You'll be fine. Just back away slowly."

Eric hesitated. Maybe he should stay close to Dusty. He was the expert around here. But Dusty was just messing with him about moose, right? And there was less vegetation on the other side, so he had high hopes there would be fewer flies.

He reached the middle of the river, where the water was up to his waist just as Dusty had predicted. The cold chilled his legs. The water moved deceptively fast, pressing against him with unyielding persistence. Maybe he should've listened to Dusty.

He kept going. He was in the best shape of his life. He had nothing to fear from a river this size, right? His foot struck a smooth rock and he slipped. He raised the pole high over his head as he floundered for a moment to regain his balance. His phone lurched, but he caught it before it could disappear in the watery depths.

Yikes. That was close. It took some effort to right himself, but no harm done. He looked sheepishly back at Dusty, who seemed not to have noticed.

When he climbed out of the river on the other side, Eric wrung out the bottom of his tank top and looked around. The water had created an embankment on this side as well, but unlike the side where he'd left his bag, this side left little room to stand along the edge. No matter. If there were fewer horseflies, it would be worth it.

He held the rod the way Dusty had shown him and repeated Dusty's casting instructions to himself as he swung the top of the pole back and tried to hold his wrist steady. *"No flicking,"* Dusty had said. Eric's first cast hit the water with a splash, and he flinched. Not exactly the "delicate presentation" Dusty had recommended. His second cast landed a foot in front of him, and he kicked at it. He must look like an idiot. When he glanced at Dusty, he still appeared to be paying him no mind.

Then why did Eric get the feeling Dusty was scrutinizing his every move?

He took a deep breath and squared his shoulders. He could

do this. He gripped the rod and tried again. The caddis fly sailed up and back, light as a feather, and Eric grinned as he wrenched the rod forward, sure this was it. The perfect cast, finally. But the fly did not return.

His rod stopped short, leaving him frozen mid-cast. He tugged but there was no give. His heart sank as he lowered the rod to waist level and turned his head to look behind him.

The embankment was about five feet high and steep. The line stretched from the tip of his pole into the sparse brush and disappeared, the fly up there somewhere, hooked. Probably on a moose. Oh, great.

Eric had read an article once about how discarded fishing line endangered wildlife. He tugged again.

Nothing.

"You need a hand?" Dusty called.

Eric couldn't look at him. "I'm fine."

Dusty's voice moved closer. "Don't break my tippet."

As Eric pondered what to do—should he climb up there?—the horseflies found him. He could've sworn they were the same ones. They crossed the river just to get to him. The first thing he was going to do when he got home was search online for some high-quality bug repellant.

One of the thumb-sized black demons bit him right in the middle of his back, and he swung an arm around to swat at it, somehow tangling himself in the fishing line. He struggled halfheartedly, remembering Dusty's warning. *"Don't break my tippet."*

"Mighty fine mess you've got yourself in, champ." Dusty had crossed the river and appeared on the bank beside him without Eric noticing.

Eric's cheeks warmed. "I've got it."

"I'm sure you do." Dusty appeared to be fighting a smirk. "But I'm pretty attached to that pole so I'm going to help you before something happens to it."

Eric's shoulders drooped. "Sorry."

Dusty laughed. "Don't go thinking you're the first fisherman to ever get their fly caught in the bushes. It happens to the best of us. Now, I want you to stay right there."

"But—"

"Don't move." Dusty climbed the embankment. "Give it a little tug when I tell you."

As Dusty picked through the brush, Eric inched closer to the embankment. "Let me help."

Dusty turned toward him as he moved away. "Stay where you are." He gave a big grin. "I think you've helped enough."

He took another step backward, still grinning at Eric, then froze. Eric could just barely hear a hollow rasping sound over the river talking. Dusty's smile disappeared.

"What?" Eric froze. "What is that?"

It almost sounded like a rattle. He made a move toward Dusty, but Dusty held up his hands. "No, don't—"

A flash of movement made Eric jump. Dusty's eyes bulged. He cried out. And a sand-colored, four-foot-long snake with dark brown patches slithered away through the dirt.

twenty-four

Eunice sat on Eric's front step with slumped shoulders, watching Cinderella chase grasshoppers through the yard. It had already been a couple of hours since he and Dusty left. She had somehow managed to avoid actually getting in the Jeep for this long—she'd gone back home to change, she'd eaten a snack, she'd checked on her garden—but she couldn't put it off any longer. It was true what she'd told Eric. By afternoon she'd be too spent to trust herself to go anywhere, and it was already eleven o'clock.

She thought she'd been prepared for this. After Wanda's twisted version of a pep talk last week, she'd told herself it was time to face another old friend. But she'd expected Eric to be with her. Something about having another person along to take her home if something went wrong gave her a little extra courage.

Why had she jumped at the chance to borrow his Jeep and drive herself? She leaned her elbows on her knees and groaned. Because she thought she was stronger than she was.

She could accept defeat, return Eric's keys when he got home, and ask him if he was available next weekend instead. But what if he was busy again? What if something came up? What if she . . . didn't make it that long?

No. She could do this. She didn't need Eric. And he didn't

need to know about *all* the mistakes she'd made. Or that her driver's license had expired.

"Oh, Lo-ord." Her words blended with the hot air and disappeared. "You wanted Wanda to light a fire under my butt so I wouldn't keep waiting, right? Which means you must be okay with the driver's license thing, *right*?"

With a groan, she rose to her feet. No more excuses. She would be careful.

JoJo hung silently and solemnly from her lower abdomen as Eunice trudged to the Jeep and climbed in, reminding Eunice that she'd need to get back home before the pouch required emptying. Her destination was way out there, near the river, but if the conversation was short—and she suspected it would be—she could be back in an hour and a half.

The steering wheel felt strange under her hands. The pedals strange beneath her feet. Even though it had only been a couple of months since she'd last driven a car, it took a minute for her body to remember what to do. She backed out of the driveway slowly, senses on high alert.

"Okay, God." She reached up and pulled down the sun visor. "Let's do this."

Eric's mind raced. No, *raced* wasn't a strong enough word. It dashed, sprinted, galloped through the possibilities. Should he call 911? No, his phone had no service. Could he carry Dusty back over to the truck? No, he was too big, and the water too swift. Should he leave Dusty, cross over himself, and drive to town to get help? No, he didn't want to leave him alone.

"You look like you've seen a ghost. I'm the one that's bit."

Dusty's pained voice brought Eric back to the cold reality of their situation. He didn't have time for running scenarios. It was time for action. "We need to get you some help."

Dusty was sitting on the ground, sweating. He'd pulled up his pant leg to examine the snakebite, revealing two clear puncture marks that oozed blood on his calf.

He jerked his thumb over his shoulder. "I know that green truck over there. Belongs to an old buddy of mine. It'll have keys in it."

Eric looked where Dusty pointed and saw the truck that had gone by a while ago parked along a fence a half mile away. It took a second for Dusty's words to sink in, but when they did, Eric looked down at his feet. At least he hadn't worn flip-flops.

He handed Dusty his phone for safekeeping, then gave him a look he hoped was confident and reassuring. "I'll be right back."

And then he ran. His weeks of training served him well as he covered the distance in no time, trying to focus on the task at hand rather than the two holes in Dusty's leg to keep himself from panicking. He'd never seen a rattlesnake before.

Was Dusty going to lose his leg? Would he die?

Eric ran faster.

When he reached the truck, he flung open the driver's door. Sure enough, a set of keys dangled from the ignition. Good thing people around here trusted others not to steal their vehicles, because Eric needed to steal this truck.

He hopped in and cranked it up, creating a turbulent brown cloud as he whipped a U-turn and hit the gas. He sped toward the spot where he'd left Dusty, cringing at the gas gauge. The needle was on E. How far to the hospital? Did Tukston even have a hospital? His wallet was in his backpack on the other side of the river. How would he buy more gas?

He slammed the truck into park and hurried over to Dusty, who was looking pale and uncomfortable. "How are you doing?"

"Help me up."

Eric helped Dusty to his feet and into the passenger seat. "There's hardly any gas. How far to the hospital?"

"I don't know if the clinic will have the antivenin. Might have to go to Butte."

Eric ran around to the driver's side. "How far is that?"

Dusty winced as the truck jerked into drive. "About an hour."

An hour? No, there was no time for that. Eric pressed harder on the gas, then realized he had no idea where to go.

"Right up there on the left, see?" Dusty pointed. "Before the bridge—that's where Winnie lives."

"Winnie? As in my receptionist?"

"She'll have some gas on hand."

Winnie lived all the way out here by herself? How could that be safe? And how did she still manage to beat him to the office every morning?

Eric steered the truck down her driveway toward the house and sent gravel flying as he hit the brakes and parked. Winnie's car was parked out front, and an unfriendly-looking black mutt barked as Eric stepped out.

Had he mentioned he hated dogs?

"Easy, boy." He held out a hand. "Where's Winnie?"

The dog bared its teeth and growled. Eric swallowed. It wouldn't help Dusty if he got bit, too. He took a step back.

"What in blazes is going on?" Winnie appeared from around the side of the garage, wearing the white sweatshirt with the cats. "Sparky, sit."

The dog stopped growling, but otherwise didn't budge. Neither did Eric.

"Spark Plug," Winnie shouted. "Sit. Now."

The dog sat, and Winnie walked over, staring through the truck window at Dusty. "What are you two doing here? Where's Ranger?"

"We need gas."

"That's Ranger's truck."

Eric kept one eye on the dog. "We borrowed it. Dusty got bit by a rattlesnake."

Winnie gasped. "Is it bad?"

"Well, it's not good."

She opened the passenger door and looked at Dusty's leg with a scowl. She pointed to the center console. "Hand me that pen."

Dusty gave her the pen with a shaky hand, and she drew a circle on his calf around the bite, then dropped the pen in his lap. "We've got to get to Butte."

Eric hesitated. "Won't that take too long?"

She glared at him. "Everyone in my car. Now."

Eric was in no position to argue. He tried to help Dusty out of the truck, but Dusty waved him off.

"I got it." Dusty limped to the back seat of Winnie's car and crawled in. "I'm fine."

The lines on his face told Eric he was most definitely not fine, but Eric slid into the passenger seat of the Buick LeSabre as Winnie fired it up. Apparently she kept her keys in the ignition, too.

More gravel flew as Winnie charged down the driveway and over the bridge.

"Don't worry." Winnie pushed her glasses up her nose and gripped the wheel with resolve. "I'll get you there before you can say 'The cows are out.'"

twenty-five

Freezing air from the Jeep's A/C blew on Eunice as she slowly drove out of town, but she didn't dare try to turn it off. Everything was so fancy and high-tech. For all she knew, the whole thing might shut down or sprout wings and fly if she hit the wrong button. She'd already turned the windshield wipers on by accident when she tried to signal a turn.

The sun glared, and she wished she had thought to wear her sunglasses. She squinted and shivered, puttering along at ten miles under the speed limit. What kind of music was this? Didn't Eric have any respect for his eardrums? If the person on her list wasn't home after all this, she might have to cry.

Tukston disappeared in the rearview and Eunice relaxed a little. It was unlikely she'd see many other vehicles out here, if any. She felt a little guilty about telling Eric she wasn't going "far," but this was the kind of thing that happened when people were desperate. They lied and broke the law.

When the river came into view, her heart squeezed and twisted like a dishrag God was wringing out. This had been Charlie's favorite place.

She wanted to stop and stare at it and memorize every stone and every glint of light. To soak it in and remember her care-free, joyful terrier chasing the ripples, so she could see it even when she closed her eyes and never forget there was a place on earth like this.

What if she never saw it again? Were there rivers in heaven? Were there dogs?

"God." Something choked her words, and she wasn't sure if it was grief or fear or something else. "I don't want to die."

Saying it out loud didn't bring any relief. Only an empty feeling in her chest that even the sight of the river couldn't fill.

She blinked back tears and shifted in her seat. The Jeep had slowed to a crawl, but she needed to get back on track if she was going to accomplish anything today. A deep breath in and out and she forced her attention back on the road.

A flash in the rearview mirror caught her eye, and she gulped. Blue lights behind her. Blue-and-red lights, to be precise.

Super.

She pulled the Jeep to the side of the road with a grumble and began brainstorming what kind of speech she could give the officer to convince him not to write her a ticket.

I haven't had a chance to renew my license because my neighbor broke my scooter, sir.

I wouldn't be driving without a license if it wasn't an emergency, sir.

I'm dying, sir.

She put the Jeep in park and sighed. What difference did one ticket make anyway? She'd just pay it and get on with her life.

On with her life. Right.

The police car approached, and Eunice's only prayer was that the whole thing wouldn't take too long. She wondered if someone had seen her driving through town and reported her. Probably Brenda Wallace. But then the car swung over to the far side of the road and sped by in a blur of black and white and dust.

She gaped. Oh. Whatever that officer was worried about, it wasn't her.

Phew. Her heart rate slowly returned to normal as she pulled back onto the road. That was close. She continued on a few more miles, finally summoning the courage to at least turn down the volume on the radio, until she reached a one-lane bridge. Her heart squeezed again. How many times had she crossed this bridge with her mother? Why had it taken her so long to return?

As she crept over it, her blood began to hiss in her ears like static. There was the police car again. Two of them actually. Parked in front of the house.

Her heart plummeted into a cold, dark cavern and struck the bottom with a note of finality. Something had happened to her mother's oldest, dearest friend and mentor.

She was too late.

It was probably improper to try and involve herself, but Eunice pulled into the gravel driveway and parked off to the side. She had to find out what was going on. One of the officers was waiting for her before she even unbuckled.

She opened the door. "What's going on? What happened to Winnie?"

"Was she expecting you?" He held a notebook in his hand, poised to write down her answer. "When was the last time you spoke to her?"

Eunice rubbed her temple. A headache was forming. The air outside was shockingly oppressive after the brisk atmosphere inside the Jeep.

"I—uh, no. She wasn't. I haven't."

"Do you have any idea as to her whereabouts?"

"No." Eunice hung her head. Her mother would be ashamed of her for never checking in on Winnie. Never making an effort. "No. I just came here to tell her . . ."

"We're doing everything we can, but I'm afraid you might not get the chance, ma'am." The officer looked back at the house, the burden of responsibility clearly pressing down on him. "She's been kidnapped."

186

He and Winnie made such a sorry pair as they sat in the waiting room that Eric almost had to laugh. With his wallet baking in the sun somewhere along the Madison River, and Winnie's purse at home on her kitchen table, left behind in her rush to help Dusty, they'd been forced to stare longingly at the vending machines for the past forty-five minutes.

Well, maybe only the last thirty minutes. It took the first fifteen for Eric's adrenaline and body temperature to normalize enough to realize how hungry and thirsty he was, although it was hard to think about anything besides Dusty's swollen and discolored leg. Was he going to be okay?

Winnie sat on the edge of her seat so her feet would reach the floor. "I left a perfectly good lunch warming in the toaster oven."

Eric thought of Eunice's recent experience with a toaster oven and huffed. "Is there anyone you can call about that?"

"I would call Ranger, but he can't exactly drive over to my house and check, can he?" She peered at him over her glasses. "Seeing as how you stole his truck."

"We *borrowed* it."

"And I left my phone on the table with my purse."

"You can use my phone."

She harrumphed. "You think I remember his phone number off the top of my head? I just press the *R* and his name comes up and it calls him."

Eric folded his arms across his chest. "Are there any phone numbers you do remember?"

She shook her head. "If my house burns down, it will be your fault."

He sat up straighter. "You can't blame me for that. Dusty's the one who stepped on a rattlesnake."

She gave him a pointed look. "I wonder why he wasn't looking where he was going."

Eric stared at the floor. Okay, maybe the whole thing *was* his fault. He eyed the vending machine again. What he wouldn't give for that bag of Fritos and a Pepsi. Some wild creature was probably raiding his backpack for protein bars right this minute.

He stuck his hands in the pockets of his swim trunks to find his phone but came up empty. Had he left it in the car? He was about to push out of the chair and go check when he remembered. He'd given it to Dusty at the river before he ran after Ranger's truck. Dusty must still have it on him.

"Why doesn't the clinic in Tukston carry antivenin if there are rattlesnakes around?" he asked.

Winnie shrugged. "They might have some. But I didn't want to risk wasting time at the clinic, only to find out their only vial expired two years ago. And I knew if there were any complications, they'd send us here anyway."

Eric wasn't quite sure that justified the hour drive, with poor Dusty miserable in the back seat the whole way, but he kept that to himself. "Why did you draw a circle on his leg?"

"To track the spread of the infection."

"Oh." He leaned back and set his right ankle on his left knee. "Aren't you supposed to suck out the poison or something?"

She lifted her glasses and rubbed the bridge of her nose. "Why on earth would you do that?"

Well, he'd seen it in the movies.

A good-looking nurse in blue scrubs appeared in the doorway. She gave his tank top and biceps a once-over before meeting his eyes and smiling. "Dusty Dillard asked me to find Eric and Winnie. Is that you two?"

Eric jumped up from his chair. "Yes. How is he? Is he okay?"

Winnie slid off her chair as well, and they followed the nurse as she began to walk down the hall. "He's not a hundred percent out of the woods yet, but his prognosis is good."

The nurse's auburn hair swung back and forth in a ponytail. Eric loved the color of it, but he wasn't a fan of her clunky black earrings. They didn't suit her at all. The scrubs did nothing to hide her attractive figure, though, which Eric secretly admired from behind. Or not so secretly, because Winnie smacked him on the arm and gave him a scolding look.

They reached Dusty's room, and the nurse held open the door. "Here we are."

He glanced at her name badge and aimed his dimples at her. "Thank you, Jennifer."

"Oh, brother." Winnie pushed past him with a huff. "We're here to see Dusty, not fill our dance cards."

Eric found the pink blush that appeared on Jennifer's cheeks very appealing. She must be around twenty-eight if he had to guess, and her left hand was indisputably bare. He should ask her if she had any plans for dinner. Always his favorite line. But who knew if he'd still be in Butte by dinnertime?

Jennifer left the room, and Winnie scurried to Dusty's bed-side. "You look fine."

Dusty chuckled. "You disappointed?"

"I wanted the trip to be worth it at least. What am I supposed to tell people? That it wasn't serious but I drove you all the way out here so you could be pampered by a cute young nurse?"

Eric choked on a chuckle.

"The doctor said you got about four hours after a bite to take the antivenin." Dusty shook his head. "If I'da known that, I would've told you to slow down on the curves."

"You won't lose a limb?" Winnie's voice was more serious now.

"Naw." Dusty leaned his head back. "Be right as rain by tomorrow."

"I wouldn't quite say that." A doctor appeared at the door. "You might experience some pain for a couple days, and you'll need to be on the lookout for side effects."

Dusty nodded. "Okay, but I'm good to go, right?"

"Not so fast." The doctor lifted the sheet covering Dusty's legs to take a peek at the wound site. "I'm not ready to remove your IV yet. Let's give it a couple more hours and see where we are."

"A couple more hours?" Dusty threw his hands up and slumped back. "Best fishing day of the year and I'm stuck in here with you."

The doctor smiled. "Were they biting?"

"Were they ever!"

The doctor patted Dusty's uninjured leg with a smile and headed for the door. He called over his shoulder, "Just try to relax."

As the door closed behind him, Dusty huffed. "Relax? I left my favorite pole at the river."

"And it'll be right there when you get back." Winnie pulled an overstuffed gray chair closer to the bed and sat down. "Have you had anything to eat?"

"You don't have to stay. I'm fine."

Winnie clucked her tongue. "We're not going anywhere."

Eric shifted on his feet, feeling like the outsider he was. "I'm glad you're okay. You had me worried."

Dusty gave him a friendly look. "I've never seen anyone run that fast in sandals. I could've been in real trouble if you hadn't been there. You been able to let Ranger know about his truck yet?"

Eric looked at Winnie. Winnie looked at the ceiling. "Well . . ."

Eric squeezed the back of his neck. "I don't suppose you have his number?"

"My phone's still at the river."

"What about mine? Do you have it?"

Dusty scratched at his mustache and gestured toward the bedside table. "It must be in that bag over there."

Eric retrieved the bag, which held Dusty's watch, belt, and shoes, along with the phone. His brow furrowed as he pulled the phone out and checked the screen. Three new voicemails and one text message that said *Call me please*. All from Eunice.

Uh-oh. He knew better than to loan her his vehicle. What kind of trouble had she gotten herself into?

Winnie must've seen the look on his face. "What's the matter?"

"I'm not sure." He walked over to the window for a little privacy. "I need to make a phone call."

Eunice answered right away. "Eric, I need your help."

Yep. It was just as he'd feared. She was in a ditch somewhere, and he was probably going to have to call a tow truck and—

"Have you and Dusty seen anything suspicious along the river today?"

Suspicious? What was she talking about? "Uh . . ."

"You need to be on the lookout. There's a manhunt going on all up and down the Madison."

"A manhunt?"

Winnie was out of her chair and by his side in an instant. "A manhunt? Who are you talking to?"

So much for privacy. He put his finger to his lips to signal Winnie to be quiet. "Are you okay?"

"I'm fine." Eunice was talking loudly as if she was outside. "But there's been an abduction."

Winnie was leaning close and straining to hear. Deaf as she was, she must have heard the word *abduction* because she gasped. Eric's eyebrows rose. A manhunt *and* an abduction?

"Wow." He never expected this kind of thing to happen in a place like Tukston. Then again, there were probably a lot of places to hide a body up in those hills.

Eunice sounded grave. "I'm surprised you haven't seen all the police. Everyone's out looking for her."

"Looking for who?" Winnie whispered loudly. "Ask who was taken."

Eric gave up on privacy and adjusted the phone so Winnie could listen in with him. "Who was taken?"

"An elderly woman." Eunice's voice sounded strained, and

she sniffed as if she'd been crying. "About five-foot-one. Curly white hair and glasses."

Eric narrowed his eyes at Winnie. She touched her hair and frowned.

"The suspect is a male in his twenties. Dark brown hair and wearing an orange tank top and flowery shorts."

Eric's chest tightened. He and Winnie both looked down at his clothes, then back up at each other. Their eyes met and widened.

"Guess we won't be staying after all, Dusty." Winnie stuck a finger in Eric's face. "I've got to turn this kid in to the police."

twenty-six

y the time Winnie drove her car back over the one-lane bridge and into her driveway, Eric had sorted out the whole story over the phone with Eunice. Apparently, Ranger had seen Eric get into his truck and reported it stolen because "That guy in them flower shorts definitely looked suspicious." When the police had found the nearly-out-of-gas truck at Winnie's house, but Winnie and her car missing, they could only conclude that the truck thief had ditched the truck and taken them both.

The left-behind purse and phone, a distressed Spark Plug, and the burned lunch in the oven had only added to their certainty that something sinister had befallen dear old Winnie. Not to mention Eunice had been under the impression Winnie had retired from Larson Financial, so she never considered there being a connection between them.

Eunice told Eric she explained everything to the sheriff, yet his stomach was still in knots as he slowly got out of Winnie's Buick, careful not to make any sudden moves as Spark Plug watched his every step.

His Jeep was still here, but where was Eunice? This day was refusing to get any better. And there was the burly giant of a sheriff, waiting.

"Pete?" Winnie slammed her door shut and shouted, "What are you still doing here?"

"I sent everyone else home, but I couldn't leave until I saw you were safe with my own eyes." Pete made a broad gesture with one arm. "You caused quite a stir around here."

She snorted. "It's hardly my fault you all jumped to conclusions."

"I called the hospital in Butte to confirm your story and talked with Dusty. Sounds like he's going to be okay."

"Thanks to this guy." Winnie jerked her thumb at Eric. "Pete, meet your thieving kidnapper. This is Eric Larson."

Pete held out a beefy hand for Eric to shake. "Looks like you got yourself quite a sunburn today."

Eric's stomach growled. "Yes, sir."

"You catch anything before all this happened?"

He'd caught a few scraggly twigs and some decent-sized bushes. "No, sir."

"All right, well, as long as you're okay"—he turned back to Winnie—"I better head on out. Someone reported gunshots out past Dick Samson's place just before you got here."

"You can see I'm fine." She shooed him with her hands. "But you know they're only shooting gophers over there."

"I know." Pete grinned. "But I still gotta check it out."

He folded his oversized frame into an old patrol car and gave a wave out the open window. Eric let out a long breath as he watched him pull out of the drive. What were the chances Uncle Jack would never hear about this?

Winnie clapped her hands together once and headed for the house. "Come on then. Let's get you some aloe for those shoulders and some food for that stomach."

Spark Plug inserted himself between Eric and Winnie as Eric followed her warily to the front door. Eunice must be in there. Winnie had been strangely quiet when he'd explained Eunice was the one who had gone to her house and discovered all the confusion and chaos. Was Winnie the person Eunice needed to reconcile with, or had his neighbor ended up here for some other reason? She had assured him she wasn't going far in his Jeep. So much for that.

That was one thing they hadn't covered in all their back and forth over the phone.

The inside of the house smelled like burnt toast, and three large box fans positioned around the main room kept the air circulating. It was a small house but organized neatly. Eunice was sitting on a short plaid couch, her face pale and drawn. For the first time, Eric realized how thin she really was. How fragile.

"My heavens, Eunice." Winnie froze when she saw her, and an unreadable expression clouded her face. "You look like death warmed over."

Eunice wanted to be at home, sitting on her stool with her cheek against the cool countertop. Alone. She wanted to empty her ostomy pouch in her own bathroom and get a drink of water from her own sink, though she had to admit the well water from Winnie's faucet tasted better than the town water from hers.

But here she was. And she wasn't leaving until Winnie forgave her.

"What are you doing here?" Winnie asked.

Though the words weren't spoken harshly, Eunice flinched. Winnie had never asked her that before. In the past, she could've shown up at three o'clock in the morning in a clown costume and Winnie would've just opened the door and said, "Come on in. I'll make coffee." But now, her mother's old friend looked at her as though she were a stranger. Or worse, an intruder.

Eunice gave Eric a desperate look, and he raised one finger in the air. "I'm going to go get a drink. I'll be in the kitchen if you need me."

"Help yourself to anything in the fridge," Winnie said without taking her eyes off Eunice. "Except the banana cream pie. That's mine."

"Yes, ma'am."

Winnie's big black dog followed Eric around the corner with a vigilant look on his face, and one corner of Winnie's mouth lifted. "Sparky won't let Eric touch that pie. He knows I've been saving it."

Eunice nodded. "Good dog."

Winnie walked over and sat on the other end of the couch, facing Eunice. "You look like you haven't slept in weeks. You got coon eyes."

"Dusty's going to be okay, right?"

"Oh, he'll be fine." Winnie chuckled. "He'd be back on the river already if the doctor would allow it."

"Good." Eunice picked at the edge of the couch cushion. "Winnie, I . . ."

Winnie waited. Eunice noticed her feet touching the floor and remembered how Dusty had adjusted the legs of this couch years ago to accommodate Winnie's short legs. He and Nate had a knack for taking people's discarded furniture and turning it into a blessing for someone else. She'd loved watching them work together at the Kitchen Sink. She'd loved how Dusty was willing to do whatever it took to provide for his son. She'd felt at home there with them.

Why did he still let her work enough hours to qualify for the store insurance? He didn't need her help with the online sales. He could've cut her off a long time ago.

"I'm sorry I haven't been around." Eunice took a deep breath. "Haven't stopped by."

Winnie's hands fidgeted in her lap. "I'm sure you've been busy."

Eunice almost laughed. No, she hadn't. But she was sure Winnie had, if Eunice knew her at all. The woman had never been content to sit around.

"How have you been?" she asked.

"Fine, fine." Winnie narrowed her eyes at her. "How have *you* been?"

This morning, Eunice had felt better than she had in days. Bertie had helped her wash her hair before she left yesterday, and Eunice's body was actually doing what she asked it to do for once. JoJo had even been cooperating. But that was hours ago. Now she felt only a soul-deep, unshakable weariness.

"Fine," she said.

The corner of Winnie's right eye twitched. Eunice pressed her lips together. Winnie deserved more than that. What was the point of coming here, putting herself through all this, if she was going to hold back?

Eunice sat up a little straighter. "Actually, I'm not fine. And I won't be fine until I know that you can forgive me for the way I acted after Mom and Dad died. It wasn't fair of me to blame you. Or abandon you. You were never anything but kind to me."

Winnie looked away. Clasped her hands in her lap. "I encouraged her to go on that trip because I saw how happy it made her. How it gave her a purpose. She needed to live her own life and stop trying to live yours."

Eunice hung her head.

"I don't blame you for blaming me." Winnie's voice cracked, and she picked at a fingernail. "Lord knows I blamed myself. I was the one who first gave her the idea, did you know that? She wanted to buy an RV and take a road trip up and down the West Coast."

Eunice looked up. "I didn't know that."

Winnie slumped back and shook her head. "I told her to dream bigger. I said, 'The sky's the limit.' She was like a daughter to me. I—I'm so sorry."

An uncomfortable weight pressed on her chest as Eunice mulled over Winnie's words. What if her parents had bought that RV? Spent a month driving through Oregon and California?

Would they still be here now? Or would it have changed nothing but the location of their accident?

Had they died because of their trip, or had they just happened to be on a trip when the time came for them to die? How did it work? And what about her? Would she die soon with or without her illnesses because her time was up? Or was she dying because she was sick?

"Something else is bothering you." Winnie gave her a concerned look. "You can tell me."

Eunice didn't want to keep Eric waiting forever, alone in the kitchen with Spark Plug. And she didn't want the truth to make Winnie think she had to feel sorry for her or pretend everything was fine between them. But this was the woman she used to confide in about everything. The woman who had been her mother's mentor—and hers, too, by extension.

"I'm sick."

The myriad wrinkles around Winnie's eyes deepened. She hesitated and opened her mouth twice before getting any words out. "Is it serious?"

Eunice fought to maintain control with what little strength she had, but a sob escaped as she nodded.

Winnie scooted closer on the couch and put a hand on Eunice's knee. "Oh, Neecy. I'm so sorry."

"No, I'm sorry." Eunice's words were jagged and broken. "You were always good to me. You made all the arrangements after they died when I couldn't even . . ."

She drew in a deep breath, and it made her cough. Winnie rubbed her back as she heaved and sputtered.

"I was angry. Angry at them for leaving me. Angry at you for encouraging them to go. Angry at myself for spending so many years resenting my mom. Taking her for granted. She was overbearing, but she was there. Then, all of a sudden, she wasn't. I was all alone."

Winnie took her hand and squeezed. "But you weren't alone."

"Being around you reminded me of her. I was afraid to come here."

"I should've come to you." Winnie nodded slowly. "I wanted to give you some space, but maybe I gave you too much space. It was easy for me to fill my life with other things."

"It wasn't easy for me."

"You've experienced so many disappointments."

"Will you forgive me?"

"Yes." Winnie put an arm around her shoulders. "Yes, of course. Good grief, you're nothing but skin and bones. Oh, Eunice." Her voice caught. "Will you forgive *me*?"

Eunice sniffed as she nodded, Winnie's forgiveness blowing over her like a gentle breeze, easing a bit of her burden. Why had she taken so long to come here?

"Now." Winnie ran a finger under her glasses to wipe her eyes, then slapped her hands on her knees. "How about some banana cream pie?"

twenty-seven

The seat belt rubbed painfully against Eric's burned shoulder as he drove the Jeep back to Tukston, gripping the wheel a little tighter than he should. The text he'd received from his father while hiding out in Winnie's kitchen had burrowed under his sunburned scalp and left him with a desire to scratch until he bled. *Please text me back. I'd like to catch up.* No "I'm sorry." No "How are you?" Just his dad thinking only of what he wanted and not caring how his actions affected other people.

Typical.

His hands ached as he gripped tighter. Did his dad even want to catch up with him or was this Uncle Jack's doing? Uncle Jack had probably convinced Dad to send the text since he obviously felt the need to meddle in their relationship. Yes, that made sense. Dad would be relieved if Eric didn't respond. He was just trying to get his big brother off his back.

What a day it had turned out to be. He wasn't even going to go for a run tonight. He was going to veg out in front of the TV and eat something unhealthy. Maybe even ice cream. He could always run extra miles tomorrow.

He glanced over at Eunice. When he'd pulled off the road to climb down the embankment and retrieve his and Dusty's gear from the riverbank, she'd nodded off while waiting for him to return. Her eyes were open now, but she seemed far away.

"Eunice?"

She blinked.

"What about the people who owe *you* an apology?"

She blinked again and slowly turned her head toward him. "What?"

"I mean, you did some things to some people and you want to make it right, and I respect that. But what about the people who've hurt *you*?"

She looked out the windshield with a pensive expression as if seeing something in the world passing by that he couldn't. "There's nothing I can do about that. I've forgiven them. I'm only concerned with my own debts now."

Eric frowned. He'd seen the way she was treated around town by certain people. He'd watched Dick Samson berate her in front of his friends. She didn't care about that?

"If they knew you were dy—uh, sick, don't you think they would feel bad and apologize? Why don't you want anyone to know?"

"What kind of apology would it be if they only did it because they felt sorry for me?"

He pressed his lips together. An apology was an apology, wasn't it? Uncle Jack's words popped into his head. *"I understand you're still angry with him. I know he was wrong. But it's been twenty years."*

Did Uncle Jack really expect Eric to forgive his dad when he wasn't even sorry for what he'd done? Why should it be up to Eric to try to restore the relationship when the whole thing was his dad's fault?

"Aren't you angry that they hurt you, but they just go on with their lives as if nothing happened?"

Eunice folded her arms across her stomach. "Not anymore. I don't have enough life left for anger."

They continued driving in silence, although the thoughts in Eric's head were loud. He had enough life left for anger.

201

He swallowed. That was probably what Eunice had thought, too, up until a few months ago.

Eunice kept her arms wrapped tight around herself. As he directed the Jeep through Tukston, he clicked off the A/C and lowered his window. Warm air filled the car, and he noticed how many people were around town. Meeting for milk shakes at Good Food. Walking dogs in the park. Barbecuing in their backyards. Some of them waved at him as he passed, and he raised his hand in reply. It made him smile. These were good people. Maybe they didn't live exciting lives by Seattle standards, but they seemed . . . happy.

He started dreaming about ice cream when they reached Prairie Dog Road. Winnie had filled him up before they left, but he hadn't gotten a single bite of her pie. He steered around Eunice's single-horse trailer and prepared to turn into his driveway but hit the brakes. Why was there a rental car at his house? Why was there a woman on his porch?

Eunice's brow furrowed. "Is that Tiffani with an *i*? I didn't know she was coming to visit."

He carefully parked next to the rental and shook his head. "Neither did I."

Tiffani's long tan legs brought her down the steps and to his door. She flipped her hair over her shoulder and leaned through the open window to kiss his cheek. "Hello, lover. Surprise."

"Wow. Hi." He didn't even try to hide his shock. "I can't believe you're here."

He glanced over at Eunice, unsure how to proceed now that two women needed his attention. Should he help her get back to her house? He could tell the day's stress had taken a toll.

Tiffani followed his gaze and frowned. "Who's this?"

"This is my neighbor, Eunice. Eunice, this is Tiffani."

Eunice gave a sluggish nod. "Nice to meet you."

Tiffani gave a little wave, yet her expression was hard to

read behind her big black sunglasses. "How can you wear those long sleeves when it's a hundred degrees? I'm dying out here."

Eunice shrugged and slowly slid out of the Jeep. "Thanks for the ride, Eric."

He lowered his voice. "You going to be okay?"

She shut the door and lifted one hand in response.

Tiffani watched her walk away. "She's worried about something."

Eric peeked at Tiffani from the corner of his eye. It never ceased to amaze him that someone so hard to understand could be so good at understanding others. She was the only one in his group of friends who could tell when he was having a bad day.

"And she should really do something about those split ends." Tiffani tugged on his arm. "Come on, I want to see your house. And would you be a dear and get my suitcase from the car?"

His head spun. She never let her thoughtful side show for long.

She glided back to the porch before he could respond, knowing he'd do whatever she asked. He couldn't believe she was really here. She'd always been spontaneous, but he never imagined she'd deign to visit "cowboy country," as she'd called it when he first told her where he was going. His heart tugged at the sight of her climbing his front steps. It felt good to see someone from home.

The suitcase weighed at least thirty pounds, making him wonder how long she planned to stay. As he dragged it up the steps, he noticed Cinderella was nowhere to be seen. Probably holed up somewhere shady and cool.

"Did you drive the whole way?"

Tiffani wrinkled her cute little nose. "Of course not. I flew to some tacky little airport in Butte after flying all the way to Salt Lake City first. Then I couldn't order an Uber, so I had to rent a car. I hate driving."

Eric's chest puffed up a little. She'd done all that for him?

He unlocked the door and let Tiffani inside. It felt good to have someone in his house, too.

"Everything's so nineties in here." She spun around, taking it all in. "It's just like that condo we rented in Seaside that time, remember?"

He chuckled. "I remember you sweet-talking the manager into an upgrade."

She grinned and held up her hands. "He was *happy* to accommodate the 'close, personal friend of Mr. Lindor.'"

They laughed together, reveling for a moment in the memory, until her eyes landed on the bowling ball sitting on the hallway floor. "Oh my gosh, do you bowl now?" She squealed. "Like at an actual bowling alley? I didn't know those still existed."

"Alas, no. It's Eunice's."

"Oh." Tiffani pulled off her sunglasses and dropped her Alexander McQueen purse on the couch. "Why do you have her stuff over here?"

"It's a long story." He set the suitcase against the wall with a thud. "I'm surprised your dad let you come here."

She flicked her wrist. "He doesn't know."

"He'll know when he checks his credit card statement." Or maybe not. Tiffani's dad was the type of guy who thought his money could replace his presence in his daughter's life. Hence the unrestricted access to his credit cards.

She brushed his words away and moved close enough that he could see the rosy sheen of her lip gloss and smell the citrusy sunshine of her hair. "I didn't come here to talk about my dad."

All the talk about dads put an uneasy feeling in his stomach. He didn't want to talk about that either. "Why did you come here?"

"Because, silly." Her mouth formed a pout as her fingers reached out to dance across his pecs. "I missed you."

She pressed her perfect little self against him and leaned toward his lips. His body responded as he kissed her, but his mind refused to move on from the whole dad thing. Wasn't this exactly what his dad would do in a situation like this? Get physically involved with a woman he didn't currently have a real relationship with?

Tiffani sensed his hesitation and pulled back to look at his face. "What's wrong?"

How could he explain it? He'd never turned down her advances before. This uncertainty was brand-new. "It's just . . . I've had a long day."

Her eyes narrowed. "Does this have anything to do with Eunice?"

He denied it, even as Eunice's words rang loud and clear in his mind. *"I suppose you can afford to be picky and only pay attention to supermodels."* Eric drew Tiffani back into his arms and rested his chin on top of her head with a deep breath. There was no doubt she was supermodel material, but surely his interest in her wasn't limited to her looks. She'd been a good friend to him. Helped build his confidence in dealing with wealthy clients. Introduced him to influential people.

He wasn't the kind of guy who only cared about a woman's appearance. Was he?

His shoulders tensed, and he squeezed Tiffani tighter. He would *not* be like his dad. Before he let anything else happen between him and Tiffani, he was going to make sure their relationship had more than a physical foundation.

She relaxed in his arms, her own long day no doubt catching up to her, and he kissed her hair. Even though her appearance was unexpected, it was good she'd shown up here. Her sudden nearness made him realize he was tired of the whole on-again-off-again routine. It was time they considered getting serious. He was thirty-two, after all. Had an established career. Would soon be promoted. He needed to know where he stood with this beautiful woman.

He pulled away and gave her a reassuring smile. Yes, he and

Tiffani would spend some time together. Would get to know each other without the hustle and bustle of the city and discuss their future. He would prove to Eunice—and himself—that he wasn't some shallow playboy.

He was nothing like his father.

twenty-eight

Eric blew out a relieved breath as his last client left at five-thirty on Tuesday. He knew Tiffani would not so patiently be awaiting his return to the house.

"Long day?" Max asked.

Eric pasted on a smile. He couldn't even make a private facial expression around here. He'd updated the mailing address for the cubicle wall and expected delivery any day now.

He tidied up his desk and grabbed his briefcase. "The usual."

"Did you hear from Jerry about his decision?"

Eric turned toward the exit and fought off a grimace. Jerry had left a message letting him know he would prefer to meet with Max from now on. "Yes."

"I think he just felt a little rushed when he talked with you." Max lifted one shoulder. "People around here like to know a feller really hears them, really cares, before they decide to trust him. Don't take it personally."

Eric pressed his lips together. How could he not take it personally? He'd given Jerry his full attention for almost an hour. Had answered all his questions.

But.

Maybe he'd been a little short with his responses, trying to get the appointment over with so he could take care of other business. And he'd cut Jerry off when he started talking about his grandpa's farm where he used to work as a boy. Eric hadn't thought that was relevant to Jerry's current financial situation. Yet maybe it was relevant in other ways.

"All right." He nodded halfheartedly. "Guess I'll see you to-morrow."

Max gave him a quizzical look. "Everything else okay? You seem kind of distracted this week."

Distracted? Ha. If Max only knew just how distracted he was. Every minute of the day, he was wondering what Tiffani was doing while he was gone. Thinking about what he could do to keep her entertained. Dreaming about kissing her soft, full lips and running his fingers through her long hair. She wasn't making his current chastity vow easy on him, traipsing around the house in tiny pajamas and leaving the bathroom door cracked when she showered. He wasn't sure how long he was going to last.

"I'm fine." He forced another smile, loosened his tie, and headed for the door.

The lobby was empty. Today's clients had all been taken care of, and Winnie always left at five-thirty on the dot on Tuesdays. Eric couldn't remember if Tuesday was bridge club or water aerobics, but he was glad Winnie wasn't around to keep teasing him about being late for work this morning. The first time he'd been late since arriving in Tukston.

It was all Tiffani's fault. She hadn't even been up yet when he left for work, but he'd still been late after sleeping through his alarm. He'd been having trouble sleeping since she arrived, his mind spinning for hours as he thought about their relation-ship. Their past together. Their future. It was driving him crazy.

But that would all change tonight if things went according to plan.

He shut the front office door behind him. As he stepped out onto the sidewalk, Benson came hurrying after him.

"Eric, wait up."

Eric slowed down. He was never going to get out of here. At

least Benson had finally stopped calling him Mr. Larson. "Hey, Benson. Good work today."

The kid was quiet but sharp. He seemed to know what files or stats Eric would need before he even asked.

"Thanks." Benson fell into step beside him. "I was wondering if I could ask you something."

"Sure."

They reached Eric's Jeep, and Eric turned to Benson expectantly.

Benson kicked at a pebble. "When I first started here, Jack—uh, Mr. Larson told me he'd help with my tuition if I would come on as associate advisor here after I graduated."

Eric nodded. He hadn't known that, but it sounded like something Uncle Jack would do, and it seemed like a wise investment for the company. "Go on."

"I turned him down because my parents—I mean, I just didn't know if that's what I wanted. Mr. Larson said I could have a lifelong career here, or I could go to any branch I chose if I would give him five years."

Eric suspected Benson's parents had had a lot of influence on the kid's decision. Or, more specifically, Benson's dad. Dick Samson didn't seem like the kind of guy who valued a college education. "Sounds like a pretty good option. But you weren't sure at the time?"

Benson shoved his hands in his pants pockets. "I never thought of leaving Tukston before that. Wasn't sure I could leave my family."

"But you could be an associate here as long as you wanted without ever leaving. Eventually even senior advisor." Eric fought the desire to check the time on his phone. Tiffani was going to flip out if he wasn't home by six. "It's a great job, and someday you might want to get married. Have a family. You'll need financial security."

"I know." Benson lifted his foot to kick at another rock but stopped himself. "I'm having second thoughts. Do you think I already missed my chance?"

"You've been paying for your own tuition?"

"Yeah."

"And you're wondering if Jack's offer still stands?"

Benson nodded. "I'll finish my associate's degree at the end of summer semester. I could transfer to U of M Western in Dillon. Get my bachelor's there."

Eric ran a hand through his hair. "I'll talk to him."

Benson's face brightened. "Really?"

"Sure. You're a good worker. A smart guy." Eric punched Benson's shoulder and smiled. "If we could just get you to come out of your shell a little bit, I think you'd make a great advisor."

Benson's cheeks reddened. "Thanks."

"I've got to run." Eric reached for the Jeep's door handle. "I'll bring it up to Jack, okay?"

He hopped in the Jeep and gave Benson a wave as he backed out onto the road. Maybe this could solve the problem of finding another advisor for the Tukston branch. Eric had seen enough to know Max could take over as senior advisor—clients apparently preferred him anyway—and if Benson came on as associate, Eric was confident they could handle the caseload here.

The only flaw in the plan was the question of time. How long would it take Benson to get his bachelor's degree? Eric wasn't about to fill in for two years. Could Max skate by for a couple of years while he waited for Benson? If Benson kept working part-time, he could start taking on more responsibilities, even before he graduated.

It just might work.

Eric pushed thoughts of Larson Financial from his mind as he sped home, his stomach in a twist. On Sunday, he'd shown Tiffani around town—which hadn't taken long—and she'd gushed about how "charming and peaceful" everything was. But then last night, when he'd made her dinner at the house after work, she'd complained about being alone all day and wondered how the quiet hadn't driven him crazy. He admitted it had come close, then removed her hand from where it had been resting on his thigh.

Tonight, however, he had a plan. He was going to take Tiffani to dinner at Good Food so she could experience a real hometown diner. Then he would order pie to go and drive her out to the Madison River so they could admire the view and talk about their future. From inside the Jeep, of course. He wasn't ready to face those flies again.

As he walked toward the house, he scanned around for Cinderella but didn't see her. She hadn't been around since Tiffani arrived. Was she okay? Where was she laying her eggs now?

Tiffani flung open the door as he climbed the steps. "Where have you been? I'm so borrred."

He almost chuckled. In Seattle, he often worked late, sometimes putting in fifty or sixty hours a week. Tiffani had never noticed because she was always too busy to spend time with him until eight or nine at night anyway. Now all of a sudden six o'clock was the end of the world.

"I got off as soon as I could." He caught the scent of her perfume as he went inside and shut the door. "You look nice."

She was dressed up and had curled her hair. The makeup around her eyes gave her a smoldering look that did something to his heart rate.

She picked up on his appreciation and did a little spin. "You said we were going out."

He nodded but didn't have the heart to tell her that her finery would go utterly unappreciated at Good Food. "Just let me get changed. Are you hungry?"

She lifted one dainty, beautiful shoulder. "If it gets me out of this house."

He kissed her on the forehead. "Give me five minutes."

She sulked as he walked away. He did feel bad leaving her

cooped up alone all day. Cinderella wasn't even around to talk to. But he couldn't skip work just because she'd had one of her spur-of-the-moment ideas.

He quickly changed and found Tiffani sitting on the couch, scrolling on her phone. She jumped up when she saw him. "Where are we going?"

"Remember the diner we walked past the other day?"

Her face fell. "We're going to a diner?"

He held the front door open for her and winked. "There aren't a lot of options around here. At least we'll be together."

She pouted as they got into the Jeep. "Couldn't we go to that Butte place? At least it had a few stoplights and hotels. There must be a decent bar and grill there."

"It's an hour away." He backed out of the driveway.

"So?"

"So, I have to work tomorrow."

"Since when did your work schedule ever keep you from staying out late?"

It was true. There'd been no hour too late for a rendezvous with Tiffani in the past. Maybe Tukston was starting to get to him.

He cranked up his dimples to eleven. "This will give me a chance to show you off around town. Make all the other cowboys jealous."

Her lips turned up. "You're not a cowboy."

"Aha, there's a smile." He reached over to squeeze her hand. "Just give it a chance, it's not that bad. They have really good fries."

She scoffed. "As if I'm going to eat *fries*."

He laughed. "They've got an avocado chicken salad, too."

The parking around Good Food was almost filled up, and Eric's scalp itched at the crowd inside the restaurant. He'd been hoping for more of a quiet evening. But as he'd already explained, there weren't many other options. And Good Food's service was fast, so they'd be on their way to the river in no time.

He led Tiffani inside and felt a dozen pairs of eyes on them as they found a booth along the far wall. He was used to people staring at him, and he knew Tiffani was, too. She thrived on it. But these looks were different. Not like people admiring their clothes or their looks, but more like curious people wanting to check up on him.

No privacy at work, and no privacy outside of work either, apparently.

Tiffani slid into the seat across from him and tucked her glimmery purse into the corner. "Hasn't anybody around here seen a Valentino dress before?"

Eric shook his head. "People aren't used to someone as gorgeous as you walking around."

She eyed one of the plastic-covered menus and gingerly picked it up by the corner with two fingertips. "It's sticky."

"Have mine." He traded her.

Dee appeared with two sets of silverware rolled in white paper napkins. "Howdy, Eric. You haven't been in since that Cowboy Deluxe night. I was afraid we'd scared you off."

He pulled out his most charming grin, desperately wanting to avoid talking about Cowboy Deluxe night. "Of course not. I've just been busy. I ordered takeout a couple times."

"Don't be working too hard now." Dee raised her eyebrows at Tiffani. "And who do we have here?"

"This is my, uh, friend Tiffani." Eric swallowed. "From Seattle."

"Aren't you a pretty little thing." Dee pulled out her notebook with a wink. "What can I get you kids to drink?"

Tiffani didn't look up from her menu. "Water with two slices of lemon."

"Okay."

"Same for me, please." Eric shifted in his seat. "And what is the special tonight?"

"You're in luck." Dee's face lit up. "We got Rocky Mountain

oysters this week. Probably the only time we'll have 'em this summer, so now's your chance."

Tiffani perked up. "Oysters?"

"Well, they're not the—"

"I'll have that." Tiffani slapped the menu down on the table. "And hurry with the water. I'm parched."

Dee frowned. "Okay. How about you, Eric?"

Despite growing up on Puget Sound, he'd never developed a taste for seafood. "I'll have the avocado chicken salad, please."

Dee jotted down their orders and scurried away.

Tiffani glanced around, taking in the other diners and the local artwork on the walls. "There's a lot of denim in here."

"You get used to it."

"Why would you want to?"

Something tinged her voice, but he wasn't sure what it was. His smile wavered. "I didn't say I *wanted* to. I'm making the most of it while I'm here, is all."

She met his eyes for a second, and he would've sworn he saw a flicker of vulnerability before she looked away. "But you aren't thinking of staying, are you?"

"Of course not. I—"

"Why, if it isn't Eric Larson." A woman slid onto the bench seat next to him and brazenly kissed his cheek. "I owe you a drink."

Oh, great.

Pickles.

Eric's brow furrowed. "You do?"

She set a manicured hand on his forearm. "Turns out you were right about me. I *am* a ringer. Me and old Hazel won the horseshoe tournament at Max's party."

"Oh." He glanced warily at Tiffani. She was glaring at Pickles. "That's great. I'm glad you had fun."

Pickles scooted closer, leaning the top of her low-cut tank top toward him. "Thanks to you. So, how about that drink?"

"Maybe another time." He gestured toward Tiffani. "We're having dinner."

"Oh, my." Pickles put her hand on her chest and gave an exaggerated gasp. "I am *so* sorry. I didn't realize you were with someone." She held out a hand to Tiffani. "I'm Pickles. And you are . . . ?"

Tiffani scowled, keeping her hands clasped on the table. "On a date with my boyfriend."

"How strange," Pickles said, her smile sickeningly sweet. "Eric never mentioned he was seeing anyone."

Eric squirmed. This evening was going downhill fast. And he didn't like the way Pickles said his name.

Tiffani was unfazed. "He never mentioned the people around here were named after food either."

Pickles waved a dismissive hand. "My daddy always called me that, God rest his soul. Because I loved pickles so much as a kid. It just sort of stuck."

"What a fascinating story," Tiffani deadpanned. "Now if you'll excuse us . . ."

"Of *course*. I didn't mean to interrupt." Pickles stood and wiped her thumb across Eric's cheek with a giggle. "Oops, I left a little lipstick there. I'll catch up with you for that drink some other time."

Eric opened his mouth to respond but then thought better of it. Instead, he made what he hoped was a noncommittal gesture and forced all his attention back to Tiffani as Pickles walked away.

Tiffani's expression remained indecipherable. "You went to a party with her?"

"No. She was there, is all. There were tons of people there."

"You went by yourself?"

"Well . . ." He pulled at the collar of his shirt. "Technically I went with Eunice, but—"

"Eunice again? What is it with you and that woman?"

"Nothing. She's my neighbor and she needs help getting around. That's it."

"Why do you have to be the one to help her?"

No one but him and Eunice knew the whole story. That had been part of the deal. But Tiffani wouldn't be here long, and if it put her mind at ease . . .

"Look, I had a run-in with her the day I moved here. I almost ran her over. She threatened to sue me if I didn't help drive her around, so—"

"She's blackmailing you?" The pitch of Tiffani's voice rose sharply. "How dare she."

Uh-oh. She'd have her father's high-powered lawyers involved in no time if Eric wasn't careful.

"No, it's not like that. I mean, it started out that way, but—"

"Here you go, kids." Dee set two plates down on the table with a *thunk thunk*. "One avocado chicken salad, and one order of Rocky Mountain oysters, fresh out of the fryer. Do you want any hot sauce for those, hon?"

Tiffani shrank back. "They're fried?"

"Of course."

"They don't look like oysters."

Dee nodded. "That's because they're, you know, bull balls."

Eric's stomach clenched. Wait a minute. He'd overheard Max talking about this once. Did she mean . . . ?

"You know, Montana tendergroin," Dee continued. "Swinging beef."

Tiffani's face paled. Eric's heart sank.

"Like I said, you're lucky you came in when you did." Dee smiled. "These testicles will be gone by the end of the week."

twenty-nine

Eric leaned against the doorframe of the guest bedroom. "Can we please talk about this?"

Tiffani threw clothes into her suitcase. "I hate it here. She did that on purpose."

"You've only been here three days."

"Four, technically. And that's been more than enough."

He squeezed the back of his neck. He'd wanted to pack up and leave town a few times since the day he arrived in Tukston, too. But he didn't want Tiffani's visit to end like this. "Maybe I can take a couple days off work. We can spend some quality time together."

She paused, a pair of studded ankle boots in her hand. "I'm listening."

He crossed the room and sat on the end of her bed. "Come here."

She reluctantly set the boots down and joined him, sitting close enough that her smooth, bare leg touched his. The material at the bottom of her very short dress was like the surface of Puget Sound under the moonlight. Maybe it wasn't the best idea to be with her on her bed after three nights of avoiding this very scenario.

He shifted enough to put an inch or two between them. "I had planned to drive you out to the river tonight so we could talk."

She bumped him with her shoulder and gave a teasing smile. "Talk? Or *talk?*"

A blush warmed his cheeks. "I mean really talk. About us."

Her smile remained, though something in her eyes changed. "What about us?"

"We've been together off and on for a long time now." He'd had a whole speech planned, but now his words sounded lame and impulsive. "I thought maybe it was time to decide if we want to get more serious."

They hadn't had much opportunity yet to discover if there was more to their relationship than a physical attraction, but he was willing to keep trying. There had to be something there. Otherwise, why had he kept going back to her all this time? Why was she here now?

She closed the small amount of distance between them and pulled his arm around her waist. Her breath was warm on his skin as she leaned in. "We have too much fun together to get serious."

She pressed her lips to his neck and made a sexy purring sound. His heart pounded. It would be so easy to give in. His body screamed at him to do so. But his father's voice hounded him as that memory from when he was twelve replayed. *"You can do better,"* his dad had said about the girl Eric liked at the time. But maybe his dad had really been talking about himself. He thought *he* could do better. Could walk away from his family and replace them with something *better*.

Eric had spent the last twenty years pushing himself to go far beyond better and become the best. He wanted to scream. *Why did I ever listen to you?*

He summoned the full strength of his willpower and gently pulled Tiffani's hands out from where they'd found their way under his shirt. "You're not making this easy."

She simpered, "That was my plan."

He took a deep breath, trying to get his blood pressure under control. Time to go for broke. "Can you see yourself with me long term? Do you think there's a future for us?"

She looked over at her suitcase, then back at him. "I don't know."

"Maybe you could stay a few more days and think it over." He tried not to let his voice sound too desperate or hopeful but suspected he failed. "I can show you the river. We can go running together. Maybe drive to Butte for a movie."

He knew it wasn't much of an offer—wasn't the lifestyle Tiffani was used to—but it was all he had right now.

"Can't we figure this all out when you get back to Seattle?" She bent to pick the ankle boots up off the floor again. "I want to go home."

"Come on, Tiff," he pleaded. "It's not that bad here."

She clutched the boots to her chest. "You said you weren't thinking of staying."

He held up his hands. "I'm not. But—"

"You're supposed to be miserable without me." Her voice was suddenly soft, and she poked at the carpet with her toe. "You're supposed to be dying to come back."

Her words floated in the air like dust motes caught in a ray of sun, and Eric stared at them. She was right. If he truly had feelings for her . . .

"That's what I'm trying to say." He pressed his sweaty palms against his knees. "I want us to spend more time together and figure out where we stand."

She hesitated. "Eric . . ."

"Please." He pushed off the bed and touched her arm. "There are places I want to show you. And you haven't even met Cinderella yet."

She tossed the boots into the suitcase and threw up her hands, the sharpness back in her voice. "Why do all the people around here have such weird names?"

"Cinderella's not a person. She's my chicken."

219

Tiffani stared at him.

He shifted on his feet. "Well, she's not really mine, but she lives here. Sort of." He was grasping at straws now. Why would Tiffani care about a chicken? "You should see her. She's hilarious."

Tiffani narrowed her eyes. "Is that the weird black-and-white thing I saw on your porch the other day?"

He pulled out his dimples. "So you *did* meet her."

"It crapped right on the top step." Tiffani put her hands on her hips. "I shooed it away."

He fought to keep from frowning. Maybe that was why he hadn't seen Cinderella around lately. "I thought you liked animals."

"In zoos, Eric. Not pecking at my feet. How can you stand it around here, with chickens at your house and fried testicles at the diner and trashy rednecks everywhere you turn?"

The corner of his jaw twitched. "They're not trashy. They're good people."

She hung her head and tugged on the zipper of her suitcase. "I'm sorry. I shouldn't have said that. I just want everything to go back to the way it was before."

Eric rubbed the back of his neck. The way it was before? He wanted to go back to Seattle, but did he want to go back to the way things were before?

"Maybe I'm ready for something different. Something more."

Emotions flashed across her face like lightning. "We're good together, Eric. We make sense. Just tell me nothing's changed."

She'd helped him navigate higher social circles than he'd ever dreamed of. She'd shown him how to look and act the part. He cared about her. He owed her. But . . .

"I'm not sure I can do that."

Her shoulders fell as she let out a long breath. "Then I'm not sure I can stay."

Eunice waited until it was almost dark to check on her garden. She didn't want anyone to see her, and she didn't like the way the oppressive heat made her feel. Like she was moving in painful slow motion through a bad dream.

Tiffani's rental car was still parked in Eric's driveway. She was even more stunning and fashionable than Eunice had imagined. Like she'd stepped right out of a magazine. Eunice had almost been tempted to go over and say hello this morning, knowing Tiffani would be alone while Eric was at work, but she'd looked at her reflection in the mirror and chickened out. Her pale, haggard face and stringy hair appeared infinitely more tragic when compared to Tiffani's youthful tanned skin and thick wavy locks.

She pulled a few weeds and stuck her finger in the dirt to test the moisture level. Dry. Everything was dry. The summer had become an arid beast. She turned on the sprinkler and leaned against the fence, close enough the water sprayed her purple Crocs.

"You should get a timer for that."

The voice startled her, and she gasped.

Eric leaned his forearms on the fence and gave her a half smile. "Sorry."

"What are you doing out here? Where's Tiffani?"

He shrugged like he didn't care to talk about it and held up her new bowling ball.

"Just drop it over the fence," she said. "Timer for what?"

"For the sprinkler. You can set it for an hour or two hours or whatever, so you don't have to come back out and turn the water off later."

He reached the ball over the fence, and it landed in the dry grass with a muted thud.

"Oh." She watched the sprinkler move back and forth, back and forth. The water droplets falling made a soothing sound.

"I'll pick one up from Hardware Hank's tomorrow," he said. "Thanks."

They stood in silence for a minute as darkness fell. She could already see the benefit of the timer because she wished she could go to bed now and not have to wait up. Why hadn't she turned the hose on earlier? Her brain just wasn't working like it used to.

"How long will Tiffani be staying?"

Eric straightened and stretched his arms above his head. "She's leaving tomorrow."

"Oh."

She didn't know what else to say. There were plenty of questions. Why had Tiffani come here? What did she think of Tukston? Was Eric happy she'd surprised him? But the words wouldn't come.

"She's a city girl, you know." Now he bent to touch his toes, stretching his hamstrings. "Tukston is a little rustic for her."

He bent his arms and twisted his torso back and forth.

"What are you doing?"

He gave her a sheepish look. "I stretch when I'm stressed."

"That's a good coping strategy, I guess." She gave a weary smile back. "Better than drugs."

He bent his right knee and held on to his right foot from behind. "You're not going to ask what I'm stressed about?"

Eunice folded her arms across her stomach. "I don't like it when people ask *me* questions, so . . ."

"Gotcha." He switched to the other leg, and she could see his dimples even in the dark. "So, can I ask you a question?"

A month ago, she would've snapped at him for that, just to prove his boundless charm wouldn't work on her. Now she was too tired. Plus it was kind of nice having someone to talk to.

She still tried to sound annoyed, though. "I guess if you have to."

"Didn't you ever want a normal bucket list?"

222

That wasn't what she was expecting. She'd thought maybe he needed relationship advice. Which she wasn't qualified to give.

"What do you mean, *normal?*"

He pulled one arm across his chest. "You know, like *Go to Disneyland. Try every flavor of ice cream. See the ocean.* That sort of thing."

Was that the normal thing to do?

She looked at the sky as she pondered his question and stared at the waning full moon. The sky in Montana was vast. Clouds piled up like foam on the seashore. Storms came and went like waves, an endless cycle of changing colors and moods. Tides moving in. Tides moving out.

She blinked. "I've seen the ocean."

"Okay." He switched to the other arm. "But isn't there anything you wish you could do before it's too late?"

She thought of the dog bed on the floor of her living room. The cat collar with the little silver bell. "It's already too late."

"That's hooey."

Her stomach squeezed. "You sound just like your uncle."

He snorted. "He'd be thrilled to hear that. Can I ask you another question?"

She grimaced. "Fine. But only if I can ask you one."

"Were you ever married?"

"No." She didn't hesitate. The answer was easy. The reason was hard. But she couldn't risk any follow-up questions. "My turn. Do you love her?"

He lifted the toes of his right foot to stretch his calf. "I don't think so. I've known her a long time. She's done a lot for me. But when she told me she was leaving tomorrow . . ."

Eunice waited.

Eric sighed. Switched to the other foot. "I didn't put up much of a fight."

She looked back up at the sky. The stars were coming out, flickering into place one by one. She could say something about

223

how it was probably for the best, but she remembered how it felt when her mother said the same thing after convincing Eunice to break off her engagement to the only man she'd ever loved. It was true Eunice hadn't been hard to convince. She'd been eighteen. Not ready for marriage. Still, her mother's words . . .

The only thing she could think of to say to Eric were the words she wished so badly her mother would've said instead. "Maybe you made a mistake."

thirty

It had been a week since Tiffani peeled out of his driveway in her rental car without a backward glance. Eric had texted her once, to ask if she made it home okay, but she hadn't responded. Her last words to him before she left were *"I shouldn't have come."* But the words that haunted him most were Eunice's.

"Maybe you made a mistake."

He picked at his lunch in the sweltering heat of Tukston Park. The temperature had taken away his appetite. If only he could go for a swim in Puget Sound. Walk along the beach in bare feet. He tugged at his tie and barely stopped himself from scratching at his shoulders. They had finally stopped peeling yesterday.

"You'd look better without it."

Eric glanced up. Winnie never left her post during the lunch hour, but here she was, gracing him with an inscrutable expression. She gestured toward his chest. "Your tie."

He looked down. He considered it part of his uniform. Part of his identity. He had to dress as sharp as his clients, move with ease through their world, if he wanted to be successful at Larson Financial.

He blew out a breath and pulled off his tie. "Maybe just for today."

Winnie smiled and joined him on the shaded bench. "It's too hot for frippery."

She wore a light pink crewneck sweatshirt with the words *Summer Vibes and Sunshine* in gold print on the front. She caught him looking at it and laughed. "My honorary granddaughter got this for me. Remember, the one I told you about?"

He remembered, all right. The one with the "lovely personality."

Winnie patted his knee and spoke loudly. "I still think you two should hook up sometime. It'd be good for you to hang out with someone your own age once in a while."

Eric covered up a smile and glanced around, hoping no one else could hear their conversation. Winnie clearly had no idea that the term *hook up* had multiple meanings. "I appreciate your concern."

"Fine, fine." She threw up her hands. "If you don't want to listen to me about your social life, at least listen to me about work. We do work in the same office, you know."

"Okay." He unbuttoned the top button of his shirt. "What about work?"

"I'm worried about Benson."

His eyebrows shot up. He'd expected something about coffee machines or tables or unscheduled office visits. "Benson?"

"Surely you can see how much potential he has. Are you going to keep him filing papers forever?"

"Well, I—"

"I know he doesn't assert himself, but he's not cut out to be a townie. I don't know how I know, I just know."

"A townie?"

"Someone who's content to stick around Tukston forever, reliving their glory days and following in their father's footsteps. Nothing wrong with that, but that's not Benson."

Eric scrunched his lips to one side. How did she know? How did anyone ever know if they were on the right path or if they were meant for something else?

"I've been meaning to talk to my uncle about him actually."

226

Eric took a drink from his water bottle. Why did he have to be here for the hottest summer in Montana history? "About sending him to Dillon to get his bachelor's so he can take Max's place."

Winnie put a hand to her chest and practically shouted, "You're firing Max?"

"No, of course not." He flinched and glanced over his shoulder, wishing she would keep her voice down. "Max would become senior advisor."

"What about you?"

"I'm only going to be here three more weeks. I think Max and Benson can handle it." He pulled out a smile. "With your help."

He remembered Uncle Jack's words the last time they'd talked about Eric moving back to Seattle. That "we'll see" still echoed in his brain, but he wasn't about to accept that as the final answer. Now that he had a plan for the Tukston branch, he just needed to convince Uncle Jack.

"You're going back to the big city?" Winnie asked.

If there were any "big things" on his horizon, he wasn't going to find them here. "That's the plan."

"Huh."

Huh? What was that supposed to mean? He needed to return to Seattle. He missed it. He missed his friends, his brother. And he couldn't lose himself in Tukston, no matter how many clients he had or miles he ran. And if he couldn't lose himself . . . well, he might accidentally find himself instead.

The sooner he got out of here, the better.

"You came all the way over here to talk to me about Benson?"

"No. I also wanted to thank you."

"For what?"

"For helping Eunice."

His shoulders drooped a little. Eunice. He'd stopped by her house twice in the past week, first to drop off the timer for the sprinkler and then just to make sure she was still breathing. She hadn't brought up her list, but if he had counted correctly, she still had two names left now that Winnie's was crossed off. He hoped she wasn't planning to give up.

"She told you about . . . ?"

Winnie nodded. "It doesn't seem fair. Here I am, almost eighty-one years old and fit as a fiddle. And poor Eunice is just . . ." She shook her head. "Well, the Lord's ways are mysterious. Who am I to say what's fair?"

Eric's eyes narrowed. "You think it's God's fault she's sick?"

"I don't think *fault* is the right word. But it's certainly in His hands."

"Then why would He do that?"

Winnie stood and brushed off the back of her pants. "Like I said, His ways are mysterious. I've had a long, full life, and she's lost so much. But you know what the Psalm says. Long life or short, we are all but dust in view of the Lord."

Eric tilted his head. "Butt dust?"

"Yes. Nothing but dust. And I would trade places with Neecy in a heartbeat, but we each have our own path to walk. Only God knows why we have the path we do."

Eric stood, too. "How do you know He knows?"

Winnie glanced over at him as they walked back to the office. "Didn't your uncle ever teach you about faith?"

Eric shortened his steps to keep pace with her. "He's talked about it, but it's not really my thing."

"What *is* your thing?"

He bristled as they crossed the street. She could somehow magically see that Benson had potential and wasn't "cut out to be a townie," but she couldn't see he lived and breathed finance?

They reached the office, and he held the door open for her. "You know our motto. 'Your financial security tomorrow is our leading goal today.' That's my thing."

Winnie scurried around her oversized desk and hopped up onto her chair. The chains on the arms of her glasses swung back and forth as she swiveled herself into place, then lowered her chin to peer up at him. "That's not what I meant."

Before shutting down his laptop at the end of the day, Eric checked the Track Package feature for the cubicle wall he'd reordered. He frowned. It still said IN TRANSIT. That was what it had said for days now. How could they be doing this to him again?

At least he didn't have to worry about finding a suitable console table anymore. He'd gone to check on Dusty after he was released from the hospital and told him to go ahead with whatever he had in mind for the bench. "We'll get it all spiffed up for you," he'd said. "Then I'll have Nate deliver it."

Winnie would be thrilled. Uncle Jack, too.

Ah, yes. Uncle Jack.

Eric had been putting off calling him. When Uncle Jack would call and leave a message, Eric would text back any necessary information. He was sure Uncle Jack knew he was avoiding him. He was also sure his uncle knew why.

Winnie's words from earlier returned to his mind: *"That's not what I meant."* Then what had she meant?

Max's shadow fell across his desk as he packed his briefcase. "I heard you talking to the Millers earlier."

Eric struggled not to scowl. Of course he had. Just like Eric had heard him talking with Mrs. Grimshaw at his last appointment about selling 4-H pigs instead of financial portfolios. No wonder profit growth was so hard to come by around here.

"I know you mean well," Max continued, "but those kids are in no position to take the kind of risks you were proposing."

"All investments come with a certain amount of risk." He looked up at Max. "What do you want them to do? Keep the money in a savings account and earn less than a quarter percent in interest?"

The Millers were a nice young couple with two little kids. Sam Miller had a good job as a plumber. Sarah worked part-time at the community library. They didn't have tons of money, but they kept to a tight budget and had managed to save up a modest sum. At their age, he felt they could afford to push the envelope a little. They had lots of time to let their investments grow. Or to recover if the worst should happen and the market crashed.

"I'm just saying there are safer options." Max rapped his knuckles on Eric's desk. "Around here, when a recession hits or the market falls or unemployment rises, it's awful hard to bounce back. Small towns don't just suffer through a downturn, Eric. They die."

Eric stood, briefcase in hand, and met Max's eyes. "Uncle Jack said Tukston's been around since 1874. I don't think it's going anywhere."

"And you're willing to bet Sam and Sarah's future on that? Their kids' future?"

Finance was a high-stakes business. The bigger the risk, the bigger the reward. He had clients back in Seattle who lived for the adrenaline rush of a big payoff. Who would make a hundred grand and tell him to turn around and put it all back in something even more chancy. He knew things were different here, but his pushing for a greater reward made sense. It would help both the Millers and Larson Financial. It was a win-win.

He walked around his desk and stood next to Max. "I'm not betting anything. It's the Millers' decision to make."

Max nodded. "But they're counting on you to steer them right. They're putting their trust in you."

Another lecture from Max about clients and trust. Eric was well aware of his responsibilities and the trust his clients put in him. He didn't need Max's approval or permission.

He put on the most diplomatic expression he could muster. "I hear what you're saying. I appreciate your concern."

He turned to head for the door, but Max called after him. "And another thing."

Oh, great. What other mortal sins had he committed today? He reluctantly stopped. "Yes?"

"You're coming for dinner and a trim at our house tonight. I can't spend one more day looking at that scruff on your head."

Eric's eyes bulged. "*You're* going to cut my hair?"

"Don't be ridiculous. Ceci's worked at the salon for over fifteen years. She'll set you to rights."

Eric ran his fingers through his hair as he tried to come up with a response. It was much longer than he liked, and he did sort of have a Brad Pitt in *World War Z* vibe going on. But what would Ceci do to it? What if she cut it too short?

"Sorry, pal." Max clapped him on the shoulder. "She's already made up her mind."

thirty-one

Eric held his breath as Ceci waved a mirror in front of his face.

"What do you think?"

He'd never had a haircut in the great outdoors before. He squinted in the sun and peeked at his reflection with no small amount of dread.

Oh. Not quite the same style he was used to, but it looked good.

"I like it." He smiled. "Thank you."

A scrappy-looking goat tried to chew on his chair, and Ceci shooed it away. "No, thank *you*. Now I won't have to hear Max complain about it anymore."

She made a face as if Max were a nuisance, but he'd been watching how they were with each other. It was clear they were best friends. They were in love. Over dinner, he'd heard all about how their two kids had grown up and moved away, yet he saw no evidence they were depressed about being empty nesters. They were just happy to have each other.

He thought about Tiffani and tried to picture them together the way Max and Ceci were together—growing older, growing closer—and he couldn't. Eunice had wondered whether Eric had made a mistake, but he knew now he hadn't. At least not about letting Tiffani go.

He'd made other mistakes where Tiffani was concerned, though.

As Ceci removed the cape from his shoulders, he ran his fingers through his hair. "What do I owe you?"

"This one's on me." She held up her hand when he started to protest. "I insist. But feel free to make an appointment at the salon next time. We don't bite."

He stood and brushed off a couple clumps of hair that had bypassed the cape. "I'll keep that in mind."

The goat returned and gently rammed its head into Ceci's knees. She put her hand on its head. "Are you getting tired, Mellie?"

The goat gave a plaintive bleat, and Ceci laughed. "She wants me to let her in so she can lie down. Poor old thing."

"In?"

"In the house."

Eric tried to hide his surprise. The goat slept in the house?

"I know she stinks." Ceci rubbed the goat's ears. "That's why people call her Smellie Mellie. But I don't mind her sleeping in the laundry room."

Max returned from cleaning up dinner. "Dishes are done. Hey, you look like a brand-new man."

Eric touched his head. "You were right."

"Of course I was." Max patted his stomach. "Anyone up for ice cream?"

Mellie's ears perked up. Eric thought again of Tiffani. Her unexpected arrival had prevented him from having the ice cream binge he'd craved after his day of "fishing" with Dusty, but he was still stuffed from dinner.

He jerked his head toward where his Jeep waited out front. "I better not. I've got to get home."

Max smirked at him. "What for?"

"Don't hassle him, dear." Ceci gave Eric a hug. "You come back anytime."

"Thanks for dinner."

Max, Ceci, and Mellie walked him to the Jeep, where the couple waved as he drove away. Max's arm was around Ceci's shoulders, and the sight made Eric's heart twinge. Had his parents ever been that happy and at ease with each other? He'd thought so as a kid. When his dad packed his bags one day, it had been a complete shock. There had been no yelling or fighting. No long periods of silence. Just normal life and then a divorce.

It wasn't until later he'd learned the reason behind his father's disappearance.

As he drove home, he called Chase. It had been a while since he'd actually talked with his brother instead of texting.

Chase's voice was upbeat when he answered. "Hey, guess what? Only twenty-three days until you come back."

Eric laughed. "You're counting down the days?"

"Only because of Move-In Day."

"I see how it is," Eric teased. "You don't actually care about seeing me. You just want to make sure I'm around to help carry your stuff."

"Something like that."

"Figures. You're going to save all the heaviest boxes for me because you can't hack it with your puny little arms."

Chase huffed. "Shows how much you know. I've been working out with your old weight sets."

Eric raised his eyebrows. "That wouldn't happen to have anything to do with Darcy, would it?"

He'd learned the pink-haired girl's name was Darcy, she was a year older than Chase, and she was a cross-country runner. He didn't know much else about her except that Chase thought she was "pretty cool."

Chase hesitated. "Maybe."

Eric was pleased his brother was taking an interest in fitness—he'd never been successful at convincing Chase to exercise with him—but something about his tone of voice gave Eric pause.

"You trying to impress her?"

"I want to look good for college."

"If she really likes you, she won't care how big your arms are."

"Easy for you to say." Chase's voice morphed from upbeat to defensive. "Girls always drool over you."

It was true Eric rarely had trouble getting a girl's attention, but this was different. Chase already had Darcy's attention. "You're already a great guy, just the way you are."

"Are you worried I might get stronger than you or something?"

"Of course not." Eric turned onto Prairie Dog Road. "I just don't want a girl to turn you into someone you're not."

"How do you know what I am or not? You don't know everything about me. You work out every day, why can't I?"

Whoa. Chase's voice was downright hostile now. What was going on? His brother never talked to him this way.

"I'm sorry, bro. I was just trying to help."

"Fine. Whatever. Can we talk about something else?"

Eric parked the Jeep in his driveway and leaned his head back against the seat. "Okay, how's Mom?"

Chase groaned. "Something besides that."

"All right, maybe you pick the topic then."

"Look, I should probably go. I'm meeting Darcy and some of her friends at the beach."

"Oh. Okay, I guess I'll talk to you later."

"Okay."

Chase hung up, and Eric opened his door. What had all that been about? Maybe Chase was wound up because Darcy was the first girl he'd ever dated. It was a good thing Chase was starting to care more about his appearance, right?

"Girls always drool over you." Chase wasn't the kind of guy who wanted girls drooling over him, though, was he? *"You don't know everything about me."*

No, apparently he did not.

He was happy to see Cinderella on the porch as he walked up the driveway. "Hey, crazy lady."

"Are you talking to me or the chicken?"

Eric winced and looked over at Eunice, standing in her yard. "The chicken?"

Eunice stared at him. "You got your hair cut."

He touched his head. "Ceci did it."

"She's nice."

"Yeah."

Eunice kicked at the purple bowling ball at her feet. "I'm trying to find the right place to put this."

It was the new one Dusty had given her. How had she carried it up here from the backyard with those stick arms? He thought of how he'd called Chase's arms *puny* and cringed.

"You need me to move it somewhere?"

She studied the ball, sitting there in the middle of the yard. "Actually, I think I like it right where it is."

"Okay."

"How's Dusty doing?"

He chuckled. "He's still mad about having his fishing day cut short, but otherwise he's fine. He likes to show off the fang marks in his leg to everyone who comes into the store."

The ghost of a smile passed over her face. "I used to work there, you know."

"He told me."

"You wouldn't believe some of the crazy stuff people would drop off. But he and Nate always found a way to turn it into treasure. I wish I could see inside one more time. I have so many fond memories."

"I'll take you."

She took a long moment to answer. "I don't want him to see me like this."

Eric didn't know what to say. Dusty had already seen her the other day. She wore those awful purple Crocs and the long

236

sleeves and long pants he'd become accustomed to seeing her in. Her hair was . . .

"Hey. You got a haircut, too."

She wrapped her arms around herself. "Wanda did it."

"Wanda?"

"One of my home nurses."

He nodded. The nurse had cut Eunice's long, thin hair to just past her chin.

"It looks nice."

She blinked.

"Well, I better get inside." He gestured toward his house. "Let me know when you're ready to conquer the next name on your list."

She didn't answer. He turned and went inside. It no longer bothered him when she acted like that, although it did make him wonder. What had she been like when she was his age?

He checked the temperature and groaned. Still eighty-two degrees at eight-thirty. Maybe he'd put his evening run off a little longer and hope it dropped into the seventies. He plopped onto the couch and pulled out his phone, mindlessly scrolling through social media as he thought back to the image of Max and Ceci standing on the side of the road, smiling and waving. How could his dad have given that up for another woman, then another, then another? And now he had no one.

A picture popped up on his screen, and he stopped scrolling. It was Greg on his boat, cuddled up with a smiling brunette in a gleaming white bikini. They were raising glasses of wine toward the camera, and the caption read *Sweeties and sunsets*, with a whole row of lip and heart emojis. Ugh.

Thoughts of Tiffani returned. She'd been spending a lot of time with Greg earlier in the summer from what he could tell. She'd mentioned him more than he liked when they would text or talk on the phone. Who was Greg's new girl? Did Tiffani know about her?

He drew in a sharp intake of breath as it all became clear. Of course she did. That was the real reason she'd come. She'd been burned and had run to him looking for a rebound. Expecting him to do whatever she wanted without question, like he always had before. No wonder she'd balked at his talk of getting serious. All she'd wanted was to reassure herself she could still count on Eric for a diversion and get her mind off Greg.

A spark of indignation flared up in his chest, but it sputtered out as quickly as it came. Yes, maybe she'd been using him to make herself feel better after being rejected. Yes, maybe she'd been thinking only of herself when she came here. But he . . .

Eric shook his head, the truth as clear as a Montana morning. He'd done it, too. He'd been using Tiffani for years.

thirty-two

Eunice stared at the empty wall. The faint outline of the large painting that used to hang there made her wonder how faint of an outline she would leave behind when she was gone. How closely would people have to look to be able to tell she'd been there?

Dr. Mullins's words from her appointment earlier in the day echoed in her mind. *"Your numbers aren't looking good,"* he'd said. *"I'd like to bump your home nurse visits to twice a week."*

The last thing she needed was Bertie and Wanda telling her how pathetic she was twice as many times. Her headache intensified. Another month of her life was gone.

She shifted her eyes to the list hanging on the fridge. Five names crossed off, two to go. Three, to be precise, since number six was actually a pair of names. She tapped a single finger against the counter as she stared at the yellow piece of paper. The closer she got to the end of her list, the more two sentiments warred within her.

One was a feeling of peace and satisfaction at the reconciliation she had found. The forgiveness she'd been given. Even though Marlene hadn't remembered her transgression, Dick had refused her, and Diane needed more time, there had still been one more burden lifted from her shoulders with every name she drew a line through with her pen.

The other was a growing feeling of trepidation, as if the

239

names ticked off her list were like the sands of time ticking down. She needed to complete her task before she died, but at the same time, completing her task made her death seem nearer. She was tempted to put it off. As if she could prolong her life by avoiding it.

With a grumble, she trudged across the kitchen floor and moved the piece of paper from the front of the fridge to the side, where it competed with an array of stoma-related brochures and pamphlets and scraps of paper she'd written numbers on. It was less intimidating there. Less inevitable. Then before she could talk herself out of it, she tapped her phone to wake it up. Her fingers moved sluggishly as she brought up Eric's number and texted him a message.

> Are you busy Saturday?

It was late on a Wednesday night. He would've returned from his evening run by now. She'd seen him run past her living room window every night at the same time for the past two weeks. After a minute, he responded.

> No. Do you need a ride?

Tears stung the corners of her eyes.

"Oh, Lo-ord." Her voice was ragged and ricocheted through the empty house. "I'm thankful you brought Eric along to help me. I really am. But I don't want him to see . . ."

He'd already seen too much. Her desperation. Her humiliation. Her decline. Better him perhaps than anyone she'd known and cared about her whole life. Still, it left her feeling exposed to think of his bearing witness to the next task she needed to accomplish. She'd rather have her stoma on display for the whole world to see.

She typed a response.

Maybe.

It was the best she could do. The biggest commitment she could make in her current state.

I think you should do it. You don't want to keep putting it off.

Ha. As if she didn't know that.

thirty-three

ric rubbed his chin in frustration. This was not what he wanted to be doing with his Saturday. "I called to talk about Benson and the branch, not my dad."

"I know," Uncle Jack said. "All I'm asking is that you think about it."

Think about it? *Think about it?* All he'd been able to do for the past two weeks was think about it. Meanwhile, his dad's texts remained unanswered and his relationship with Uncle Jack became more and more strained.

He slumped in his deck chair. "How do I know you aren't putting him up to the whole thing?"

The time it took Uncle Jack to answer was revealing. "I encouraged him to reach out, yes. Because I care. But I'm not putting him up—"

"I knew it."

"He needed a little push, is all."

It figured. His dad had to practically be forced to communicate with him.

"Look, I promised Benson I would discuss his education with you. That's the only reason I called."

Uncle Jack sighed. "I already gave Benson a chance to come on as an associate. He wasn't interested."

"He was a teenager then. You can hardly expect an eighteen-year-old to know what he wants to do with his life."

"He's only twenty now. What's changed?"

"I think he's starting to realize there's more to the world than Tukston. I knew what I wanted to do when I was twenty. So did you. You've told me a hundred times about how no one took you seriously when you said you were going to own your own finance company one day."

"And do you remember the only person who believed in me?"

"Yes." Eric gritted his teeth. He shouldn't have brought that up. "My dad."

Uncle Jack let the words hang there for a minute. "Okay. I think Benson's a great kid. You can tell him I would be happy to have Larson Financial sponsor his continued education if he'll commit to five years at the branch."

"Okay." Eric let out the breath he'd been holding. "Thanks. I'll tell him."

"Now, hold on. I have one stipulation. If he's going to do it, he needs to go to school full time. No sense in dragging his degree out for years by taking a few classes here and a few classes there like he's been doing."

Eric scrunched up his nose. "But then he wouldn't be able to put much time in at the office. Max would be practically alone over there."

Uncle Jack's silence spoke volumes.

"No." Eric jammed his fingers through his freshly shorn hair. "It's August already. I'm only planning to be here two and a half more weeks."

"We can't leave Max hanging."

"Which is why you were supposed to find him another associate. How can there not be a single qualified candidate in the state of Montana?"

"It's not just about qualifications, Eric. I want to find someone who's the right fit."

"Well, it's not me." Eric's raised voice caused Cinderella to stop chasing grasshoppers and look over at him.

"Last time I checked, it was still my company. Not yours."

Eric bit his tongue. He was walking on thin ice here. Uncle Jack was still his boss.

He worked to get his voice under control. "You said you'd bring me back."

"And I will. But I need to do what's best for the company."

"What about what's best for me?"

"I'm not sure you know what that is, my boy."

Eric's jaw clenched. "I'm not sure *you* do. And don't call me that."

Uncle Jack chomped his gum into the phone for a few seconds. "We'll talk again soon, okay?"

Eric hung up the phone with a painful jab of his finger. He hated being at odds with Uncle Jack. He hated the thought of his uncle having to beg his father to contact him. He hated having so little control over his life. But he was done playing whatever this game was with Uncle Jack. He would be home by the end of the month, no matter what his uncle said.

Cinderella strutted over to where he sat, bobbing her head. She'd been laying eggs on his porch again, but it didn't bother him anymore. He'd even fried one up, just to see, and found it to be richer and more delicious than a store-bought egg.

"What are you going to do when I'm gone?"

She studied him with one eye and made a low murmuring sound. Would the new renters run her off? Maybe he should try to find her another place to live before he left town. He could place an ad in the *Tukston Times*. "Friendly Polish chicken. Free to good home."

He stood and stretched, reaching both hands above his head and leaning side to side. Then he bent forward to touch his toes. It was about time for his evening run, but a large metal windmill in Eunice's yard caught his eye as the blades spun lazily in the summer breeze. What was she up to? She'd never gotten back to him about going out today.

Her plants had grown a lot since he first arrived, and they appeared a little unkempt as he stared over the fence. When he thought about it, he couldn't remember the last time he'd seen Eunice out there working. Was she okay? He hadn't heard from her since Wednesday night. Didn't she want to cross another name off her list? What was she waiting for?

He crossed the yard and hopped the fence onto her property. Wait a minute. What if she was . . . ? He shuddered, imagining poking around her house and discovering her lifeless body. He'd never seen a dead person before. How would he know? Would he have to touch her?

Morbid? Yes. Possible? Also yes.

He opted to remain in the yard and tried to focus his thoughts on getting to work. It was hot, as usual, though the breeze blew over his sweaty skin and cooled him just enough. He busied himself pulling weeds and trimming around all the raised beds with a Weedwacker he found leaning against the corner of the house.

While the work kept his hands occupied, his thoughts kept returning to Eunice. First, he had the ridiculous thought that surely she would've called him if she was about to die. Then he had the even more ridiculous thought that if he were the one to find her body, he would be blamed for her death.

Finally, he reached the point where he couldn't take it anymore. He had to find out if she was okay. He spun toward the house to march to the back door with determined steps but then came to an abrupt stop.

She was standing at the sliding glass door, watching him. Arms wrapped around her stomach. Her pee bag hung just below her shirt, and he hated that he didn't know a better name to call it than a pee bag. Her face was pinched as if she was in pain, and he hated that he didn't know of a way to make her feel better.

She raised one hand in a small wave. He resumed his march to the house and slid open the door.

"Hey."

She took a step back and peeked around his shoulder at the yard. "You don't have to do that."

"I don't mind."

"Thank you."

"Do you have any plans for next Saturday?"

She snorted, and he mentally kicked himself. Of course she didn't.

What would it be like to know every Saturday could be your last?

He tried again. "Are you up for an outing?"

Her shoulders slumped. "I don't know . . ."

"We don't have to do a name if you don't want to. We could do something else."

She tugged her shirt down. "Maybe."

"Tomorrow morning I'll mow back here."

"You don't—"

"Have to do that. I know." He pulled out his dimples but not to impress her. Just to let her know he was sincere. "I want to."

She nodded slowly. She seemed so fragile.

He said good-night and put the Weedwacker away. When he hopped back over the fence and looked back, she was gone from the doorway. He walked to his house, thinking back through all the interactions with women he'd had over the past twenty years, since the time his dad told him "You can do better." Had he ever spent as much time talking with a woman he wasn't attracted to as he had spent talking with Eunice this summer?

No. He hadn't. He'd always found any excuse to disqualify a woman from being good enough for him, whether it was her clothes or her hair or the way she laughed. Tiffani had been easy to be around. She was so outwardly perfect and seemed to want the same things he did. She was good for his ego and his image. Yet he was realizing he probably knew more about

Eunice, whom he'd known for two months, than Tiffani, whom he'd known for over four years. Tiffani had been all for show.

He pulled off his sweaty T-shirt, tossed it into the hamper, and studied his abs in the mirror. Maybe he was all for show, too.

Maybe he was just like his father after all.

thirty-four

Eunice looked at the list in her hand. How had another week gone by already? She'd only agreed to go out with Eric today because he was leaving soon. And because Wanda—who now came every Tuesday, while Bertie came every Friday, thanks to Dr. Mullins's decree—had not so subtly reminded her of how few chances she had left to see all the beautiful things around Tukston one last time. But she hadn't decided whether she had the strength to cross a name off her list today or not.

She stuck the crumpled piece of paper in her pocket, slung her survostobag over her shoulder, and opened the door. She would wait and see how she felt after driving around for a while.

Eric was wiping the wheels of his Jeep with a rag when she walked over to his driveway.

"Hey."

He stood and gave her a lopsided smile. "Good morning. Are you ready for an adventure?"

She grimaced. "Do I look like I'm ready for an adventure?"

His smile never faltered. "You look like you could use one."

She remembered resenting those endearing dimples and infuriatingly enchanting blue eyes at first, afraid he would use them against her. Afraid she might be tempted to actually like him if she gazed too long into those cerulean depths. Now she just appreciated that he was around.

"I think your debt to me has been paid," she said. "You don't owe me anything. I'll take your secret to the grave."

"Said the dying woman gravely."

Her lips quirked. "I'm the only one allowed to joke about my impending death."

He made a mockingly serious face. "Who's joking?"

She put her hands on her hips and jerked her chin at the Jeep. "Well, are you ready to go or not?"

"Would I be out here if I wasn't?" He laughed and opened the passenger door. "Your chariot awaits."

She rolled her eyes as she climbed in, but it felt good to have an inside joke with someone other than JoJo. Eric walked around to get in the driver's side. He was wearing green golf shorts dotted with tiny pink flamingos and a pink polo shirt. Any other man would've looked like he was trying to be something he was not. But Eric just looked like Eric. She felt suddenly protective of him, indignant that the rest of the world only noticed his looks and charm and didn't bother to notice the man underneath.

She sure hadn't.

As he backed out of the driveway, a teeny, tiny spark of anticipation fluttered in her chest. "Where are we going?"

"Well." He lowered his window and rested a tanned and muscular left arm on the frame. "Since you don't have your own bucket list of things you want to do before, uh—"

"Before I die."

"Right. Since you don't have your own, I made a list of things *I* want to do before I leave Tukston."

"What *you* want to do? Why do you need to drag me along, then?"

Oh, super. There they were. The dimples.

"If you have any of your own ideas, I'd be happy to amend our plans."

She didn't. And he knew she didn't. "As long as we're not gone too long."

He winked. "Home before lunch."

The Jeep quickly worked its way through town and headed north, but before Eunice could get nervous about how far away they were going to get, Eric turned off the road and parked near the wooden *Welcome to Tukston* sign. He turned off the Jeep and hopped out.

She frowned. "Um . . ."

He waved an arm. "Come on."

With a sigh, she slowly climbed out. What was so interesting about a sign? Eric walked past the sign toward the five giant wheels sitting behind it. Ah. The rope drive compressor wheels. She'd grown up in Tukston, and the wheels had always been there. She hardly noticed them anymore.

Eric stopped at a historical marker in front of the wheels. "Aren't these cool?"

She lifted one shoulder. "They're wheels."

He raised one eyebrow. "They're not just wheels." He turned to the marker and read the first couple of lines. "They're twenty-two-foot-tall wheels from 1903 that were used to make compressed air to power mining machinery. I've never seen any-thing like this."

His enthusiasm was contagious. She took a step closer. "Read the rest of the marker."

He was silent for a minute as he read. She could tell which part of the marker he was reading by the look on his face. She knew all about how each wheel had twenty-two grooves that ran about half a mile of rope between it and an electric motor, but watching him learn about it for the first time made it feel new.

"Wow." He took a step back from the marker. "Amazing. Twenty tons *each*? How did they ever move them here from Butte Hill?"

She shrugged. "I wish I could've seen it."

"Here." He held his phone out to her. "I want a picture of me standing next to one."

She grimaced at the phone, not reaching for it. It looked confusing. And expensive.

He picked up her hand and set the phone in it. "Please?"

"Fine. Show me how."

She had a smartphone, but it was an older model, and she never used the camera. What would she take pictures of? And for who?

In a flash, Eric readied the camera app and pointed to the circle at the bottom. "Just hit that button when you're ready."

"Okay."

He hurried to the first wheel and leaned against the rusty rim. In his colorful clothes with the deep blue sky behind, she had to admit it was a striking picture. He smiled, and she pushed the button several times, hoping her hand was steady enough to keep the photos from blurring.

He walked back to her. "Thanks." He held out his hand for the phone. "Now it's your turn."

Her eyes widened. "I don't think—"

"Do you already have a picture of yourself beside the wheel?"

"No."

"Then you're doing it."

He gave her a gentle push. Some nerve this guy had. Pushing around an old lady. Because boy did she feel old today.

She was glad for her long pants as she approached the wheels. Scratchy, dry weeds grew everywhere, and grasshoppers zinged out of the grass like six-legged fireworks as she waded through them. She remembered Dusty's encounter with a rattler and slowed down, taking a little more care where she placed her feet.

"Do you need any help?" Eric called.

The wheel towered over her, casting an eerie but captivating shadow. How could she have lived near these things for forty-six years and never been this close? Eric was right. They were cool.

"I'll just stand in front," she called back.

The steel was warm to the touch as she turned toward Eric and leaned her back against it. A barren breeze blew strands of hair across her face, and she brushed them away and tried to smile. As Eric held his phone up to take a picture, a memory from years ago popped into her mind. A memory she hadn't thought of in a long time.

Her parents had taken her up to Hyalite Lake. She was about ten. The scenery was breathtaking. She was sunburned and dirty and having the time of her life when her dad decided he wanted a picture of her and her mom together, with the mountains in the background. Back then they used real cameras, not phones.

He directed them where to stand and looked into the camera, trying to frame the scene the way he wanted. *"Move a little to the left,"* he'd said. *"Now your faces are in the shadow— take two steps back."* She and her mom had dutifully obeyed, only to find the rocks behind them were much slicker than expected. Eunice had slipped and reached out frantically for her mother, only to find she had slipped at the same time. They both ended up with their rear ends in the water, laughing until they cried.

Eric said something, and Eunice snapped back to the present. "What?"

He put his phone back in his pocket. "I said that was a good one."

She grunted and followed Eric back to the Jeep. She didn't think any picture with her in it could be a good one, but when she tried to think of any recent photos she had of herself, she couldn't. Should this stage of her life be documented like all the others? Who would ever see that picture?

Back in the Jeep, Eric gave her a concerned look. "You okay?"

"Yeah."

"All right, then on to our next stop."

Part of her wanted to ask how many stops he was planning

to make, but another part didn't want to know. He drove back into town and parked in front of Hoagies and Grinders. She kept her thoughts to herself, but inside she grumbled. The last thing she wanted was a sandwich. And Eric had been here before. Why was it on his so-called bucket list?

As if reading her mind, or maybe just her face, he turned off the Jeep and chuckled. "You'll see."

The light was dim inside the shop, but even before her eyes adjusted Eunice could see the girl behind the counter noticeably brighten as Eric walked in. Was this girl the reason Eric wanted to come here? Which family did she belong to? Eunice didn't know any of the young people anymore.

Eric led Eunice to a small booth and slid onto the bench across from her. He rested his crossed forearms on the table and leaned forward with the same eager puppy look she'd found maddeningly adorable since the beginning. "Have you ever heard of the Huckleberry Meltdown?"

She set her survostobag next to her and narrowed her eyes. "Yeees . . ."

He hopped back out of the seat as if he couldn't contain his excitement. "We're going to eat one."

She gulped. "We?"

"Okay, mostly me." He grinned. "But you have to at least try a bite."

The Huckleberry Meltdown? Was he crazy? Before she could form a response, he swaggered over to the counter. Eunice was afraid the girl behind the counter was going to lunge over it and tackle Eric to the ground, the way she looked at him. She fluttered her eyelashes so hard, Eunice wondered if she had a condition.

Eric flashed his dimples. "Hi, Jessica."

Of course he knew her name.

"Hi," Jessica chirped. "It's so sweet of you to take your mom out on a date."

What? Eunice gasped. His *mom*? Of all the pea-brained, nonsensical things to—

"It's my duty as a son." He glanced over his shoulder at her and winked.

Eunice fumed. Fine. If he wanted her to play his mom, she would act the part and boss him around.

Jessica tucked her hair behind her ear. "I didn't expect to see you two days in a row."

"We're here to try that Huckleberry Meltdown you told me about."

Oh, so this was all Jessica's fault. Figured.

Jessica smiled. "Coming right up."

Eric helped himself to two glasses of water from a pitcher and returned to the table.

Eunice gave him her most withering look. "You're a lousy son if you don't even ask your mother what *she* wants to eat."

He smacked the table and laughed, loud and completely uninhibited.

"You're right." He wiped his eyes. "You can pick next time."

Next time. He'd be gone in less than two weeks, and she was dying. There wouldn't be a next time.

She pointed at his shirt. "Aren't you worried about what the Huckleberry Meltdown might do to the dozens of abs you have hiding under there?"

He waved a hand in the air. "There are only six."

"What, do you count them?"

He gave her a sheepish grin.

"Oh my word, you do."

"Maybe I check them once in a while. Just to make sure they're all still there."

"You're unbelievable."

He leaned back with a shrug, and Eunice felt her insides loosening a little. Eric was fun to be around. Irritating, but fun. Sometimes he reminded her of . . .

No. She didn't want to think about him.

Jessica appeared at the table, holding what would more accurately be described as a platter than a plate. She set it down, along with two spoons, and gave Eric an admiring look. "Here you go. And remember, if you finish it, it's on the house."

Eric nodded. "Thank you."

He picked up a spoon and held it out to Eunice as Jessica walked away. "Do you want to go first?"

She stared at the giant mound of fudge brownie, huckleberry ice cream, chocolate syrup, and whipped cream, sitting in a puddle of huckleberry sauce and topped with white chocolate shavings. It was the size of a toaster and made her teeth hurt just looking at it. But it also looked really, *really* delicious.

She took the spoon from Eric's hand and scooped a small, tentative bite. It was soft and gooey and smelled like satisfaction when she held it in front of her face.

She hesitated, and Eric cocked his head. "Come on, *Mom*. It's not like you have anything to lose."

The nerve. She glared at him and put the spoon in her mouth. "Mmm."

Eric smiled. "Good?"

"Mm-hmm."

He picked up the other spoon and took a big bite. His eyes twinkled as he chewed. "Jessica was right. This is amazing."

First the compression wheels were "amazing," now this dessert. Eric was far too easily impressed.

Eunice smirked as she took another tiny taste. "Has anyone ever finished one of these?"

Eric swallowed his bite. "Jessica said it happens once in a while. It's only supposed to count if a single person eats the whole thing by themself, but she said she'd let it slide if you help me a little."

The corner of Eunice's mouth twitched. "I'm sure she did.

This wouldn't have anything to do with needing to prove yourself after the Cowboy Deluxe incident, would it?"

His eyes bulged. "How'd you hear about that?"

She shrugged nonchalantly. "Sometimes Dusty fills me in on local news when he emails me pictures of the items he wants me to research and post."

"How did *he* hear about it?"

She pointed her spoon at him. "You know Dee from Good Food?"

"The waitress? Yeah."

Eunice took a long sip of water, making him wait. "She's his sister."

"Of course she is." Eric palmed his forehead. "Well, I don't know what it is with this town and outlandish food items, but this has nothing to do with the Cowboy Deluxe."

"Sure." She scooped another bite off the platter. "Keep telling yourself that."

He laughed again, and she chuckled, too. As she chewed, her hand found its way into her pocket and took hold of the piece of paper, now soft from wear and frayed around the edges. She was actually enjoying herself this morning like a normal, non-terminal person. Did she really want to bring up her list?

Eric made a decent dent on his side of the platter before slowing down. Looked like they would not be getting this dessert for free.

"You're not going to go into a sugar coma, are you?" she asked.

He took a gulp of water. "I can't make any promises."

"How many more stops were you planning?"

"Just one more." He set his spoon down. "Is that okay? How are you feeling?"

It was almost jarring how quickly he could go from teasing and charming to serious and concerned.

"I'm fine. I was just wondering . . ."

"Did you have something else in mind? My idea can wait."

She used her spoon to swirl the melting ice cream in the huckleberry sauce, forming a pretty purple design. "Yes. I think it's time."

thirty-five

$\mathcal{E}$ric's stomach felt as if he'd swallowed one of Eunice's bowling balls as he climbed into the Jeep and backed onto the road. Though he had come close to finishing off the Huckleberry Meltdown, in the end he'd decided it wasn't worth it. Jessica had tried to give him credit for his valiant effort, but he'd insisted on paying.

He glanced at Eunice. "Which way?"

"Left."

The lighthearted, sarcastic tone she'd had in the diner was gone, replaced by something much heavier. He followed her instructions and drove toward the far southwest corner of town, a residential area he hadn't explored yet. They passed house after house without any indication from Eunice they'd arrived at the right place. Finally they reached the edge of town. There were no houses left.

"You can park along the fence," she said.

A long row of chain-link fence corralled a stand of old juniper trees and stretched west for a hundred yards. He parked and turned off the Jeep, waiting for Eunice to make the first move.

She looked out the window. "Do you know where the name Tukston comes from?"

He shook his head. "No."

"From the Nez Perce word for sunshine."

That made sense. Aside from the occasional late-afternoon

258

thunderstorm, he'd seen more sun this summer than the past two years in Seattle.

"My dad taught me that."

He didn't know what she was getting at, but he didn't want to push. After a minute, she opened her door. "Will you come with me?"

She'd never asked that before. He got out of the Jeep and hurried over to Eunice's side in case she needed help. From there, he noticed the sign hanging from the fence a ways down. *Tukston Memorial Cemetery: Rest in the Sun.*

Oh.

Eunice walked slowly to a small gate, and Eric reached around her to open it. The metal was warm to the touch. They passed through and reached the other side of the trees, where a large plot of land dotted with headstones lay, fenced in on all sides and yet appearing boundless.

He hung back a little, wanting to give her space. She wound her way through the collection of stones until she reached a four-sided monolith about two feet tall and made of white marble. It was pointed at the top and had simple decorative touches on each corner.

He strained to read the inscription. *Dan and Lisa Parker. Died August 13, 2002.*

"That's today." His words spread out across the cemetery and disappeared, absorbed by dried-up flower bouquets and long-forgotten memories.

"My parents," she said.

He spied a cement bench off to the side and turned in that direction. "I'll be over here. Take your time."

The cement was still cool, having been shaded by the trees until only moments ago. He sat and let the quiet peacefulness settle over him. He'd only been in a cemetery a couple of times before. Once when his grandpa died, and once when a good friend of his mother's was killed in a car accident. Those memories were vague. But he had a feeling he wouldn't forget this cemetery visit for a long time.

Birds sang, and somewhere in the distance a tractor droned. He watched Eunice as she shifted back and forth on her feet, saying something to the stone. He couldn't make out her words. Why were her parents' names on her list? How could you reconcile with someone who was already dead? Wasn't it too late?

His mind began to wander, and he thought about his dad. What if he got sick? What if he died? What had Eric left unsaid? So many things.

The slew of emotions about his father that he'd been wrestling with since his arrival in Tukston rose up with renewed force. Now that he'd realized how much he'd grown to be like his dad, could he still hate him for who he was? Eric resented how he'd abandoned Eric's mother for a younger woman, but hadn't Eric spent the last twenty years scrutinizing every girl he met based on her appearance? His dad would say those girls hadn't been good enough for him, but maybe he wasn't good enough for them. Hadn't they all been beautiful?

Out of the corner of his eye, he saw Eunice sink slowly to the ground. The sun shone on her head, glinting off streaks of silver. She was beautiful, too, in her own way. How had he never seen it?

He had slumped on the bench and almost nodded off by the time Eunice walked over to say she was ready to go. He stood and followed her back to the gate, closing it behind them after they'd passed through.

He started the engine but left the Jeep in park. They sat in silence for what felt like ten minutes but was probably only two.

Finally, he got up the courage to ask, "What did you do to them?"

"What?"

"Your parents."

"It's what I didn't do."

"Okay, what didn't you do?"

It suddenly felt very important that he know.

"I didn't appreciate them enough. I didn't give them the benefit of the doubt. I didn't take responsibility for my own decisions, because it was too easy to blame them, especially my mom. I was so angry at them."

Eric dropped his hands from the steering wheel. "Do you think they heard you?"

"I don't know."

"I haven't talked to my dad in a long time. He left us when I was twelve. My uncle says he's changed, but . . ."

Eunice turned knowing eyes on him. "But you're scared of being hurt again."

Eric swallowed. "Are *you* scared? Of . . . the end?"

She rubbed the edge of her shirt between two fingers. "Not of being dead necessarily. But of dying?"

He waited.

"Yes."

His eyes narrowed. "But the thought of being dead doesn't scare you?"

She didn't answer.

He could feel his chest tightening. Maybe it was the thoughtful solitude of the cemetery, or the harsh reality of names carved into stone, but he couldn't help but wonder.

"It doesn't bother you that you'll never hear another bird sing? Never feel the wind on your face or see the blue of the sky?"

"You're getting poetic on me."

He stared at the trees along the fence. His throat was tight now, too.

She let out a long breath. "I don't really know how I feel. This is all new to me. But I do know that where I'm going, the sky is bluer than we can imagine, Eric. We don't even know what blue is."

"You mean heaven?"

She nodded.

"How do you know?"

"Faith is the certainty of things hoped for and the proof of things we've not yet seen."

He looked over at her with a question in his eyes, and she gave him a half smile. "That's a paraphrase. From the Bible."

He looked away. How could anyone be certain of something they hadn't seen? He recalled his conversation with Winnie when she'd mentioned the Bible, too. *"Didn't your uncle ever teach you about faith?"* He didn't believe in that stuff like they did. But if it made them happy, if it allowed Eunice to face the end of her life with a little less fear, who was he to question it?

He backed the Jeep up and headed for home, instinctively knowing Eunice had had enough for today. No, he wouldn't question her faith. He was glad she'd found something to give her a little peace. She was the one dying, not him.

Then why did her words open a black pit in his heart that felt as though it wanted to swallow him whole?

Weariness enveloped her as Eric brought the Jeep to a stop in his driveway, yet Eunice felt light and happy. It wasn't any big deal—taking pictures with the compression wheels, being defeated by a dessert—but . . . well, yes, it was a big deal. To her, it was.

"Thank you," she said.

Eric's face was hard to read. "I'm leaving soon, but you still have one name left."

She picked up her survostobag from the floor and set it on her lap, needing something to do with her hands. She'd saved the hardest and most important name for last.

"I don't need your help with that one."

"We could do it tomorrow."

No. They couldn't.

"It's okay. I have a plan."

She shouldn't be telling lies this close to the pearly gates, but she didn't want to burden Eric any more than she already had.

"Are you sure?"

She nodded and opened her door. "Thanks again."

"I'll mow the backyard and get everything cleaned up and weeded one more time before I go."

"You don't have to do that."

"That's what you always say." He smiled. "It'll give me a chance to stop in and say goodbye."

Her heart squeezed. *Goodbye.* Such a merciless word.

"Okay." She waved and trudged toward her house.

How was it that he'd been a better friend to her than she'd been to people she'd known her whole life?

The air inside her house felt cool compared to the heat outside. She headed straight for the bathroom to empty her pouch, her mind drifting to other things as her hands went through the motions of draining the bag. She'd said some things at the cemetery that she'd never had the chance to say to her parents when they were alive. Was it always like that? Were there always things left unsaid?

It had given her a measure of peace to speak her piece—ha, see what she did there?—but the truth was it hadn't been her parents in that ground. Just bits of bone and dust.

"Oh, Lo-ord." She pulled her shirt back down and washed her hands. "Will I see them when I get there? Is there still a chance to tell them I'm sorry in person?"

Outside, her wind-chime collection began to sing as a gust of wind blew through the yard. The music was like words, as if God were answering her. Maybe in heaven you didn't talk the same as on earth. Maybe it was more like music.

She opened the window in the kitchen so she could hear the

chimes better, then crossed her parents' names off her list with the stub of a pencil she found on the counter. She had hope she'd see them again. Talk with them. That everything would be made right between them. Even though she couldn't see it yet, she had faith. But what if her faith was only as strong as her desire to have something to believe in?

She stuck the piece of paper to the side of the fridge. *"You still have one name left,"* Eric had said.

The name she could never forget. Would he speak to her? Did he think of her? She thought of him every day.

She lay down on the couch, ready for a nap but trying not to think too much about falling asleep and never waking up. Eternal slumber.

The wind chimes played their lilting song.

thirty-six

The next week and a half passed quickly as Eric spent as much time in the office as possible before he left Tukston in the dust. He wasn't going to leave Max hanging, as Uncle Jack had said. He was setting Max up for success. He couldn't see any reason why Max wasn't already senior advisor at this branch anyway. Why hadn't Uncle Jack given him the job?

Halfway through the morning three days before his departure, Winnie rang Eric's desk.

"There's someone here to see you." Her double voice rang out loud and clear.

Neither he nor Max was expecting their next client for thirty minutes, and he'd hoped to do some research so he could give Bob Crowley his best possible pitch if he stopped in again. Bob was his last hope for securing profit growth that might impress his uncle.

But Eric didn't want to keep anyone waiting. "Send them back."

"No, you're going to need to come out here."

His brow furrowed. Was someone harassing Winnie? She'd never called him up front before. He hung up the phone and hurried through the glass-paneled doors.

Nate was standing in the lobby with a wide smile on his face. He pointed at the wall, where a console table sat. The bench from the Kitchen Sink had been polished to a rich shine, and the ornate legs of what he guessed had been a chair had been skillfully attached to the bottom of the bench legs, giving it just the right amount of height.

"Oh." Eric looked back and forth between Nate and the table. "It's amazing."

"He can't read your lips if you don't look him in the face," Winnie scolded.

Heat spread from Eric's cheeks to the tips of his ears as he turned to Nate, held out his hand, and tried again. "It looks great. I'm impressed. Thank you."

Nate shook his hand and beamed. Then he waved at Winnie and headed out the door. Eric turned back to the table and studied it. He would've never guessed when he first saw the bench in the store that it could turn into something like this. And now he only had a couple of days left to enjoy it.

Winnie hopped down from her chair and came to stand beside him with her hands on her hips. "I suppose there's no getting rid of the Keurig now."

"Not a chance." He grinned. "I'll move everything to the new table on my lunch break."

She shuffled back to her desk, muttering just loud enough for him to hear, "Okay, but it's getting awfully cluttered in here."

He loved the look of the table. He only wished he would've given the green light for its creation sooner. Uncle Jack had been right, and Eric had a sinking feeling Winnie would make sure he knew it.

A quick glance at the wall clock revealed there was still time to get a little research done before his next client. He headed for his desk, then spun around to look when he heard a sound at the front door.

The FedEx guy held the door open with one foot while he tried to maneuver a dolly carrying two oversized boxes into the lobby. The boxes were so tall the man could barely see around them. Eric hurried over to help him.

"Thanks." The man grunted as he pushed the dolly over the threshold. "These suckers are huge."

Eric shut the door. "What have you got there?"

The man tipped the dolly to lean the boxes against the wall next to the new table. "Cool table." He pulled a handheld mobile scanner from a holster at his hip and read the screen. "Two sets of cubicle walls for Eric Larson."

Eric's mouth formed an o. Two? "But I only ordered one." And he'd given up on it ever making an appearance.

The man shrugged and pointed at the scanner. "Not according to this. Sign here, please."

Eric could feel Winnie's glare as he quickly signed the digital pad and thanked the delivery man. He reached up to loosen his tie but found he wasn't wearing one. He hadn't put one on in a couple of weeks and hadn't missed it like he thought he would. Except when he was nervous.

Winnie peered down at him from her throne. "What on God's green earth are you planning to do with two sets of cubicle walls?"

He was sure he'd canceled the first order before placing the second one. They'd even issued a refund. "Uh . . ."

"What's going on out here?" Max appeared from the back. "What are those?"

Winnie's expression was grim. "Eric decided we needed more walls."

Max scratched his head. "Where are we going to put more walls? It's already crowded in here."

They looked over at Eric expectantly.

He pulled out the biggest smile he could muster. "There's been a mistake. I only —"

"I'll say there has," Winnie huffed.

Eric coughed into his fist and looked at Max. "I only meant to order one set. Not two. To go between our desks."

Max blinked.

Eric shifted on his feet. "For privacy."

"You didn't think to talk to me about it first?"

Eric swallowed. "Uncle Jack told me to be on the lookout for any improvements that could be made."

"And you think sticking these ugly pieces of particle board between our desks would be an improvement?"

Eric threw up his hands. "I can hear everything you say."

"Only when I'm not being discreet."

"Shouldn't you always be discreet with a client's financial information?"

Max pressed his lips together for a moment. "And how much financial information have you overheard, exactly?"

Eric hesitated, thinking back over the last two and a half months. He'd often overheard Max talking with clients about their families, their pets, their jobs. But he couldn't remember a single time he'd actually heard anything specific about their finances.

His face heated. Max had heard plenty of confidential information come out of Eric's mouth, however.

"Do you know how long I've worked here, Eric?" Max asked.

Eric had read up on the office and its employees before he arrived. "Since 2000, when this branch opened."

"That's right. Twenty-two years now. And do you know what I did before that?"

"You were in rodeo. You told me."

"I quit rodeo in 1994."

"Oh. So you went to school?"

Max shook his head. "Rodeo had already taken care of my education. I got a full four-year scholarship. But when I didn't have rodeo anymore, I didn't know who I was. What to do. I hit a rough patch."

Winnie clucked her tongue. "You don't have to do this, Max."

He held up a hand. "More than a rough patch. I hit the

bottle. Hard. I went from one job to the next, never lasting more than six months before I got fired. I was on the verge of losing everything—my house, my wife, my kids—when your uncle sent word he wanted to open a branch out here and needed my help."

Max tucked his thumbs into the pockets of his jeans and leaned against Winnie's desk. "I didn't learn until later that he didn't need me at all. He could've gotten anyone. Or sent someone from out of town. But he'd heard I was in a bad way and chose me." Max gave Eric a pointed look. "This office saved my life."

Eric reached for his missing tie again, then folded his arms across his chest instead. If he'd known Max's history and how much Larson Financial meant to him, maybe he would've included him in his decision to purchase the cubicle walls. But none of this changed the fact he felt the setup in the office was unprofessional. Why was this turning into such a big deal?

"I—"

The door opened, and Max's next appointment walked in. Max greeted Jerry, then turned to Eric. "To be continued."

Eric watched Max and Jerry disappear into the back, surprised to find Jerry's rejection of him still stinging his pride even now. He'd been wrong about how to handle clients, wrong about the table, wrong about Tiffani. Maybe he'd been wrong about the walls, too.

What else had he been wrong about?

He shook his head. He couldn't dive too deep into that right now. His next client would be here any minute, as well.

Winnie gave an exaggerated clearing of her throat and gestured toward the two huge boxes. "You're not going to leave those there, are you?"

Eric muttered to himself as he hurried down the sidewalk to Hoagies and Grinders on his break. His last client before lunch had been Brenda Wallace. Again. He was beginning to think she made appointments just to flirt with him and bring up her dog walker rather than for any actual financial concerns.

A BLT sandwich on whole wheat and a hazelnut latte with almond milk from the little shop had become his Friday tradition. Jessica always had his sandwich and coffee ready for him when he arrived and would smile at him and throw in an extra bag of chips. And he always gave her a big tip. He still thought she was cute. But she was still too young.

He greeted Jessica and paid for his meal. Sometimes he ate at a table inside, but today the weather was perfect so he headed for the door to take his food outside. There were three little black bistro tables on the sidewalk, each with two chairs.

When he opened the door, his napkin flew from his hand, and he ran after it. There was nothing he hated more than litter. He'd read that nine billion tons of litter ended up in the ocean every year. The napkin flitted down the sidewalk toward a man in cowboy boots, who spotted it and pinned it with his foot. He bent down to retrieve it and held it out to Eric.

"Thanks." Eric took the napkin and tensed. He knew this guy.

Dick Samson.

"Not sure I've ever seen a man in a suit chasing a napkin before."

Eric's dress slacks and button-down shirt hardly qualified as a suit, especially without a tie, but he decided not to point that out.

He forced a smile. "These BLT sandwiches can get pretty messy."

Dick grunted, unimpressed, and made a move to push past Eric and keep walking, but Eric held up a hand. "Wait."

Dick stopped and raised his eyebrows.

270

"I need to talk to you." Eric tucked the napkin in his pocket and set his food on one of the tables. "Got a minute?"

Dick looked him up and down with a hard expression. "I got nothing to say to you."

"It's about Benson."

Dick's face softened slightly. "He says you're an okay guy, even though you're friends with Eunice."

"He's a great kid." Eric pulled out one of the chairs. "Please, just five minutes."

Dick grunted again but acquiesced. Eric joined him at the table and quickly sorted his thoughts. He'd spoken with Benson last week about Uncle Jack's decision. Told him about his uncle's stipulation regarding full-time classes. Benson had seemed relieved and excited at first, but the more they talked, the more reluctant and nervous he had become.

Benson had said he wasn't sure if he was ready to make the commitment. He still hadn't given Eric an answer. Eric feared Benson was going to repeat the same mistake he'd made the first time Uncle Jack made the offer, and Eric had a feeling he knew what—or more specifically *who*—was holding Benson back.

"Your son is a really smart guy," he began. "Has a ton of potential."

Dick glared at him. "You think I don't know that?"

Eric was not easily intimidated, yet something about Dick Samson set him on edge. He put on his financial advisor face, friendly and sincere but also firm and confident. "Of course you do. I'm sure you also know that solid career opportunities don't come along every day around here."

Dick didn't respond, although he appeared to be listening.

"It would be a shame if Benson passed up another chance to have his degree paid for and get fast-tracked into a career he is clearly suited for."

Dick's eyes were full of fire. "What are you saying?"

Eric leaned back, trying to appear casual. "I'm just saying

that Jack probably won't offer this opportunity again. You need to think about Benson's future."

Dick abruptly pushed back his chair and stood.

"Just think about it," Eric said. "If it would help to have more information about the job, I'd be happy to answer . . ."

His words faded away as Dick stormed off.

That went well.

When he returned to the office, he was still thinking over his encounter with Dick. Maybe he shouldn't have said anything, but securing a degree and five-year commitment for the branch from Benson was the perfect plan. He'd reassured Uncle Jack of that very thing yesterday when he'd told him he was returning to Seattle at the end of the week whether his uncle liked it or not.

Eric wasn't about to let Dick Samson stand in the way.

He had about fifteen minutes to transfer everything onto the new table as Winnie had reminded him he'd promised to do. He set to work with his head down right away, hoping to avoid another conversation about the cubicle walls, but Winnie had finished her customary canned fruit and cottage cheese lunch, and her gaze bored into his back like the horns of a bull.

"Did you have a nice lunch?" she asked.

He carefully lifted the Keurig off the old table. "Yes."

"Why'd you look like you lost your favorite tie when you came back, then?"

He made a face as he finished moving the rest of the items to the new table. "I ran into Benson's dad, and we had a little chat."

"About Benson?"

"Yeah." He stepped back to look at the new table. It was the perfect size. "Where do you want me to put the old table?"

When Winnie didn't respond, he turned to look at her. "Should we send it to the Kitchen Sink?"

"What exactly did you say to Dick?"

His forehead wrinkled. Why did her voice sound like that? "I told him it would be a shame if Benson passes up Uncle Jack's offer a second time. Opportunities like this don't come along every day in a place like Tukston. That's all."

Winnie knew all about the decision Benson needed to make. She'd been the one going on and on about giving Benson a push. Why did she look like he'd told her Spark Plug ran away?

"Oh." She frowned. "Oh dear."

"What?"

She rubbed her temples and shook her head. "You just kicked the hornet's nest, hon."

thirty-seven

£ric pulled up to the office forty minutes early on Thursday, his last day of work, and stared at the building. He hadn't spoken with Uncle Jack since the other day when he'd told him about his decision to return to Seattle, but their conversation still rumbled through his brain. *"I'd like you to reconsider,"* Uncle Jack had said, the displeasure clear in his voice. *"I'm not sure you're ready for the tenth floor."*

They had a meeting scheduled for Monday morning, and Eric had a feeling it was going to be more of a painful lecture than a debriefing. But Eric had done all the considering he planned to do. He needed to get back to his life. If Uncle Jack couldn't understand that, Eric might have some hard decisions to make in the near future.

Surely it wouldn't come to that.

He pushed through the front door, and Winnie was there, drinking a cup of Valu Brew.

"We're going to miss you." She pushed her glasses up her nose. "And you never got to meet my granddaughter."

He winked. "She's better off without me."

Winnie laughed. "You might be right about that."

He picked his way around the two huge boxes sitting in the corner of the office to get to his desk. He probably shouldn't leave those here for his replacement to deal with—if a replacement ever came. Max had made it clear he didn't want the walls set up anywhere in the room, though Eric held on to a small shred of hope that a new guy would come in and talk Max into it.

Max sauntered into the office a few minutes before eight, carrying a large ziplock plastic bag filled with homemade cookies. He tossed it onto Eric's desk.

"These are from Ceci. She doesn't want you to go hungry on your drive home."

Eric eyed the bag with appreciation. "Tell her thanks for me."

"Will do. And, Eric . . ." Max scratched the back of his head. "We should have a talk before you go. I don't want to leave anything between us."

Their relationship had been cordial and professional but strained since the cubicle walls had arrived. Eric nodded. "Sounds good."

Eric's first client was right on time, and Eric gave him his full attention—letting him talk for as long as he needed to—so he didn't notice until the man left that Benson hadn't arrived. He picked up his desk phone to ring Winnie. "Any word from Benson?"

"Not yet," she shouted.

"It's not like him to be late."

Come to think of it, Benson hadn't been himself yesterday. He'd been jumpy and distracted and had bolted out of the office as soon as he could.

"Let me know if he calls."

At twelve-thirty, Max left for lunch. At one o'clock, Benson still hadn't contacted the office, and Eric was beginning to worry. He stopped at Winnie's desk on his way out for his own lunch break.

"Has he ever done this before?"

She hesitated. "Once."

He didn't like the look on her face. "Once? What was it about?"

275

"Look, you can't blame yourself." She fidgeted with her pearl earring. "You had no way of knowing."

"What are you talking about?" Eric cocked his head.

"That thing with Benson's dad . . ."

A jolt of alarm punched Eric's gut. Benson's dad wouldn't hurt him, would he? Dick Samson had at least fifty pounds on his son.

"Dick never even knew about Jack's offer to pay for Benson's school the first time. Benson never told him."

Eric slammed his fist against Winnie's desk. "Because his dad would freak out. Shoot. I'm an idiot."

"No." Winnie glanced around and lowered her voice for once. "His dad's not the problem. He never told Dick because he knew Dick would try to talk his mom into letting him do it. He's never been Dad of the Year or anything, but there's nothing he wants more than to see Benson make something of himself. Get out of Tukston if he can."

What? Dick wasn't the one unsupportive of Benson's aspirations? "His mom doesn't want him getting his degree?"

Winnie twirled the other earring. "She doesn't really know what she wants. Her mind has always been . . . fragile. She had a few good years when their kids were younger, but after the divorce . . ."

Eric pictured Dick's face as he chewed out Eunice in that field. It had seemed like such an overreaction at the time. It hadn't really been her fault. But it sounded like there was a lot more pain and baggage involved than he realized.

"You think Benson is helping his mom right now?"

Winnie pulled on the sleeve of her sweatshirt uneasily. "If Dick confronted her about the job opportunity—if he tried to convince her to let Benson go—she might be having an episode. And Benson's the oldest. He thinks it's his responsibility to take care of her."

The alarm in Eric's gut grew. He really *had* kicked the hornet's nest.

"Is there anything I can do?"

Before she could answer, the door swung open. Bob Crowley entered, and the faint but acrid smell of smoke followed.

"Your Bronco on fire, Bob?" Winnie asked.

He shuffled over to Eric. "Smoke's setting in from the fire over to Jenkinsville. You hear about it?"

"I heard." Winnie nodded solemnly. "They ever find out how it started?"

"Best they can figure, it's from a cigarette someone flicked out their window. Don't know how anyone could be so stupid when it's this dry."

The talk of fire did nothing to ease the discomfort in Eric's stomach. "What's on fire?"

"The hills northeast of here."

"Where Max lives?"

"It's miles away." Bob clapped him on the shoulder. "You got a few spare minutes for an old man?"

Eric ran his fingers through his hair and sucked in a quick breath. There was nothing he could do about Benson or the distant wildfire at the moment, so he might as well check something else off his to-do list.

"Sure. Let's talk in my office."

Bob took a seat, and Eric maneuvered around the cubicle wall boxes for a second time to sit behind his desk. Bob's white hair was sticking up in all directions as if he'd driven to town with the top down.

Bob caught Eric looking and reached up to pat it down with a chuckle. "The wind's starting to blow out there."

Eric smiled.

"I hear you're leaving tomorrow." Bob's expression was guileless and unguarded. "Back to the big city."

"Yes, I'm eager to get home. But I'm glad you stopped in. I've been wanting to follow up with you about everything we talked about last time."

"I shouldn't have told you."

"No, I'm glad you did. I want to help."

The office was empty. It was the perfect chance to get to the bottom of Bob's predicament and convince him to invest his fortune.

"I think it's admirable you want to leave all your money to charity in your will, and I understand your desire to keep it out of your brother's hands."

Bob rubbed a weathered hand over the scruff on his face. "But?"

"Have you considered investing it? There are—"

"How would that keep my brother from going after it when I kick the bucket?"

"Well, it wouldn't solve that problem, but—"

"That's the only problem I care about." Bob shrugged. "I got no interest in investing. My money's doing exactly what I want it to right now."

"But you could see ten percent or more a year in returns if you—"

"Look, son, I know you mean well, but I'm only concerned about after I'm gone."

Eric stifled his frustration. What would Brady the Brown-noser do in this situation? Move in for the kill? Force the issue?

Eric sat back in his chair and sighed. Did it really matter what Brady would do? Brady wasn't here. Eric was. Did it really matter if he reached his goal for ten-percent profit growth? Would that make Uncle Jack happy? Make him change his mind about Eric being ready for the tenth floor?

He'd said there were big things on Eric's horizon, but maybe there were bigger things than financial success. What did Uncle Jack *really* want from him? What if helping Bob find peace of mind about his money meant zero profit?

Eric let out a long breath. Time to take a different approach. "Okay, Bob. I hear you. Let's figure this out, then. If your main concern is what happens to the money after you're gone, why not donate it now?"

It would be a simple solution. Bob planned to donate it all anyway. He could donate a sizable portion and still have plenty to live on. He was still spry and independent at the moment, but realistically—and not to be callous here—he probably only needed enough funds to last him a few more years.

Bob fidgeted and shook his head. "I never expected to have to worry about something like this. Never thought all that land investment up in Gallatin County was going to pay off so big. But donating it now . . ."

So that was where the money had come from. Eric held up a hand. "Hear me out. Your house and property are paid off, right?"

Bob nodded.

"Your living expenses are minimal. Your social security check probably covers at least half of them each month, right?"

Bob nodded again. "More'n half."

"So, you give maybe two-thirds of the cash to whatever charities you want now, and—"

"I can't do that."

Eric leaned his elbows on the desk. "Why not?"

"I can't tell you. No one's supposed to know."

"Our meetings are confidential, Bob. I can assure you no one will ever hear it from me."

Eric cracked his knuckles uneasily. From the look on Bob's face, Eric wasn't sure if Bob was going to slap him on the back or shoot him.

Finally, Bob sighed. "I'm sorry. It's got nothing to do with you. I made a promise."

Eric scrunched his lips to one side. Did Bob have a family member coercing him? Trying to keep the money within reach? But no, he'd said there wasn't any family except his brother. He said he'd made a promise. To his late wife maybe?

"If you're not able to give the money away now, I guess your best option is—"

Max burst through the glass-paneled door in a frenzy and grabbed a set of keys from off his desk. "Eric. We need to close early. I've got to get home."

Bob pushed himself out of his chair with a grunt. "What happened?"

Max fixed Bob with a penetrating look. "The wind changed."

Bob's face paled. "How long?"

"They've already issued an evacuation notice." Max hurried for the door and called over his shoulder, "They're saying two hours at the most."

The door slammed behind him, and Bob turned to Eric. What was going on?

Bob noted the confusion on his face. "The fire changed direction. It's headed for our hills now."

Eric sat up straight. "You said it was miles away."

"It was. But it's drier'n a cow chip out there. If the wind decided to push the blaze toward Tukston, there's nothing anyone can do about it."

"What about the fire department?"

Bob laughed a humorless laugh. "Son, there's not a crew in the country that can stop a wildfire under these conditions. They'll send crews from all around to help with containment and probably get a chopper up there to drop retardant, but none of that's going to happen fast enough to spare Max's place."

Eric's heart beat a little faster and harder. "What can I do?"

Bob set his lips in a grim line and turned toward the door. "Pray the wind changes."

He left before Eric could ask what *he* was planning to do.

Winnie appeared in his place, wringing her hands. "Guess we better close up."

"I can stay. Some clients might already be on their way."

"I don't know . . ."

Eric's phone made a chirping sound. He checked the screen. A text from Eunice?

I need your help.

He frowned. He'd talked to her over the fence last night, and she'd seemed all right. But she would never send him a text like that for no reason.

"Everything okay?" Winnie asked.

He scanned the office, torn. Could he really just lock the door and leave for personal reasons? He'd never consider such a thing if he were in Seattle. But he wasn't.

"It's Eunice."

Winnie's face creased with concern, one hand flying to her chest.

"You're right, Winnie," he said. "I think we better go."

She drew herself up to full height. "You go. I'll call everyone who's left and cancel."

Eric hurriedly packed his briefcase. "You'll be all right? Will your place be safe?"

She held the door open for him to pass through and followed him into the lobby. "I don't think it'll jump the river. But don't worry about me. Go."

"Are you sure—?"

She shoved him toward the door. "Go."

He went. Outside, a dirty haze had settled over the valley, and an air of tension thicker than the smoke enveloped the town. His eyes burned as he hopped into the Jeep. What would happen to Max's home? Should he have tried to stop Max from driving up there?

He pushed the scan button on his radio to find the local station. All he knew about it was that it broadcast from Tukston High School and most of its programs were prerecorded, but he hoped it might have information about what was going on.

The scanner found the station, and he cranked up the volume as he backed onto Main Street.

"... that all residents who live on Sheridan Road, Alder Road, or Twin Bridges Road south of the Highway 87 junction are urged to evacuate immediately. Please use caution when driving, as visibility is poor due to smoke in the area. Contact the Sheriff's Department for more information."

Eric turned left at the four-way stop. There was more traffic than usual for a Thursday afternoon. A school bus, even though school didn't let out for over an hour. Two trucks pulling empty horse trailers. The radio station went on to broadcast the weather forecast, Friday's lunch menu for the school cafeteria, and an ad for Arlo's Autobody, then repeated the evacuation message.

His phone chimed again, and he glanced at it. Another text from Eunice.

Eric. Please help.

He stepped on the gas.

thirty-eight

Eunice's head pounded, the pain like a railroad spike being driven into her skull, the Tylenol she'd taken a mere apparition, taunting but powerless. After four trips back and forth from her house to the horse trailer, breathing that awful smoke, all she wanted to do was curl up on the grass somewhere in the shade and cry until she fell asleep. But she couldn't do that. Not yet.

Where was Eric? Why hadn't he responded to her texts?

The trailer door shut with a metallic bang, and she slid the latch and wiped her hands on her pants. It was a small trailer, and old, but it would do for the task at hand. She remembered seeing it for sale in the paper five years ago. The price had been reduced three times, but still no one had wanted it. She'd felt compelled to bring it home. Just like she'd felt compelled to bring home the cat carrier someone had in the Free pile at their garage sale, and the leashes she'd purchased on clearance when the old pet store in Butte went out of business.

She hadn't been able to believe all those items had nothing left to offer. Had no life left. Surely they could still serve a purpose. And maybe . . . maybe she could, too.

Eric's Jeep came speeding down Prairie Dog Road, and she stepped out to where he could see her and waved an arm. As she'd hoped, he pulled the Jeep to a stop where she stood instead of parking in his driveway.

283

"What's going on?" He hurried out of the car. "Are you okay?"

His expression was one of concern, and she was touched by it. But this was no time for sentimentality.

"I'm okay, but—"

"You don't look okay. And you said you needed help."

She probably looked a fright, and her headache had not eased even a little. "I do. I need you to hook this trailer to the back of your Jeep."

He blinked. Opened his mouth to speak. Closed it.

"Please. Everything's loaded and ready to go—we just need to hitch it up."

Her words snapped him out of his daze. He inched closer to the trailer to try to look in the window. "What's loaded? Where are we going?"

"You heard about the evacuation."

"Yeees."

He was not making the connection, but why would he? They didn't exactly have wildfires in the big city. And he hadn't been here all those years ago when an uncontrolled fire threatened homes in a different area, east of Tukston, and the whole town had mobilized to dig trenches, donate food and water to the firefighters, and rescue a total of twenty-seven horses from the blaze.

She'd joined in the efforts because she thought she could help. She had experience and knew how to handle a frightened horse. And of course Charlie had gone with her. They'd done everything together.

"Right now, people are scrambling to throw as many of their belongings in their trucks as possible and get out of the hills ahead of the fire," she said. "Do you know what people do with their animals when they're in that situation?"

He shook his head.

"If they can't quickly and easily get them in their vehicle,

284

or if they don't fit, they set them loose. And hope—" her voice caught—"hope they can outrun the flames."

She never knew what made Charlie take off like he did. Maybe fear or disorientation. She'd screamed at him to come back. Screamed until her voice was gone. But he never did.

Her hands clenched. She couldn't load a bunch of horses into this tiny trailer, but there would be other critters up there she could help. Headache or not, she would not sit around while there were animals running through the hills terrified and alone, like Charlie. She would not leave them behind. And she knew how frantically she would hope against hope to be reunited with her pets if she were the one who had to flee her home.

Eric waved an arm in the direction of the fire. "We can't go up there. It's too dangerous."

"Please. I, uh, *we* have to help."

"You're in no condition to—"

"We can just drive close enough to watch for any animals that might come running out. They're going to need someone to pick them up. Give them water." Her desperation revealed itself in her voice. "We can do that much at least."

She'd loaded four one-gallon jugs of water. She would've filled more but that was all she had.

He rubbed the back of his neck and grimaced.

"Come on." She knew there wasn't much time. "You've got friends up there. Don't you want to do something?"

She wanted to. Needed to.

He hesitated. "I guess we can drive over and see what's going on, but—"

"Thank you."

"But I don't want you getting out of the car."

She wanted to throttle him. She wasn't a child. He wasn't her boss. But she needed him.

"Okay. Deal. I promise."

Again with the lies. She'd ask God for forgiveness later.

Eric reluctantly got back in the Jeep and backed up closer to the trailer. She'd already cranked up the level of the hitch before he'd arrived, and even though she'd never used this trailer before, she knew exactly what to do. She'd done it many times before with a different blue-eyed man by her side.

She made sure she was standing on the driver's side when they were finished.

Eric stood back to survey their work. "Are you sure about this?"

She nodded. "I just need my survostobag from the house."

"Your what?"

"The bag I always carry." She gestured toward her stomach impatiently. "It has my personal supplies in it. I can't go anywhere without it."

"Oh." His cheeks flushed. "I just thought it was a purse."

"Will you get it for me? It's in the bathroom."

He gave her a look she couldn't quite interpret, then nodded. "Be right back."

He really was a good guy. It was a shame she had to put him through this.

As he neared the house, she inched closer to the driver's door. He'd left the Jeep running.

"Oh, Lo-ord." Her voice sounded scratchy and sluggish. "Don't let him turn around."

He didn't. The moment the front door closed behind him, she let out the breath she'd been holding and scrambled into the Jeep. She jammed the car into drive, whispering a prayer of thanks that she'd had practice driving this thing only a few weeks ago.

Her chest buzzed with adrenaline. Her hands shook. She didn't know what awaited her up in the hills or if she'd ever make it back. But she knew with a certainty born of tried-and-tested faith that this was a mission God had prepared her to accomplish. And this time she would not come home empty-handed.

thirty-nine

The survival bag, or whatever she called it, was not in Eunice's bathroom. Eric checked the kitchen. Wasn't there. He checked under the couch. Nope.

Was it really such a good idea to intentionally take a terminally ill woman near a dangerous situation? She was so weak and frail. She should be in bed resting.

And he hated fire.

He hesitated before peeking into her bedroom. It felt wrong to intrude on her personal space, but he couldn't think of anywhere else the bag could be. The room was dimly lit and as sparse as the rest of the house. Even after packing up all his things in preparation for leaving tomorrow, his rental was still not as bare as Eunice's house.

He found the bag on the floor in her closet. The top was open, and he fought the impulse to rifle through the contents. He'd seen some of the supplies before when he raided her bathroom for a first-aid kit, but what exactly did the emergency travel kit for a person with a urostomy consist of?

Yes, urostomy. He knew the proper term for it now. He'd Googled it and frankly couldn't believe he'd never known what a wonder of science and invention a stoma was.

He closed the bag and headed for the front door, all the while trying to think up a way to change Eunice's mind about her mission of mercy. There must be other ways they could help.

287

Maybe he could call the Sheriff's Department, as the radio had said, and find a way to donate food to whatever emergency shelter they must be scrambling to set up.

When he opened the door, it took three or four steps before it registered in his brain that there was no trailer parked in front of the house. No Jeep. And no Eunice.

No, no, no.

He threw up his hands and ran to the street, scanning up and down the road. No sign of her. He dropped the bag on the ground and jammed his fingers in his hair. How could she do this? He shoved a hand in his pocket for his phone but came up empty. A groan escaped. He'd left his phone in the Jeep.

Great.

Just great.

He paced up and down the yard, his mind racing. He couldn't call anyone to intercept Eunice. He had no other car to hop in and chase after her—

Wait. The scooter.

He jogged to Eunice's garage and flipped on the overhead light. The Honda's back tire was flat but the air compressor she must've used last time was sitting right next to it. He had no hope of catching her on that old thing, even if he could get it on the road, but he had to do something. He couldn't sit around waiting for her return. Maybe he could catch Winnie before she left the office.

The noise from the air compressor reverberated through the garage. How long would the tire hold air? Couldn't it fill any faster? From the corner of his eye, he saw a movement and startled. Cinderella.

"What are you doing here?"

She wandered over, giving the noisy air compressor a wary look, and hopped onto the floor of the scooter.

Eric waved his free hand at her. "Get off there. Shoo."

She bobbed her head, unconcerned, and hopped up to the

seat. He checked the tire and decided it was good enough. Too much time had already gone by.

Unhooking the compressor, he set it aside and pushed the scooter out of the garage by the handlebars. Cinderella rode it out, pecking at the padding from the seat that was poking out through cracks in the black fabric.

By the time he reached the road, he was coughing. The smoke was getting worse. The mountains in the distance were completely obscured. The sky was orange and gray.

He glared at Cinderella. "Time to get off now."

She moved to the small metal rack attached to the back and wrapped her toes—were they called toes?—around the bars. He waved his hands at her, yet she was unfazed.

"I don't have time for this."

He'd never touched her before, but she was leaving him no choice. He gulped and reached out to pick her up. She pecked at his fingers, and he snatched his hand away.

"Ow."

She turned her head and leveled one unblinking eye at him as if daring him to touch her again.

"I thought we were friends."

This was ridiculous. He wasn't scared of a chicken, was he? All he had to do was lift her up, set her on the ground, and ride away.

He reached out again, and she squawked. He jumped back and glanced around to be sure no one had seen.

"Fine. Suit yourself."

She'd fly down as soon as the scooter started moving, he was sure. He sat on the beat-up seat. What about a helmet? Could he get pulled over? He'd never driven a scooter before . . .

He hurried back to Eunice's garage to look around. The only helmet he found was her silver one with purple stars. There had to be something else.

A quick and frantic search yielded no other options. He

shoved the silver helmet on his head with a frustrated grunt. This was crazy. If Eunice managed to survive whatever adventure she was on, he was going to kill her.

He hopped on the scooter and cranked the key. The engine sputtered but didn't turn over.

"Come on, come on."

He tried again, and the engine roared to life.

"Last chance, Cinderella," he shouted.

She clung desperately and defiantly to the metal rack, and he pulled out onto the road.

After the third time listening to the recorded message about the evacuation, Eunice turned off the radio. Her hands clutched the wheel. Sweat formed on her temples and under her arms. What had Eric's face looked like when he came out of the house? She knew the survostobag wasn't in the bathroom. She was really racking up the lies these days.

She hoped eventually he would understand, because she did not plan to wait somewhere out of danger for any animals that might come running her way, as she'd implied, and she couldn't let him put his life at risk. *Her* life? Well, she was already as good as dead. But Eric? He was about to go back to his high-flying life in Seattle. Back to his little brother. Back to people who would miss him.

She'd already passed three horse trailers coming down the hill on her way to Alder Road. Everyone else had gotten there ahead of her and was already heading back to town, rescued animals in tow. But her body trembled with anticipation and purpose as she urged the Jeep onward.

Or maybe it was her internal organs shutting down.

The smoke thickened the closer she got to the turnoff, and a harrowing memory assaulted her. In the distance she could see a blackened swath across Heeb Hill, where the fire had already consumed whatever fuel it could find. Hot spots of visible flames dotted the rest of the hillside. Ahead on the road, an empty patrol car was parked in her lane, lights flashing, preventing anyone else from going up. But the other lane was unblocked, which meant there were still people up there they hoped would make it down in time.

She decreased her speed, her heart pounding painfully in her chest. A fire truck was parked on the side of the road, and a fireman in full gear paced alongside it while shouting into a walkie-talkie. He spotted the Jeep and pointed resolutely behind her before resuming his animated conversation. The implication was clear. *Go back.*

No one else was in sight. Where had the policeman gone?

She thought about all the nights she'd lain awake wondering what death was going to be like. Trying to convince herself she was ready but never quite getting past her fears. She thought about the mistakes she'd made and the people she'd hurt. She thought about a blazing fire nipping at the heels of an exhausted, terror-stricken terrier with a missing ear.

There was still one name left on her list. Still one man out there who deserved to hear her say she was sorry. Who, if she continued up this hill, might never get the chance.

If she ever did face him, would her words be penitent enough to bridge the chasm between them? Would the grace in his heart be powerful enough to extend forgiveness? Would they be able to make peace with each other?

"God, I've made my peace with you." She swerved into the other lane and smashed her foot against the gas pedal. "And that *is* enough."

forty

Perspiration poured down Eric's face, stinging his eyes. He'd made it to Larson Financial just in time to see Winnie driving away in her Buick. He'd earned more than a few stares as he waved his arms, hoping she'd catch sight of him in her rearview mirror.

On second thought, it was possible those people had been staring at his glitzy helmet and Polish sidekick.

He turned off the scooter, hoping to formulate a plan. Only then did he notice the gas gauge on the Honda was pointing to an undefinable area somewhere below the E. What was he supposed to do now? How had he managed to keep commandeering nearly empty vehicles?

He longed for some water but didn't have his keys to get into the office. Should he track down a police officer to ask for help? He walked the scooter over the sidewalk and into Tukston Park, looking around. Every officer Tukston had was probably up on the hill right now.

He slumped onto a bench and pulled off the helmet. Cinderella pried her fingers—maybe that was what they were called?—from the bars and hopped onto the dry grass. There were plenty of bugs to keep her busy.

"What in tarnation are you doing, champ?"

Eric held his hand above his eyes to shade them from the sun. "Dusty?"

Dusty joined him on the bench with a bemused look on his face. "I recognize that scooter. Where's Eunice?"

Eric groaned and wiped his face. "She stole my Jeep and drove it up the hill pulling a trailer full of water jugs and dog beds."

"Dog beds?"

Eric threw up his hands. "I don't even know what she had back there. She thinks she can go up and help the animals for some reason. I rode the scooter over here to find help. Where's your truck?"

Dusty sat back with a heavy sigh. "At the store. But how long ago did she leave? We'll never catch her."

Eric stood, his dress shirt sticking to his back. "We have to try. She's risking her life . . ."

Dusty gave him a solemn look. "Is she risking it? Or using what's left of it for good?"

Eric hesitated, then sat back down. "You know?"

Dusty lifted one shoulder. "I set it up so all her medical bills—uh, I mean, health-insurance claims come through the store. I know how many there've been."

Eric's brow furrowed. How could Eunice still have insurance through Dusty's store?

"I figured she must be pretty sick," Dusty continued. "And she was in bad shape when I saw her at your house."

Eric watched Cinderella peck at the ground without a care in the world. "She never told me why she didn't want anyone to find out."

"I've known her a long time." Dusty rested his hands on his knees and looked off into the distance. "She's a complicated woman."

Eric snorted. *Complicated* didn't begin to describe Eunice. "What should we do?"

"*I'm* going to pick Nate up and go help out at the emergency shelter they're setting up in the high school gym. *You* should go home. She's going to come back at some point, and I have a feeling she's going to need you."

After Dusty had gone, Eric grumbled about the whole world going crazy and talked himself into rolling up the bottom of his gray slacks. It had to be at least ninety-five degrees, and he didn't care what he looked like at this point. His legs were suffocating.

His stomach reminded him he'd missed lunch, and his throat declared that if he didn't get some water soon, he was going to start cramping up. The grocery store and Good Food were both a mere two blocks away, but he'd left his wallet in his briefcase. Which was still in the Jeep.

Dusty was right. He'd better go home.

Eric limped along, muttering to himself. He'd managed to start the scooter despite its dire gas gauge warning, but apparently it had only enough fuel to get him out of the downtown area. His Italian loafers were great for the office. Not so great for walking.

Pushing the scooter while simultaneously trying to ignore the chicken that had decided to roost on his shoulder and the pain in his feet was a difficult task. He'd have blisters by the time he got home, and the digits of Cinderella's feet—which he now determined must be called claws—poked into his skin. Yes, he'd stripped off his button-down and was walking along the side of the road in his undershirt.

If only his friends from Seattle could see him now.

The upside was that he didn't have to wear that awful helmet anymore. He focused on putting one foot in front of the other and dreamed about taking a cool shower. Without his phone, he had no idea what time it was or how much time had passed since Eunice took off. About two hours, if he had to guess.

What if she never made it back?

He was almost to Prairie Dog Road. An engine roared behind him, and he moved over as far as he could, but there was no shoulder. He was teetering on the edge of the road as it was. The vehicle blew by him with a rush of wind, and he lost his balance. As he tumbled over the scooter and into the ditch, he caught a glimpse of the car that had passed.

A bright blue Jeep, pulling a single-horse trailer.

forty-one

As a child, Eunice couldn't think of anything better than working with animals every day instead of people. But her mother had discouraged the idea, describing in detail all the schooling that would be required to become a vet and the gory surgeries she would have to perform. What would her life have been like if her mother hadn't tried to make all her decisions for her? What would it have been like if Eunice hadn't let her?

And perhaps the most agonizing question: What if she hadn't done the same thing to her blue-eyed man? She never gave him a chance to decide for himself. She'd believed he'd be better off without a sick and barren wife and had made sure he would move on and leave her behind.

What would he have done if she'd told him the truth?

She slammed on the brakes with a yelp. "Oh, my goodness. There's my house."

How had she arrived already? She could hardly recall driving back to Tukston. Any recollection of the last two hours was veiled in smoke and eclipsed by pain.

She parked and turned off the Jeep, an assortment of smells suddenly assailing her. Ash and dank fur and . . . urine? It would be easy to blame the two dogs crowded in the back seat, but all except one of those odors were coming from her. Where was Eric?

With a groan, she slid from the car. The bottom of her shirt and top of her waistband were wet, but she couldn't worry about that now.

"Sorry, JoJo."

Instead of convincing her unwieldy fingers to pull open the passenger door, she patted the front seat and urged the dogs to climb through the middle. "Come on, Charlie. Come here."

They trembled as they obeyed, their tongues lolling. Heads hanging.

No, not Charlie.

She swallowed hard. "Let's get you some water."

They followed her around the front of the Jeep to the yard. Tears pricked her eyes. How was she going to get all the animals into the backyard? Fill up all their water dishes? Find them all food? Her heart was beating far too fast. Her vision was far too murky.

"Eunice."

She turned to find her neighbor. "I don't have any food."

The puzzled look on his face quickly morphed into concern. "Let's get you inside. Get you something to drink."

"No." She said it as firmly as she could, but it wasn't much more than a whisper. "Not until we take care of the animals."

Eric glanced around at the dogs in the yard, the Jeep, and the trailer. "Fine. But you go sit in the shade and let me handle this."

Her body trembled. "Promise you'll take care of them."

He jerked his chin once and put his hands on his hips. "I promise."

She let out her breath. Drooped her shoulders. Okay, she would sit.

Just for a minute.

Eric hurried to the side gate, slapping his thigh in hopes the dogs would follow. They did. He let them into the backyard and turned on the garden hose, first taking a deep draught himself, then laying it on the ground for the dogs. It would do until he could get them proper bowls.

He closed the gate and cautiously approached the Jeep. Cinderella had conveniently abandoned him and returned to his house. A banging sound coming from the trailer made his hands turn clammy. What was back there? Surely not a horse?

He would deal with that in a minute.

He flung open the passenger door of the Jeep. "Um. Hello."

A frazzled-looking goose honked at him from inside a cat carrier. The interior of his Jeep smelled like a campfire, swamp, and sewer all mixed together. He lifted the carrier out and set it on the grass.

"And what do we have here?"

A turtle lay in a rectangular aquarium. He shook his head. Where had she found a turtle? What had happened up there?

He called to Eunice, "Do you want these guys in the backyard or the house?"

She sat on the ground, slumped against a post, and made an ambiguous gesture.

He looked at the goose. "I think that means in the house."

He carried them inside and set the tank on the kitchen counter. Would the turtle be able to drink from a bowl, or would a bowl be too tall? He settled on a saucer of water and a pile of precut honeydew he found in the fridge—thank goodness for that—then carried the goose into the bathroom. He couldn't leave it stuffed in the carrier, but he wasn't about to give it free rein of the house.

The goose did not appreciate being pulled out by its feet, but it seemed to be happy in the bathtub. Eric left a trickle of water running from the tub faucet and shut the bathroom door, his thoughts turning to Max. How many of his belongings had he been able to rescue? Had the fire reached his house?

The smell of smoke hit him with renewed force as he went

298

back outside. Eunice's eyes were closed, her head leaning against the post, but her chest moved up and down. He had a feeling she was in worse shape than any of the animals, but he would complete her mission before confronting her. Clearly the safety of the animals was a bigger concern to her than her own health.

More banging and some other indistinguishable sounds came from the trailer as he reached to undo the latch. He braced himself as the door swung open.

Two creatures covered in black streaks stared at him with wild eyes. The larger one of the two must be a pony. Its nostrils flared in fear. The smaller one was . . . another dog? Eric looked closer.

"Smellie Mellie?"

The pony stamped its feet nervously, and the goat gave him a pitiable bleat. Eric rubbed his temples. This was *not* happening.

"Come on then." He stepped to the side and waved his arm.

Neither creature moved, but they had to come out. There was no way he was getting in there with them. He looked back at Eunice.

Her eyes had opened. "Water."

Of course. The jugs she had loaded earlier were gone, though an empty bucket rolled around on the floor. He grabbed it and quickly filled it with water from the spigot.

When he held the water bucket in front of the door, Mellie took a hesitant step forward. The pony sniffed the air.

"Come on. I won't hurt you."

They emerged tentatively from the trailer as he slowly backed away, holding the bucket in front of him. He led them to the backyard and set the bucket down. As they fought over it, he went in the house through the sliding door. He took every pet dish he could find outside and filled them with water, then turned off the hose and eyed the goat warily. He remembered Max saying something about how Mellie was an escape artist.

Fortunately, Eunice had a dog collar, leash, and metal chain sitting right there in the laundry room, as if somehow she'd known this moment would come one day. He grabbed it all. Mellie was chewing on the already-empty bucket and hardly noticed him slip the collar over her neck. He attached the leash to the fence, then thought better of it and exchanged it for the chain. It wasn't ideal—his PETA friends would throw a fit—but it would have to do for now. Until Max could come claim her.

Now, what to do about the pony?

He studied the creature for a minute. It appeared to be in shock. It just . . . stood there. Could a pony this size jump over a fence?

He'd find out soon enough.

Eric shut and latched the gate with tense shoulders. What the heck was he doing? What had happened to Max? What had happened to Eunice?

Her eyes were closed again.

"Eunice?"

She didn't move. His heart twinged. He put his hand in front of her nose and felt a faint wisp of air.

"Eunice?"

Still nothing.

"That's it."

He scooped her up and carried her to the Jeep. The clinic wasn't far. What had she said the name of her doctor was? Would the clinic be equipped to help her?

As he struggled to buckle her in, he noticed the dampness of her clothes and the smell of ammonia. He shut the passenger door and jogged around to the other side. She'd been fighting against time for months. Now it was his turn.

forty-two

Once again Eric found himself in a waiting room, hoping for good news. At least this time he had money to buy food, even though the vending machines at Sunshine Medical Center left a lot to be desired.

"What on earth are you wearing?"

Eric dropped the bag of mini pretzels in his lap and looked up with a start. Winnie. He'd called her as soon as he arrived.

He huffed. "It's been quite a day."

His gray slacks were still rolled up to mid-calf, and the loafers were covered in bits of grass and mud. His sleeveless undershirt was streaked with dirt and damp with sweat.

She sat down beside him. "What happened to your shoulder?"

He craned his neck to look where she pointed. His right shoulder was covered in red scratches from Cinderella's claws. "It's a long story."

"How's our girl?"

Eric offered his bag of pretzels to Winnie. She shook her head.

"Haven't heard anything yet. I'm hoping we can go back and see her soon. She'll be glad you're here."

"I don't know about that." Winnie folded her hands in her lap and hung her head. "I've let her down. She didn't have a single person to talk to when she got the news about her diagnosis. I should've been there."

Eric wasn't sure how to respond. He was the outsider here. Eunice and Winnie and all the other people from her list had long histories together.

"I know I've only known her a short time," he said, "but I don't think she has any hard feelings about that. She told me she's only concerned with her own debts. Not anyone else's."

They sat in silence for a few minutes. Eric finished off the pretzels and tossed the bag in the trash. Winnie rummaged in her purse for an Altoid.

A soft-spoken older man appeared in the doorway. "Are you Eunice's friends?"

Eric scrambled to his feet. "How is she? Can we see her?"

"Hold on a minute." The man held up his hands. "One thing at a time. I'm Dr. Mullins. Eunice is stable and resting for now, but—"

"What does that mean?" Winnie joined Eric on her feet. "For now?"

Dr. Mullins's face took on a serious and compassionate expression, one Eric guessed he'd perfected over many years of delivering bad news.

"Eunice's body is shutting down. She doesn't have much time. I'm very sorry."

Winnie gasped and leaned into Eric's side. He put an arm around her shoulder. "Can we see her?"

Dr. Mullins nodded. "Follow me."

Eunice's room was quiet and dim. Against the stark white sheets and pillows, she seemed to have withered. She was nothing but a thread, laid across a cot.

Eric stood by her bed, but she didn't move. He'd known she was sick. She'd told him she was dying. But somehow he wasn't prepared to see her like this. He thought he'd be long gone before the end came.

"She'll probably be asleep for a while." Dr. Mullins held the door open with one arm. "I'll check back in a bit."

When he was gone, Winnie pulled a chair up to the bedside, just as she'd done in Dusty's hospital room. At how many bedsides had she kept vigil in her lifetime?

"You better head home." She pulled a book from her large, lumpy purse. "I'll stay."

Eric scoffed. "I'm not going to leave you here. I'm the one who asked you to come."

She tilted her chin down and scrutinized him over her glasses. "You look like a hobo in those clothes, and your stomach hasn't stopped growling since I got here. Besides, there's only one chair."

He hesitated.

"Go home and get changed," Winnie continued. "Get some food. Then call me."

No wonder she was so good at running the office at Larson Financial. She was bossy.

He watched Eunice for a moment. The doctor was probably right. She wasn't going to wake up for a while. He had time to take care of a few things.

"Oh." He smacked his forehead. Speaking of taking care of things . . . "What am I supposed to do about the animals?"

Winnie lifted one eyebrow. "Animals?"

Her eyes filled with moisture as he explained about the turtle, goose, goat, pony, and two dogs waiting at Eunice's house.

Winnie ran a finger under her glasses. "She saved them?"

He nodded.

"Of all the stupid, stubborn, reckless things to—" Her voice caught and broke.

One corner of Eric's mouth lifted in a sad half smile. "I guess it was the one thing she thought she could do to help."

"Leave it to Eunice to care about a turtle in all this." Winnie sighed. "You remember how to get to my house?"

"Yes."

"I've got a big bag of dog food and some hay in the barn.

And lettuce and carrots in the fridge. That should get you through the next couple of days. By then they'll probably all be gone."

"Gone?"

"Their owners will come get them once they find out where they are."

"How are they going to find out?"

"I'm sure there's already a bulletin board up at the police station or something. We'll figure that all out later."

Eric let out a long breath. "Okay."

He wanted to have a plan. He wanted to know the timeline. But he'd made a promise.

<hr />

As he pulled back up to Eunice's house, the empty trailer clattering behind, Eric yawned. The day was starting to catch up to him. He unloaded the food from Winnie's place and took the dog food and hay straight to the backyard. The dog food was for the dogs, the hay for the pony, he knew that much. But what about the goat?

He closed the gate behind him before any animals could escape and groaned. The pony was helping itself to Eunice's garden.

"Here, pony, pony." He waved a handful of hay. "Here's some nice hay for you."

He felt like an idiot. The pony ignored him. But the goat went for the hay, so at least that answered *that* question.

He left two dishes for water and filled two with dog food, then put the dog food bag in the garage. Inside the house, he found the turtle had eaten some honeydew and seemed content, as far as he could tell. He refilled the saucer with water.

What was that sound coming from down the hall? It didn't sound like a goose.

His phone rang, and he swiped to answer it without looking, expecting Winnie. "Hello?"

"Are you all packed?"

Chase.

Eric blinked. Crap. In the chaos, he'd completely forgotten he was supposed to go home tomorrow. Caring for these animals wasn't the only promise he'd made. "Hey, bro. How are you?"

They hadn't talked since Chase had blown up about the whole working-out thing.

"Feeling pretty nervous about this weekend. What time are you planning to get here tomorrow night?"

Eric's heart took a nosedive. How could he leave now? The animals needed him. The office needed him. Maybe Eunice needed him most of all. "I'm really sorry, but I don't think I'm going to make it."

Silence. Stony, angsty silence.

His brother needed him, too.

Chase attending UW had been all Eric's idea from the beginning. He'd coaxed and encouraged and prodded him. Told him he'd be there every step of the way. And he wanted to be. But what he was dealing with here in Tukston was a lot bigger than what he wanted.

"There's a wildfire, a bad one, and my friend needs my help. She's in the hosp——"

"Fine. No big deal. It doesn't matter." Chase's voice contradicted his words.

"It does matter." Eric gripped the phone. There was that weird noise again. He moved toward the hall. "I promised you I'd be there. But you wouldn't believe . . ."

His voice trailed off. His eyes widened. A growing puddle of water flooded the hallway, coming from underneath the bathroom door.

Oh no.

"Look, Chase, I'll have to call you back later. I'm so sorry."

"Don't worry about it." Chase's voice was cold. Distant. "I don't need you anyway."

Eric winced as his brother hung up the phone, but the water continued seeping steadily toward him. He had no time for regrets or reflection. He braced himself and pulled open the bathroom door.

Eric couldn't remember the last time he'd been so exhausted. He lay in bed, his feet aching. Eyes wide open. He wanted to sleep. He really did. But he couldn't get the image of Eunice's fragile frame out of his mind. Or the words his brother had said. *"I don't need you anyway."*

He'd called Chase back at least a dozen times, wanting to explain, but his brother never answered. He'd try again in the morning.

It had taken way too long to clean up the watery mess. Best he could figure, the dumb goose had stepped on the stopper and accidentally closed the drain in the tub. What he *couldn't* figure was how one solitary goose could produce that much poop in such a short time. But at least he'd gotten the house almost back to normal. If he'd stayed at the hospital with Winnie as he'd planned, the whole place would've been underwater.

After cleaning everything up, he'd changed his clothes, put his blistered feet into a pair of flip-flops, and eaten the only food left in his kitchen. Three organic granola bars, two hard-boiled eggs, and half an avocado. Then he'd driven back to the medical center.

Winnie had scolded him for not calling first, but he hadn't wanted her to try to talk him out of it. Eunice had still been sleeping. "I'll stay the night in case she wakes up," Winnie had insisted. He'd protested, but she said she'd already missed enough time with Eunice and wasn't about to miss any more.

Eric rolled onto his side. Tomorrow he would need to figure out how to get in touch with the owners of all the animals. Max hadn't returned his call. The local news station had reported firefighting attempts had only managed fifteen-percent containment.

A honking sound echoed through the house. Oh yeah, by the way, he'd been forced to relocate the goose to his own bathroom. He was afraid the dogs would eat it if he left it in the backyard, and he wasn't willing to lock it in Eunice's bathroom again. He didn't trust the ugly thing not to cause a problem. It seemed like the type of creature that would do that kind of thing on purpose.

He definitely had not left the water running in the tub this time.

He rolled to his other side and tugged at the bedsheet. At Larson Financial, he was responsible for large sums of money, and it didn't faze him. Ever since moving out of his mom's house, he'd been responsible for keeping himself clothed and fed. Paying his own bills. Getting himself where he needed to be. But he'd never been wholly responsible for another living thing before.

This was not the kind of pressure he thrived on.

At least the turtle was easy.

forty-three

*E*unice was surprised when she opened her eyes. She expected to be alone in her bedroom or at the front gates of heaven. Instead, she was in a hospital room with not one but two friends. Somehow, there were still two people left in the world who cared about her.

She thought about Bertie and Wanda and Dusty. Maybe there were more than two.

The room was quiet and unclear. She blinked. It was daylight, yet she had a feeling it wasn't the same daylight she'd closed her eyes to.

"Nice of you to finally join us, Neecy." Winnie patted her hand. "Did you have a good nap?"

Eunice's voice was hoarse. "There was a fire."

Winnie nodded solemnly. "Yes. But don't worry about any of that. You just need to worry about getting rested up."

Eunice was glad Winnie didn't say *getting better*. She knew there would be no getting better.

"What happened up there?" Eric had been pacing, but now he stopped and peered down at her. "How did you end up with a turtle?"

"Leave her alone," Winnie admonished. "None of that matters right now."

Eunice swallowed slowly. "It was out on the road."

Someone must have set it free, hoping it would find a safe

place. Or maybe it had escaped in the chaos. She only knew that when she saw it, she had to save it.

"Why did the turtle cross the road?" Eric joked.

Winnie shot him a stern look. Eunice chuckled weakly. It was good to laugh. Up on the hill, she'd started to cry. She couldn't save every animal. Couldn't go any farther into the flames. Couldn't make much of a difference. And her fear of death had roared up on her like a grizzly, powerful and terrifying.

She'd told Eric weeks ago, that night in her kitchen, that fire makes everything clear. And things had never been clearer than in that moment on the hill. The blaze—beyond her control, beyond her comprehension—revealed to her what mattered most. The sickening smoke had brought everything into sharp focus.

She'd stopped crying and smiled then, amazed at how little was left when unimportant things were stripped away. When past mistakes and earthly desires turned to ash in light of eternity. And she'd done what she could with peace in her heart.

"Can I get you anything?" Winnie asked. "Are you hungry?"

She took a minute to answer. Was she hungry? She felt disconnected from her body, as if her spirit were already pulling away. "Water."

Winnie scrambled from her chair. "Coming right up."

Eunice's gaze struggled to follow Winnie out the door, then make its way back to Eric. Her eyes moved sluggishly, as if fighting their way through her mother's layered Jell-O. Her hands and feet were cold and stiff. How much longer did she have?

Eric gave her an inscrutable look. "Why *did* the turtle cross the road?"

She tried to sit up. "They're all okay, right? The animals?"

"They're fine." He set one hand on her shoulder, gently pushing her back. "You saved them."

She sank into her pillows, impossibly heavy and weightless at the same time. They were safe. The animals were safe.

"There's one more person."

"I know." Eric's expression intensified. "Whoever it is, I'll take you to see them as soon as they let you out of here. We'll get that name crossed off."

"No." She tried to shake her head. She didn't care about her list anymore. She'd done what she could. "I mean you."

He cocked his head. "Me?"

"I'm sorry for how I treated you. I'm sorry I wasted so much of your time."

His eyes sparked. For eyes like that she'd almost be willing to fight for more time. Blue eyes like the Montana sky.

He covered her hand with his. "It wasn't a waste."

"But it didn't change anything."

"It changed me."

She breathed in. Breathed out. "Promise me one more thing."

He hesitated. "Okay."

"Promise you won't wait too long to make peace."

His face clouded. "With my dad? I don't know if he even wants to. I don't know where we stand."

She shook her head. "In the end, it only matters where you stand with one person, and it's not your dad."

He looked down. She couldn't read his face. The room was too dim. Why was everything in shadow?

She closed her eyes. Tried to smile. "To get to the other side."

The steady *beep beep beep* of Eunice's heart monitor infused the small room with a measure of composure Eric didn't feel and reassured him whenever the space between Eunice's breaths felt interminably long.

"I hope she's not in pain," Winnie said.

He glanced over at her. How long had they been sitting here? "There's got to be something they can do."

Winnie's sigh was long-suffering. "I know it's hard to watch, but it's time to let her go."

Eric folded his arms across his chest. What did that even mean? *Let* her go? As if he had any control over it.

"You don't have to stay." Winnie touched his elbow. "She would understand."

Eunice had closed her eyes hours ago and never reopened them. Her body continued to go through the motions, but there was no sign she was aware of her surroundings. No sign she would wake up again.

"No. I'm not leaving."

He was supposed to be on the road right now, driving home to Seattle. He was supposed to be thinking about his brother and rejoicing that he would finally be able to order from Starbucks and eat authentic Thai food again. But for some reason, he could not bring himself to leave this room and the beeping sound that meant Eunice was still holding on.

"She said that in heaven, the sky is bluer than we can imagine." He unfolded his arms and braced his palms on his knees. "But she couldn't possibly know that, right? I mean, no one actually knows, do they?"

Not that he believed in heaven.

Not that he didn't.

Winnie's eyes never left Eunice's face. "She'll know soon enough."

Eric grumbled to himself. That wasn't an answer.

"I've watched a lot of loved ones die." The chains on Winnie's glasses swung back and forth as she wiped her eyes. "You don't get to be my age without a whole lot of loss. And I don't know how I could've faced all that without the promise of heaven."

He didn't want to ask, but he had to know. "What if . . ." His voice was low and husky. "What if it isn't real?"

She turned to look at him, eyes clear and blazing. "What if it is?"

He looked away and stared at the buttons that moved Eunice's mattress up and down, the question sitting heavy on his shoulders. *What if it is?* Then, a movement from the bed.

Winnie gasped and leaned closer. "We're here, Neecy. You're not alone."

There was no response. No further movement. Eric held his breath as Eunice expelled hers, slowly, slowly . . . slowly. He watched her chest, willing her lungs to refill. Watched the monitor, willing the resolute beeping to continue, realizing how much he didn't want to lose her. She was his friend. One of the best he'd ever had.

He should've told her that. He should've helped her more. He should've—

A short sob startled him, and he set a gentle hand on Winnie's shoulder as she cried.

Eunice was gone.

forty-four

The goat nibbled at Eric's shirt as he scooped dog poop in Eunice's backyard.

"Knock it off."

Mellie bleated and went after the bottom of his shorts. He pushed her away.

The pony was eating from the garden again. "Hey. You. Get away from there." Eric set the shovel down and approached it.

"There's perfectly good hay over there." He pointed, his voice rising. "She didn't plant all this for you."

The pony didn't budge, and Eric's chest tightened. Maybe she had. Maybe all this produce was meant for this stupid little horse all along.

The sun was starting to get low, the blue sky deepening from turquoise to bottomless ocean. Was it evening already? Sitting in the hospital for hours on end had caused him to lose all sense of time.

Dying was different than what he'd imagined.

He returned the shovel to the garage and stood for a minute blinking at the red Honda scooter, his eyesight blurring. When he tried to take a deep breath, the air caught on a jagged piece of memory sticking out of his heart. He'd never forget the day he moved to town and saw her on that scooter, wearing that ridiculous silver helmet and purple trench coat. He'd been in such a hurry—always in a hurry—thinking he had to go fast to get the most out of life. More, more, more. Now he wondered if going fast only got you where you were going with less.

How could she be gone?

He went in the house through the sliding door to check on the turtle he'd named Chicken. His throat constricted. It was so empty in here. So quiet. She'd never be here again.

He shook his head and pinched the bridge of his nose but couldn't stop a single tear from falling. He was going to miss her and those purple Crocs. *"To get to the other side,"* she'd said. Her last words. It was the answer to his joke about the turtle, but he couldn't shake the feeling it was so much more than that.

His phone rang, and he startled out of his thoughts. He checked the screen and groaned.

"Hi, Uncle Jack."

"My boy! Hope you made it okay. I wanted to remind you about our meeting. First thing Monday morning."

Right. The meeting. Where they were supposed to "debrief" about Eric's time in Tukston and discuss what Uncle Jack had planned for Eric's future.

"I don't think I'm going to make it." Eric dropped some zucchini he'd picked up at the grocery store into Chicken's tank. "I haven't left yet."

"Isn't Chase's move-in day tomorrow?"

"Yes."

Uncle Jack waited. Eric tapped a finger against the counter. How much should he tell him?

"There's a wildfire going on over here, up in the hills. They've almost got it contained, but it sounds like they're going to have to let it burn itself out for the most part."

"Is it bad? Was anyone hurt?"

Eric pictured Eunice sitting slumped against the front porch post as he scrambled to take care of the creatures she'd saved. "Yeah."

"Is it near Max's place? Are he and Ceci okay?"

"They're fine, but they won't know what happened to their house until they let people back up there. No one knows when that will be."

"Where are they staying?"

"At the motel."

He'd talked briefly with Max earlier. Told him he'd watch over Mellie and Larson Financial for as long as was needed. It was the least he could do.

"That's a real shame." Uncle Jack's voice changed. Turned pensive. "I'm sure Max will appreciate your sticking around a little longer to keep the office running while he deals with all that."

"Why didn't you make Max senior advisor when Stan left? I could tell he was qualified after my first week here."

He'd planned to ask that question in person, during the Monday morning meeting, but now he had no idea when he'd see Uncle Jack face-to-face again.

"I knew he was qualified."

"Then why?"

"I asked him to wait."

Eric paused. "For me."

"Yes. I wanted you to get a feel for what it's like to run your own office."

Realization dawned on him. "And you had Max reporting back to you on how I was doing the whole time. I wasn't there to bring experience and growth to the branch. It was . . ." He pressed a fist to his chin. "It was the other way around."

He thought back to the day the cubicle walls arrived at the office. "*You didn't think to talk to me about it first?*" Max had asked. Eric mentally kicked himself. What a self-centered jerk he'd been. It had been Max's office all along.

"Yes." There was a smile in Uncle Jack's voice now. "I was hoping for big things. Not out of the office, my boy. Out of *you.* I needed to know what kind of man I would be handing this company over to someday."

Eric plopped down on Eunice's couch and looked out the front window at the horizon, stretching on for miles in the promising light of early evening. If he was going to take the helm at Larson Financial one day, he had a lot to learn. He wasn't about to give up his tenth-floor ambitions or anything, but maybe this place wasn't quite done with him yet.

He sank back into the cushions. "Have you found anyone to help Max until Benson completes his degree?"

He was still holding out hope that no matter what was going on with Benson and his mom, Benson wouldn't change his mind about school. He had a bright future ahead of him.

"I'll email you the information on three promising candidates," Uncle Jack said. "Maybe you can help me choose."

"Okay." Eric's lips turned up a tiny bit. "I can do that. But I better get going. I've got a few animals depending on me for their dinner."

His stomach rumbled at the mention of dinner. Maybe when he had seen to all the animals, he'd stop in at Good Food.

"Animals?"

"I'll tell you about it some other time." It was too hard right now. Too tender.

"Okay. But I've got to say one more thing before you go."

Eric's eyes narrowed.

"Your dad's not the same person he was twenty years ago. His wanting to reconnect with you has nothing to do with me. I give you my word on that."

Eric wished he could see his uncle's face. See for himself if he was telling the truth. He sounded sincere.

"It would mean a lot to him if you reached out," Uncle Jack continued. "But I realize it's not my place to force you into anything if you're not ready. I won't bring it up again."

Eric stared at his phone for a long time after his conversation with Uncle Jack ended. If it was true about his dad, why had Uncle Jack had to talk his dad into contacting him? What kind of man had to be manipulated into talking to his own son?

Then again, he hadn't made it easy. He'd made it clear to his dad a long time ago that he didn't want him in his life. Didn't want him to keep showing up, trying to act like he hadn't ruined everything.

Eunice's words to him earlier—had that really only been a few hours ago?—rang through his mind. *In the end, it only matters where you stand with one person, and it's not your dad.* If it wasn't his dad, who was it? God?

He wasn't sure what that would even look like, seeking reconciliation with God the way Eunice had sought it with all those people on her list. Wasn't sure he was ready for that. But maybe making peace with his dad would be a step in the right direction.

forty-five

Saturday morning, Eric drove to Good Food with a ravenous appetite. He never had made it in for dinner last night. After talking to his uncle, he'd gotten a call from the very grateful and relieved man who owned one of the rescued dogs. While Eric waited for him to come pick up his dog, he'd secured his backyard and filled up a small plastic wading pool with water in hopes the goose could move out of his bathroom. Then he switched out Mellie's short chain for a longer one he'd borrowed from Winnie. Finally, he refilled everyone's food and water.

By the time the dog's owner had come and gone, the diner was closed.

He pulled up next to a 1982 Ford Bronco in front of Good Food. Bob was here. The bell chimed as he entered, and he scanned the room for the old man. He wanted to say hello.

"Good morning." Dee bustled by with three plates of food balanced on her arms. "Seat yourself."

A raised arm caught his attention from the corner of his eye, and he turned to find Bob flagging him down.

He approached Bob's table, and Bob gestured toward the empty seat across from him. "Why don't you join me?"

Eric sat, his stomach practically turning inside out with desperation at the smell of bacon and hash browns. Bob's plate was almost empty, and his left hand curled around a black mug with the words *Good Food* printed on it in white.

"This place is really called Good Food?" Eric asked. "Officially?"

Bob chuckled. "That's the sign they put up when they first opened, so people would know what they were up to. They never planned to leave it that way, but no one ever thought of anything better."

Dee set another black mug on the table, filled it with coffee from the pot in her hand, and slid it in front of Eric. "What can I get you?"

He grinned up at her. "One of everything, please. And a glass of orange juice."

She returned his smile. "Coming right up."

He took a tentative sip of the liquid gold. It smelled and tasted like it had been sitting in the pot for over an hour. More liquid brass than gold. But he was surprised to find he didn't really mind.

"How're you getting on with all them critters?" Bob asked.

Eric set his mug down. "I forget how fast news travels in a small town."

Bob raised his eyebrows. "You think Tukston is small? We got towns less than a quarter of its size. You ever heard of Wilsall?"

"No."

Bob raised his mug as if to toast. "And I don't expect you ever will."

Eric pondered that for a minute. What would it be like to live in a town of two or three hundred people?

"In a place like that . . ."

Bob took a swig of coffee and watched him.

Eric lifted one shoulder. "What does everyone do?"

Bob laughed from his belly, his mug shaking up and down. "A whole lot of checking up on each other, that's what."

Dee reappeared at the table and set a glass of juice and two plates down with a *thunk*. "Think that'll be enough for you, hotshot?"

Eric eyed the food. A stack of pancakes, sausage, bacon, two fried eggs, hash browns, toast, and a ham-and-cheese omelet. Flashbacks to the Cowboy Deluxe incident flickered through his mind, and he started sweating. Then he remembered his new role as host to all manner of omnivorous animals.

He gave Dee a wink. "It's perfect, hot stuff."

She blushed and swatted at his shoulder, then left a miniature bottle of Tabasco sauce on the table and hurried to the next customer. The diner was busy.

"A lot of extra customers right now," Bob said, "what with all the people coming to help with the fire and folks not being able to go back to their homes."

"Has this ever happened before?"

"Not as bad as this. I'm afraid the hills aren't going to be the same for a long time."

Bob finished off his coffee while Eric started on his pancakes. The amount of carbs represented on his two plates was cringe-worthy, but much like with the mediocre coffee, he didn't really care. After eating enough to take the edge off his hunger, he glanced up at Bob. He was looking around the room at all the people with an unassuming smile on his face.

"Looks like I'm going to be around a little longer." Eric took a sip of juice. "You should come by the office so we can continue our conversation."

He knew he shouldn't let his personal feelings interfere with his role as financial advisor, but he couldn't help but be concerned about Bob and his future. And they still hadn't figured out the best way to handle Bob's will. Not that Eric's role as financial advisor covered the creation or modification of a will, but Eric wasn't only interested in Bob's will from the perspective of a financial advisor anymore. He was interested as a friend.

Bob wiped his mouth with the back of his hand. "No need. I'm going to take your advice. Give it all away."

Eric's mouth fell open. "I thought you said you couldn't do that."

Bob looked down at the table. "Things are different now."

Eric chewed a strip of bacon for a minute, thinking. What could've changed his mind in such a short time?

"Okay. Well. We still have a lot to discuss. You should stop in."

"We'll see." Bob pushed away from the table and stood by Eric's chair until Eric looked up at him. He put his hand on Eric's shoulder. "I'm glad you're still here."

"I'm—" Was it true? "I'm glad too."

Bob headed for the door, stopping at the register on the way out to pay for his meal in cash. Eric ate a few more bites as he listened to the din of the place. He really was glad. Not that he planned to stay here forever, but it wasn't so bad.

As he waited for Dee to make the rounds back to his table, he checked his phone. Still no reply from Chase. He'd called and texted a dozen times, wanting to hear how the big move was going, wanting to tell Chase how sorry he was to be missing it, but apparently Chase wasn't ready to talk to him yet. He'd said he didn't even care if Eric was there or not. But had he meant it?

Eric pressed his lips into a tight line. He'd said the same sort of thing to his father many times. Had *he* meant it?

Dee finally passed by, and Eric caught her attention. "Could I get a to-go box and my check, please?"

She huffed. "I'll bring you a box, but Bob already paid for your meal. Along with everyone else's."

She scurried off, working hard to keep up with the rush. Eric looked around at all the customers, mentally tallying up how much money it must have cost to pay off every tab. Then he pulled a twenty from his wallet to leave as a tip.

By Sunday afternoon, Cinderella and the goose had become best friends. Eric had found a purple cat collar with a silver bell in Eunice's laundry room and put it on the goose so he could keep track of it. It jingled and jangled now as the two creatures chased each other around his yard and splashed in the wading pool. They made a funny pair, the goose tall and white and grumpy, and Cinderella with her black feathers and persistent friendliness—if one could call a chicken *friendly*. The steady honk-and-squawk chatter that went back and forth between them sounded like a real conversation.

Maybe it was.

Eric redialed Chase's phone and let it ring through to voice-mail before hanging up. His heart squeezed a little tighter every time his brother ignored his call. He wanted to believe Chase was too busy having fun to call him back. But the truth was he'd really blown it.

He'd sent two texts already this morning, but one more wouldn't hurt, right?

> How was your first night on campus? How's your roommate?

He grabbed the fence and swung himself over to Eunice's yard to check on the animals. They'd made a funny pair, too. He and Eunice. Which of them was the goose and which the chicken?

As he got to work cleaning up the yard, an unfamiliar red car pulled up and parked behind the horse trailer. A well-dressed woman got out and stood in the grass, staring at the house.

"Can I help you?" Eric called.

She twisted the straps of her purse in her hands. "You must be Eric."

322

He passed through the side gate and approached her. "If you're looking for Eunice, she isn't here. She's . . . uh . . ."

"I know." The woman put one hand on her chest. "I'm sorry. I shouldn't have come."

She turned to go.

Eric held up his hand to stop her. "Wait. What's your name?"

She looked into his eyes as if afraid of what she might find there. "Diane."

He gave her a reassuring smile. "Were you a friend of hers, Diane?"

"We hadn't talked in a long time. We were . . . at odds. But Eunice came to see me a few weeks ago to ask for my f-forgiveness."

Diane sucked in a breath, and her hand flew to her mouth as she covered a sob. Eric shifted uneasily on his feet while she composed herself. This must be the woman Eunice had taken her scooter to see. Brenda's sister.

After a minute, she sniffed and wiped her eyes. "I should have given it to h-her when she asked. Now it's t-too late. If only I would've known . . ."

Before Eric could think of what to say, Diane spun on her heels and hurried back to her car. Eric watched her go, remembering again Eunice's words. *I'm only concerned with my own debts now.* The anguish on Diane's face had hit him in the gut. Maybe if he could find Eunice's list, he could show it to Diane. Show her the line through her name so she would know Eunice believed her business with Diane was complete.

What would his list look like if he made one? Who would he need to . . . ?

Tiffani. Whenever he finally made it back to Seattle, he would apologize to Tiffani. He'd gained a lot from their relationship—expensive gifts, social connections, physical benefits without any real commitment—but had given next to nothing in return.

He walked back to the gate. The pony's owner would be here

in less than an hour to get her, and it wouldn't be a moment too soon in Eric's opinion. He didn't like the way that pony looked at him. No respect.

What were the animals going to do while he was at work all day tomorrow? Why did they require so much attention?

The weight of responsibility pushed down on his shoulders. Not just for the animals, but for the office and Benson's future and Chase's success at college. After thirty-two years of caring for no one but himself, he was unaccustomed to this sort of burden.

He resumed his caretaking tasks, wishing he would see Eunice watching him through the sliding glass door. Wishing he would've realized how much it took from her just to stand there as he worked. How much had she been suffering these past few weeks? She never complained, but he'd noticed the home health nurses coming more frequently. Noticed the bottles of pain medication in her bathroom.

His phone buzzed in his pocket, and he scrambled to pull it out. Maybe Chase had finally texted him back.

No such luck. It was from his dad.

> Heard you got bad fires over there. Hope you're okay.

Eric let out a small growl of frustration. Uncle Jack had clearly been talking with his dad again. Hadn't he said he was going to stay out of it? Well, not exactly. He'd only said he wouldn't bring it up to Eric anymore. Could Eric really blame Uncle Jack for wanting to keep in touch with his younger brother? It was the same thing Eric wanted to do.

He shoved the phone back in his pocket and sat down on the edge of Eunice's small back patio. The sun glared off the cement, and he covered his face with his hands. No. He was not okay.

He smelled Mellie a few seconds before he felt her nibble on the strap of his sandal.

"Leave me alone." His voice was strained.

She butted his knee with her head. He reached one hand out and patted her warm neck. She leaned into his touch, her stench increasing as he rubbed her mangy fur. He chanced a look into her face and was surprised by the solemnity he saw in her eyes. As if she understood what he was feeling. But of course that was ridiculous, right?

"What have you seen in your lifetime?" Eric noticed for the first time a scar on her right flank. A bald spot above her left eye. Ceci had said Mellie had been around a lot of years. "What kinds of secrets are you keeping in that thick skull of yours?"

With a jolt, he remembered Dusty's words. *"Me and Bob, we share all kinds of secrets."* And then the pieces clicked together in Eric's brain, and he knew exactly why Bob had changed his mind.

forty-six

Monday morning dragged on. Eric tried to focus on his work but couldn't help worrying about the animals. Did they have enough water? Were Cinderella and her new best friend still getting along? Maybe the goose's owner would be willing to take the chicken as well when they finally came for their pet. If he ever heard from them.

Should he run home during his lunch break?

The glass-paneled door flew open, and Max entered the office.

Eric dropped the financial reports he'd been studying on his desk and stood. "What are you doing here?"

Max gave him a wry look. "I work here, don't I?"

Eric swallowed, thinking about what Uncle Jack had said about Max and the senior advisor position. "Of course. Sorry. I just didn't expect you to be in this week."

Max hooked his thumbs in his leather belt. "I'm just here to check in and pick up a few things. Still no Benson, huh?"

"He called first thing." Eric maneuvered around the desk and cubicle wall boxes to stand beside Max. "Said he'll be in after lunch."

"That's good." Max nodded. "I've been worried about him."

"Me too."

"How's Mellie?"

Eric wrinkled his nose. "She smells like raw hamburger left out on the counter too long."

Max laughed. "She's fine then?"

"Yeah." Eric shifted on his feet. "Look, Max, I want to apologize for not asking you about the walls. You've been here a lot longer than I have, and I should've talked to you before making any big decisions."

One corner of Max's mouth lifted. "I'm sorry too. I overreacted. It's just that when your uncle and I first started this branch, it was never about money. Never really even about business. It was about people and service and community. That's why this place pulled me out of the hell I was in. Not because it gave me a job, but because it gave me a purpose." Max looked down at his cowboy boots. "I guess I was afraid the office might lose its heart. Get all impersonal and start caring more about dollar signs than people's lives."

Eric flinched. Max had no idea how close his fears were to the truth.

"But now that I've given it some thought," Max continued, "I believe you might be right."

Eric's eyebrows shot up. "About the cubicle walls?"

"Heck no." Max shook his head. "Those things belong in the dumpster. But maybe it would be a good idea to look into rearranging the layout in here a little better, once things settle down. Find a setup that we all feel comfortable with."

The word *we* rolled around in Eric's head like a sparkly purple bowling ball. Why had he ever thought he had the right to decide what was best for this office when he hadn't even planned to stay? And what about now?

"I better get going." Max retrieved a couple of folders from his desk and the thermos he had left in his hurry to get home last week. "Got a bunch of stuff to untangle with our insurance about the barn."

It had been the only building they'd lost in the fire.

"Good luck."

Max left, and Eric returned to his desk. What was he supposed to do with these walls? He might be able to return one, but how would he return the other when it wasn't supposed to exist? A smile played on his lips. Maybe he could use them in the yard to keep Mellie out of the dog food.

His desk phone rang, and he picked it up.

Winnie's warbly double voice rang out. "Your ten-thirty is here."

A haze of smoke still hung in the air over Tukston as Eric drove to the Kitchen Sink. It tasted like mourning. He cranked up the A/C, and the cool air ruffled the hair on his forearms. Why had it taken him so long to switch to wearing a lightweight, short-sleeved polo shirt to work?

He parked in front of the store. He'd been eating his lunch when a text came through from Dusty asking him to stop in.

Inside, Eric was surprised to see how much new inventory was on the floor. How did such a small town have so much to give away?

"Howdy." Dusty appeared, hair in his signature ponytail with his salt-and-pepper handlebar mustache as Wyatt Earp-y as ever. "Thanks for coming by. I've got something for you."

Eric followed Dusty toward the back of the store. He seemed to be moving a little slower than the last time Eric was here. Maybe the leg that had been injured was still bothering him. Or maybe there was a pain deeper than that weighing him down.

Eric spoke to Dusty's back. "I figured out what you and Bob have been up to."

Dusty froze for a second, his back rigid, but didn't turn around. "I don't know what you're talking about, champ."

Eric didn't press. Dusty reached the cash register and bent

behind the counter. With a grunt, he pulled out a bright orange bowling ball. It had black stripes like a tiger and had been polished to a high sheen.

Dusty held it out to him. "I thought you might like to have this."

Eric took the ball and swallowed the lump in his throat. "Thank you."

"She would've got a kick out of that one, don't you think?"

Eric nodded. He would find a place to display it. Somewhere he could see it every day and think of her.

"Did she know?"

"That she was like family to me?" Dusty hung his head. "No. She was never as alone as she thought she was."

Eric looked over his shoulder to be sure no one else was around. "What about the other thing?"

Dusty ran a hand over his mustache. "No. Only me and Bob know about that. And now you."

Eric shook his hand, knowing they would never speak of it again. "I'll never tell."

forty-seven

ric was starving by the time he got home from work, changed his clothes, and saw to all the animals. But it felt kind of good to take care of someone else's needs before his own for once. He threw together some dinner and dropped into his favorite chaise lounge on the deck.

Cinderella and the goose, which he had begun referring to as Gramps, were never far from each other's side. He was a little miffed he could be so easily replaced in Cinderella's heart, but it was for the best. She'd been an unexpected friend to him and now she deserved a friend of her own.

He thought of another friend he had made. Benson. He respected the care the young man had for his family, even if Eric never thought it was fair that Benson would have to give up his own goals and aspirations for the sake of his mother and younger siblings. He'd told him as much earlier when Benson came in to work a half day.

"My dad agrees with you," Benson had said. *"He didn't know how bad things were getting with my mom. He's going to move my brother and sister in with him for a while so my mom can get some help. And I'm going to accept Mr. Larson's offer."*

Eric had a feeling Benson would be running a much larger branch than Tukston one day.

He finished his dinner and pulled out his phone. Still no response from Chase. Should he take the hint and leave him alone?

He dialed Chase's number. It rang. And rang. Eric's stomach dropped. What was it going to take to get his little brother to talk to him again?

"Hey."

Eric sat up so fast he almost dropped his phone. "Hey. Chase. It's me." He panicked. Of course Chase knew who it was. Why had he not made a plan for what to say? "How are you?"

There was a pause—a brief but interminable pause—and then a sigh. "Good."

"Yeah? How's your dorm? How's the campus? Did you have class today?"

"Orientation today. Classes start tomorrow."

"I'm really sorry I couldn't be there, bro. I wanted to, but—"

"I heard about the fire. Saw some news articles about it online. That must've been pretty crazy."

"It was scary. A lot of people lost their homes. And I lost . . . a friend."

"Oh." Chase hesitated. "That really sucks, man."

"Yeah. And now I have a turtle."

"A turtle? Cool."

"Are you nervous about going to class? Are you getting along with your roommate? How's Darcy?"

"Do we have to do an interrogation right now?"

Eric stood and paced the deck. "Sorry. I just haven't talked to you in a while. We have a lot to catch up on."

"Then you should come home."

Eric jammed his fingers through his hair. "Maybe I can come visit over Labor Day weekend."

"That's not what I meant."

"I know, but I have responsibilities here that I can't walk away from right now. I'm going to stick this out."

Chase was silent for a minute. Eric glanced at his screen to make sure his brother hadn't ended the call. He still had so many questions for him. He wanted to know if Chase was still working out. If Chase was still seeing Darcy. If he regretted his decision to attend UW. But Eric couldn't bring any of that up right now. What would be a safe topic?

He smiled. "How'd Mom handle the goodbyes?"

Chase groaned. "Oh man, she blubbered all over the place. It was so embarrassing. Did she do that to you?"

"No, she couldn't wait to get rid of me."

"Guess we know who her favorite is."

Eric laughed. "I'm not even mad about it. You're my favorite, too."

When Chase replied, there was a smile in his voice. "Darcy likes me, too. I guess I'm doing pretty good."

Eric pumped a fist in the air and gave a silent shout of joy but kept his tone casual. "Don't let it go to your head."

"Like you don't?"

Eric grimaced. "I deserved that."

"Look, I better go. Everyone in the dorm is supposed to go to this meeting in the Commons tonight."

"Okay. Talk to you soon."

Eric's step felt a hundred times lighter as he pocketed his phone. There was still a distance between him and his brother that hadn't been there before, and he was going to do everything he could to eliminate it, but it had been great to hear Chase's voice.

He eased back into his chair and watched Cinderella and Gramps fight over a grasshopper as an uncomfortable thought nagged at his brain. Was his dad torturing himself, checking his phone for a response from Eric over and over as Eric had done with Chase? Did his dad have the same hollow feeling in his chest when there was no reply day after day?

Part of Eric's heart doubted it. Like eighty-seven percent. But what if . . . ?

He scrolled to his dad's last message and read it again.

> Heard you got bad fires over there. Hope you're okay.

Eric looked over at Eunice's house and thought about their last conversation. It still hadn't fully sunk in that she was gone. How did a body have life one moment, and the next . . . ?

He tapped on his dad's message and began to type. It wasn't an earth-shattering response. Wasn't necessarily going to change anything. But it was a start.

> I'm okay. How are you?

As the sun was setting, Eric noticed clouds gathering in the west. Wouldn't it figure if a lightning storm came along and started more fires. He hoped the clouds would skirt around Tukston.

He wandered over to Eunice's to fill water dishes. He hated leaving Mellie on a chain all the time but had no idea where she might go if he set her loose. He didn't want to be responsible for losing Max's goat. At least it was a long chain.

He remembered how Mellie slept in the laundry room of Max and Ceci's house at night. Should he . . . ? Could he . . . ? No, he wasn't ready for that.

He went in the house to check on Chicken the turtle.

"When is your owner going to call me?"

The turtle lifted its head slightly, and Eric frowned. Did it seem depressed? Should he put something in the aquarium besides a water dish? Did turtles play with toys? He was planning to stop at the feed store later in the week because he was low on dog food and wanted to find some grain for Mellie. Maybe someone at the store would know about turtles and could help him figure out what to do.

After giving Chicken some food, he walked around to the other side of the counter to sit on the stool beside the one Eunice had always used. He wondered what she would've thought of having a turtle in her house. He had a feeling she would've loved it.

"What kind of home did you live in before, Chicken?" Eric leaned his elbows on the counter and watched the slow-moving creature through the glass. "Do you miss your family?"

His phone buzzed, and he pulled it out. Oh. His dad hadn't wasted any time.

> Thanks for responding. I've been thinking about you a lot.

Eric read it again. And again. His thumb hovered over the reply box for a second, but then he pulled it away. He had no idea what to say. The phone buzzed a second time.

> There are so many things I'd like to talk to you about. How would you feel about me coming to Tukston for a visit?

Eric's scalp itched. His dad come here? That would be awkward. Would he stay with Eric? What would they do? What did he want to talk to Eric about? Maybe it would be better to wait until Eric went back to Seattle to try to meet up. That would give Eric more time . . .

Time.

He looked over at Eunice's favorite stool. Its edges were worn down from use. From day after day of climbing on and sliding off.

Another text.

> Just think about it.

Eric's shoulders relaxed a tiny bit. He could do that. He texted back.

Okay.

He was relieved when his dad left it at that. He would think about it. They could talk about it again another day. *Don't wait too long*, Eunice said in his head.

"Like you can talk," he replied out loud.

He stood and stretched, wishing he could go for a run. As soon as the smoke cleared enough, he vowed he'd put in at least ten miles.

Something caught his eye, and he looked across the kitchen over the top of Chicken's tank. He saw the corner of a piece of yellow paper sticking out from behind some other papers on the side of Eunice's fridge. His heart beat a little faster as he approached it, pinched the corner between his fingers, and pulled.

It was her list. He looked back at the fridge. There were dozens of pamphlets and paper scraps, all stuck haphazardly to the fridge with a variety of funky magnets. Someone could've thrown all of it away and never known Eunice's list was tucked away in there.

He scanned the wrinkled paper, recalling each mission of reconciliation he had participated in. The names had been crossed out with one deliberate stroke of the pen. Then his eyes came to rest on the last name, the one Eunice had not lived long enough to face. The one Eric had always believed must be the most important.

His head jerked back as he read it. His heart stuttered. How . . . ?

He blinked and read it again. Even in spite of Eunice's shaky handwriting, there was no mistaking what it said.

Jack Michael Larson.

335

forty-eight

"Hey there, my boy." Uncle Jack answered Eric's call after the first ring. "I was just thinking about you. Have you gotten an answer from Benson yet?"

Eric paced his back deck, just as he'd done earlier when talking to Chase, his phone in one hand and Eunice's list in the other. "Benson? Oh. Yeah. He said yes."

"Perfect. I'll have an official contract drawn up for him to sign and—"

"Uncle Jack, why is your name on Eunice's list?"

There was a moment of silence, then a low rumble of thunder in the distance and a *chomp chomp chomp* in his ear.

"What list?"

"She had a list of people she wanted to apologize to before she died. You're number seven. I want to know why."

"I—what?" Uncle Jack's tone changed. Deepened. Darkened. "What do you mean, 'before she died'?"

Eric's heart squeezed. Uncle Jack didn't know. Eric slammed his palm against his forehead. Of course he didn't know.

"Eunice passed away, Uncle Jack. On Friday."

"No." His uncle's voice was tight with emotion. "No, I— What happened?"

"She was really sick. Terminal. Her time was already short, but then she stole my Jeep and went up into the hills during the fire to rescue animals. I had no way of stopping her. I swear I would have. I'm so sorry."

Eric gripped the phone tighter. Eunice had made her choice, though he still wished he would've come out of the house soon enough to stop her from driving up in the hills alone. If only he would've found her bag faster. If only he didn't have to be the one to break the news to his uncle.

"She had a fierce love for animals," Uncle Jack finally said. "You could've never talked her out of it."

"What happened between you two? Why are you on the list?"

"I've known Eunice a long time." Uncle Jack spoke slowly, as if he had to work hard to pull the words out. "We were going to get married."

"You fell in love with her when you were here setting up the branch?"

Even though he'd grown to appreciate Eunice for who she was, he still had a hard time picturing someone as unpolished as Eunice winning over Uncle Jack's heart. Then again, what had she been like before everything that happened to her?

"No, I fell in love with her when she was still a teenager. I used to spend summers in Tukston working on a ranch that belonged to one of my dad's cousins. I became close with a lot of folks during that time. Bob and Dusty were my best friends. But Neecy and I were inseparable. Even got engaged. Her parents weren't too thrilled about it, though. I was ten years older than her."

Eric had no idea that his uncle had been to Tukston prior to the year he set up the branch with Max. He'd always assumed Uncle Jack had discovered Tukston through a wealthy client in Seattle who owned land out here or something.

"Neecy broke it off. Broke my heart. I wanted to take her back to Seattle with me. It took a long time for me to realize I should've been more patient. Given her more time. She was so young, and just because I was ready to start a family didn't mean she was."

Another rumble of thunder caused Eric to look at the sky. "Is that why you came back here in 2000?"

"When Dusty told me about Max and asked if there was anything I could do, I thought it would be the perfect opportunity to help an old friend, help the town, and win back the only woman I ever cared about."

The wheels in Eric's brain were churning through ideas like the wheels on the Jeep off-roading up a mountain. If he remembered correctly, that was about the time Eunice's health began to decline. Had Uncle Jack known about that? Had he purposefully placed Eric next door to Eunice?

"Was she sick then?"

Uncle Jack thought a moment. "I don't know. She never said anything. We spent time together, and I thought it was going to work out that time. My feelings for her hadn't changed. But all of a sudden she broke it off again. Pushed me away. I never understood why."

Eric stopped pacing and stood staring at Eunice's house as a wind gust kicked up that smelled like damp soil. Maybe she'd been afraid Uncle Jack wouldn't want to be tied down to a sick woman. Maybe she'd known even then that she wouldn't be around long and thought Uncle Jack would be better off without her. Maybe they would never know.

"I don't know why either, but I do know that if she wrote your name down, that means she wanted to tell you she was sorry." Eric steeled himself. He knew exactly what he was supposed to do. "She would want me to ask for your forgiveness, Uncle Jack."

Silence screamed at him through the phone. No chomping. No breathing. Then a choked sob.

"I left town the second I felt the office was ready so I could come back here and lick my wounds. I made Bob and Dusty promise they'd look after her for me."

One side of Eric's mouth lifted. They had done that, all right.

"I'll send you a picture of her that I took."

"I'd like that." Uncle Jack's voice was thick now. "I—I can't believe she's gone. Did she . . . was she alone?"

"No." Eric shook his head emphatically as a spatter of raindrops hit the top of his head. "I was there. And Winnie."

"Thank you." Uncle Jack's voice sounded as if it were spiraling through a portal to the past. "If it couldn't be me, I'm glad it was you."

forty-nine

Eric hurried out the door early Thursday morning. It had been almost a week since Eunice had . . . died. She'd tease him for struggling to say it if she were here. But it was such an unmovable word.

He needed to stop at the feed store before going to the office. The animals were going to mutiny if he didn't bring anything home for them after work. Luckily the feed store opened bright and early.

The air was crisp and clean as he drove to the store with his windows down. The rainstorm earlier in the week had helped put out the fire and clear out the smoke. And now that he had slowed down enough to see it, he had a hard time imagining life without this view.

He still missed Puget Sound, though.

The feed store was a brick building that had dog, cat, horse, and cow prints painted on the sidewalk out front leading up to its entrance. He'd driven by before but had never been inside.

An older man greeted him when he entered. "Can I help you find anything?"

"I need dog food. And grain for a goat."

"No problem."

"And do you have anyone around who knows anything about turtles?"

The man scratched his chin. "You're going to want to talk to Mason. She's the small animal expert around here."

"All right. Where can I find her?"

"She should be stocking dog food as a matter of fact. Aisle three." The man pointed. "You can kill two birds with one stone."

Eric nodded his thanks and headed in that direction. What was he supposed to do if he didn't hear from the remaining animals' owners soon? He knew they probably had a lot to deal with right now, especially if their homes had not survived the blaze, but he wished they would call.

He turned down aisle three and stopped. Blinked. Swallowed.

A young woman with a forty-pound bag of dog food in her arms and red Chuck Taylors on her feet smiled up at him. Strands of honey-colored hair that had escaped her messy ponytail framed her face. "Hello. Do you need any help?"

"I, uh—I think something's wrong with Chicken." His face heated. "I mean, the turtle, um . . ."

She tilted her head. "You've got a problem with your chicken?"

"No." He rubbed the back of his neck. "It's a turtle. Named Chicken."

Her chestnut eyes gleamed. "I bet there's a story behind that."

He nodded dumbly.

When he didn't speak, she set the bag down and stepped closer. "What seems to be the problem?"

"He . . . well, I don't know if it's a he. It could be a she. I don't know how to tell." His eyes widened. What on earth was he talking about? What was his problem? "Chicken seems lonely. I wondered if there was anything I could put in the tank to"—*oh no, don't say it*—"cheer him up?"

He said it. He mentally kicked himself.

She moved a little closer and gave him an encouraging look. "What do you have in there now?"

"A water dish."

"That's it? What about a light?"

Eric shook his head.

"There's your problem." She started walking and gestured for him to follow. "Turtles need UV light to stay healthy."

He walked behind her in a daze, watching her ponytail swing back and forth. He was mesmerized. Hopelessly enchanted. This had never happened to him before.

". . . and maybe a ramp." She looked back at him expectantly.

He had a sinking feeling she had just given him a list of all the things Chicken needed. He forced a smile. "Sure. Great. I'll take one of each."

She laughed. "Okay."

"You're Mason."

She did that head tilt thing again, and his heart wobbled.

He jerked a thumb over his shoulder. "That guy told me. I'm Eric."

"Here we are." She stopped by a shelf full of aquarium paraphernalia and her eyes sparked. "Wait, you're Eric Larson?"

Uh-oh. Why did she say it like that? How did she know him? What had she heard?

"My grandma keeps talking about you." She lifted one shoulder in the most adorable half shrug he'd ever seen. "Well, she's not *really* my grandma."

He opened and shut his mouth a couple times before the words would come. "Do you mean Winnie?"

It couldn't be. Winnie's unofficial granddaughter?

Mason nodded. "She says her office hasn't been the same since you came to town."

"She calls it *her* office?"

Mason chuckled. "Yep. Just like my aunt Dee. She calls Good Food *her* diner."

The hairs on the back of Eric's neck stood up. Aunt Dee? Dee from the diner whose niece was a "nice girl"?

"Why are you looking at me like that?" Mason asked.

He shifted on his feet. "You don't happen to walk Brenda Wallace's Pomeranian every Tuesday, do you?"

"Pumpkin?" Mason grinned. "That dog's a spoiled brat, but I love him to pieces. How did you know?"

She stood there looking at him as his head spun. How . . . ?

He knew he was staring, but he couldn't stop. She was pretty but not in a flashy way. Her hair, her clothes, her manner were all simple. Plain even. So why did he feel as though he'd just grabbed hold of an electric fence?

Eunice's voice cut through the buzzing electricity in his brain. *Don't wait too long.*

He thought about all the things she had left unsaid—undone—and a sense of urgency prodded him as if she were poking him in the side with her finger, telling him what to do. Demanding, more like it.

He cleared his throat and tried to smile. "I was wondering . . ." Where were his dimples when he needed them the most? "Do you have any plans for dinner?"

Acknowledgments

Thank you to all the readers who have supported me. I could not do this without you.

Thank you to my team at Bethany House. I'm so humbled and grateful to be part of such a wonderful organization.

Thank you to my early readers: Sarah Carson, Emily Conrad, Kerry Johnson, and Janice Parker. I don't know where I'd be without your steadfast support, encouragement, and feedback. And a special shout-out to my QTs, who make this writing life more fun and meaningful than I ever expected.

Thank you to my agent, Keely Boeving. You are basically the best.

Thank you to Steve White for your fly-fishing expertise, and to Pat O'Brien Townsend for your patience with all my stoma-related questions. You were both excellent guides. Any errors or misrepresentations related to these topics should be attributed to me alone.

Thank you to Tammy Partain for all that driving and baby-sitting. You have been such a blessing in my life. I'm not sure this book could've happened without your help.

Thank you to my husband, Andy, for never complaining when I disappear into a story and forget to do laundry. Thank you to my kids for making me a better person and accepting me for who I am. Thank you to my mom for your unwavering support. I love you all very much.

Thank you to my heavenly Father for being the Anchor of my life, and thank you to my earthly father for teaching me that death is not the end. Someday I will see you again, where the blue sky begins.

About the Author

Katie Powner, author of *A Flicker of Light* and *The Sowing Season*, grew up on a dairy farm in the Pacific Northwest but has called Montana home for almost twenty years. She is a biological, adoptive, and foster mom who loves Jesus, red shoes, and candy. In addition to writing contemporary fiction, Katie blogs about family in all its many forms and advocates for more families to open their homes to children in need. To learn more, visit her website at katiepowner.com.

Sign Up for Katie's Newsletter

Keep up to date with Katie's latest news on book releases and events by signing up for her email list at katiepowner.com.

More from Katie Powner

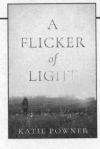

Widower Mitch Jensen is at a loss with how to handle his mother's odd, forgetful behaviors, as well as his daughter's sudden return home and unexpected life choices. Little does he know Grandma June has long been keeping a secret about her past—but if she doesn't tell the truth about it, someone she loves will suffer, and the lives of three generations will never be the same.

A Flicker of Light

You May Also Like . . .

Forced to sell his family farm after sacrificing everything, 63-year-old Gerrit Laninga no longer knows what to do with himself. 15-year-old Rae Walters has growing doubts about The Plan her parents set to help her follow in her father's footsteps. When their paths cross just as they need a friend the most, Gerrit's and Rae's lives change in unexpected ways.

The Sowing Season by Katie Powner
katiepowner.com

In 1910, rural healer Perliett VanHilton is targeted by a superstitious killer and must rely on the local doctor and an intriguing newcomer for help. Over a century later, Molly Wasziak is pulled into a web of deception surrounding an old farmhouse. Will these women's voices be heard, or will time silence their truths forever?

The Premonition at Withers Farm by Jaime Jo Wright
jaimewrightbooks.com

Fashion aficionado Iris Blakely dreams of using her talent to start a business to help citizens in impoverished areas. But when she discovers that Ekon Diallo will be her business consultant, the battle between her desires and reality begins. Can she keep her heart—and business—intact despite the challenges she faces?

To Win a Prince by Toni Shiloh
tonishiloh.com

◆ BETHANYHOUSE

More from Bethany House

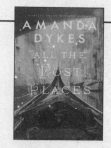

Discovered floating in a basket along the canals of Venice, Sebastian Trovato wrestles with questions of his origins. Decades later, on an assignment to translate a rare book, Daniel Goodman finds himself embroiled in a web of secrets carefully kept within the canals of the ancient city and the mystery of the man whose story the book does not finish: Sebastian.

All the Lost Places by Amanda Dykes
amandadykes.com

After uncovering a diary that leads to a secret artifact, Lady Emily Scofield and Bram Sinclair must piece together the mystifying legends while dodging a team of archeologists. In a race against time, they must decide what makes a hero. Is it fighting valiantly to claim the treasure or sacrificing everything in the name of selfless love?

Worthy of Legend by Roseanna M. White
THE SECRETS OF THE ISLES #3
roseannamwhite.com

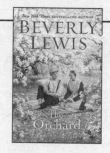

For generations, Ellie Hostetler's family has tended their orchard, a tradition her twin brother, Evan, will someday continue. But when Evan is drafted for the Vietnam War, the family is shocked to learn he has not sought conscientious objector status. Can Ellie, with the support of a new beau, find the courage to face a future unlike she imagined?

The Orchard by Beverly Lewis
beverlylewis.com